REDISCOVERY

SCIENCE FICTION BY WOMEN

(1958 – 1963)

Vista, CA
JOURNEY PRESS
2019

Journey Press
P.O. Box 1932
Vista, CA 92085

Managing Editor: Gideon Marcus
Editing and Arrangement: A.J. Howells, Janice Marcus and Erica Frank

ISBN: 978-1-951320-00-3

August 2019
www.galacticjourney.press

CONTENTS

Acknowledgements:

Napoléon: Thank you for the tremendous graphic design work you did on the cover, and especially for your patience with our changes and mistakes.

E.L.F. (the one that lives in California): Thank you for all your help with the layout, as well as your wise insight into how this whole thing works.

A.J.: Thank you for making this anthology happen.

FOREWORD
by Dr. Laura Brodian Freas Beraha

Have you ever heard of an author by the name of Marilyn Ross? How about Clarissa Ross? They were writers of Federalist Era (the American equivalent of English Regency Era) romances in the 1970s. They were also the pen names of the same author who wrote the entire series of *Dark Shadow* novels: a Mr. W. E. Dan Ross. "Why did he use those female noms de plume?" you might ask. According to Dan, no publisher—or reader, for that matter—would ever believe that such expressions of the hearts and souls of young women could ever have been felt, understood, or written by a man.

By the same token the reverse sentiment was evident about female science fiction writers well into the 1960s. After all, the genre had been dominated by men: Asimov, Heinlein, DeCamp, and Clark, to name a few. Science fiction was perceived to be read by a male audience. The advertising market quantified that at the time the readership was about 92% male and the average age was 29–30. Back then it was unlikely that readers would buy fiction by writers of the female gender. After all, it was supposed, given the preponderance of science fiction written by men, whatever could women know about the genre?

What could possibly account for this bias against women writers of science fiction? Was it strictly a matter of economics or was it something else? Early science fiction mostly revolved around hard science, and the assumption was that to write about science, a writer had to know science. In point of fact, although outnumbered by men, women *even then* had made significant contributions to the field. However, they typically faced many roadblocks to getting their works published in respected journals. Hence, women science fiction writers and the publishers anticipated little respect or interest, and therefore limited marketability.

Many addressed this issue by using initials. The first fan letter received by C. L. Moore was from a gentleman thinking that he was writing to a man. Katherine MacLean originally submitted to John Campbell as K.A. MacLean. Sonya Dorman was initially published as "S. Dorman". She did not go by Sonya until she was published in *Galaxy* in June 1966, well after she had become established. Sydney Van Scyoc, Rosel George Brown, Kit Reed, and Otis Kidwell Burger (their real names) may or may not have been recognized as women. Some women authors used male pen-names, Andre (Alice) Norton being the archetypical example. Pauline Ashwell appeared on the 1959 Hugo ballot under both her name and as Paul Ash. Of course, many women submitted and were published under their own names: Joy Leache, Anne Walker, Maria Russell, Judith Merril, Jane Rice, Doris Pitkin Buck.

Even making it into print has not ensured the endurance of these names, despite the worthiness of their creations. Which is a shame because these women were pioneers, not only writing excellent stories, but also establishing the foundation for the current paradigm—in 2019, more than 80% of the Hugo nominees were women.

Science fiction as a genre encompasses more than just hard science. I discovered science fiction in 1972 and became an avid reader. I enjoyed the sensation of its otherworldliness and was fascinated following ordinary people under extraordinary situations. I compared the pictures in my head to the published illustrations—of course I preferred mine. When I married Frank Kelly Freas (who painted the cover of this anthology), he looked over my drawings from the art classes I took at the School of Fine Arts at Indiana University (I was working on my doctorate in music education). I had always thought that all readers saw pictures in their heads. Kelly said that the ability to do that was reserved for illustrators and that I should become one. Under his tutelage I began working for *Weird Tales, Analog*, and other magazines; I also did some book covers and full color frontispieces. As an illustrator, my job was to communicate the words of authors in an evocative and immediate way. I read and digested the science fiction manuscripts months before the stories ever got to the readers. As a reader and as a science fiction artist I discovered that there were various themes in science fiction beyond hard science: there was also the extrapolative, the speculative, and the dystopian.

Female authors wrote stories about coming of age. There are cautionary tales of what the world will be like if current trends continue. There are stories set beyond our universe with perspectives from both sides of a human and nonhuman encounter. You'll find these themes and more in this anthology.

I hope that as you read their stories you don't try to ferret out "feminine" versus "masculine" elements. What you are about to read is really good science fiction, plain and simple. I certainly enjoyed the journey and have every expectation that you shall, too.

INTRODUCTION
by Gideon Marcus

Why *Rediscovery*? Why now?

Science fiction began as a male-dominated, predominantly white endeavor. Eventually, it managed to overcome these limitations. Of late, more and more diverse writers are finally receiving recognition for their talent and hard work.

That's today. What about yesterday?

I've attended lots of conventions, and when the subject of classic female SF authors has come up, fans have rarely been aware of more than a few. It's not surprising, since only a handful of names tend to get the most press: Ursula K. LeGuin, James Tiptree Jr., Joanna Russ, Anne McCaffrey. Sometimes, a person might remember Leigh Brackett and Andre Norton, or note that the entire genre began with Mary Shelley's *Frankenstein*. But that's about it. As far as many modern day fans know, women writing science fiction is a relatively new thing.

It's not.

About ten years ago, I started living in the past. Specifically, I began reading the science fiction and fantasy of exactly fifty-five years prior; in 2009, I dove headfirst into the genre as it existed in 1954. It quickly became immersive. I read the digest-sized magazines "as they came out" once every month. I bought an AM broadcaster so that 670 kHz formed the soundtrack for my journey—back then, it was Laverne Baker and Bill Haley; ten years later, it's The Beatles and The Supremes. In 2013 (1958), filled with several years of inspiration and fired up by the newly inaugurated Space Race, I began Galactic Journey, a window into the past that had hitherto been mine alone.

My original goal had simply been to review the science fiction and space shots of the time. But another agenda quickly became imperative. I wanted to use the Journey to spotlight the women who wrote science fiction.

There were two reasons for this. One was that I was discovering all these great female science fiction authors that few seemed to have heard of. By 1962, when LeGuin was first published in *Fantastic*, I had already counted more than thirty active women writing SF. And while some of them only dipped their toes in the genre, others were prominent and recurring names: Margaret St. Clair/Idris Seabright, C.L. Moore, Miriam Allen DeFord, Mildred Clingerman, Evelyn Smith, Rosel George Brown, Kit Reed, Zenna Henderson, Katherine Maclean, Judith Merril, Kate Wilhelm, and on and on.

The other was that I tended to like the pieces written by women better than the stuff done by male authors. Annually, I made a list of what I felt were the year's best stories, and women-penned tales usually made up about a quarter of the entries. And yet, women were only responsible for about 10% of the total SF output.

Why did women consistently outperform their male counterparts in my tallies? I don't think it's just my personal taste. After all, women made up half of the Best New Author nominees on the 1959 Hugo ballot.

I've come up with a few reasons why science fiction by women stood out:

Diverse writers write diverse characters.

Most Silver Age science fiction and fantasy was written by men and starred men. Female characters generally existed to be romantic foils or scenery (if they were included at all). When Anne McCaffrey gave us female protagonists in "The Woman in the Tower" (1959) and "The Ship Who Sang" (1961), when Rosel George Brown made women leads the norm in her stories, when Evelyn Smith positively portrayed a queer couple in "They Also Serve" (in 1962!), those pieces stood out. Not just because they were good but because they were blessedly, refreshingly different.

Diverse writers write in a different style and from a different perspective.

At that time, authors like Andre Norton and Marion Zimmer Bradley composed in a pulpish style, but they were the exception rather than the rule. Many women wrote in a manner shaped by the context in which society attempted to confine them. Their work frequently emphasized emotions and relationships rather than hardware and technical solutions. There is often the bitter tinge of the downtrodden. They wrote about issues particularly relevant to them; for instance: motherhood (e.g. "Henderson's Return" [1961]) and workplace discrimination (e.g. Smith's "Softly While You're Sleeping" [1961]).

I daresay that the New Wave of science fiction, which began in the early 1960s and shifted the course of the genre irrevocably, was strongly heralded by the work done by women in the 1950s.

Woman authors had (and often still have) to try harder.

In the Silver Age, women who wanted to write SF had to overcome barriers: the spoken and unspoken bias against ladies in a field that was largely stag, and the pervasive cultural assumption that science and science fiction were "not for women." Self-censorship undoubtedly contributed to the low publishing numbers. Even when they did submit, many felt they would only be taken seriously if they sent in their work under male or ambiguous names: K.L. Maclean, Sydney van Scyoc (who otherwise went by her middle name, Joyce), S. Dorman. That they hid their gender even from editors who touted or might have been favorably disposed toward women authors (e.g. *Astounding*'s John Campbell, Fantastic and *Amazing*'s Cele Goldsmith) is telling. In fact, the only haven for women SF authors in the Silver Age appears to have been *F&SF*, which not only published the greatest percentage of women, but also was up front about their Miss or Mrs. status (Ms. not yet having come into vogue).

This is not to say that women couldn't write bad stories—Sturgeon's Law applies to everyone.

But given the prevailing wisdom of the time that women just didn't write SF, women felt (and often knew) that they needed to write better stories than men to be considered for print. By the time a woman gathered the courage to submit a piece, she'd probably worked especially hard on it, discarding many earlier drafts.

So those that overcame the pressure to self-censor and the prevalent (if in some cases unconscious) social bias were the overperformers. Also, exceptional quality was likely a requirement to get a story with a non-traditional protagonist and/or theme published. That's why stories written by women that got published tended to be better, story for story, than those written by their male contemporaries.

And that is why this volume exists. These fourteen stories you're about to read aren't just some of the best science fiction by women from the latter part of the Silver Age, but they're also some of the best stories, period. Moreover, each is introduced by a current author on the rise, any of whose work would be welcome additions to an anthology six decades hence.

Rediscovery is your chance to meet the forgotten luminaries of the past who laid the foundation for the current cast of stars...and tomorrow's bright lights.

I hope you love reading it as much as we enjoyed putting it together.

Dedicated to all the women
still waiting to be Rediscovered.

UNHUMAN SACRIFICE

by Katherine MacLean

(Originally appeared in the November 1958 issue of *Astounding Science Fiction*)

> *Born in 1925 and hailing from New Jersey, Katherine MacLean is best known for her SF short stories and novelettes, often dealing with social issues. After graduating at Barnard, her path to becoming a published author wasn't a linear one. She pursued an interest in science and was employed in a laboratory prior to her first story, "Defense Mechanism," being printed in* Astounding Science Fiction *in 1949. MacLean's writing drew heavily from her strong scientific background. Her work showcased her vast technical knowledge and mixed it with a variety of other subjects, many of which were not commonly seen in science fiction at the time, to create a style all her own.*
>
> *MacLean was one of the handful of women that were penning stories in science fiction magazines during the early 1950s. Like a number of female writers, she published some of her work under a male pseudonym. In her case, it was Charles Dye, the name of her first husband, but she also submitted "Defense Mechanism" under her initials, after her family advised her that no SF publisher would take a story by a woman (happily,* Astounding *editor John W. Campbell, Jr. was delighted to publish her under her own name).*
>
> *MacLean had a steady output during the early part of*

the 1950s that tapered off by the end of the decade, though she never stopped writing short fiction, some of which was adapted for radio and television. Her next period featured the publication of three novels: The Man in the Bird Cage *(1971),* Missing Man *(a 1975 novelized version of her 1971 Nebula Award-winning novella by the same name) and* Dark Wing *(1979). Anthologies that have compiled MacLean's work throughout the years include 1962's* The Diploids and Other Flights of Fancy, *which was followed with* The Trouble with You Earth People *in 1980. Her most recent collection is 2016's* The Science Fiction Collection.

1958's "Unhuman Sacrifice," originally featured in the same Astounding *in which she launched her SF career, perfectly illustrates what makes Katherine MacLean's work special. "Unhuman Sacrifice" is the tale of a missionary who is determined to spread his religious beliefs to the inhabitants of an Earth-like planet. He and his crew learn that the natives hold an annual coming-of-age ritual. Believing he knows best, he goes through great lengths to prevent the ceremony from taking place—with not alto- gether positive results!*

"Unhuman Sacrifice" is filled with memorable characters and vivid imagery. Seamlessly switching perspectives: between insiders and outsiders, science and belief, "Unhuman Sacrifice" shows why Katherine MacLean is an author whose work is worth seeking out.

—Natalie Devitt

"Damn! He's actually doing it. Do you hear that?"

A ray of sunlight and a distant voice filtered down from the open arch in the control room above. The distant voice talked and paused, talked and paused. The words were blurred, but the tone was recognizable.

"He's outside preaching to the natives."

The two engineers were overhauling the engines but paused to look up toward the voice.

"Maybe not," said Charlie, the junior engineer. "After all, he doesn't

2

know their language."

"He'd preach anyway," said Henderson, senior engineer and navigator. He heaved with a wrench on a tight bolt, the wrench slipped, and Henderson released some words that made Charlie shudder.

On the trip, Charlie had often dreamed apprehensively that Henderson had strangled the passenger. And once he had dreamed that he himself had strangled the passenger and Henderson, too.

When awake the engineers carefully avoided irritating words or gestures, remained cordial towards each other and the passenger no matter what the temptation to snarl, and tried to keep themselves in a tolerant good humor.

It had not been easy.

Charlie said, "How do you account for the missionary society giving him a ship of his own? A guy like that, who just gets in your hair when he's trying to give you advice, a guy with a natural born talent for antagonizing people?"

"Easy," Henderson grunted, spinning the bolt. He was a stocky, square-built man with a brusque manner and a practiced tolerance of other people's oddities. "The missionary society was trying to get rid of him. You can't get any farther away than they sent us!"

The distant voice filtered into the control room from the unseen sunlit landscape outside the ship. It sounded resonant and confident. "The poor jerk thinks it was an honor," Henderson added. He pulled out the bolt and dropped it on the padded floor with a faint thump.

"Anyhow," Charlie said, loosening bolt heads in a circle as the manual instructed, "he can't use the translator machine. It's not ready yet, not until we get the rest of their language. He won't talk to them if they can't understand."

"Won't he?" Henderson fitted his wrench to another bolt and spun it angrily. "Then, what is he doing?"

Without waiting for an answer he replied to his own question. "*Preaching*, that's what he is doing!"

It seemed hot and close in the engine room, and the sunlight from outside beckoned.

Charlie paused and wiped the back of his arm against his forehead. "Preaching won't do him any good. If they can't understand him, they

3

won't listen."

"We didn't listen, and that didn't stop him from preaching to *us!*" Henderson snapped. "He's lucky we found a landing planet so soon, he's lucky he didn't drive us insane first. A man like that is a danger to a ship." Henderson, like Charlie, knew the stories of ships which had left with small crews, and returned with a smaller crew of one or two red-eyed maniacs and a collection of corpses. Henderson was a conservative. He preferred the regular shipping runs, and ships with a regular sized crew and a good number of passengers. Only an offer of triple pay and triple insurance indemnity had lured him from the big ships to be co-engineer on this odd three-man trip.

"Oh...I didn't mind being preached at," Charlie's tone was mild, but he stared upward in the direction of the echoing voice with a certain intensity in his stance.

"Come off it, you twerp. We have to be sweet to each other on a trip when we're cabin-bound. Don't kid old Harry, you didn't like it."

"No," said Charlie dreamily, staring upward with a steady intensity. Can't say that I did. He's not such a good preacher. I've met better in bars." The echoing voice from outside seemed to be developing a deeper echo. "He's got the translator going, Harry. I think we ought to stop him."

Charlie was a lanky redhead with a mild manner, about the same age as the preacher, but Henderson, who had experience, laid a restraining hand on his shoulder.

"I'll do it," said Henderson, and scrambled up the ladder to the control room.

The control room was a pleasant shading of grays, brightly lit by the sunlight that streamed in through the open archway. The opening to the outside was screened only by a billowing curtain of transparent saran-type plastic film, ion-coated to allow air to pass freely, but making a perfect and aseptic filter against germs and small insects. The stocky engineer hung a clear respirator box over a shoulder, brought the tube up to his mouth, and walked through the plastic film. It folded over him and wrapped him in an intimate tacky embrace, and gripped to its own surface behind him, sealing itself around him like a loose skin. Just past

4

the arch he walked through a frame of metal like a man-sized croquet wicket and stopped while it tightened a noose around the trailing films of plastic behind him, cutting him free of the doorway curtain and sealing the break with heat.

Without waiting for the plastic to finish wrapping and tightening itself around him, the engineer went down the ramp, trailing plastic film in gossamer veils, like ghostly battle flags.

They could use this simple wrapping of thin plastic as an airsuit air lock, for the air of the new world was rich and good, and the wrapping was needed only to repel strange germs or infections. They were not even sure that there were any such germs; but the plastic was a routine precaution for ports in quarantine, and the two engineers were accustomed to wearing it. It allowed air to filter by freely, so that Henderson could feel the wind on his skin, only slightly diminished. He was wearing uniform shorts, and the wind felt cool and pleasant.

Around the spaceship stretched grassy meadow and thin forest, and beyond that in one direction lay the blue line of the sea, and in another the hazy blue-green of distant low mountains. It was so like the southern United States of Charlie's boyhood that the young engineer had wept with excitement when he first looked out of the ship. Harry Henderson did not weep, but he paused in his determined stride and looked around, and understood again how incredibly lucky they had been to find an Earth-type planet of such perfection. He was a firm believer in the hand of fate, and he wondered what fate planned for the living things of this green planet, and why it had chosen him as its agent.

Down in the green meadow, near the foot of the ramp sat the translator machine, still in its crate and on a wheeled dolly but with one side opened to expose the controls. It looked like a huge box, and it was one of the most expensive of the new inductive language analyzers, brought along by their passenger in the hope and expectation of finding a planet with natives.

Triumphant in his success, the passenger, the Revent Winton, sat cross-legged on top of the crate, like a small king on a large throne. He was making a speech, using the mellow round tones of a trained elocutionist, with the transparent plastic around his face hardly muffling his voice at all.

And the natives were listening. They sat around the translator box in a wide irregular circle, and stared. They were bald, with fur in tufts about their knees and elbows. Occasionally one got up, muttering to the others, and hurried away; and occasionally one came into the area and sat down to listen.

"Do not despair," called Revent Winton, in bell-like tones. "Now that I have shown you the light, you know that you have lived in darkness and sin all your lives, but do not despair..."

The translator machine was built to assimilate a vast number of words and sentences in any tongue, along with fifty or so words in direct translation, and from that construct or find a grammatical pattern and print a handbook of the native language. Meanwhile, it would translate any word it was sure of. Henderson figured out the meaning of a few native words the day before and recorded them in, and the machine was industriously translating those few words whenever they appeared, like a deep bell, tolling the antiphony to the preacher's voice. The machine spoke in an enormous bass that was Henderson's low tones recorded through a filter and turned up to twenty times normal volume.

"I...LIGHT...YOU...YOU...LIVED...DARK...LIFE..."

The natives sat on the green grass and listened with an air of patient wonder.

"Revent Winton," Harry tried to attract his attention.

Winton leaned toward the attentive natives, his face softened with forgiveness. "No, say to yourselves merely—I have lived in error. Now I will learn the true path of a righteous life."

The machine in the box below him translated words into its voice of muted thunder. "SAY YOU...I LIVED...I...PATH...LIFE..."

The natives moved. Some got up and came closer, staring at the box, and others clustered and murmured to each other, and went away in small groups, talking.

Henderson decided not to tell the Revent what the machine had said. But this had to be stopped.

"Revent Winton!"

The preacher leaned over and looked down at him benevolently. "What is it, my son?" He was younger than the engineer, dark, intense and sure of his own righteousness.

"MY SON," said the translator machine in its voice of muted thunder. The sound rolled and echoed faintly back from the nearby woods, and the natives stared at Henderson.

Henderson muttered a bad word. The natives would think he was Winton's son! Winton did not know what it had said.

"Don't curse," Winton said patiently. "What is it, Harry?"

"Sorry," Henderson apologized, leaning his arms on the edge of the crate. "Switch off the translator, will you?"

"WILL YOU..." thundered the translator. The preacher switched it off.

"Yes?" he asked, leaning forward. He was wearing a conservative suit of knitted dark gray tights and a black shirt. Henderson felt badly dressed in his shorts and bare hairy chest.

"Revent, do you think it's the right thing to do, to preach to these people? The translator isn't finished, and we don't know anything about them yet. Anthropologists don't even make a suggestion to a native about his customs without studying the whole tribe and the way it lives for a couple of generations. I mean, you're going off half cocked. It's too soon to give them advice."

"I came to give them advice," Winton said gently. "They need my spiritual help. An anthropologist comes to observe. They don't meddle with what they observe, for meddling would change it. But I am not here to observe, I am here to help them. Why should I wait?"

Winton had a remarkable skill with syllogistic logic. He always managed to sound as if his position were logical, somehow, in spite of Henderson's conviction that he was almost always entirely wrong, Henderson often, as now, found himself unable to argue.

"How do you know they need help?" he asked uncertainly. "Maybe their way of life is all right."

"Come now," said the preacher cheerfully, swinging his hand around the expanse of green horizon. "These are just primitives, not angels. I'd be willing to guess that they eat their own kind, or torture, or have human sacrifices."

7

"Humanoid sacrifices," Henderson muttered.

Winton's ears were keen. "Don't quibble. You know they will have some filthy primitive custom or other. Tribes on Earth used to have orgies and sacrifices in the spring. It's spring here—the Great Planner probably intended us to find this place in time to stop them."

"Oye," said Henderson and turned away to strike his forehead with the heel of his hand. His passenger was planning to interfere with a spring fertility ceremony. If these natives held such a ceremony—and it was possible that they might—they would be convinced that the ceremony insured the fertility of the earth, or the health of the sun, or the growth of the crops, or the return of the fish. They would be convinced that without the ceremony, summer would never return, and they would all starve. If Winton interfered, they would try to kill him.

Winton watched him, scowling at the melodrama of his gesture.

Henderson turned back to try to explain. "Revent, I appeal to you, tampering is dangerous. Let us go back and report this planet, and let the government send a survey ship. When the scientists arrive, if they find that we have been tampering with the natives' customs without waiting for advice, they will consider it a crime. We will be notorious in scientific journals. We'll be considered responsible for any damage the natives sustain."

The preacher glared. "Do you think that I am a coward, afraid of the anger of atheists?" He again waved a hand, indicating the whole sweep of the planet's horizon around them. "Do you think we found this place by accident? The Great Planner sent me here for a purpose. I am responsible to Him, not to you, or your scientist friends. I will fulfill His purpose." He leaned forward, staring at Henderson with dark fanatical eyes. "Go weep about your reputation somewhere else."

Henderson stepped back, getting a clearer view of the passenger, feeling as if he had suddenly sprouted fangs and claws. He was still as he had appeared before, an intense, brunet young man, wearing dark tights and dark shirt, sitting cross-legged on top of a huge box, but now he looked primitive somehow, like a prehistoric naked priest on top of an altar.

"Anthropology is against this kind of thing," Henderson said.

Winton looked at him malevolently from his five foot elevation on the crate and the extra three feet of his own seated height. "You aren't an anthropologist, are you Harry? You're an engineer?"

"That's right," Henderson admitted, hating him for the syllogism.

Winton said sweetly: "Then why don't you go back to the ship and work on the engine?"

"There will be trouble," Henderson said softly.

"I am prepared for trouble," the Revent Winton said equally softly. He took a large old-fashioned revolver out of his carry case, and rested it on his knee.

The muzzle pointed midway between the engineer and the natives.

Henderson shrugged and went back up the ramp.

"What did he do?" Charlie was finishing his check of the fuel timers, holding a coffee cup in his free hand.

Angrily silent, Harry cut an exit slit from the plastic coating. He ripped off the gossamer films of plastic, wadded them up together and tossed them in a salvage hopper.

"He told me to mind my own business. And that's what I am going to do."

The preacher's impressive voice began to ring again from the distance outside, and, every so often, like a deep gong, the translator machine would speak a word in the native dialect.

"The translator is still going," Charlie pointed out.

"Let it. He doesn't know what it is saying." Sulkily, Henderson turned to a library shelf, and pulled out a volume: "The E. T. Planet, a manual of observation and behavior on extraterrestrial planets, with examples."

"What is it saying?"

"Almost nothing at all. All it translated out of a long speech the creep made was 'I life path.'"

The younger engineer lost his smile. "That was good enough for others. Winton doesn't know what the box is saying?"

"He thinks it's saying what he is saying. He's giving out with his usual line of malarkey."

"We've got to stop it!" Charlie began to climb the ladder.

Henderson shrugged. "So go out and tell him the translator isn't

9

working right. I should have told him. But if I got close to him now, I'd strangle him."

Charlie returned later, grinning. "It's O.K. The natives are scared of Winton, and they like the box; so they must think that the box is talking sense for itself, and Winton is gibbering in a strange language."

"He is. And it is." Henderson said sourly. "They are right."

"You're kind of hard on him." Charlie started searching the shelves for another copy of the manual of procedure for survey teams. "But I can see what you mean. Anyhow, I told Winton that he was making a bad impression on the natives. It stopped him. It stopped him cold. He said it would put off preaching for a week and study the natives a little. But he said we ought to fix up the translator, so that it translates what he says." Charlie turned, smiling, with a book in one hand. "That gives us time."

"Time for what?" Henderson growled without looking up from his book. "Do you think we can change Winton's mind? That bonehead believes that butting into people's lives is a sacred duty. Try talking any bonehead out of a Sacred Duty! He'd butt into a cannibal banquet! I hope he does. I hope they eat him!"

"Long pig," Charlie mused, temporarily diverted by the picture. "Tastes good to people, probably would taste foul to these natives, they're not the same species."

"He says he's planning to stop their spring festival. If it has sacrifices or anything he doesn't like, he says he'll stop it."

Charlie placed his fists on the table and leaned across toward Henderson, lowering his voice. "Look, we don't know even if the natives are going to have any spring festival. Maybe if we investigate we'll find out that there won't be one, or maybe we'll find out that Winton can't do them any harm. Maybe we don't have to worry. Only let's go out and investigate. We can write up reports on whatever we find, in standard form, and the journals will print them when we get back. Glory and all like that." He added, watching Henderson's expression: "Maybe, if we have to, we can break the translator."

It was the end of the season of dry. The river was small and ran in a narrow channel, and there were many fish near the surface. Spet worked rapidly, collecting fish from fish traps, returning the empty traps to the water, salting the fish.

He was winded, but pleased with the recollection of last night's feast and hungry in anticipation of the feast of the evening to come. This was the season of the special meals, cooking herbs and roots and delicacies with the fish. Tonight's feast might be the last he would ever have, for a haze was thickening over the horizon, and tomorrow the rains might come.

One of the strangers came and watched him. Spet ignored him politely and salted the fish without looking at him directly. It was dangerous to ignore a stranger, but to make the formal peace gestures and agreements would be implying that the stranger was from a tribe of enemies, when he might already be a friend. Spet preferred to be polite, so he pretended not to be concerned that he was being watched.

The haze thickened in the sky, and the sunlight weakened. Spet tossed the empty trap back to its place in the river with a skillful heave of his strong short arms. If he lived through the next week, his arms would not be strong and short, they would be weak and long. He began to haul in another trap line, sneaking side glances at the stranger as he pulled.

The stranger was remarkably ugly. His features were all misfit sizes. Reddish brown all over like a dead leaf, and completely bald of hair at knees and elbows, he shone as if he were wet, covered all over with a transparent shininess, like water, but the water never dripped. He was thick and sturdy and quick moving, like a youngling, but did not work. Very strange, unlike reality, he stood quietly watching, without attacking Spet, although he could have attacked without breaking a peace gesture. So he was probably not of any enemy tribe.

It was possible that the undripping water was an illusion, meant to indicate that the stranger was really the ghost of someone who had drowned.

The stranger continued to watch. Spet braced his feet against the grass of the bank and heaved on the next trap line, wanting to show his strength. He heaved too hard, and a strand of the net gave way. The stranger waded out into the water, and pulled in the strand, so that no

11

fish escaped.

It was the act of a friend. And yet when the net trap was safely drawn up on the bank, the brown stranger stepped back without comment or gesture, and watched exactly as before—as if his help was the routine of one kinfolk to another.

That showed that the brown one was his kin and a member of his family. But Spet had seen all of his live kinfolk, and none of them looked so strange. It followed reasonably that the brown one was a ghost, a ghost of a relative who had drowned.

Spet nodded at the ghost and transferred the fish from the trap to the woven baskets and salted them. He squatted to repair the broken strand of the net.

The brown ghost squatted beside him. It pointed at the net and made an inquiring sound.

"I am repairing the trap, Grandfather," Spet explained, using the most respectful name for the brown ghost relative.

The ghost put a hand over his own mouth, then pointed at the ground and released its mouth to make another inquiring noise.

"The ground is still dry, Grandfather," Spet said cordially, wondering what he wanted to know. He rose and flung the trap net out on its line into the river, hoping that the brown ghost would admire his strength. Figures in dreams often came to tell you something, and often they could not speak, but the way they looked and the signs they made were meant to give you a message. The brown ghost was shaped like a youngling, like Spet, as if he had drowned before his adult hanging ceremony. Perhaps this one came in daylight instead of dreams, because Spet was going to die and join the ghosts soon, before he became an adult.

The thought was frightening. The haze thickening on the horizon looked ominous.

The brown ghost repeated what Spet had said, almost in Spet's voice, blurring the words slightly. *The ground is still dry Grandfather.* He pointed at the ground and made an inquiring noise.

"Ground," said Spet thinking about death, and every song he had heard about it. Then he heard the ghost repeat the word, and saw the satisfaction of his expression, and realized that the ghost had forgotten how to talk, and wanted to be taught all over again, like a newborn.

That made courtesy suddenly a simple and pleasant game. As Spet worked, he pointed at everything, and said the word, he described what he was doing, and sometimes he sang the childhood work songs, that described the work.

The ghost followed and helped him with the nets, and listened, and pointed at things he wanted to learn. Around his waist coiled a blind silver snake that Spet had not noticed at first, and the ghost turned the head of the snake towards Spet when he sang, and sometimes the ghost talked to the snake himself, with explanatory gestures.

It was very shocking to Spet that anyone would explain things to a snake, for snakes are wise, and a blind snake is the wise one of dreams—he who knows everything. The blind snake did not need to be explained to. Spet averted his eyes and would not look at it.

The ghost and he worked together, walking up the river bank, hauling traps, salting fish, and throwing the traps back, and Spet told what he was doing, and the ghost talked down to the snake around his waist, explaining something about what they were doing.

Once the brown ghost held the blind silver snake out toward Spet, indicating with a gesture that he should speak to it.

Terrified and awed, Spet fell to his knees. "Tell me, Wisest One, if you wish to tell me, will I die in the hanging?"

He waited, but the snake lay with casual indifference in the ghost's hand, and did not move or reply.

Spet rose from his knees and backed away. "Thank you, oh Wise One."

The ghost spoke to the snake, speaking very quietly, with apologetic gestures and much explanation, then wrapped it again around his waist, and helped Spet carry the loads of salted fish, without speaking again, or pointing at anything.

It was almost sundown.

On the way back to his family hut, Spet passed the Box That Speaks. The black gibbering spirit sat on top of it and gibbered as usual, but this time the Box stopped him and spoke to him, and called him by his own name, and asked questions about his life.

13

Spet was carrying a heavy load of salted fish in two baskets hung on a yoke across one sturdy shoulder. He was tired. He stood in the midst of the green meadow that in other seasons had been a river, with the silver hut of the ghosts throwing a long shadow across him. His legs were tired from wading in the river, and his mind was tired from the brown ghost asking him questions all day; so he explained the thing that was uppermost in his mind, instead of discussing fishing and weather. He explained that he was going to die. The ceremony of Hanging, by which the almost-adults became adults, was going to occur at the first rain, five younglings were ready, usually most of them lived, but he thought he would die.

The box fell silent, and the ghost on top stopped gibbering, so Spet knew that it was true, for people fall silent at a truth that they do not want to say aloud.

He made a polite gesture of leave-taking to the box, and went toward his family hut, feeling very unhappy. During the feast of that evening all the small ones ate happily of fish and roots and became even fatter, and the thin adults picked at the roots and herbs. Spet was the only youngling of adult-beginning age, and he should have been eating well to grow fat and build up his strength, but instead he went outside and looked at the sky and saw that it was growing cloudy. He did not go back in to the feast again, instead he crouched against the wall of the hut and shivered without sleeping. Before his eyes rested the little flat-bottomed boats of the family, resting in the dust behind the hut for the happy days of the rain. He would never travel in those boats again.

Hanging upside down was a painful way to become an adult, but worth it, if you lived. It was going to be a very bad way to die.

Hurrying and breathless with his news, Revent Winton came upon the two engineers crouched at the river bank.

"I found out..." he began.

"*Shhh*" one said without turning.

They were staring at a small creature at the edge of the water.

Winton approached closer and crouched beside them. "I have news that might interest you." He held his voice to a low murmur, but the triumph sounded in it like a rasp cutting through glass, a vibration that drew quick speculative glances from the engineers. They turned their attention back to the water's edge.

"Tell us when this is over. Wait."

The young preacher looked at what they were staring at, and saw a little four-legged creature with large eyes and bright pointed teeth struggling feebly in the rising water. The younger engineer, Charlie, was taking pictures of it.

"Its feet are stuck," Winton whispered. "Why don't you help it?"

"It's rooting itself," Henderson murmured back. "We're afraid that loud noises might make it stop."

"Rooting itself?" Winton was confused.

"The animal has two life stages, like a barnacle. You know, a barnacle is a little fish that swims around before it settles down to being just kind of a lump of rock. This one has a rooted stage that's coming on it now. When the water gets up to its neck it rolls up underwater and sticks its front legs out and starts acting like a kind of seaweed. Its hind feet are growing roots. This is the third one we've watched."

Winton looked at the struggling little creature. The water was rising toward its neck. The large bright eyes and small bared teeth looked frightened and uncomprehending. Winton shuddered.

"Horrible," he murmured. "Does it know what is happening?"

Henderson shrugged, "At least it knows the water is rising, and it knows it must not run away. It has to stand there and dig its feet in." He looked at Winton's expression and looked away. "Instinct comes as a powerful urge to do something. You can't fight instinct. Usually it's a pleasure to give in. It's not so bad."

Revent Paul Winton had always been afraid of drowning. He risked another glance at the little creature that was going to turn into a seaweed. The water had almost reached its neck, and it held its head high and panted rapidly with a thin whimpering sound.

"Horrible." Winton turned his back to it and pulled Henderson farther up the bank away from the river. "Mr. Henderson, I just found out something."

He was very serious, but now he had trouble phrasing what he had to say. Henderson urged him, "Well, go on."

"I found it out from a native. The translator is working better today."

15

"Charlie and I just recorded about four hundred words and phrases into it by distance pickup. We've been interviewing natives all day." Henderson's face suddenly grew cold and angry. "By the way, I thought you said that you weren't going to use the translator until it is ready."

"I was just checking it." Winton actually seemed apologetic. "I didn't say anything, just asked questions."

"All right," Henderson nodded grudgingly. "Sorry I complained. What happened? You're all upset, man!"

Winton evaded his eyes and turned away, he seemed to be looking at the river, with its banks of bushes and trees. Then he turned and looked in the direction of the inland hills, his expression vague. "Beautiful green county. It looks so peaceful. God is lavish with beauty. It shows His goodness. When we think that God is cruel, it is only because we do not understand. God is not really cruel."

"All right, so God is not really cruel," Henderson repeated cruelly. "So what's new?"

Winton winced and pulled his attention back to Henderson.

"Henderson, you've noticed that there are two kinds of natives, tall, thin ones that are slow, and quick, sturdy, short ones that do all the hard work. The sturdy ones we see in all ages, from child size up. Right?"

"I noticed."

"What did you think it meant?"

"Charlie and I talked about it." Henderson was puzzled. "Just a guess, but we think that the tall ones are aristocrats. They probably own the short ones, and the short ones do all the work."

Thick clouds were piled up over the far hills, accounting for the slow rise in the river level.

"The short ones are the children of the tall thin ones. The tall thin ones are the adults. The adults are all sick, that is why the children do all the work."

"What..." Henderson began, but Winton overrode his voice, continuing passionately, his eyes staring ahead at the hills.

"They are sick because of something they do to themselves. The young ones, strong and healthy, when they are ready to become adults they...they are hung upside down. For days, Henderson, maybe for

16

more than a week, the translator would not translate how long. Some of them die. Most of them...most of them are stretched, and become long and thin." He stopped, and started again with an effort. "The native boy could not tell me why they do this, or how it started. It has been going on for so long that they cannot remember."

Abruptly, and, to Henderson, shockingly, the preacher dropped to his knees and put his hands together. He tilted his head back with shut eyes and burst into prayer.

"Oh Lord, I do not know why You waited so long to help them to the true light, but I thank You that You sent me to stop this horrible thing."

Quickly he stood up and brushed his knees. "You'll help me, won't you?" he asked Henderson.

"How do we know it's true?" Henderson scowled. "It doesn't seem reasonable."

"Not reasonable?" Winton recovered his poise in sudden anger. "Come now Harry, you've been talking as if you knew some anthropology. Surely you remember the puberty ceremonies. Natives often have initiation ceremonies for the young males. It's to test their manhood. They torture the boys, and the ones who can take it without whimpering are considered to be men, and graduated. Filthy cruelty! The authorities have always made them stop."

"No one around here has any authority to order anyone else to stop," Harry grunted. He was shaken by Winton's description of the puberty ceremony, and managed to be sarcastic only from a deep conviction that Winton had been always wrong, and therefore would continue to be wrong. It was not safe to agree with the man. It would mean being wrong along with Winton.

"No authority? What of God?"

"Well, what *of* God?" Henderson asked nastily. "If He is every-where, He was here before you arrived here. And He never did anything to stop them. You've only known them a week. How long has God known them?"

"You don't understand." The dark-haired young man spoke with total conviction, standing taller, pride straightening his spine. "It was more than mere luck that we found this planet. It is my destiny to stop

17

these people from their ceremony. God sent me."

Henderson was extremely angry, in a white-faced way. He had taken the preacher's air of superiority in the close confine of a spaceship for two months, and listened patiently to his preaching without letting himself be angry, for the sake of peace in the spaceship. But now he was out in the free air again, and he had had his fill of arrogance, and wanted no more.

"Is that so?" he asked nastily. "Well, I'm on this expedition, too. How do you know that God did not send *me*, to stop *you*?"

Charlie finished taking pictures of the little animal under water as it changed, and came back up the bank, refolding the underwater lens. He was in time to see Winton slap the chief engineer in the face, spit out some profanity that would have started him on an hour of moral lecture, if he had heard either of them emit such words. He saw Winton turn and run, not as if he were running away, but as if he were running to do something, in sudden impatience.

Ten minutes later Henderson had finished explaining what was bothering the preacher. They lay on the bank lazily looking down into the water, putting half attention into locating some other interesting life form, and enjoying the reflection of sunset in the ripples.

"I wish I could chew grass," Henderson said. "It would make it just like watching a river when I was a kid. But the plastic stuff on my face keeps me from putting anything into my mouth."

"The leaves would probably be poisonous anyhow," Charlie brushed a hand through the pretty green of the grass. It was wiry and tough with thin round blades, like marsh grass. "This isn't really grass. This isn't really Earth, you know."

"I know, I wish I could forget it. I wonder what that creep Winton is doing now." Henderson rolled on his back and looked lazily at the sky. "I've got one up on him now. I got him to act like a creep right out in the open. He won't be giving me that superior, fatherly bilge. He might even call me Henderson now instead of Harry."

"Don't ask too much," Charlie clipped a piece of leaf from a weed and absently tried to put it into his mouth. It was stopped by the transparent plastic film that protected him from local germs and filtered

18

the air he breathed.

He flicked the leaf away, "How did that creep get to be a missionary? Nothing wrong with him, except he can't get on with people. Doesn't help in his line of work to be like that."

"Easy, like I said," said Henderson, staring into the darkening pink and purple of the sky. "They encouraged him to be a missionary so he would go far far away. Don't ever tell him. He thinks that he was chosen for his eloquence." Henderson rolled back onto his stomach and looked at the river. It was a chilly purple now, with silver ripples. "More clouds over the mountains. And those little clouds overhead might thicken up and rain. If the river keeps rising, there might be a flood. We might have to move the ship."

"Winton said that the native mentioned a flood." Charlie got up lazily and stretched. "Getting dark out here anyhow. We'll have to find out more about that interview."

They went in search of the preacher.

What he told them was disturbing, and vague.

"That was Spet," Henderson said. "That was the one I was learning words from all afternoon. And he told you he was going to die?"

Winton was earnest and pale. He sat crouched over the chart table as if his resolution to act had frightened him. "Yes. He said he was going to die. He said that they were going to hang him upside down in a tree as soon as the next rain starts. Because he is old enough."

"But he said that other young males live through it? Maybe he's wrong about dying. Maybe it's not as tough as it sounds."

"He said that many die," Winton said tonelessly. His hands lay motionless on the table. He was moved to a sudden flare of anger. "Oh those stupid savages. Cruel, cruel!" He turned his head to Henderson, looking up at him without the usual patronizing expression. "You'll fix the translator so that it translates me exactly, won't you? I don't want to shoot them to stop them from doing it. I'll just stop them by explaining that God doesn't want them to do this thing. They will have to understand me."

He turned his head to Charlie standing beside him. "The savages call me Enaxip. What does that mean? Do they think I'm a god?"

19

"It means Big Box," Henderson cut in roughly. "They still think that the box is talking. I see them watch the box when they answer, they don't watch you. I don't know what they think you are."

That night it did not rain. Winton allowed himself to fall asleep near dawn.

To Spet also it made a difference that it did not rain.

The next day he fished in the river as he always had.

The river was swollen and ran high and swiftly between its banks and fishing was not easy at first, but the brown ghost returned, bringing another one like himself, and they both helped Spet with pulling in the fish traps. The new ghost also wanted to be told how to talk, like a small one, and they all had considerable amusement as the two ghosts acted out ordinary things that often happened, and Spet told them the right words and songs to explain what they were doing.

One of them taught him a word in ghost language, and he knew that he was right to learn it, because he would soon be a ghost.

When Spet carried the fish back along the path to his family hut that evening, he passed the Box That Talks. It spoke to him again, and again asked him questions.

The spirit covered with black that usually gibbered on top of the box was not there. Nothing was on top of the box, but the brown ghost who had just been helping him fish stood beside the box and spoke to it softly each time it asked Spet a question. The box spoke softly back to the ghost after Spet answered, discussing his answers, as if they had a problem concerning him.

Spet answered the questions politely, although some of them were difficult questions, asking reasons for things he had never thought needed a reason, and some were questions it was not polite to ask. He did not know why they discussed him, but it was their business, and they would tell him if they chose.

When he left them, the brown ghost made a gesture of respect and mutual aid in work, and Spet returned, warmed and pleased by the respect of the ghost-relative.

He did not remember to be afraid until he was almost home.

It began to rain.

Charlie came up the ramp and into the spaceship and found Henderson pacing up and down, his thick shoulders hunched, his fists clenched, and his face wrinkled with worry.

"Hi," Charlie did not expect an answer. He kicked the lever that tightened the noose on the curtain plastic behind him, watched the hot wire cut him loose from the curtain and seal the curtain in the same motion. He stood carefully folding and smoothing his new wrapping of plastic around himself, to make sure that the coating he had worn outside was completely coated by the new wrapping. All outside dust and germs had to be trapped between the two layers of sterile germproof plastic.

He stood mildly smoothing and adjusting the wrapping, watching Henderson pace with only the very dimmest flicker of interest showing deep in his eyes. He could withdraw his attention so that a man working beside him could feel completely unwatched and as if he had the privacy of a cloak of invisibility. Charlie was well mannered and courteous, and this was part of his courtesy.

"How're things," he asked casually, slitting open his plastic cocoon and stepping out.

Henderson stopped pacing and took a cigar from a box on the table with savage impatience in his motions. "Very bad," he said. "Winton was right."

"Eh?" Charlie wadded up the plastic and tossed it into the disposal hopper.

"The natives, they actually do it." Henderson clenched the cigar between his teeth and lit it with savage jerky motions. "I asked Spet. No mistake in the translator this time. He said, yes, they hang the young men upside down in trees after the first spring rain. And yes, it hurt, and yes sometimes one died, and no, he didn't know why they had to do this or what it was for. Ha!" Henderson threw the cigar away and began to pace again, snarling.

"Oh yes, the translator was working fine! Generations of torturing their boys with this thing, and the adults can't remember how it started, or why, and they go on doing it anyway…"

Charlie leaned back against the chart table, following his pacing with his eyes. "Maybe," he said mildly, "there's some good reason for the custom."

"A good reason to hang upside down for a week? Name one!"

Charlie did not answer.

"I just came from the native village," he said conversationally as though changing the subject. "Winton has started. He's got the translator box right in the center of their village now, and he's sitting on top of it telling them that God is watching them, and stuff like that. I tried to reason with him, and he just pointed a gun at me. He said he'd stop the hanging ceremony even if he had to kill both of us and half the natives to do it."

"So let him try to stop them, just by talking." Henderson, who had stopped to listen, began to pace again, glowering at the floor. "That flapping mouth! Talking won't do it. Talking by itself never does anything. I'm going to do it the easy way. I'm going to kidnap Spet, and keep them from getting him.

"Charlie, tribes only do things at the right season, what they call the right season. We'll turn Spet loose after the week is up, and they won't lay a hand on him. They'll just wait until next year. Meanwhile they'll be seeing that the trees aren't angry at them or any of that malarkey. When they see that Spet got away with it, they'll have a chance to see a young male who's becoming a healthy adult without being all stretched out and physically wrecked.

"And maybe next year, Spet will decide to get lost by himself. Maybe after looking at how Spet looks compared with an adult who was hanged, some of the kids due for hanging next year would duck into the forest and get lost when it's due."

"It's a good dream," Charlie said, lounging, following Henderson's pacing with his eyes. "I won't remind you that we swore off dreaming. But I'm with you in this, man. How do we find Spet?"

Henderson sat down, smiling. "We'll see him at the stream to-morrow. We don't need to do anything until it starts raining."

Charlie started rummaging in the tool locker. "Got to get a couple of flashlights. We have to move fast. Have to find Spet in a hurry. It's already raining, been raining almost an hour."

Darkness and rain, and it was very strange being upside down. Not formal and ceremonial, like a story-song about it, but real, like hauling nets and thatching huts, and eating with his brothers. The world seemed to be upside down. The tree trunk was beside him, strong and solid, and the ground was above him like a roof being held up by the tree, and the sky was below his feet and very far away...and looking down at the clouds swirling in the depth of the sky he was afraid of falling into it. The sky was a lake, and he would fall through it like a stone falling through water. If one fell into the sky, one would fall and fall for a long time, it looked so very deep.

Rain fell upward out of the sky and hit him under the chin. His ankles and wrists were tightly bound, but did not hurt, for the elders had used a soft rope of many strands tied in a way that would not stop circulation. His arms were at his sides, his wrists bound to the same strand that pulled at his ankles, and the pull on his arms was like standing upright, carrying a small weight of something. He was in a standing position, but upside down. It was oddly comfortable. The elders had many generations of experience to guide them, and they had chosen a tall tree with a high branch that was above the flood. They had seemed wise and certain, and he had felt confidence in them as they had bound and hung him up with great gentleness, speaking quietly to each other.

Then they had left him, towing their little flat-boats across the forest floor that was now a roof above his head, walking tall and storklike across the dim lit glistening ground, which looked so strangely like a rough, wet ceiling supported by the trunks of trees.

The steady rain drummed against the twigs and small spring leaves, splashing in the deepening trickles of water that ran along the ground. Spet knew that somewhere the river was overflowing its banks and spreading into the forest and across meadows to meet and deepen the rain water. In the village the street would be muddy, and the children would be shouting, trying already to pole the boats in the street, wild with impatience for the rising of the river, to see again the cold swift flow of water and watch the huts of the town sag and flow downward, dissolve and vanish beneath the smooth surface.

For a month in the time of floods everyone would live in boats. His tribe would paddle and pole up the coast, meeting other tribes, trading baskets and fishhooks, salt fish for salt meat, and swapping the old stories and songs with new variations brought from far places. Last time they had been lucky enough to come upon a large animal caught in the flood, swimming and helpless to resist the hunters. The men of the enemy tribe had traded skin for half the roast meat on a raft, and sang a long story song that no one had heard before. That was the best feast of all.

Then the horde of small boats would come home to the lakes that were draining meadows and forest, and take down the sick and dying young men who had been hanging in the trees, and tend and feed them and call them "elder." They would then travel again for food, to fight through storms to salt the meat of drowned animals and hunt the deep sea fish caught in the dwindling lakes.

When the rains had stopped and the land began to dry, they would return to the damp and drying land to sing and work and build a village of the smooth fresh clay left by the flood.

But Spet would not see those good times again. He hung in his tree upside down with the rain beating coolly against his skin. It was growing too dark to see more than the dim light of the sky. He shut his eyes, and behind his shut eyes were pictures and memories, and then dreams.

Here he is. How do we get him down. Did you bring a knife. How do we get up to him. It's slippery. I can't climb this thing. Wait, I'll give you a boost.

A flash of light, too steady for lightning, lasting a full second, Spet awoke fully, staring into the darkness, looking for the light which now was gone, listening to the mingled voices in the strange language.

"Don't use the flashlight, it will frighten him."

"Going to try to explain to him what we're doing?"

"No, not right away. He'll come along. Spet's a pal of mine already."

"Man, do these trees have roots. As big as the branches!"

"Like mangroves."

"You're always claiming the South has everything. What are mangroves?"

"Florida swamp trees. They root straight into deep water. Give a

hand here."

"Keeps raining like this and they're going to need their roots. How high can we climb just on the roots anyhow?"

"Think you're kidding? Why else would they have roots like this? This territory must be underwater usually, deep water. This flat land must be delta country. We're just in the dry season."

"What do you mean delta country? I'm a city boy, define your terms."

"I mean, we're at the mouth of one of those big wandering rivers like the Mississippi or the Yellow River that doesn't know where it's going to run next, and splits up into a lot of little rivers at the coast, and moves its channel every spring. I noticed that grass around the ship looked like salt water grass. Should have thought about it."

A dark figure appeared beside Spet and climbed past him toward the branch where the rope was tied. The next voice was distant. "You trying to tell me we landed the ship in a riverbed? Why didn't you say something when we were landing?"

"Didn't think of it, then." That voice was loud and close.

"It's a fine time to think of it now. I left the ship wide open. You up there yet?"

"Uh huh. I'm loosening the rope. Going to lower him slow. Catch him and keep him from landing on his head, will you?"

"Ready. Lower away."

The voices stopped and the world began to spin, and the bole of the tree began to move past Spet's face.

Suddenly a pair of wet arms gripped him, and the voice of the brown ghost called, "Got him."

Immediately the rope ceased to pull at Spet's ankles, and he fell against the brown ghost headfirst and they both tumbled against slippery high roots and slid down from one thick root to another until they stopped at the muddy ground. The ghost barked a few short words and began to untie the complex knots from Spet's ankles and wrists.

It was strange sitting on the wet ground with its coating of last year's leaves. Even rightside up the forest looked strange, and Spet knew that this was because of death, and he began to sing his deathsong.

25

The brown ghost helped him to his feet, and said clearly in ordinary words, "Come on, boy, you can sing when we get there."

His friend dropped down from a low branch to the higher roots of the tree, slipped and fell on the ground beside them.

In Spet's language the standing one said to the other. "No time for resting, Charlie, let's go."

It was very dark now, and the drips from the forest branches poured more heavily, beating against the skin.

The ghost on the ground barked a few of the same words the relative-ghost had made when he had fallen, and got up.

The two started off through the forest, beckoning Spet to follow. He wondered if he were a ghost already. Perhaps the ghosts had taken him to be a ghost without waiting for him to die. That was nice of them, and a favor, possibly because they were kinfolk. He followed them.

The rain had lightened, and become the steady, light falling spray that it would be for the next several days. Walking was difficult, for the floor of the forest was slippery with wet leaves, and the mud underneath was growing soft again, remembering the time it had been part of the water of the river, remembering that the river had left it there only a year ago. The ghosts with him made sputtering words in ghost talk, sometimes tripped and floundered and fell, helped each other up and urged him on.

The forest smelled of the good sweet odors damp earth and growing green leaves. The water and mud was cooling against his hurting feet, and Spet unaccountably wanted to linger in the forest, and sit, and perhaps sleep.

The floods were coming, and the ghosts had no boats with them.

"Come on, Spet. We go to big boat. Come on, Spet."

Why did they stumble and flounder through the forest without a boat? And why were they afraid? Could ghosts drown? These ghosts, with their perpetually wet appearance—if they had drowned once, would they be forced to relive the drowning, and be caught in the floods every year? A bad thing that happened once, had to happen again and again in dreams. And your spirit self in the dream lived it each time as something new. There is no memory in the dream country. These ghosts were dream people, even though they chose to be in the awake world.

They were probably bound by the laws of the dream world.

They would have to re-enact their drowning. Their boat was far away, and they were running toward the watercourse where the worst wave of the flood would come.

Spet understood suddenly that they wanted him to drown. He could not become a ghost, like these friendly brown ghosts, and live in their world, without first dying.

He remembered his first thoughts of them, that they carried the illusion of water over them because they had once drowned. They wanted him to be like them. They were trying to lure him through waters where he would stumble and drown as they had.

Naturally as they urged him on their gestures were nervous and guilty. It is not easy to urge a friend onward to his death. But to be shaped like a young one, merry, brown, and covered with water, obviously he had to be drowned as they were drowned, young and merry, before the hanging had made a sad adult of him.

He would not let them know that he had guessed their intention. Running with them toward the place where the flood would be worst, he tried to remember what verse he had stopped singing his death song, and began again from that verse, singing to stop the fear-thoughts. The rain beat coolly against his face and chest as he ran.

Each man in his own panic, they burst from the forest into the clearing. The engineers saw with a wave of relief, that the spaceship was still there, a pale shaft upright in the midst of water. Where the meadow had been was a long narrow lake, reflecting the faint light of the sky, freckled with drifting spatters of rain.

"How do we get to it?" Charlie turned to them.

"How high is the water? Is the ramp covered?" Henderson asked practically, squinting through the rain.

"Ramp looks the same. I see grass sticking up in the water. It's not deep."

Charlie took a careful step and then another out into the silvery surface. Spongy grass met his feet under the surface, and the water lapped above his ankles, but no higher.

"It's shallow."

They started out toward the ship. It took courage to put their feet down into a surface that suggested unseen depth. The shallow current of water tugged at their ankles, and grew deeper and stronger.

"Henderson, wait!"

The three stopped and turned at the call. The path to the village was close, curving away from the forest toward the distant river bank, a silvery road of water among dark bushes. A dark figure came stumbling along the path, surrounded by the silvery shine of the rising water. Ripples spread from his ankles as he ran.

He came to the edge where the bushes stopped and the meadow began, saw the lake-appearance of it, and stopped. The others were already thirty feet away.

"Henderson! Charlie!"

"Walk, it's not deep yet. Hurry up." Charlie gestured urgently for him to follow them. They were still thirty feet out, standing in the smooth silver of the rising water. It was almost to their knees.

Winton did not move. He looked across the shining shallow expanse of water, and his voice rose shrilly. "It's a lake, we need boats."

"It's shallow," Charlie called. The rain beat down on the water, speckling it in small vanishing pockmarks. The two engineers hesitated, looking back at Winton, sensing something wrong.

Winton's voice was low, but the harshness of desperation made it as clear as if he had screamed.

"Please. I can't swim—"

"Go get him," Henderson told Charlie. "He's got a phobia. I'll herd Spet to the ship, and then head back to help you."

Charlie was already splashing in long strides back to the immobile figure of the preacher. He started to shout when he got within earshot.

"Why didn't you say so, man? We almost left you behind!" He crouched down before the motionless fear-dazed figure. "Get on, man. You're getting taxi service."

"What?" asked Winton in a small distant voice. The water lapped higher.

"Get on my back," Charlie snapped impatiently. "You're getting transportation."

"The houses dissolved, and they went off in boats and left me alone.

28

They said that I was an evil spirit. I think they did the Hangings anyway, even though I told them it was wrong." Winton's voice was vague, but he climbed on Charlie's back. "The *houses* dissolved."

"Speak up, stop mumbling," muttered Charlie.

The spaceship stood upright ahead in the center of the shallow silver lake that had been a meadow. Its doors were open, and the bottom of the ramp was covered by water. Water tugged against Charlie's lower legs as he ran, and the rain beat against their faces and shoulders in a cool drumming.

It would have been pleasant, except that the fear of drowning was growing even in Charlie, and the silver of the shallow new lake seemed to threaten an unseen depth ahead.

"There seems to be a current," Winton said with an attempt at casual remarks. "Funny, this water looks natural here, as if the place were a river, and those trees look like the banks."

Charlie said nothing. Winton was right, but it would not be wise to tell a man with phobia about drowning that they were trying to walk across the bed of a river while the water returned to its channel.

"Why are you running?" asked the man he carried.

"To catch up with Henderson."

Once they were inside the spaceship with the door shut they could ignore the water level outside. Once inside, they would not have to tell Winton anything about how it was outside. A spaceship made a good submarine.

The water level was almost to Charlie's knees and he ran now in a difficult lurching fashion. Winton pulled up his feet nervously to keep them from touching the water. The plastic which they wore was semi-permeable to water and both of them were soaked.

"Who is that up ahead with Henderson?"

"Spet, the native boy."

"How did you persuade him to stay away from the ceremony?"

"We found him hanging and cut him down."

"Oh," Winton was silent a moment trying to absorb the fact that the engineers had succeeded in rescuing someone. "It's a different approach. I talked, but they wouldn't listen." He spoke apologetically, hanging on to Charlie's shoulders, his voice jolting and stopping as Charlie tripped over a concealed tuft of grass or small bush under the water. "They didn't even answer—or look at me. When the water got deep they went off in little boats and didn't leave a boat for me." Charlie tripped again and staggered to one knee. They both briefly floundered waist deep in the water, and then Charlie was up again, still with a grip on his passenger's legs, so that Winton was firmly on his back.

When he spoke again Winton's tone was casual, but his voice was hysterically high in pitch. "I asked them for a boat, but they wouldn't look at me."

Charlie did not answer. He respected Winton's attempt to conceal his terror. The touch of water can be a horrifying thing to a man with a phobia of drowning. He could think of nothing to distract Winton's attention from his danger, but he hoped desperately that the man would not notice that the water had deepened. It is not possible to run in water over knee height. There was no way to hurry, now. The rain had closed in in veiling curtains, but he thought he saw the small figures of Henderson and the native in the distance reach the ramp which led to the spaceship.

If the flood hit them all now, Henderson and Spet could get inside, but how would he himself get this man with a phobia against water off his back and into the water to swim? He could visualize the bony arms tightening around his throat in an hysterical stranglehold. If a drowning man gets a clutch on you, you are supposed to knock him out and tow him. But how could he get this non-swimming type off his back and out where he could be hit?

If Winton could not brace himself to walk in water up to his ankles, he was not going to let go and try to swim in water up to his neck. He'd flip, for sure! Charlie found no logical escape from the picture. The pressure of the strong bony arms around his throat and shoulders and the quick irregular breathing of the man he was carrying made him feel trapped.

The water rose another inch or so, and the drag of it against his legs became heavier. The current was pulling sidewise.

"You're going slowly." Winton's voice had the harsh rasp of fear.

"No hurry," with difficulty, Charlie found breath to speak in a normal tone. "Almost there."

The curtain of rain lifted for a moment and he saw the spaceship, dark against the sky, and the ramp leading to its open door. The ramp was very shrunken, half covered by the rising water. It seemed a long way ahead.

As he watched, a light came on.

In the archway of the spaceship, Henderson flipped a switch and the lights went on.

Spet was startled. Sunlight suddenly came from the interior of the hut and shone against the falling rain in a great beam. Rain glittered through the beam in falling drops like sparks of white fire. It was very unlike anything real, but in dreams sunlight could be in one place and rain another at the same time, and no one in the dream country was surprised. And these were people who usually lived in the dream country, so apparently they had the power to do it in the real world also.

Nevertheless, Spet was afraid, for the sunlight did not look right as it was, coming out in a great widening beam across the rippling rain-pocked water. Sunlight did not mix well with rain.

"Sunlight," Spet said apologetically to his relative-ghost.

The brown ghost nodded and led him down the slope of the ramp through the strange sparkling sunlight, with the ramp strange and hard underfoot.

"Don't go inside until I return," the ghost said, mouthing the words with difficulty. The ghost placed his hands around the railing of the ramp. "You hang on here and wait for me," said the brown ghost of someone in his family, and waded down into the water.

Spet followed him down into the comfortable water until his sore feet were off the end of the ramp and in the cooling soft mud, and then he gripped the rail obediently and waited. The water lapped at his waist like an embrace, and the wind sang a death-song for him.

The bright glare of the strange sunlight on the dancing water was beautiful, but it began to hurt his eyes. He closed them, and then heard a sound other than the wind. Two sounds.

One sound he recognized as the first flood crest crashing through the trees to the north, approaching them, and he knew he must hurry and drown before it arrived, because it was rough and hurtful.

The other sound was the strange voice of the black spirit which usually gibbered on top of the Box That Talks. Spet opened his eyes, and saw that the gibbering spirit was riding on the shoulders of the brown ghost, as he and his friend, the other brown ghost, moved through the waist-deep water towards Spet and the ramp.

The black spirit gibbered at him as they passed, and Spet felt a dim anger, wondering if it would bring bad luck to him with its chants, for its intentions could not be the same as friendly ghosts.

"Spet, come up the ramp with us. It's dry inside. Don't look like that, there's nothing to be afraid of now, we'll go inside and shut the door, it will keep the water away, it won't get in... Come along Spet."

The black spirit suddenly leaped down on the ramp with a strange scream. *"Aaaaiiii... He's turning into a seaweed. Quick, get him out of the water! Help!"*

The spirit with the black skin and white face possibly wanted him for his own dark spirit world. He was coming down the ramp at Spet, screaming. He was too late though, Spet knew that he was safe for the dim land of the drowned with the friendly ghosts who had come for him. He felt his feet sending roots down into the mud, moving and rooting downward, and a wild joy came over him, and he knew that this was the right thing for him, much more right and natural than it would have been to become a tall sad adult.

He had been feeling a need for air, panting and drawing the cold air into his lungs. Just as the clawed hands of the dark spirit caught hold of his neck, Spet had enough air, and he leaned over into the dark and friendly water, away from the painful beauty of the bright lights and moving forms. The water closed around him, and the sound of voices was lost.

He could still feel the grip of the spirit's bony arms around his neck, pulling upward, but he had seen the brown ghosts running towards them, and they would stop it from doing him any harm...so he dismissed the fear from his mind, and bent deeper into the dark, and plunged his hands with spread fingers deep into the mud, and gripped his ankles as if he had always known just how to do this thing. His hands locked and became unable to unfold. They would never unfold again.

He felt the soft surge that was the first flood wave arriving and passing above him, and ignored it, and, with a mixture of terror and the certainty of doing right, he opened his mouth and took a deep breath of cold water.

All thought stopped. As the water rushed into his lungs, the rooted sea creature that was the forgotten adult stage of Spet's species began its thoughtless pseudo-plant existence, forgetting everything that had ever happened to it. Its shape changed.

The first wave of the flood did not quite reach up to the edge of the ship's entrance. It caught the two engineers as they dragged a screaming third human up the ramp toward the entrance, but it did not quite reach into the ship, and when it passed the three humans were still there. One of them struck the screaming one, and they carried him in.

Winton was hysterical for some time, but Henderson seemed quite normal. He worked well and rationally in compiling a good short survey report to carry to the planetary survey agency, and when the waters dried around the spaceship he directed the clearing of mud from the jets and the overhaul of the firing chambers without a sign of warp in his logic.

He did not want to speak to any native, and went into the ship when they appeared.

Winton was still slightly delirious when they took off from the planet but, once in space, he calmed down and made a good recovery. He just did not talk about it. Henderson still seemed quite normal, and Charlie carefully did not tell Winton that Henderson kept a large bush in a glass enclosure in the engine room.

Ever since that time Henderson has been considered a little peculiar. He is a good enough risk for the big liners, for they have other engineers on board to take over if he ever cracks.

He has no trouble getting jobs, but wherever he goes, he brings with him an oversized potted plant and puts it in the engine room and babies it with water and fertilizer. His fellow officers never kid him about it, for it is not a safe subject.

When Henderson is alone, or thinks he is alone, he talks to the potted bush. His tone is coaxing. But the bush never answers.

Charlie runs into him occasionally when their ships happen to dock at the same spaceport around the same planet. They share a drink and enjoy a few jokes together, but Charlie takes care not to get signed onto the same ship as Henderson. The sight of Henderson and his potted bush together make him nervous.

It's the wrong bush, but he'll never tell Henderson that.

WISH UPON A STAR

by Judith Merril

(Originally appeared in the December 1958 issue of *Fantasy & Science Fiction*)

I love "organic" science fiction, where biology is as relevant to the story as machinery. I love the mix of starships and pollination, of computer calculations and the richness of dark earth waiting to hold new life. "Wish Upon a Star," a tale of generation ship colonization of another star, begins with children and plants and family relationships that obviously aren't the ones we have on earth.

Judith Merril was a founding member of the Futurian Society, one of the earliest science fiction fans-and-writers clubs. They shaped the culture of science fiction for decades, until it was solid and well-known enough that no one organization could reach all of it. Futurians split from other SF clubs over ideologies: They wanted fiction that reached for a world where people were treated fairly, where technology was used to improve everyone's lives, where war only happened if someone or something had failed. This stood in stark contrast to the conquer-the-galaxy militaristic science fiction that filled many of the pulps. Merril, specifically, wrote fiction that had families, not just "heroes."

Merril became known for her writing and editing during a time when many women felt they had to hide their gender to get published at all. Although she wrote sports stories under pseudonyms, and some of her works were first published under male names, Judith Merril mainly published under her own name. She slowly pushed her way into a male-dominated field, sometimes with fiction, and sometimes by collecting and curating the stories of others. She edited SF: The Year's Greatest Science Fiction and Fantasy *in 1956 and for three more years, joining Asimov (another Futurian) and Bleiler in the quest to recognize and share the best of each year's stories. In fact, Merril is acknowledged as one of mid-Century SF's most important anthologizers, collecting pieces not just from the SF mags, but from mainstream sources like* Playboy, Harper's, *and* Rogue.

"Wish Upon a Star" is an excellent example of her writing talents. Even in a scant few thousand words, she draws several disparate elements together (people, technology, politics, intentions), showcasing them rather than explaining, and lets the reader find the connections between them and grow to understand the plot as the characters and setting are revealed.

When she first introduced Lieutenant Johnson, a woman, I thought, "Huh, isn't that rather progressive for when this was written?" And I assumed Merril was making a state-ment: Look, women can be starship officers! Later, I realized that wasn't quite the point she was making. She was talking about communities, not the military: Look, if you need emotional stability and group cohesion, put women in charge.

I found myself fascinated. I wanted to know what happened to young Sheik next—next week, next year, next decade. In the more distant future, Sheik's descendants will have colonized a new planet. I wish I could read those stories. For now, I can see both hope and worry, and I want to know which wins out in the end.

The year "Wish Upon a Star" was published, Nikita Khrushchev had risen to prominence in the Soviet Union, denouncing Stalin's violence and promising to focus on

36

improving the lives of everyday citizens. Mao Zedong's "Great Leap Forward" intended to bring China out of rural agricultural poverty and into the technological era. Schools in the US were ordered to integrate; racial bias was no longer a valid reason to deny someone an education. President Eisenhower sent the first message "from space," through the world's first communication satellite: "I convey to you and all mankind America's wish for peace on earth and good will to men everywhere."

Not all of those bright beginnings turned out well, and dark forces threatened to overcome the chance of a better future: McCarthyism was in full swing, Cold War tensions could explode any day, and the civil rights movement still faced many social and legal barriers. Still, there was room for hope—and wishing on stars.

"Wish Upon a Star" is a feminist story. While some aspects of its women-are-equal message are directly stated, others are more subtle. The culture of the adults is ours, or something like it, but the children's is not. Their community, purposely designed to meet the needs of space travel, is not shaped around the biases that are woven into every civilization on earth. What will these people be like after they've reached their destination and set up a society that's not driven entirely by survival? How will their future grow from these seeds?

What could we learn from them, these children of the children of the stars?

—Erica Frank

I wish, I wish, I wish…

Sheik sat under the shadow of a broad-leaf shrub, his head back, eyes closed against the glare from overhead, mouth open for a shout of protest he could never voice.

He stifled the thought with the sound, pushed it out of his head as he pushed his body backward, throwing his weight straight-armed on the flat palms of his hands behind him. Flexing his calves below bent knees, he pulled against the long thigh sinews and tightened the slanting muscles of his back, driving all tension from his mind into his body as he raised his buttocks up off the ground and hung suspended, arching from knees to elbows, hands and feet rooted to the soil. Wholly intent on the immediate physical effort, he stayed so till the blood rushing to his head choked in his throat, and arms and legs were trembling beyond control. Then with a last summoning of purpose, he flipped over and sprawled contentedly collapsed on chest and stomach, head turned so one cheek also rested on the resilient softness of the granular stuff that made the plant beds. With each great breath of air his nostrils sucked up the rich sweet damp aroma of the roots.

For a moment there was peace; and then, again, *I wish, I wish, I wish*...

Tears filled his eyes. He sat up and angrily and brushed them off. He was too old for crying. Crying wouldn't help. He was too old to be sitting idle here, wasting time, wasting wishes on absurdities. Old enough not to be bothered by anything Naomi said or did...but not yet old enough (smart enough?) to know better than to try to tell her anything.

She had listened so meekly, watched so quietly, while he repaired the rootpack she had broken, holding the torn parts—just *so*—together, tamping the soil down—just *so*—around the fiber, explaining as he worked why it was just *this* way. He let her silence fool him; well, it was no one's fault but his own. He should have known better by now.

When he was finished, she smiled, very sweetly. "It's so *comforting* to know you'll be here, Sheik," she said, "when *I'm* in charge. You're so *efficient*." Then a quick glance at the chrono, which she must have been watching all the time from the corner of her eye, or she couldn't have timed it all so perfectly. "Oh-oooh! I better run! I'm late for Sessions now..." And she was off, flashing a hand free of dirt or work, leaving him, trowel in hand, to realize he had just finished doing her job for her.

It wasn't fair. Naomi was twelve and a half, more than a year younger than he was. In Standard School she was behind him in almost everything; and never, never as long as she lived, would she be able to handle a plant, to feel it and *understand* it, as he did. But she was the one in Special Sessions classes now, learning the things he ought to know. They'd make her read all the books *he* wanted, whether she cared or not, and put her to learn in the lab, mastering all the mysteries and intricacies of advanced Bichem. While he, Toshiko, would go on day after day, trowel in hand, taking her jibes now, and later—much later, when he replaced Abdur in charge of the plantroom—taking her orders as Ab took his orders from Lieutenant Johnson.

It just wasn't *fair!*

I wish, I wish I was...

He stopped it, cut it off sharply. He was not going to think that way any more. *I wish Sarah was here*, he finished the thought instead. Tonight, maybe, she would ask him again. He had nursery duty, but if he told Bob...*if* she asked him, that was...well, if she did, he'd get off duty somehow...

Without even closing his eyes, he could see her there now, as she had been the night before last, sprawled on the rootpacks beside him, her shining long legs golden under the ultras, her face in the shadow of the leafy shrub a deep dark brown, but somehow giving out the gold-glow, too. Her eyes were closed and her hand, smooth and cool, soft and small, lay inside his as he watched her in warm and perfect comradeship.

For most of an hour, they had barely moved or talked: they just lay there together in the private shadow, sharing what had been his alone, thinking and dreaming silently but not separately at all.

Nothing Naomi said or did ought to matter now, because things-as-they-were had given him this special thing, a place and a significance, to share with Sarah. Never before had he told anyone about the shadows—how he felt about them. (No one but Ab, of course, but that was different; Ab *knew*.) She had seen them, naturally, most every day of her life; everyone in the ship had. The nursery-age children spent at least an hour each day hullside, for ultra exposure and exercise as well as their basic Bichem. When they started with Standard School class-work, they were required to spend a half hour of playtime every day under the lamps. But it was the light they came for; the shadows belonged to Sheik.

When he was just old enough to be allowed to go about alone, he started coming down hullside every chance he had; the shadows drew him. Later, the plants became important, too, and now he knew that they would be his work all his life. That was good in itself, but better because the shadows were part of the plants.

Nowhere else in the whole ship was there anything like it. Once in a while, the floorlight or one of the walls in the regular living and work rooms would go out of whack, and for a brief time the diffusion would be distorted and patches of dark-and-bright showed when people moved. But only here, where the thick rootpack lined the whole inner shell of the ship's hull, where there were only struts instead of walls, and the great ultra lamps glared day and night overhead, only here were there real *shadows*, under the plants, stationary, permanent, and shaped.

The ultras were never dimmed. They shone, Sheik thought, with the same brilliant fixity of time and purpose as the pinpointed stars on the black satin of the lounge viewplate. And in the center of this same clump of shrubbery where he lay now there was a hollow spot where some of the oldest, tallest plants grew so thick no light could penetrate, where it was dark, *black*, almost as black as the space between the stars: the way, he thought, a planet's night must be.

And this spot, where he had taken Sarah, was—depending where you held your head—a moonlit planet night, a 'twilight,' 'morning,' or 'afternoon'...all words in books, until they took on meaning here where the leaves and lights produced an infinitude of ever-changing shades and combinations of black, gray, green, brown, and gold.

He had never told anyone how he thought about that. Not Abdur; not even Sarah, yet. But if she asked him to take her here again, he thought, he could tell her; she would really understand.

He sat up sharply, the faint rustling sound like an answer to a prayer. *Sarah?*

Two plant stalks parted cautiously and a small, round, brown face stared into his own.

"What are *you* doing down here now?" Sheik demanded. How had the fool kid found him here?

"I *told* 'm I'd find you," Hari said triumphantly. "I *told* 'm I could. You better hurry. Ab's mad at you. He has to work onna mew-tay-

40

shuns," the small boy said the new word carefully, "an' you're supposed to be our teacher this time."

Sheik scrambled to his feet. Nursery class here already? *That* late? He'd spent half the afternoon doing nothing, dreaming... Ab must be mad, all right!

"You forgot about us," Hari said.

He hadn't forgotten; he had just forgotten time. "Come on, shrimpy," he told Harendra gruffly. "Better hop on if you want to get back *quick*." He squatted and Hari climbed on his shoulders—a rare and special treat; it would make up for his seeming to forget. He started for Abdur's workroom at a trot.

Harendra was three years old now, almost four, but he was Toshiko's favorite in the nursery still. He had been Sheik's first full-charge baby; sometimes he didn't seem too sure himself which one was his father, Abdur or Sheik. Certainly he didn't care; he loved them both with the same fierce intensity. And it upset him if Ab was angry with Sheik.

Abdur had been spending all his time the past few days struggling to save a planting of mutant seedlings newly developed in the Bichem lab. It was a high-protein lentil with a new flavor, but some mysterious lack in rootpack nourishment—the kind of thing that showed up only in actual growth conditions—made it essential to nurse each plant with extra care while the lab techs tried to find the cause of the trouble.

The intricate, patient skill with which Abdur tended the delicate young plants was fascinating to Sheik. And the young children, he thought, would be interested in the luminous unfamiliar yellow of the sickly leaves.

Abdur agreed with evident satisfaction to having the children visit the sick patch. He rebuked Sheik only briefly and without heat for his forgetfulness, and set out immediately for his plants, taking the way cross-ship, through the central living section, to reach the area on the other side of the hull without further delay. Toshiko took his troupe of six around by the hullside route, routinely replying to the inevitable routine questions at each step: why was this plant taller, the other stalk thicker, a leaf a darker green or different shape. To most of the grown people on board, the endless rows of plants covering the whole inner

41

surface of the ship's hull were monotonous and near identical. Abdur knew better; so did Sheik; and the nursery kids noticed things sometimes that Toshiko hadn't seen himself.

But this time he didn't want to stop at every plant. It was a slow enough trip with their short legs, and he hurried them past spots where he might otherwise have tried to show them something new or slightly changed. Then Dee, silly dimpled shrieking Dina, who, at barely two, should not (in Sheik's opinion) have come into the nursery class as yet, sat herself down on the rootpacks and refused to budge.

Toshiko bent to pick her up. He'd carry her, rather than waste time coaxing now. But she pointed to one root, growing wrong, malformed and upended, and stopped progress completely by spilling out a spurt of only half-coherent but entirely fascinated inquiry.

Well, he had been wrong; she *was* old enough. Sheik sat down beside her and got to work, framing his answers to her questions carefully, trying to give her a new mystery each time to provoke the next useful question. He pulled packing away from around the upended root, dug down, and placed the root where it belonged, giving all the children a chance to see how the other roots lay in the pack before he covered it. He explained how the roots drank nourishment from the soil, and floundered attempting to explain the action of the ultraviolet lamps.

All the while, Hari hung over his shoulder, watching; the boy had seen it all before, when Dina was too little to care, but he drank in every sight and every word as if it were the first time for him, too.

"It's like being tucked in," he broke in suddenly, offering his own level of lucidity in place of Sheik's complications. "Like when your daddy tucks you in at night and kisses you and you feel warm and good all over you and you grow in your sleep."

Dina's black eyes were shining with excitement. "I know," she said. "Every night when I sleep I grow." She lifted a hand to prove the point. "*Way* up!"

"Well, that's how it is," Hari nodded commendation to his pupil. "Only the lights don't have to go out for the plants to sleep, because they're asleep all the time. Underneath there. *That's* why they never go anyplace."

His voice lost some confidence at the end. He looked to Toshiko for approval, and Dina looked for confirmation.

Sheik hesitated, failed to find words for a more adequate explanation, and decided Hari had probably put across more than he could for right now. He nodded and smiled at them both. "Come on, now, or we won't have time to see the new plants." They all ran after him.

Lieutenant Johnson was on duty at the children's supper that evening. She strolled casually from one of the four tables to another, listening to a scrap of conversation here, answering a question there, correcting a younger child somewhere else, reminding Fritzi—who at eleven had just become a table leader—to keep her group quieter.

At Sarah's table she paused only briefly; the officer on duty never had to stop there except for a greeting. Sarah and Sheik had seven in their group, more than anyone else, but they never had trouble. They were a good combination; Sheik glowed inwardly with his awareness of this, and with the feeling that the same thought was passing through Johnson's mind as she looked from one end of the table to the other. He didn't need any smiles from Johnson to keep him happy tonight, though. In the lounge, just before, Sarah *had* asked him. As soon as he could swap his evening duty, he was to meet her and take her down hullside again.

He caught her glance across the table as the Lieutenant walked away, and saw her wink at him. With astonishment he thought, *She's as happy as I am! She wants to go, too!*

He knew, though he could not see as she bent over the carving, how her breasts had begun to swell under her shirt, and he knew by heart, though they were hidden behind the table, the long clean curves of those golden legs. Mechanically he added lentils to carrobeet top and passed a plate down, reminding Adolph Liebnitz that there was a fork at his place, and he should use it. He answered a question of Irma's without ever knowing what she asked, filled another plate, kept his eyes off Sarah thinking, *This time...this time I'll...* Added a little extra greens to Justin's plate, skimping on the carrobeets the kid hated... *This time I'll...* Looked up, caught Sarah's eye again, felt himself going hot and red, and dropped the thought.

He was in a warm daze still when Lieutenant Johnson mounted the rostrum to conclude the meal with the evening prayer. Sheik chanted the familiar words of thanksgiving, suddenly meaningful, and looked directly at Sarah as they finished, saying to her and her alone, "Survive in Peace!"

The Lieutenant read off the cleanup assignments, and then, just as casually as if she were making a routine announcement instead of delivering a stomach punch, added, "There will be game-room play for Classes Three and Four till bedtime. Special Sessions girls are invited to attend a staff meeting in the wardroom immediately after senior supper."

Sarah threw him a look of mild disappointment. "Tomorrow?" she mouthed. He didn't answer, pretended not to see. Tomorrow? Sure. What difference did it make to *her*?

And then he was angry at himself. It wasn't Sarah's fault. And you couldn't blame her for being excited about a wardroom meeting. It had to be something *big* for the Sessions to get asked into wardroom. He tried to meet her eye again, but everyone was getting up; people were moving; he caught a glimpse of her back, and then couldn't see her at all. Desultorily, he drifted with the other older children to the lounge and stood staring at the big screen.

The sun was big now, filling one whole sixteenth sector. Maybe the meeting...? He couldn't get excited. There'd been too many false alarms when they began decelerating almost a year ago, rumors and counter rumors and waves of excitement about how the tapes were coming out of the calckers, how it was *the* planet... No, it was poisonous, ammonia atmosphere... No, it was just a barren sun... It was the right one after all; it had a perfect earth-type atmosphere, one-third the mass...

Meaningless words, after all, to those who had been born on board *Survival*; words out of books. The older people had been more excited than the kids. "Earth-type" *meant* something to them.

But that was a year ago, and every day since the sun had grown bigger on the plate, and no day had brought any real news, except somewhere along the way it had been confirmed officially that there *were* planets—type as yet unknown. Bob said he thought it would be four or five more months before they came in close enough to give the calckers anything to work on.

Last year, when they first began decelerating, Bob had talked a lot to Sheik, times when they were by themselves in quarters, the little ones napping or asleep for the night. It was the first time, really, since Toshiko's nursery years that he and his father had been close. From the time he was six, when he was assigned for training in the plant rooms, Abdur had grown to fill the role of father-advisor more and more. But when the bright sun started to grow faintly brighter on the viewscreen, Bob's excitement was uncontainable; he poured it out on his son, a boy incredibly grown to where, by the time a landing was likely to take place, he would be in effect one of the men.

And the men, Bob told him, would have to work together when that happened. Things on a planet would not be quite the same as on board ship. For weeks, Bob reminisced and daydreamed, talking about Earth and its homes and families and governments, about the launching of the ship, *Survival*, and how and why things were set up on board ship as they were.

Some of it Sheik had heard in class; other parts he was cautioned to forget except in private. Everyone knew that the *Survival* was Earth's first starship, a colonizing expedition sent to find a planet—*if* there was one suitable for the spillover of the world's crowded billions. Everyone knew the voyage might take years or decades; the ship was completely self-contained; the ion drive made it possible to carry fuel enough for a hundred years. There were living quarters on either side of those now in use that had never been unlocked; if a third or fourth generation grew up on board ship, they'd be needed.

But if it took that long, it would do Earth no good. If the ship could not return with news of an established colony within fifty years, then it was under orders not to return at all, but to remain and start over altogether in the new place.

This much was common knowledge, and one further fact: that the original crew of twenty-four had included twenty women and four men for obvious biological race-survival reasons.

What they didn't tell in classes was why all of the men were subordinates, none of them trained for astrogation, electronics, communications, or any of the skilled jobs of ship control; why all the officers were women. The children took it for granted as they grew; the ship was the way things were and always had been; the readers that spoke of families and pets and churches, towns and villages and lakes and oceans, aircraft and weather, were fascinating, and in a quaint way, true, no doubt; but reality was the ship with its four family units, domestic fathers, energetic women, school dorms, communal meals.

Bob's talk of men who "ran their own families" and ruled their homes, of male supremacy in the environment of a hostile world, of wives and husbands cleaving one to one faithfully, first intrigued Sheik, then excited him, while he regarded it as fairy-tale stuff. But when his father pointed out one day that there were just as many boys as girls among the children—a fact Toshiko somehow had not thought about before—everything the old man said struck home in a new way.

"Then *why* did they put the women in charge of everything?" he demanded for the first time.

Bob's answer was incoherent, angry and fantasizing. Later Toshiko took his puzzlement to Ab, who explained, tight-lipped, that women were considered better suited to manage the psychological problems of an ingrown group, and to maintain with patience over many, many years, if needed, the functioning and purpose of the trip.

"Then when we land...?"

"*When* we land, there will be time enough to think about it! Who's been talking to you about all this?"

"Well, I was asking Bob," Sheik said cautiously. "But..."

"But nothing," Abdur said sharply. "If you're smart, Sheik, you'll forget it now. If anyone else hears this kind of talk from you, your father will be in trouble. Or I will. Forget it."

And for the most part, he did. Bob never spoke of it again. And Ab spoke only as he always had, of sun and rain, forests and gardens, sunsets and hillsides and farmlands *outdoors* on a planet.

Sheik stared at the giant sun on the viewscreen; if they had found their planet, if they landed here, he was almost a man...

No. He *was* a man. He could do everything a man could do, and he was very strong, stronger than any of the girls. And Sarah, he thought, was very close to womanhood. She was the oldest of the girls; it would be natural. One man and one woman, Bob had said...the thought was exciting. There was no other woman he would want to have. Naomi or Fritzi or Beatrice, the other older girls, were *nasty*. As for the crew— Lieutenant Johnson, maybe, but—but when he thought of Sarah the idea of being at the call of four others besides was obscene somehow.

Sheik laughed abruptly and turned and left the lounge. He had spent enough time today dreaming fantasies. There was work to do.

Still, when the last of the little ones was tucked in bed, and the quarters were quiet, Sheik found himself pacing restlessly in the tiny pantry-service room. He had his schoolbooks with him, and had meant to study for the morning's class. But when he tried to read, plant shadows and Sarah's legs and all the things Bob had said raced through his mind, blurring the print. He wished Bob would come back from wherever he was. The kids were asleep; there was only one hour till he himself had to be in dorm, and he was obsessed with the need to go hullside, to find his cool shadow-corner and lie there where peace was always to be found.

And obsessed, foolishly, with the idea that after the meeting Sarah might, just *might*, go down to look and see if he was there...

Bob didn't come. After a while Toshiko closed his book, wrote a quick note, "Hullside. Back in a minute," and went out.

He had never done such a thing before. He had broken rules, yes, but not when the children were in his care. But, really, what could happen? If one of them woke up, if anything went wrong, half an hour could not mean life or death. And...

And he didn't care. He *had* to go.

Quickly and quietly, exhilarated beyond previous experience by the sense of his guilt, he went down companionways towards the hull. He closed the last hatch behind him and stood on the top step looking down into the shadowed vastness of hullside. He was above the lamps. Beneath them was bright yellow light; then pale green, new leaves at the top of the plant stalks. Darker green below. Brownish-green stalks, some slender swaying things, some thick as his own arm. And underneath, the shadows. He started down, quietly still, but beginning already to feel more at ease.

Then he heard the voice. Bob's voice. Urgent, persuasive.

"I tell you it's *true*. This time it's true. I got it straight."

"Hell, Bob, every time they send in a tech to film something secret, you think that's *It*. You said the same thing six months ago, and how many times before that?" That was Sean, Sarah's father, who ran the livestock rooms.

"This time I know I'm right," Bob said quietly. His voice was convincing, even to Sheik.

"Well, if it is, what do you want us to do, Bob?" Abdur, this time, also quiet. The voices were coming, Sheik realized, from Abby's little private room near the seedbeds.

"Just that I think it should have been announced. I want to know what they're up to, with that meeting. Ab, have you ever stopped to think that maybe when the time came, the *women wouldn't want to land?*"

Silence, shocked silence; Sheik stood like a statue on his step.

"Come off it, man." Sean. "They're not *that* crazy."

"It's not so crazy, Sean," Abdur said thoughtfully, and then: "But I don't see what we could do about it if they didn't. *And* I don't think they'd hold back, even if they wanted to."

"You got a lot of trust in human nature, Ab."

"No-o-o-o. Well, yes. I guess I do. But that's not why. Listen, Robert, what do you think kept you from going off your nut those first five years?"

"What do you want me to say?" Bob asked bitterly. "God?"

"Well, He may have helped. But that wasn't what I meant. You were in bad shape for a while. After Alice…"

"Watch yourself, Ab." Bob growled.

"Take it easy and listen a minute. After what happened—how come you didn't do the same thing?"

Sheik eased himself down to a sitting position on the top step and listened.

A lot of it made no sense. Alice had been one of the women, of course; there were nineteen now. Funny he'd never thought of *that* before! She must have died when he was still a baby. Most of the kids wouldn't even know the name.

48

And Bob, Bob had had something to do with Alice. The conversational scraps and fragmentary references were incomplete, but Sheik had a picture, suddenly, of something that had happened to his father, of something like what was, maybe, happening with him and Sarah, and wasn't *supposed* to happen.

He tried to think how he would feel, what he would do, if Sarah suddenly—were no more. He could not imagine it. Nobody ever died. Nobody on the ship was more than forty-five. If Bob had felt that way, and then Alice died, he could see why his father was—*funny*, sometimes. Why he imagined things and made up stories about the time on Earth.

The twin revelation—the knowledge that what he thought and felt for Sarah had happened to *other* people, often, and the shocked glimpse of grief inside his father—almost obscured the more immediate importance of what the men said down there.

"Indoctrination," Ab was saying.

Alice was the only one who hadn't had it. She had been the ship's doctor; "they," the planners, had thought someone on board, the "stablest" one, should be free of "post-hypno." Words, some new, some old but out of context here. *Indoctrinated...*the women were indoctrinated, too; they *couldn't* refuse to land the ship. Ab said so.

The others agreed with him. Bob didn't, at first, but after a while, though he kept arguing, Sheik knew even Bob was convinced.

Gradually, the voices turned more casual; the conversation slowed. Sheik thought it must be getting close to dorm curfew. He raised the hatch above him cautiously, hoisted himself up through it and let it down with silent care. He reached his own family quarters again without meeting anyone.

Inside, he put his note down the dispostll, checked on the sleeping children, and arranged himself in the galley with a book on his lap, his feet on the counter, and a yawn of boredom on his face. When Bob returned, he hung around hopefully a little while, but Bob was not feeling talkative.

Sheik had a few minutes till curfew still; without planning it, he found himself in the nightlit empty lounge, at the big screen, watching the giant sun, almost imagining he could see it grow bigger and closer against the dead black of space, straining his eyes absurdly for the planet…

Planet!

The pieces began to come together.

Voices came down the corridor, and a far part of his mind remembered the wardroom meeting, Sarah, the evening's plans. Just coming out now? Maybe he could see her still. That was silly—curfew soon. Well, tomorrow… Just coming out *now?* That was some meeting…

Meeting! And Bob said he knew *for sure* this time the tapes on the planet were through: It was a good one. They could land on it, and live.

Live on a planet.

His stomach felt funny for a minute, and he thought that was foolish, what was there to be *afraid* of?

Live on a planet. He thought the words slowly and purposefully. Planet. Plants. Plants on a planet. On a planet, plants grew everywhere, by themselves, *naturally*. That's what Ab said. He said they grew all over, so you'd have to *tear them out* to make a place to build your house.

House. Family. Inside-outside. They were all words in the books. Hills, sunsets, animals. *Wild* animals. Danger. But now he wasn't afraid; he *liked* the thought. Wild animals, he thought again, savoring it. Houses, inside and outside; inside, the family; outside, the animals. And plants. The *sun*shine…daytime…and night…

Shadows!

The light brightened around him. On a planet, there would be shadows all the time everywhere.

"Sheik…"

"Yes, Ma'am." He turned. The response was automatic… "indoctrinated?" …even before his mind reoriented.

The room was daylit again. Five of the women were standing just inside the door. Lieutenant Johnson was smiling, watching him.

"Better hop, boy. Curfew."

"Yes, Ma'am." He moved past the others. Johnson, closest to the doorway, reached out a hand and rumpled up his hair.

"Do your dreaming in bed, Sheik," she said tenderly, as if he were in the nursery still. But something was in her eyes that made him know she did not think he was a little boy. He felt better when he got outside.

The girls' dorm was to the right; he could see the last of the senior class girls disappearing through the door. If he moved faster…

He turned to the left, walked up to the boys' dorm, and almost missed hearing the sharp whispered noise from the cross-corridor beyond.

He looked back. No one in sight. Raced up the corridor, and she was *there*, waiting. Waiting for *him*.

"Sheik! Shhh…I just wanted to make sure…Tomorrow night?"

"Sure," he said.

Her eyes were shining. Like the Lieutenant, she was looking at him *differently*. But it was a different kind of difference, and he liked it. Very much.

"Sure," he said again. "Tomorrow night for sure." But neither one moved. A gong sounded softly. Curfew time.

"You better get back," she said. "I have a pass." Even her whispering voice was different. She was vibrating with excitement. It was *true!*

"Okay," he said. "Listen, Sarah. Let's not wait. What about tonight?"

"*Tonight?*"

"After inspection."

"You mean…?"

"Sneak down. It's easy," he promised out of the practice of an hour ago, and lied. "I've done it lots of times."

"Who with?"

He smiled. From inside the lounge they heard voices. "Listen, I got to get back. Right now. I'll meet you in Cargo G in half an hour. Then I'll show you how."

"But, Sheik…"

He didn't wait for her answer. He didn't dare. Johnson or one of the others would be out for inspection any minute now. He ran on his toes, silently, back down the corridor, tore off his clothes, jumped into bed,

51

pulled covers up, and did not open his eyes even to peek and see what officer it was when she came in to inspect the row of beds. He just lay there, astonished at what he had said and what he was—beyond hesitation—going to do.

He thought of the times he had waited and wanted and hoped for Sarah to ask him, to notice him, to pick him to dance with or play with or for a work partner. Now, all of a sudden, he had thrown himself at her head, suggested...

He began to be horrified. It wasn't the idea of breaking curfew rules. Yesterday, even this afternoon, that would have shocked him, but now—knowing about the planet changed all *that*. What bothered him now was the brazenness of it, the way he had practically begged her to come, and hadn't even waited to find out...

He wouldn't go. She'd never go. He was crazy to think...

She was laughing at him now.

I wish, he thought miserably, *I wish I was...*

Only he didn't. He didn't envy girls any more.

He lay very quietly in bed for fifteen minutes. Then he got up and pulled on his shorts. He looked at the six other beds in the schoolboys' dorm. Joel, the youngest, was nine, still a kid. The others were twelve, thirteen, eleven, eleven, twelve. Five of them who would soon be men. Like Bob and Ab, Bomba and Sean, and Sheik himself. He left the dorm, slipped down the corridor, thinking as he went of the words he had read somewhere, that he "moved like a shadow."

I wish, he thought, and turned round a corner to safety, *I wish that she comes.* And then: *I wish that we land on a planet* very *soon.*

A MATTER OF PROPORTION
by Anne Walker

(Originally appeared in the August 1959 issue of *Astounding Science Fiction*)

Born September 26, 1924 in Buffalo, NY, Anne Walker Gutterman is remembered in her obituary not as an SF author, but as an elementary school teacher. Anne was a member of the DAR, a Vassar graduate and member of Phi Beta Kappa. After the death of her husband, Arthur Gutterman, she continued in education, teaching English as a second language. She died at 91 in Fishersville, VA.

The world Anne Walker was writing for had seen a generation face death, deprivation and disability. They knew men who had inhaled mustard gas and seen the first generation of cyborgs try to hug their children and relearn to love their wives. Anne wrote "A Matter of Proportion" for The Magazine of Fantasy & Science Fiction *in 1959, her first story of two, and reading it, it's clear that she'd had the misfortune to see more than one generation maimed by war.*

In "A Matter of Proportion" Walker combines the fantasy of the super-soldier with cyborg science to introduce us to protagonist Willie and his experience with, and impressions of, a legendary soldier by the name of Scott. We then learn the reality of Scott's experience from his much more sobering personal perspective.

I remember the first time I read a story about a wounded soldier from Operation Storm, and the freedom of a replacement limb. The story was meant as a feel-good tale of a returning hero. We look at Senator Tammy Duckworth, and we imagine that her sacrifice of both legs turns her valor into, as Walker puts it in Willie's words, "big music and stars over the gorge."

But war is not the only thing that robs us of the use of our bodies. Disease doesn't come with Medals of Honor or write-ups in Parade magazine. No one considers life using a wheelchair noble.

I can already see the reply to that: "You wouldn't know anything about it." The spittle is visible even in text. "You're not one of us."

How do I explain that my apparent health and wellness is a façade that carefully conceals a lifetime of chronic illness...illnesses that landed me in the hospital regularly as a child and any day now could rob me of...well, anything. That's the real joy of the disease I have—you literally don't know what might be taken away from you, when. Today I can walk. That might not be true tomorrow.

I've seen it all too often: "We do our best to accommodate..." Walker, too, was familiar with the phenomenon. Though her story was written sixty years ago, it still rings true: a new computer receives more accommodation than a human being. I had to climb over one curb to get to the door, or walk to the skirt at either end of the large convention center's front entrance. Today I can do that. That might not be true tomorrow.

Tomorrow I might have to "multiply distances by five, heights by ten, and slickness by twenty" as Scott describes the challenges of functioning in a world built for the able. I might have to, like Scott, climb steps I am not able enough to navigate to prove I am worthy of a noble death.

War isn't the only thing that robs us use of our bodies, but it's the only time that theft is honored. Anne Walker wrote in the near aftermath of World War Two and the Korean War. She faced the very real fact of soldier cyborgs returning from a not-war, watched them fighting for freedoms they were no longer able to access, without a record that told the truth for another 50 years—until most of them were dead. She would have understood that.

As I read "A Matter of Proportion," I was cognizant of the daily battle for normalcy faced by those broken by our forever-war, learning skills that have little applicability to civilian life and people who face those same limitations without that same status.

Walker's story rings through with a deeply held belief: every struggle is a noble one. It seems to me we could and should award Medals of Honor to everyone who scales those icy steps, regardless of circumstance. I think that Anne Walker, Daughter of the Revolution as she was, would have agreed.

—Erica Friedman

In the dark, our glider chutes zeroed neatly on target—only Art Benjamin missed the edge of the gorge. When we were sure Invader hadn't heard the crashing of bushes, I climbed down after him. The climb, and what I found, left me shaken. A Special Corps squad leader is not expendable—by order. Clyde Esterbrook, my second and ICEG mate, would have to mine the viaduct while my nerve and glycogen stabilized.

We timed the patrols. Clyde said, "Have to wait till a train's coming. No time otherwise." Well, it was his show. When the next pair of burly-coated men came over at a trot, he breathed, "Now!" and ghosted out almost before they were clear.

I switched on the ICEG—inter-cortical encephalograph—planted in my temporal bone. My own senses could hear young Ferd breathing, feel and smell the mat of pine needles under me. Through Clyde's, I could hear the blind whuffle of wind in the girders, feel the crude wood of ties and the iron-cold molding of rails in the star-dark. I could feel, too, an odd, lilting elation in his mind, as if this savage universe were a good thing to take on—spray guns, cold, and all.

We wanted to set the mine so the wreckage would clobber a trail below, one like they'd built in Burma and Japan, where you wouldn't think a monkey could go; but it probably carried more supplies than the viaduct itself. So Clyde made adjustments precisely, just as we'd figured it with the model back at base. It was a tricky, slow job in the bitter dark.

I began to figure: If he armed it for this train, and ran, she'd go off while we were on location and we'd be drenched in searchlights and spray guns. Already, through his fingers, I felt the hum in the rails that every tank-town-reared kid knows. I turned up my ICEG. "All right, Clyde, get back. Arm it when she's gone past, for the next one."

I felt him grin, felt his lips form words: "I'll do better than that, Willie. Look, Daddy-o, no hands!" He slid over the edge and rested elbows and ribs on the raw tie ends.

We're all acrobats in the Corps. But I didn't like this act one little bit. Even if he could hang by his hands, the heavy train would jolt him off. But I swallowed my thoughts.

He groped with his foot, contacted a sloping beam, and brought his other foot in. I felt a dull, scraping slither under his moccasin soles. "Frost," he thought calmly, rubbed a clear patch with the edge of his foot, put his weight on it, and transferred his hands to the beam with a twist we hadn't learned in Corps school. My heart did a double-take; one slip and he'd be off into the gorge, and the frost stung, melting under his bare fingers. He lay in the trough of the massive H-beam, slid down about twenty feet to where it made an angle with an upright, and wedged himself there. It took all of twenty seconds, really. But I let out a breath as if I'd been holding it for minutes.

As he settled, searchlights began skimming the bridge. If he'd been running, he'd have been shot to a sieve. As it was, they'd never see him in the mingled glare and black.

His heart hadn't even speeded up beyond what was required by exertion. The train roared around a shoulder and onto the viaduct, shaking it like an angry hand. But as the boxcars thunder-clattered above his head, he was peering into the gulf at a string of feeble lights threading the bottom. "There's the flywalk, Willie. They know their stuff. But we'll get it." Then, as the caboose careened over and the searchlights cut off, "Well, that gives us ten minutes before the patrol comes back."

He levered onto his side, a joint at a time, and began to climb the beam. Never again for me, even by proxy! You just *couldn't* climb that thing nohow! The slope was too steep. The beam was too massive to shinny, yet too narrow to lie inside and elbow up. The metal was too smooth, and scummed with frost. His fingers were beginning to numb. And—he *was* climbing!

In each fin of the beam, every foot or so, was a round hole. He'd get one finger into a hole and pull, inching his body against the beam. He timed himself to some striding music I didn't know, not fast but no waste motion, even the pauses rhythmic.

I tell you. I was sweating under my leathers. Maybe I should have switched the ICEG off, for my own sake if not to avoid distracting Clyde. But I was hypnotized, climbing.

In the old days, when you were risking your neck, you were supposed to think great solemn thoughts. Recently, you're supposed to think about something silly like a singing commercial. Clyde's mind was neither posturing in front of his mental mirror nor running in some feverish little circle. He faced terror as big as the darkness from gorge bottom to stars, and he was just simply as big as it was—sheer life exulting in defying the dark, the frost and wind and the zombie grip of Invader. I envied him

Then his rhythm checked. Five feet from the top, he reached confidently for a finger hole… No hole.

He had already reached as high as he could without shifting his purchase and risking a skid—and even his wrestler's muscles wouldn't make the climb again. My stomach quaked: Never see sunlight in the trees any more, just cling till dawn picked you out like a crow's nest in a dead tree; or drop…

Not Clyde. His flame of life crouched in anger. Not only the malice of nature and the rage of enemies, but human shiftlessness against him too? Good! He'd take it on.

Shoulder, thigh, knee, foot scraped off frost. He jammed his jaw against the wet iron. His right hand never let go, but it crawled up the fin of the strut like a blind animal, while the load on his points of purchase mounted—watchmaker co-ordination where you'd normally think in boilermaker terms. The flame sank to a spark as he focused, but it never blinked out. This was not the anticipated, warded danger, but the trick punch from nowhere. This was It. A sneak squall buffeted him. I cursed thinly. But he sensed an extra purchase from its pressure, and reached the last four inches with a swift glide. The next hole was there.

He waited five heartbeats, and pulled. He began at the muscular disadvantage of aligned joints. He had to make it the first time; if you can't do it with a dollar, you won't do it with the change. But as elbow and shoulder bent, the flame soared again: Score one more for life!

A minute later, he hooked his arm over the butt of a tie, his chin, his other arm, and hung a moment. He didn't throw a knee up, just rolled and lay between the rails. Even as he relaxed, he glanced at his watch: three minutes to spare. Leisurely, he armed the mine and jogged back to me and Ferd.

As I broke ICEG contact, his flame had sunk to an ember glow of anticipation.

We had almost reached the cave pricked on our map, when we heard the slam of the mine, wee and far-off. We were lying doggo looking out at the snow peaks incandescent in dawn when the first Invader patrols trailed by below. Our equipment was a miracle of hot food and basic medication. Not pastimes, though; and by the second day of hiding, I was thinking too much. There was Clyde, an Inca chief with a thread of black mustache and incongruous hazel eyes, my friend and ICEG mate—what made him tick? Where did he get his delight in the bright eyes of danger? How did he gear his daredevil valor, not to the icy iron and obligatory killing, but to the big music and stars over the gorge? But in the Corps, we don't ask questions and, above all, never eavesdrop on ICEG.

Young Ferd wasn't so inhibited. Benjamin's death had shaken him—losing your ICEG mate is like losing an eye. He began fly-fishing Clyde: How had Clyde figured that stunt, in the dark, with the few minutes he'd had?

"There's always a way, Ferd, if you're fighting for what you really want."

"Well, I want to throw out Invader, all right, but—"

"That's the start, of course, but beyond that—" He changed the subject: perhaps only I knew of his dream about a stronghold for rebels far in these mountains. He smiled. "I guess you get used to calculated risks. Except for imagination, you're as safe walking a ledge twenty stories up, as down on the sidewalk."

"Not if you trip."

"That's the calculated risk. If you climb, you get used to it."

"Well, how did you *get* used to it? Were you a mountaineer or an acrobat?"

"In a way, both." Clyde smiled again, a trifle bitterly and switched the topic. "Anyway, I've been in action for the duration except some time in hospital."

Ferd was onto that boner like an infielder. To get into SC you have to be not only championship fit, but have no history of injury that could crop up to haywire you in a pinch. So, "Hospital? You sure don't show it now."

Clyde was certainly below par. To cover his slip he backed into a bigger, if less obvious, one. "Oh, I was in that Operation Armada at Golden Gate. Had to be patched up."

He must have figured, Ferd had been a kid then, and I hadn't been too old. Odds were, we'd recall the episode, and no more. Unfortunately, I'd been a ham operator and I'd been in the corps that beamed those fireships onto the Invader supply fleet in the dense fog. The whole episode was burned into my brain. It had been kamikaze stuff, though there'd been a theoretical chance of the thirty men escaping, to justify sending them out. Actually, one escape boat did get back with three men.

I'd learned about those men, out of morbid, conscience-scalded curiosity. Their leader was Edwin Scott, a medical student. At the very start he'd been shot through the lower spine. So, his companions put him in the escape boat while they clinched their prey. But as the escape boat sheered off, the blast of enemy fire killed three and disabled two.

Scott must have been some boy. He'd already doctored himself with hemostatics and local anesthetics but, from the hips down, he was dead as salt pork, and his visceral reflexes must have been reacting like a

59

worm cut with a hoe. Yet somehow, he doctored the two others and got that boat home.

The other two had died, but Scott lived as sole survivor of Operation Armada. And he hadn't been a big, bronze, Latin-Indian with incongruous hazel eyes, but a snub-nosed redhead. And he'd been wheel-chaired for life. They'd patched him up, decorated him, sent him to a base hospital in Wisconsin where he could live in whatever comfort was available. So, he dropped out of sight. And now, this!

Clyde was lying, of course. He'd picked the episode at random. Except that so much else about him didn't square. Including his name compared to his physique, now I thought about it.

I tabled it during our odyssey home. But during post-mission leave, it kept bothering me. I checked, and came up with what I'd already known: Scott *had* been sole survivor, and the others were certified dead. But about Scott, I got a runaround. He'd apparently vanished. Oh, they'd check for me, but that could take years. Which didn't lull my curiosity any. Into Clyde's past I was sworn not to pry.

We were training for our next assignment, when word came through of the surrender at Kelowna. It was a flare of sunlight through a black sky. The end was suddenly close.

Clyde and I were in Victoria, British Columbia. Not subscribing to the folkway that prescribes seasick intoxication as an expression of joy, we did the town with discrimination. At midnight we found ourselves strolling along the waterfront in that fine, Vancouver-Island mist, with just enough drink taken to be moving through a dream. At one point, we leaned on a rail to watch the mainland lights twinkling dimly like the hope of a new world—blackout being lifted.

Suddenly, Clyde said, "What's fraying you recently, Will? When we were taking our ICEG reconditioning, it came through strong as garlic, though you wouldn't notice it normally."

Why be coy about an opening like that? "Clyde, what do you know about Edwin Scott?" That let him spin any yarn he chose—if he chose.

He did the cigarette-lighting routine, and said quietly, "Well, I *was* Edwin Scott, Will." Then, as I waited, "Yes, really me, the real me talking to you. This," he held out a powerful, coppery hand, "once belonged to a man called Marco da Sanhao... You've heard of transplanting limbs?"

I had. But this man was no transplant job. And if a spinal cord is cut, transplanting legs from Ippalovsky, the primo ballerino, is worthless. I said, "What about it?"

"I was the first—successful—brain transplant in man."

For a moment, it queered me, but only a moment. Hell, you read in fairy tales and fantasy magazines about one man's mind in another man's body, and it's marvelous, not horrible. But—

By curiosity, I know a bit about such things. A big surgery journal, back in the '40s, had published a visionary article on grafting a whole limb, with colored plates as if for a real procedure[1]. Then they'd developed techniques for acclimating a graft to the host's serum, so it would not react as a foreign body. First, they'd transplanted hunks of ear and such; then, in the '60s, fingers, feet, and whole arms in fact.

But a brain is another story. A cut nerve can grow together; every fiber has an insulating sheath which survives the cut and guides growing stumps back to their stations. In the brain and spinal cord, no sheaths; growing fibers have about the chance of restoring contact that you'd have of traversing the Amazon jungle on foot without a map. I said so.

"I know," he said, "I learned all I could, and as near as I can put it, it's like this: When you cut your finger, it can heal in two ways. Usually it bleeds, scabs, and skin grows under the scab, taking a week or so. But if you align the edges exactly, at once, they may join almost immediately, healing by First Intent. Likewise in the brain, if they line up cut nerve fibers before the cut-off bit degenerates, it'll join up with the stump. So, take a serum-conditioned brain and fit it to the stem of another brain so that the big fiber bundles are properly fitted together, fast enough, and you can get better than ninety per cent recovery."

"Sure," I said, parading my own knowledge, "but what about injury to the masses of nerve cells? And you'd have to shear off the nerves

---

[1] Hall, "Whole Upper Extremity Transplant for Human Beings." *Annals of Surgery* 1944, #120, p. 12.

growing out of the brain."

"There's always a way, Willie. There's a place in the brain stem called the isthmus, no cell masses, just bundles of fibers running up and down. Almost all the nerves come off below that point; and the few that don't can be spliced together, except the smell nerves and optic nerve. Ever notice I can't smell, Willie? And they transplanted my eyes with the brain—biggest trick of the whole job."

It figured. But, "I'd still hate to go through with it."

"What could I lose? Some paraplegics seem to live a fuller life than ever. Me, I was going mad. And I'd seen the dogs this research team at my hospital was working on—old dogs' brains in whelps' bodies, spry as natural.

"Then came the chance. Da Sanhao was a Brazilian wrestler stranded here by the war. Not his war, he said; but he did have the decency to volunteer as medical orderly. But he got conscripted by a bomb that took a corner off the hospital and one off his head. They got him into chemical stasis quicker than it'd ever been done before, but he was dead as a human being—no brain worth salvaging above the isthmus. So, the big guns at the hospital saw a chance to try their game on human material, superb body and lower nervous system in ideal condition, waiting for a brain. Only, whose?

"Naturally, some big-shot's near the end of his rope and willing to gamble. But *I* decided it would be a forgotten little-shot, name of Edwin Scott. I already knew the surgeons from being a guinea pig on ICEG. Of course, when I sounded them out, they gave me a kindly brush-off: The matter was out of their hands. However, I knew whose hands it *was* in. And I waited for my chance—a big job that needed somebody expendable. Then I'd make a deal, writing my own ticket because they'd figure I'd never collect. Did you hear about Operation Seed-corn?"

That was the underground railway that ran thousands of farmers out of occupied territory. Manpower was what finally broke Invader, improbable as it seems. Epidemics, desertions, over-extended lines, thinned that overwhelming combat strength; and every farmer spirited out of their hands equaled ten casualties. I nodded.

"Well, I planned that with myself as director. And sold it to

Filipson."

I contemplated him: just a big man in a trench coat and droop-brimmed hat silhouetted against the lamp-lit mist. I said, "You directed Seed-corn out of a wheel chair in enemy territory, and came back to get transplanted into another body? Man, you didn't tell Ferd a word of a lie when you said you were used to walking up to death." (But there was more: Besides that dour Scott's fortitude, where did he come by that high-hearted valor?)

He shrugged. "You do what you can with what you've got. *Those* weren't the big adventures I was thinking about when I said that. I had a team behind me in those—"

I could only josh. "I'd sure like to hear the capperoo then."

He toed out his cigarette. "You're the only person who's equipped for it. Maybe you'd get it, Willie."

"How do you mean?"

"I kept an ICEG record. Not that I knew it was going to happen, just wanted proof if they gave me a deal and I pulled it off. Filipson wouldn't renege, but generals were expendable. No one knew I had that transmitter in my temporal bone, and I rigged it to get a tape on my home receiver. Like to hear it?"

I said what anyone would, and steered him back to quarters before he'd think better of it. This would be something!

On the way, he filled in background. Scott had been living out of hospital in a small apartment, enjoying as much liberty as he could manage. He had equipment so he could stump around, and an antique car specially equipped. He wasn't complimentary about them. Orthopedic products had to be: unreliable, hard to service, unsightly, intricate, and uncomfortable. If they also squeaked and cut your clothes, fine!

Having to plan every move with an eye on weather and a dozen other factors, he developed an uncanny foresight. Yet he had to improvise at a moment's notice. With life a continuous high-wire act, he trained every surviving fiber to precision, dexterity, and tenacity. Finally, he avoided help. Not pride, self-preservation; the compulsively helpful have rarely the wit to ask before rushing in to knock you on your face, so he learned to bide his time till the horizon was clear of beaming simpletons. Also, he found an interest in how far he could go.

These qualities, and the time he had for thinking, begot Seed-corn. When he had it convincing, he applied to see General Filipson, head of Regional Intelligence, a man with both insight and authority to make the deal—but also as tough as his post demanded. Scott got an appointment two weeks ahead.

That put it early in April, which decreased the weather hazard—a major consideration in even a trip to the Supermarket. What was Scott's grim consternation, then, when he woke on D-day to find his windows plastered with snow under a driving wind—not mentioned in last night's forecast of course.

He could concoct a plausible excuse for postponement—which Filipson was just the man to see through; or call help to get him to HQ—and have Filipson bark, "Man, you can't even make it across town on your own power because of a little snow." No, come hell or blizzard, he'd have to go solo. Besides, when he faced the inevitable unexpected behind Invader lines, he couldn't afford a precedent of having flinched now.

He dressed and breakfasted with all the petty foresights that can mean the shaving of clearance in a tight squeeze, and got off with all the margin of time he could muster. In the apartment court, he had a parking space by the basement exit and, for a wonder, no free-wheeling nincompoop had done him out of it last night. Even so, getting to the car door illustrated the ordeal ahead; the snow was the damp, heavy stuff that packs and glares. The streets were nasty, but he had the advantage of having learned restraint and foresight.

HQ had been the post office, a ponderous red-stone building filling a whole block. He had scouted it thoroughly in advance, outside and in, and scheduled his route to the general's office, allowing for minor hazards. Now, he had half an hour extra for the unscheduled major hazard.

But on arriving, he could hardly believe his luck. No car was yet parked in front of the building, and the walk was scraped clean and salted to kill the still falling flakes. No problems. He parked and began to unload himself quickly, to forestall the elderly MP who hurried towards him. But, as Scott prepared to thank him off, the man said, "Sorry, Mac, no one can park there this morning."

Scott felt the chill of nemesis. Knowing it was useless, he protested his identity and mission.

But, "Sorry, major. But you'll have to park around back. They're bringing in the big computer. General himself can't park here. Them's orders."

He could ask the sergeant to park the car. But the man couldn't leave his post, would make a to-do calling someone—and that was Filipson's suite overlooking the scene. No dice. Go see what might be possible.

But side and back parking were jammed with refugees from the computer, and so was the other side. And he came around to the front again. Five minutes wasted. He thought searchingly.

He could drive to a taxi lot, park there, and be driven back by taxi, disembark on the clean walk, and there you were. Of course, he could hear Filipson's "Thought you drove your own car, ha?" and his own damaging excuses. But even Out Yonder, you'd cut corners in emergency. It was all such a comfortable Out, he relaxed. And, relaxing, saw his alternative.

He was driving around the block again, and noted the back entrance. This was not ground level, because of the slope of ground; it faced a broad landing, reached by a double flight of steps. These began on each side at right-angles to the building and then turned up to the landing along the face of the wall. Normally, they were negotiable; but now, even had he found parking near them, he hadn't the chance of the celluloid cat in hell of even crossing the ten feet of uncleaned sidewalk. You might as well climb an eighty-degree, fifty-foot wall of rotten ice. But there was always a way, and he saw it.

The unpassable walk itself was an avenue of approach. He swung his car onto it at the corner, and drove along it to the steps to park in the angle between steps and wall—and discovered a new shut-out. He'd expected the steps to be a mean job in the raw wind that favored this face of the building; but a wartime janitor had swept them sketchily only down the middle, far from the balustrades he must use. By the balustrades, early feet had packed a semi-ice far more treacherous than the untouched snow; and, the two bottom steps curved out beyond the balustrade. So…a sufficiently reckless alpinist might assay a cliff in a sleet storm and gale, but he couldn't even try if it began with an overhang.

Still time for the taxi. And so, again Scott saw the way that was always there: Set the car so he could use its hood to heft up those first steps.

Suddenly, his thinking metamorphosed: He faced, not a miserable, unwarranted forlorn hope, but the universe as it was. Titanic pressure suit against the hurricanes of Jupiter, and against a gutter freshet, life was always outclassed—and always fought back. Proportions didn't matter, only mood.

He switched on his ICEG to record what might happen. I auditioned it, but I can't disentangle it from what he told me. For example, in his words: Multiply distances by five, heights by ten, and slickness by twenty. And in the playback: Thirty chin-high ledges loaded with soft lard, and only finger holds and toe holds. And you did it on stilts that began, not at your heels, at your hips. Add the hazard of Helpful Hosea: "Here, lemme giveya hand, Mac!", grabbing the key arm, and crashing down the precipice on top of you.

Switching on the ICEG took his mind back to the snug apartment where its receiver stood, the armchair, books, desk of diverting work. It looked awful good, but…life fought back, and always it found a way.

He shucked his windbreaker because it would be more encumbrance than help in the showdown. He checked shoelaces and strapped on the cleats he had made, for what they were worth. He vetoed the bag of sand and salt he kept for minor difficulties—far too slow. He got out of the car.

This could be the last job he'd have to do incognito—Seed-corn, he'd get credit for. Therefore, he cherished it: triumph for its own sake. Alternatively, he'd end at the bottom in a burlesque clutter of chrom-alum splints and sticks, with maybe a broken bone to clinch the decision. For some men, death is literally more tolerable than defeat in humiliation.

Eighteen shallow steps to the turn, twelve to the top. Once, he'd have cleared it in three heartbeats. Now, he had to make it to a twenty-minute deadline, without rope or alpenstock, a Moon-man adapted to a fraction of Earth gravity.

With the help of the car hood, the first two pitches were easy. For the next four or five, wind had swept the top of the balustrade, providing damp, gritty handhold. Before the going got tougher, he developed a technique, a rhythm and system of thrusts proportioned to heights and widths, a way of scraping holds where ice was not malignantly welded to stone, an appreciation of snow texture and depth, an economy of effort.

He was enjoying a premature elation when, on the twelfth step, a cleat strap gave. Luckily, he was able to take his lurch with a firm grip on the balustrade; but he felt depth yawning behind him. Dourly, he took thirty seconds to retrieve the cleat; stitching had been sawed through by a metal edge—just as he'd told the cocksure workman it would be. Oh, to have a world where imbecility wasn't entrenched! Well—he was fighting here and now for the resources to found one. He resumed the escalade, his rhythm knocked cockeyed.

Things even out. Years back, an Invader bomber had scored a near miss on the building, and minor damage to stonework was unrepaired. Crevices gave fingerhold, chipped-out hollows gave barely perceptible purchase to the heel of his hand. Salutes to the random effects of unlikely causes!

He reached the turn, considered swiftly. His fresh strength was blunted; his muscles, especially in his thumbs, were stiffening with chill. Now: He could continue up the left side, by the building, which was tougher and hazardous with frozen drippings, or by the outside, right-hand rail, which was easier but meant crossing the open, half-swept wide step and recrossing the landing up top. Damn! Why hadn't he foreseen that? Oh, you can't think of everything. Get going, left side.

The wall of the building was rough-hewn and ornamented with surplus carvings. Cheers for the 1890s architect!

Qualified cheers. The first three lifts were easy, with handholds in a frieze of lotus. For the next, he had to heft with his side-jaw against a boss of stone. A window ledge made the next three facile. The final five stared, an open gap without recourse. He made two by grace of the janitor's having swabbed his broom a little closer to the wall. His muscles began to wobble and waver: in his proportions, he'd made two-hundred feet of almost vertical ascent.

But, climbing a real ice-fall, you'd unleash the last convulsive effort because you had to. Here, when you came down to it, you could always sit and bump yourself down to the car which was, in that context, a mere safe forty feet away. So he went on because he had to.

He got the rubber tip off one stick. The bare metal tube would bore into the snow pack. It might hold, if he bore down just right, and swung his weight just so, and got just the right sliding purchase on the wall, and the snow didn't give underfoot or undercane. And if it didn't work—it didn't work.

Beyond the landing, westwards, the sky had broken into April blue, far away over Iowa and Kansas, over Operation Seed-corn, over the refuge for rebels that lay at the end of all his roads...

He got set...and lifted. A thousand miles nearer the refuge! Got set...and lifted, balanced over plunging gulfs. His reach found a round pilaster at the top, a perfect grip for a hand. He drew himself up, and this time his cleated foot cut through snow to stone, and slipped, but his hold was too good. And there he was.

No salutes, no cheers, only one more victory for life.

Even in victory, unlife gave you no respite. The doorstep was three feet wide, hollowed by eighty years of traffic, and filled with frozen drippings from its pseudo-Norman arch. He had to tilt across it and catch the brass knob—like snatching a ring in a high dive.

No danger now, except sitting down in a growing puddle till someone came along to hoist him under the armpits, and then arriving at the general's late, with his seat black-wet... You unhorse your foeman, curvet up to the royal box to receive the victor's chaplet, swing from your saddle, and fall flat on your face.

But, he cogitated on the bench inside, getting his other cleat off and the tip back on his stick, things do even out. No hearty helper had intervened, no snot-nosed, gaping child had twitched his attention, nobody's secretary—pretty of course—had scurried to helpfully knock him down with the door. They were all out front superintending arrival of the computer.

The general said only, if tartly, "Oh yes, major, come in. You're late, a'n't you?"

"It's still icy," said Ed Scott. "Had to drive carefully, you know."

In fact, he *had* lost minutes that way, enough to have saved his exact deadline. And that excuse, being in proportion to Filipson's standard dimension, was fair game.

I wondered what dimension Clyde would go on to, now that the challenge of war was past. To his rebels' refuge at last maybe? Does it matter? Whatever it is, life will be outclassed, and Scott-Esterbrook's brand of life will fight back.

THE WHITE PONY
by Jane Rice

(Originally appeared in the February 1960 issue of *Fantasy & Science Fiction*)

When it comes to influential, notable female names in science fiction and fantasy, the name Jane Rice should ring a few bells. An American science fiction and horror writer, Rice was born Jane Theresa Dixon on April 30, 1913 in Owensboro, Kentucky; she made her mark with her debut work "The Dream" in the July 1940 issue of the pulp fiction fantasy magazine Unknown. *From her captivating werewolf story "The Refugee" published in the October 1943* From Unknown Worlds *anthology to "The Idol of the Flies" showcased in the June 1942 issue, Rice's work has been characterized by her ability to convey entire worlds in just a few words. Her penchant for subtle worldbuilding served her well in the atmospheric mystery short stories she wrote for* Alfred Hitchcock's Mystery Magazine *in the 80s, and in 1995, she went on to write a horror novelette* The Sixth Dog *that was published by Necronomicon Press.*

Unfortunately, she did not live to see the publication of her second book, a collection of her short fiction called The Idol of the Flies and Other Stories. *Jane Rice died at the age of ninety in 2003, months before the book was published by Midnight House in a limited run of 500 copies. Her work lives on though, still tantalizing readers with an implicative word or subtle phrase.*

No work embodies that feeling more than "The White

Pony," published in the November 1960 issue of Fantasy Science Fiction Magazine *(the last of a trio of SFF stories that seemed to spring from nowhere before and after a long hiatus in the genre). "The White Pony" follows the ill-fated romance between Bill, a writer unable to "afford to be either eccentric or gregarious" if he "wanted to stay employed and solvent," and Margie-not-Margaret, a woman new to the city with dreams of grandeur that—like many things in Rice's fictionalized future—don't quite pan out the way she intended. Rice is a master at teasing this new, foreign world with just a few casual asides, a handful of wayward phrases to let us know that life is very different from the way we know it to be now. Hints of conflicts outside the city walls color the narrative as Bill struggles to make sense of the conflicts in his own life.*

The story serves as an interesting counterpart to her more horror-themed works, pushing aside the existential dread to present a romance instead. "The White Pony" is a love story told through rose-tinted glasses, ironically set in a world where roses have long gone extinct. It is bittersweet in its simplicity and relatable in its mundanity—all of which is caught in a strange sort of dissonance when placed in front of a backdrop of post-apocalyptic fallout. Peaches, birds, and life as we know it are but a distant memory. Those who remember do so with solemnity and speak of it in wistful, nostalgic moments in between Red Caution weather warnings and Fried Browns at the suitably named Hasty-Tasty.

Love, purpose, and the ennui of coming to terms with a pipe dream being just that give Rice's "The White Pony" the whimsical weight it carries so well even today.

—T.D. Cloud

Edna is a swell wife. We get along together fine. Better than most married couples at any rate. There are occasions, however, when she puts me in mind of Fili, our cat, who still believes in birds.

Take this notion Edna has that I led a mad, erratic, unconventional life before I met her and settled down. An absurd idea.

To begin with, I had few friends. Jim and (?) Stella Tyler. Greg. I wasn't a rockbound iconoclast but I pretty much whistled a single tune. To end with, I couldn't afford to be either eccentric or gregarious, if I wanted to stay employed and solvent. Besides, I had this urge to write and writing is a lonesome road.

I remember yet my first acceptance from an Independent. I read the tape four times before I actually believed they'd bought my fiction ms and were going to issue me ninety A stamps. Ninety A stamps in a lump was WOW.

When you have one jumper, and one dustproof, and one UW dc-kit not worth a hoot, and one cramped unit in a scarred, old, rundown, honeycomb type prefab, and earn your living—if you could call it that—hacking out action items for a vdo paper—under a supervisor like "Blast-off" Switzer, ninety A stamps is a double booster shot in the ego. The main point was, though, I'd proved I could do it.

I wanted to stand somewhere high and gaze out and all around. So I went up on the roof. It wasn't any great shakes of a height but it was handy and the scenic spread of the tropolis through the smaze, with the astralights coming on and the sector divisors pinked out, was a lulu.

The new girl, with the vaguely familiar face, was up there leaning against the meshing taking it in. For a fleeting instant, I almost identified her.

"Looks as if you could make a wish on it, doesn't it," I said. It was a statement. Not a question.

"Umm," she said. She smiled absently, intent on her own wish off in the mauzy distance, like a signal from a spotter's tower. We watched the City brighten and deepen.

"What would you wish for?" she asked, after awhile. Her voice sounded misty and alight, like the view, and she had a soft up-and-down way of speaking.

"A white pony, maybe," I mused aloud, and promptly regretted it. The white pony had become a sort of symbol. I didn't care to share it, even jokingly, with anyone. Especially a chance rooftop newcomer.

"What would *you* wish for?" I countered quickly, to get out from under.

"Ummmmm...I don't know," she said. "There're so many things. Unless you're hungry. Then it narrows down to food." she tucked a blowing tendril of fair hair under her hood. "I'd choose something to eat, I suppose. A no more something. Like...well...like peaches. Remember peaches?" She sighed. "Delicious, slurpy peaches," she added, dreamily.

I remembered. Sun-ripe, blushed, velvet skinned, the golden inner meat clinging to the dimpled, dull red seedstone, and each bite dripping with sweet fruity juice. 'Slurpy.' Expressive. Choice. Descriptive. Perfect. Suddenly hungry myself, and intrigued by her ability to evoke a whole lost way of life with one word, I heard myself say, "Would you settle for a Fried Brown at the Hasty-Tasty?"

A glue-footed silence crawled out of nowhere and laid down between us. When she spoke, her tone reminded me of a limits inspector rejecting a yellow pass.

"I wasn't hinting," she said. "If I've given you the wrong impression, I'm sorry."

"Look," I said stiffly, "I'm not representing the United World Welfare League. Nor am I planning any surprise maneuvers under the table. The invitation was spur of the moment and purely impersonal."

"I didn't mean—" she began.

"Shall we have another lunge at it?" I cut in. "Do you want a Fried Brown? Or don't you."

The Hasty-Tasty was an eatery close by. It wasn't mad. Or unconventional. Or hasty. Or very tasty, for that matter. The "atmosphere" was stool-and-table and the only erratic thing in the place was a zoneboard with the weather flashed on it. The food was of the punchtab ilk. The regular "patrons" called the cashier "Mom." That's how you knew they were regulars. That and a certain worn sameness about them, as if they were all of a pattern, despite their diverse appearances, ages, and occupations. Mom called *them* "Pal." She was a dead ringer for what's-his-name, the genial robot on the Larry Wilson show, except that she was fatter and played the races. Greg once took a mention at an art exhibit for a pastiche he'd done of Mom's racedrome mementos.

A Fried Brown was a kind of grilled sandwich roll served with gravy. It was filling and it was cheap and it retained an element of novelty as you never knew what might be in it.

There were no little signs and portents that Cupid was loose and on the prowl. But that was the commence. That was when he flew in, circled, and began rubbing rosin on his bowstring. That was where it started. With Fried Browns at the Hasty-Tasty.

I learned her name was Margaret but that she preferred Margie. Margaret was "too Sunday," she said. She came from an area near the End Zone. The recent demise of a maiden aunt with whom she had lived had left her on her own with a couple of paid-up certificates. These she had turned in for the necessary wherewith to transfer to the tropolis. She wanted to "prove" herself.

She hoped I wouldn't feel she was eating "under false pretenses" but I hadn't let her explain why she was hungry, had I? It was her own fault. She'd decided to forego supper to economize for having had two lunches because she had gone without breakfast, to economize for having bought a "darling bracelet dohinky" and to "make up" for being "out" the price of a fare on the escaway on account of the token getting stuck in the "thingmadoodle."

I could visualize that stuck token. Its shape was distinctive. It had DO NOT USE ON THE ESCAWAY illuminated on it. Its raised . . . was unmistakable if you merely recognized the elementary fundamentals of warning insignia. Even the blind could tell the difference.

I could also visualize the deceased aunt. She was having a chain reaction in her slotbox and was murmuring, "To *prove* herself, did she say?" And I had finally pinned down my impression of having met her doe-eyed niece, Margie, before. It was the forehead. The forehead was the rounded intellectual brow of Sarah Ames who had been top honor back in Continuation School.

Perhaps it was this false resemblance to the sagacious Sarah that tickled my fancy and gave our conversations absurd turns and twists when we happened into each other during the following several weeks. Not that she kept up a flow of chatter. She didn't. "Ummm," was her favorite response. In fact, walking back with her from the area bakery one day, it occurred to me she was the one girl I'd ever known who didn't think talking was an essential social grace. She didn't laugh unduly either. And she took her femininity for granted. She didn't feel impelled to make me conscious of it.

And, there was the April morning we had a Red Caution weather warning and shared an equalizer to the escaway and she stayed in step and didn't hang on my arm. There was the young May evening when the green moon and its paler satellite hung in the gathering sky, and she was wearing a lavender jumper and had her hood pushed back—and, for no reason, I felt protective and muscular. There was the dull dumb Sunday when I couldn't squeeze out a paragraph and, for want of what to do, took her to a telovie. There was the dark Saturday I emerged from the archives to see her number hurrying by and, lengthening my stride to overtake her, saw the number wasn't hers after all...and was disappointed.

Our first real date was in late May when I brought her to a party at Jim and Stella Tyler's down in area 4 near the canals.

Jim and I, and Greg, had been inseparable as boys. Our friendship, while a bit frayed by Time and Change, and by Stella, and by Greg's yen for lost horizons, still held at the seams.

The party was a potluck deal, co-op style, where everybody contributed to the festal board. We took a sausage stick. Margie mixed in but she didn't "belong" and didn't attempt to. I'd suspected that was how she would be, which was why I'd asked her to go. I didn't fit in either. I seldom did in a group. It was as though they were mutations and I was a transmute. There's a distinction. Small, but it's there. It was nice to have Margie for company. The festivities dissolved fairly early because the dust squawkers were warming up.

Going home on the SSS, otherwise called the Sweat, Smother, and Stand, Margie fell asleep. She might have been entitled *Sleeping Girl*. By Greg, maybe. For all Greg's tousled trimensional approach, he believed in beauty. Beauty, he contended, was the one remaining defenseless thing left. Anywhere. Margie's lax upturned palm and the shadowed curve of her cheek would have had him squirting paint tubes all over a palette.

Summer arrived overnight, as if it had come pell-mell ahead of the sunrise and had tripped on a spotter's tower and collapsed. One minute Spring was trolloping by scattering showers and placards for the Summer Pops, and the next minute Summer had straddled us, spraddle-legged, licking a frostdip and thumbing her nose at the recently completed, highly touted and presumably adequate, citywide airwash system.

It was a good summer. Greg returned from his travels, a trifle thinner but the same easy-going Greg in a narrow studio amid a clutter of queer bright canvasses, burned matches, unwashed cups and ideas. "Blast-off" Switzer got prickly heat. The choke-and-strangle snorer who lived below me moved. I had two more stories accepted and, under this tonic influence, dived into an adventure novella.

And, my interest in Margie grew steadily in strength, like the V sirens, until it split a decibel one night in what is still called the Park. We had stopped to watch the aureola and, strolling on, hand in hand, we paused at a bend in the meshing and kissed.

Her voice comes whispering back across the intervening years. "Isn't the aureola glorious!" Which was it exactly. Same aureola, new perspective.

"It looks like kissing is, doesn't it," she said...and I wondered if I could ever make a pass at anyone so shiveringly trustful.

She was about as deep as a plate but, somehow, she could put an extra dimension into an innocuous comment. "As long as we remember how roses were, and robins, and fireflies and things, they're not really extinct." And, walking home from an open air concert, "The City isn't big. It's a place full of places, that's all." On the subject of Greg, "He's awfully *very*, isn't he?" From an observation float, "The principal difference between ups and downs is where you are."

And she had this silky hair and those hazy eyes, and quiet asleep-looking hands, and that habit of listening with her head tilted and her lips slightly parted. She was the only girl I'd ever gone with who didn't have mannerism, or who could put on her eye shield without a mirror.

There was the Hasty-Tasty, and the roof, and the Park, and the dunes, and the Ruins, and the Sunday Specials to various play centers.

There was the Sunday we went with a bunch to May Rocket, and

Greg won a floppy doll for Margie, after I'd given up, and I could've wrapped it around his neck. There was the Sunday Margie and I picknicked on the Pinnacle and both recognized, simultaneously, the shape of a wedding cake in a harmless fleecy cloud passing overhead.

And there was the August Sunday I took her to my sister Polly's in area 62, although there wasn't anything remarkable about it except that it was family...haphazard, good natured, interruptive, company first, you-kids-shut-that-wicket-and-behave-yourselves family.

At the supper table, Bub's piping, "Is Uncle Bill *her* Uncle Bill, too?" and Cissy's superior, if somewhat ambiguous, "He's her *fella*. Else why'd she be here?" provoked general laughter. And set it up in frame.

I finished the adventure novella in September, and got three hundred A stamps for it, plus a request for more of the same. I was in! EeeeeYOW! With a heady, nearly drunken, exhilaration of release I quit the vdo paper. If, like Margie, I was going to "prove" myself, the Time was Now.

I counted out three months advance room rent into Mrs. Hellwig's genteel superintendent's claw. I wanted to be rid of the sensation that I was eternally one short jump ahead of her. I wanted a long enough headstart. I even inquired about her "stummick trouble" and tsktsked sympathetically while she told me, in lurid detail. That's how happy I was. For three whole months I was freeeeeeeee.

Somewhere along in there I began to dream about the white pony again.

The summer I was twelve, the white pony had been the prize in an essay contest sponsored by a dc aerosol company. When I wasn't composing essays or scrounging aerosol labels I was fixing up our dilapidated decontamination hut for a stable, assisted by Jim and Greg. That winter we had had the cleanest, soundest, emptiest dc hut in the area.

Save for Margie's appearance in the dream, the new version didn't vary drastically from the original. Mane and tail flying, the pony eluded my pursuit through toppling ruins, a shriveled forest, over deserts, into tunnels. Margie gave me talismans to carry while I gave chase. A polished pebble of immense significance. A glove, "For sooth," she explained. A box of meat cubes, whispering, "Here are *these*."

And, it was along in there that I began to think in terms of "our." Our song, our knock, our table at the Hasty-Tasty…

Love didn't rise up *boo*. It quietly hove to and fell in step one Fall afternoon during the second-shift exodus. I had gone outside to meet her at "our" wicket outside the drome in which she was temporarily employed. (All her employments were temporary.) Swinging off the escaway, I saw her before she saw me and it came to me, like a touch on the sleeve… I'm in love with her.

Funny, the photo clarity of it. The news tape: ACTION ON TRANS-SPAN IS CITY CRY. The skinny kid bouncing a ball. The patriarch out of a Twentieth Century novel imperiously hailing a Lift—and the operator asking, conversationally, as he missed me by a hair, "You aim me slotbox you, Mac?"

The phrase "walking on a cloud" isn't apt. You walk around in it. And you see like dogs hear. The same old fluttering tell-tales on the corners were gay as flags. Each day had a song in its heart. Every street was part of a parade. Kisses were violins. Desire was a gentle ache, tender and sweet and yearning. I almost caught the white pony twice in a row. And Greg, striking a match and watching it burn, said, "So she's different. So? Take it from papa, they all are." And I wanted to clout him.

In fiction, young love wrestles a host of mighty difficulties but where to be alone, come the solstice, isn't among them, since there is no such object as a bed. Well, you can't spend the evening with the girl of your dreams in a unit where the bed is the predominant feature. You simply—cannot—do it. You sit on the ramp.

I can see it. The cracks, and the rust, and the warped rail. The buckled plate on "our" landing, on which that poor, scurrying, earless Johnson kept stubbing his built-up boot. The vacant niche in the wall which in a bygone era had probably housed a Reichert's hose. And a boy, saying, "I love you." And a girl, her face like a drowsy kitten's, saying, "I love you, too."

"What are you thinking about?"

"Ummm…how it'll be someday. A two-unit, dishes, pretty floor cushions. Doris who works next to me has a boy friend connected with Unit Allocation and she says he'll keep his eye open for us. Maybe by Spring... What are *you* thinking about?"

"A white pony."

"Oh, you. You're forever saying that."

I recall, likewise, a swift succession of scenes, on the order of a fantasy sequence starring a dance team. Thanksgiving Dinner at Polly's. Wish-shopping on 5 Street. The Author at Work. Skating on the Free Canal. Tyler's Holiday Party. Under the Synthetic Mistletoe. New Year's Eve, fusing into a fuzzy comic sketch wherein Greg and I are lugubriously singing an old sentimental folk-song for Margie, with Jim trying to harmonize and having trouble with the word "acquaintensh," and Stella acting as if she didn't know us.

Immediately thereafter came Inside January, or, Mrs. Hellwig Rides Again. Having to pay rent once more sharpened up the focus considerably. That, and Doris.

Doris and Margie visited back and forth, and set each other's hair, and went on diets. One day, when I went down to see if Doris had gone—and she hadn't—they had a generous heaping of what appeared to be quick cement spread on their faces.

Doris called me, "Willie."

"Greetings, Willie," she'd say. "How's friction?" Or, "What's the price of rust?" She had a zillion of them.

It was simply her mode of salutation. Meaningless. Fairly humorous. But there were days when I seemed to be this genetic error "Willie." Days a plot wouldn't jell, or a story rolled up its eyes and died aborning, or when one I'd counted on as sure-fire was rejected.

It was "Willie" who'd hint, *You're not good enough. You haven't got what it takes. You'll never make the climb.*

I'd shove my jaw at him. "I am. I have. I will. There's plenty of room at the top."

The top isn't having any.

"You wait," I'd tell him.

I'll wait, he'd drawl, a grin in his sneering enunciation. *Will Margie?*

As the winter drew to a close, I'd sometimes rouse in the night with a sense of urgency, as though I'd overslept or had gotten misplaced.

I remember one night I wakened, groaning, from a pony hunt in the course of which Margie slipped her ID tag in my hand. The tag had BE MINE printed on it, like the Valentines in the cases at Restorationville. The dream was so clear I sat bolt upright.

Ain't nobody here but us Willies, Willie said, and I got up and flicked on the light and peered at myself in the mirror. I looked pale and sick.

"Go head and marry the girl," Greg advised. "Stop beating yourself over the head. You don't have to stay in the City. Go to the archipelago. Or a colony. And write, write, write. This century needs artists, poets, writers. Vision. Go to one of the outer bountylands. They're safe, if you exercise reasonable precaution. Take it from papa: you can live in rare style on two C stamps a day on any of the outer bounties."

He made such a plan sound feasible as he unrolled it, resembling an outlander himself in his sandals and paint pants, surrounded by tortured colors, and the wanderlust again upon him. I could tell, invariably, when he was getting ready to shoo off. He began to pace, as if he were caged. And he ripped and tore at dissatisfactions—like the canvas that lay, slashed, where he'd hurled it after he'd mutilated it. But the image of bounty life, as he painted it on my mind, was as plain and as possible as his parting words, "Listen, you introspective lovesick ass, all you have to do is *do it*."

I left elated. A winding road, instead of the escaway. The friendly bounty people with their seeds, and determination, and courage, instead of the government boys and form sheets and commissaries. Write, write, write, and Margie. The sweet doing nothing.

I floated home. "Our" area already had the ephemeral quality that everyday localities develop prior to imminent departure. The Hasty-Tasty was "remember when." Two effusive women taking leave of each other in front of the bakery lent a further transitory aspect—emphasized by the sliding hiss of the closing door. "Our" prefab had acquired a faint nostalgic antique charm. Mrs. Hellwig, talking to Margie by the lockers, had ceased to be an ogre. I got rid of her with the greatest of ease by the simple expedient of remarking, "Whew, I feel dusty."

"I've got news," Margie said, slipping her arm through mine.

"So've I. Wait'll you hear."

I remember how golden she seemed, drifting about doing the little primping things girls do when they come in from work—powdering her nose, applying fresh lipstick—while I unfolded our future. And the crystalline moment when she pivoted, elbows uplifted, in the act of brushing her hair, and exclaimed, "Married? Married!"

Her eyes were wide and startled. "Why we're not even *engaged*. Whatever made you think—"

"Whatever made me think—" I repeated stupidly. "You're joking."

But she wasn't. It was crazy. And it went on and on. Over and over.

"Margie, you said you loved me. You said so, Margie."

"I *do*. But I'm not *in* love with you, Bill. Don't you see. Can't you understand? Loving someone and being *in* love with him isn't the same thing at *all*."

"If the prospect of living in the outlands is the stumbling block—"

"It *isn't*. I wouldn't want to, but that isn't it. No, there isn't anyone else. I know I said I love you, and I *do*, but I'm not *in* love with you. How can I marry you, Bill, when I'm not in love with you? I *know* I kept talking about a two-unit but I didn't mean with you. I meant with Doris. I *did* tell you. You didn't *listen*. That's the news I had for you. Lew found us a two-unit today. I was telling Mrs. Hellwig when you came in. Lew is *Doris'* boy friend. I *did* tell you. Months ago. If you'd just *listened* instead of half-listened. Oh, Bill. If I've given you the wrong impression, I'm sorry. What do you mean this is where you came in? Don't look at me like that. *Please...*"

I just stood there. Even when she began to cry. Unbelieving. Stunned. Waiting for it to sink in. Trying to cope with the lunatic sensation that I was an audience watching a nightmare and that the white pony would gallop past any second with my dead body bumping along behind him in a snarled tangle of stirrups and reins.

I helped Margie move. There wasn't much. Nothing really that made any appreciable gap in the furnishings but, taking a last glance around, the emptiness was a physical blow.

I didn't prolong the agony at her new quarters. Doris must've known the score for she skipped the "Willie" routine and shook hands

81

Goodbye and made herself scarce.

"Couldn't we be like before?" Margie said. "Couldn't you *try*?"

I drew her close and kissed her hair, and then I left.

I held the cubicle door as I went out for a chap who was juggling his key and a grocery pak. We exchanged noncommittal pleasantries and I thought...Is he the one? Have I shouldered by him, unknowing, somewhere in a crowd? Will they picnic on the Pinnacle? He was my height and build and he was wearing a UW-issue dustproof similar to mine, and I felt as if I were passing myself entering.

When I got to the nearest bar I went in. I guess my expression had a lot in common with the Great Crater because the barman set the bottle beside me and let me alone.

I sat there, thinking things out, picking up the pieces. I saw that Jim and Stella were pretending to be what they were not and never would be. To whit: Necessary. I saw that Greg would wind up a "character" addressed as Papa and that he was running away from, rather than searching for, himself. That was why he always came back. Underneath, where it counted, he knew. I saw it was the day-to-day stuff that was the challenge and required the most bravery and made the best story in the long run. And I saw, with a strange glassy insight, I was damn well going to be one of Mom's "Pals" if I wasn't careful.

When I stepped into the street again I was tired, as though I had gone a great distance uphill. But I knew what to do.

Which was how I met Edna. She was in my class at vocational-rehab...

I was right about Jim and Stella. I missed on Greg. Greg died that summer, of desperation possibly, while journeying towards those lost horizons of his.

And, this morning when I ran into Margie in the Flue, I wasn't too astonished. As she once said, the City isn't big. It's high, but it isn't big. Considering the lack of elbow room, it's amazing such encounters don't happen more frequently.

She was older-looking and she was wearing one of those cape businesses that apparently are in vogue this season, but she wasn't that many years ago older-looking, and she still had those enormous eyes and that habit of tilting her head.

She said, *"Bill."*

And I said, "Margaret!" and we inched out of the throng and talked for a minute. The usual polite surface scratchings. She was married. Had two healthy children, lived in New Boston…and so on.

In parting, she said, to keep it light, "Did you ever get that white pony?"

I thought of Edna, and of our strong young son Billy. I thought of my work, and our home, and our mode of life. I thought of the grass beginning to grow back, and the Hope, and how the force field is steadily pushing out beyond former points of no return. I thought of the four powerful words that once more form our universal motto: *In God We Trust.*

And I smiled at Margie and answered, "Yes. Yes, I finally got it."

STEP IV
by Rosel George Brown

(Originally appeared in the June 1960 issue of *Amazing Stories*)

Our heroine in "Step IV" starts out like many young women: feeling both fear and awe upon meeting a boy for the first time. Living in a matriarchal society, she had been warned by her elders about the dangers of men. But this one, she thinks, is different.

Rosel George Brown was a prolific writer of the '50s and '60s whose career was cut short by her untimely death in 1967. Born and raised in New Orleans, she worked as a teacher and welfare visitor throughout the state of Louisiana. She made her writing debut in 1958 with "From an Unseen Censor" in Galaxy Science Fiction. One year later, she was nominated for a Hugo award for "Best New Author," though the award ultimately went to no one. Nonetheless, the feat marked her rise in the writing world, and she went on to publish the Sibyl Sue Blue series featuring a female cop who not only is raising a teenage daughter but engaging in various interstellar adventures. The novels were praised for depicting a vibrant heroine and serving as poignant social commentary that some argued was better than other books that specialized on that subject at the time. With these accolades under her belt, it makes it all the more tragic that her death at the age of 41 left so many potential masterpieces unwritten.

"Step IV" is an example of George Brown's typical

writing style, combining elements of galactic exploration along with the experiences of womanhood. Our protagonist, Juba, is a young woman living in a female dominated culture, the men used only for servitude or gladiator battles. Furthermore, her home planet lives in isolation from the rest of the galaxy, creating the perfect environment for her youthful naivety. When Juba meets her first man, a war scout with a gentle heart whom she discovers after his ship crashes on her planet, her world view is called into question. After some conversations and shared meals, she does what most girls her age do: disobey.

The themes of youthful ignorance and adolescent misbehavior resonate with me. Growing up sheltered, I myself was unaware of how the world outside my home worked until it bitterly taught me. The innate desire to see things for oneself is something we all share, especially when we're at the brink of newfound independence. And like the protagonist, I learned bitter lessons on who I should listen to and why. I won't spoil the ending, but let's just say Juba learns too late why she should have listened to her peers. George Brown leaves us with this sobering lesson: Mother does know best.

—Andi Dukleth

The first time Juba saw him, she couldn't help recalling the description of Ariovistus in *Julius Caesar: Hominem esse barbarum, iracundum, temerarium.*

She unpinned the delicate laesa from her hair, for Terran spacemen are educated, and if they have a choice, or seem to have, prefer seduction to rape.

Step I. A soft answer turneth away wrath, leaving time for making plans.

He caught the flower, pleased with himself, Juba saw, for not fumbling, pleased with his manhood, pleased with his morality in deciding not to rape her.

Rule a—A man pleased with himself is off guard.

He was big, even for a Man, and all hair, and in his heavy arms the veins were knotted and very blue. He had taken off his shirt, letting the air blow shamelessly over him.

It was true he was wonderful to see. And Juba knew that such is the nature of our violences, if she had been born into such a body, she too, would be a thing of wars and cruelty, a burner of cities, a carrier of death and desolation.

His face softened, as though the hand of Juno had passed over it. Softly he gazed at the flower, softly at Juba.

Rule b—This is the only time they are tractable.

"Vene mecum," she bade him, retreating into the glade—what was left of it after his ship burned a scar into it. She ran lightly, so as to give the impression that if he turned, only so far as to pick up the weapon on the ground by his shirt, she would disappear.

"I follow," he said in her own language, and she stopped, surprise tangling her like a net. For she had been taught that Men speak only New-language in our time, all soft tongues having been scorned to death.

She should not have stopped. He looked back toward his gun. "Wait a moment," he said. His *a*'s were flat and harsh, his words awkwardly sequenced.

"Come with me," she said, and ran off again. She had been caught off guard.

Would he follow her? "Wait!" he cried, hesitated, and came after her again. "I want to get my gun." He reached for Juba's hand.

She shrank back from him. "Mulier enim sum." Would he get the force of the particle? What could he fear from a mere woman?

When he had followed her far enough, when he had gone as far as he would, for fear of losing his way from his ship, she let him take her hand.

"Terran sum," he said. And then, with meaning, "Homino sum."

"Then you are, naturally, hungry," Juba said. "You have no need to come armed. Let me take you to my home. There are only my sisters and I and the mother."

"Yes," he said, and took her other hand.

She blushed, because he was strangely attractive, and because the thought came to her that his ways were gentle, and that if he spoke a soft tongue, perhaps he was not like other Men.

Rule c—They are all alike.

"Come," Juba said, turning, "We are not far from the cottages."

She watched, during the meal, to see how he impressed the sisters and the mother. The little sisters—all bouncy blond curls and silly with laughter—their reaction to everything was excitement. And the mother—how could she seem so different from her daughters when they were so completely of her? They had no genes but her genes. And yet, there she sat, so dignified, offering a generous hospitality, but so cold Juba could feel it at the other end of the table. So cold—but the Man would not know, could not read the thin line of her taut lips and the faint lift at the edges of her eyes.

Juba brought him back to the ship that night, knowing he would not leave the planet.

"Mother," Juba said, kneeling before the mother and clasping her knees in supplication. "Mother...isn't he...different?"

"Juba," the mother said, "there is blood on his hands. He has killed. Can't you see it in his eyes?"

"Yes. He has a gun and he has used it. But mother—there is a gentleness in him. Could he not change? Perhaps I, myself..."

"Beware," the mother said sternly, "that you do not fall into your own traps."

"But you have never really known a man, have you? I mean, except for servants?"

"I have also," she said, "never had an intimate conversation with a lion, nor shared my noonday thoughts with a spider."

"But lions and spiders can't talk. That's the difference. They have no understanding."

"Neither have men. They are like your baby sister, Diana, who is reasonable until it no longer suits her, and then the only difference between her and an animal is that she has more cunning."

"Yes," Juba said resignedly, getting to her feet. "If thus it is Written. Thank you, Mother. You are a wellspring of knowledge."

"Juba," Mother said with a smile, pulling the girl's cloak, for she liked to please them, "would you like him for a pet? Or your personal servant?"

"No," she said, and she could feel the breath sharp in her lungs. "I would rather... He would make a good spectacle in the gladiatorial contests. He would look well with a sword through his heart."

She would not picture him a corpse. She put the picture from her mind. But even less would she picture him unmanned.

He would rather die strong than live weak. And Juba—why should she have this pride for him? For she felt pride, pangs as real as the pangs of childbirth. There are different kinds of pride, but the worst kind of pride is pride in strength, pride in power. And she *knew* that was what she felt. She was sinning with full knowledge and she could not put her sin from her.

Juba ran straight to the altar of Juno, and made libation with her own tears. "Mother Juno," she prayed, "take from me my pride. For pride is the wellspring whence flow all sins."

But even as she prayed, her reason pricked at her. For she was taught from childhood to be reasonable above all things. And, having spoken with this Man, having found him courteous and educated, she could not believe he was beyond redemption simply because he was a Man. It was true that in many ways he was strange and different. But were they not more alike than different?

And as for his violences—were they much better, with their gladiatorial combats? Supposed to remind them, of course, of the bloodshed they had abhorred and renounced. But who did not secretly enjoy it? And whose thumbs ever went up when the Moment came? And this making of pets and servants out of Men—what was that but the worst pride of all? Glorying that a few incisions in the brain and elsewhere gave them the power to make forever absurd what came to them with the seeds at least of sublimity.

Juba stood up. Who was she to decide what is right and what is wrong?

She faced the world and its ways were too dark for her, so she faced away.

There was a sound in the brush near her, and she wished the stars would wink out, for the sound had the rhythm of her Mother's approach, and Juba wanted to hide her face from her mother.

The mother frowned at Juba, a little wearily. "You have decided to forsake the world and become a Watcher of the Holy Flame. Am I not right?"

"You are right, mother."

"You think that way you avoid decision, is that not right?"

"That is right," Juba answered.

She motioned the girl to the edge of the raised, round stone and sat. "It is impossible to avoid decision. The decision is already made. What you will not do, someone else will do, and all you will have accomplished is your own failure."

"It is true," Juba said. "But why must this be done, Mother? This is a silly ceremony, a thing for children, this symbolic trial. Can we not just say, 'Now Juba is a woman,' without having to humiliate this poor Man, who after all doesn't…"

"Look into your heart, Juba," the mother interrupted. "Are your feelings silly? Is this the play of children?"

"No," she admitted. For never before had she been thus tormented within herself.

"You think that this Man is different, do you not? Or perhaps that all men are not so savage of soul as you have been taught. Well, I tell you that a Man's nature is built into his very chromosomes, and you should know that."

"I know, mother." For Juba was educated.

"There was a reason once, why men should be as they are. Nature is not gentle and if nature is left to herself, the timid do not survive. But if bloodlust was once a virtue, it is no longer a virtue, and if men will end up killing each other off, let us not also be killed."

"No," Juba said. For who would mind the hearths?

"All that," the mother said, rising and dusting off her robe, "is theory, and ideas touch not the heart. Let me but remind you that the choice is yours, and when the choice is made I shall not yea or nay you, but think on this—a woman, too, must have her quiet strength, and you spring of a race of queens. How shall the people look to the Tanaids for

89

strength in times of doubt and trouble, if a Tanaid cannot meet the Trial? The choice is yours. But think on who you are."

The mother slipped away and left Juba alone in the quiet precinct of Juno, watching how the little fire caught at the silver backs of turned leaves when the wind blew.

Yes, Juba knew who she was, though they had never made it an important thing to be a ruler. But ruler or not, she loved her land and her home and her people, and even this ringed space of quiet where the spirit of Juno burned safely. Life somehow had chosen for her to be born and had made room for her in this particular place. Now *she* must choose *it*, freely. Otherwise she would never have in her hands the threads of her own life, and there would be no life for her. Only the complete loss of self that comes to the Watchers of the Holy Flame. And that is a holy thing, and an honor to one's house, if it is chosen from the heart. But if it is chosen from fear of crossing the passageways of life—then it is no honor but a shame.

And Juba knew she could not bear such a shame, either for her house or within the depths of her soul.

"Mother Juno," she prayed, "make clear the vision of my soul, and let me not, in my vanity, think I find good what the goddesses see to be evil."

So she rose with a strong and grateful heart, as though she had already faced her trial and had been equal to it.

The rest of the night she slept warmly, so unaware are we of the forces within us.

The first fingers of the sun pulled Juba from her cot, as they pull the dew from the green things of the earth, and she pinned in her hair the first Laesa she saw that the sun's fingers had forced.

The Man was standing beside his space ship again. It was a small ship—indeed, from the angle of Juba's approach, and from the glancings of the sun, it looked smaller than the Man.

Juba's decision held firm within her, for she saw there was no humility in him. He stood there laughing at the dawn, as though he were a very god, and were allowing the earth and sky to draw off their shadows for him, instead of standing in awe and full gratitude for the gift of life, and feeling, as one should, the smallness of a person and the weakness of a person's power, compared with the mighty forces that roll earth and sky into another day.

It is in this way, Juba thought, that men seem strong, because they have no knowledge of their own weaknesses. But it is only a seeming strength, since it stems from ignorance, and the flower of it falls early from the bush.

Juba did not, however, say all this.

Rule d—A man's ego is his most precious possession.

"You are very strong," Juba said, her eyes downcast, for he was bare again to the waist, and it had come to her that she would like to string her fingers through the hair on his chest.

"Runs in the family," he said carelessly. "But come, I had dinner with you yesterday. Let's have breakfast in my ship today."

"I..." What was she afraid of? If he'd meant to do her any violence, he'd have done it already. And this would provide Juba's opportunity— "Yes," she said. "I would be delighted."

There had to be some talk, and perhaps something else, before she could make her request of him. They had to be friends of some sort before he was at all likely to agree.

It is difficult to make conversation with a man.

Finally Juba gave up trying to think of something interesting to say and asked, "What is your way of life, that you should be going around by yourself in a space ship?"

"My way of life?" He laughed. "It becomes a way of life, doesn't it? Whatever we do ends up enveloping us, doesn't it?"

For a man he was thoughtful.

"I'm a scout," he said. "I don't know that I chose it as a way of life. I was born into the Solar Federation and I was born male and I grew up healthy and stable and as patriotic as any reasonable person can be expected to be. When war came I was drafted. I volunteered for scouting because the rest of it is dull. War is dull. It is unimaginably dull."

"Then why," Juba asked, for she was amazed at this, "do you fight

91

wars?"

Again he laughed. Is there anything these men don't laugh at? "That's the riddle of the sphinx."

That is *not* the riddle of the sphinx, but Juba did not correct him.

"When you're attacked," he went on, "you fight back."

"It could not possibly," Juba said, "be as simple as you make it sound."

"Of course, it isn't," he said, and he took two square sheets that looked like papyrus, and put them each in a bowl. "There is the question of what you did, or did not do, that you should be attacked."

"And what did you do, or not do, that you should be attacked?"

He was pouring a bluish-looking milk over the papyrus thing. His hands were too large for everything he handled, and Juba wondered, if his hand were on her wrist, if he could crush it. Or, being able to crush it, if he would take care not to.

"Oh—trade agreements, immigration agreements, how many space ships can go where—who can say what either side did when or where to begin it all? Nobody is *making* it happen. Sometimes, perhaps. But not as far as this war is concerned. All I can say now is—O.K., for whatever reason I'm in a war. At this point, what can I do but kill or be killed?"

Juba mashed the papyrus into the milk with her spoon, as the man was doing. She took a bite. It tasted just like it looked.

"You could," Juba said, "refuse to have anything to do with it at all. You could simply go away and…" She stood up and the spoon clattered to the floor and she could feel the bowl of milk spill cold and sticky along her thigh. Because that's just what you can't do. You can't pull the thread of your life out of the general weaving.

She looked at her adversary, and he was as close to her as the darkness is to the evening.

"No," he said. "Life flows. A person's life or a civilization's life or all humanity's life. If it cannot flow forward it flows backward. Isn't that true? *Isn't* it?"

But she turned away from him, to recover herself a little. For she felt that he was right and her country and her foremothers were wrong and she was wrong and yet—she had made her choice last night, at the altar of Juno, and though she felt herself possessed by new understanding, she had to go on in spite of it, as though she fought wounded or blinded.

"You are perhaps right," Juba said. "I am only a woman and I do not know. But still, can you not take a few days from your war? Must you think always on that and never on anything else?"

He ate another of the paper things, not melting it first, and drank from the container.

"Look, Juba," he said, "I've been thinking on other things ever since I got here, but first I want to…"

"First," Juba interrupted, for here was her moment, "I ask one thing of you. Only that you radio incorrect coordinates back to your base. Say you have moved on, that this is a barren world."

"Let me talk to you first," he said. "I want to…"

"Please," Juba begged, moving toward him. "It is no loss to you. Only a small favor, to protect our planet from outsiders, in return for… for whatever pleasures I can provide for you, or my sisters, if I do not please you."

"All right," he said, turning to his communication equipment. "If that's the only way you're going to let me speak to you."

"Your tape," Juba said. "Turn on your tape."

"Tape!"

"I do not speak New-language. I will have to have it translated."

The Man looked at Juba hard and worked at the corner of his mouth with his tongue.

"All right," he said, flipping a switch. He turned to his equipment and spoke his strange language into it. It was rough and she liked it.

"Now," he began.

"Give me the tape," Juba interrupted.

He jostled a flat box out of the wall, held the tape up to the light and snapped off a small portion and handed it to Juba.

"Come outside," she said, taking his hand. "My world is more beautiful than your space ship."

"Can't deny that," he said, watching the branches of the Untouchable Bush draw away as they walked through it.

"Now," he said, when he was stretched out on the undulant moss. He

93

felt at the patch of moss sprouting under the warmth of his palm, and watched while an exploratory tendril curled around his little finger. "Now—do you know what it is I want of you?"

"I have," Juba said, "some idea." She hadn't known they talked about it. She thought they just did it.

"Well, you're wrong."

"Oh," she said, and stood up and walked over to the brook so he would not see her face. For she wondered wherein she was lacking and she was embarrassed. "Then," she asked, "what *do* you want of me?"

"There is, as I said, a war on. I am, as I said, a scout. I'm looking for a communications base halfway between a certain strategic enemy outpost and a certain strategic allied outpost."

"Why?"

"Why? I don't know why. Does the grain of sand know where the beach ends? And if I did know, what would it matter?"

"But why *this* planet? There are other systems. Even other planets in this system." The moss curled under her feet and pricked at her. She was not doing this right. What did she care about his war? But she did not know what to do. She had been prepared for Seduction, Step II, and had even thought up a few things to say, though conversation is not included in the manual, because there is usually a language barrier. It was his speaking the language that made the difference.

"This is the only immediately habitable planet. You don't realize how expensive and cumbersome and logistically difficult it is to set up the simplest station on an abnormal planet. Tons of equipment are needed just to compensate for a few degrees too much temperature, or a few degrees too little, or excessive natural radiation, or a slight off balance of atmosphere. Or even if a planet is *apparently* habitable, there's no way of being absolutely sure until there have been people actually living on it for a while. There isn't time for all this. Can't you just believe me?"

"I believe you," Juba said, "and the answer is no. It is not my decision to make. I cannot decide for my people. And if I could, the answer would still be no. That is exactly why we cut ourselves off from the rest of civilization. To stay out of your wars, to carry on civilization when you have laid it waste. That is why we are a planet of

94

parthenogenetic women."

"Is it?" he asked. "Was it to carry on the torch for civilization or to flee from it? Life flows, Juba. If it doesn't flow forward, it flows backward. Which way does your world go?"

Which way? The little stream scrambled over its bright rocks, flashing the sunlight like teeth laughing.

Which way? The servants, the pets, the gladiatorial contests. The old goddesses. Were we becoming weary with time? Juba wondered. What sense did it make? What future did it mold?

The Man got up and came to put his arms around Juba, crossing his arms over her chest and putting his hands on her shoulders. He leaned down until she could feel his breath on the back of her neck.

Then it was that Juba could feel from his strength that everything he said must be right, because he said it, and that he was the name for all those things inside her which had no name.

"I cannot bring you in for the Ceremonies," Juba said. "Whatever you are and whatever I am—these futures must lie with the goddesses. But sacrifice you I cannot." She turned in his arms. "Go," she said. "And quickly."

He kissed her. "I will not go," he said, and she wanted very much for him to stay, but not for the Ceremonies.

"I was to draw you into the gladiatorial contests," she said, "with rich promises. But I cannot. For those who die it is bad. But for those who live it is worse."

"Well, now you have told me and I will not be drawn," he said with that grin. "Who said women are not barbarous? It is up to you," he went on, "to free your world from its deadly isolation."

He kissed her by the vein in her neck, the heavy one, where the blood beats through. And there flashed through her head the instructions for Seduction, Step II, and she wondered that other women had been able to remember printed pages when this happened.

"You must go," Juba said, holding him so that he would not. "What do you want me to do?"

He lost his fingers in her hair, "I like blondes," he said. "And I like a

95

slender waist." There was a tension in the muscles of his lower lip and his eyes seemed to lengthen, and by this Juba knew what he felt at that moment.

But he said, "I want you to switch off your planetary directional diverter. Even if you had let me radio in the coordinates I had they would have been wrong, wouldn't they?"

"Yes," Juba said. "But the directional diverter diverts only in certain patterns, so that it might be possible to figure out..."

"I know. Maybe and maybe not. I want you to turn it off long enough for me to get up beyond your whole system and have my instruments take a fix on your orbit. Then we can planet in blind, if necessary, to set up our station."

"But as soon as you take off," Juba said, wondering if she would really do such a thing or if she would suddenly wake as from a dream and find her wits again, "they'll be on me with their questions. And what could I say to them?"

"You won't have to say anything to them," the Man said. "You'll be on the ship with me."

"With *you!*" The thought went all through Juba, as ice water does sometimes, and bubbled up into her ears. "With you." When she looked at him she really couldn't see what he looked like any more. Only a sort of shine. "You mean you'll take me away with you?"

"Do you think I could leave you?" he asked, all shiny. "Smash the thing," he said. "They'll repair it, but by that time it'll be too late."

She sat down on the moss, and he was over her, his face urgent, as for Step III. But he said, "Go ahead. Go now. And hurry."

She got up hastily, planning in her mind how she would arrange her face, so as to appear calm if anyone should see her, and what excuses she would make if there were anyone about the Machine House. They had no guards and kept no watches, for why should they?

It was at the market place, near the fish stalls, that she met her mother.

The mother tugged at Juba's robe as she went by. "It is not easy for you, is it?" she asked, low, so that no one could hear.

"No," the girl said. "It is not easy." Was it not written all over her?

Was it not on her breath and shaken out of her hair?

The mother looked closely at Juba and felt at her forehead. "Perhaps it is forcing you too soon," she said with a hesitant frown, which for a moment made her look like someone else. "It is not too late, Juba, to get someone else. Even now…"

"It is too late," Juba said, and pulled away, afraid to talk more. But although the mother's face, Juba knew, was set, and her mind winding unhappily through surmises, she would not follow the girl, out of pride.

Pride.

The machine was alone. Juba cut it off and pulled the handle of the switch out. She then opened up the face plate and jerked out all the wires in sight. She reached in and broke off all the fine points of the compass settings and pulled out everything loose she could reach.

Then she walked back quickly through the market place, so as not to seem to be skulking.

"Juba…" the mother said, standing in her path.

"Later," Juba said. "It will soon be done. Mother…I love you. All of you." And she went around the mother, quickly.

"It is done," Juba said, giving him the switch key as though it meant something all by itself. "You have at least several hours, even if they find out at this moment. And they won't. There will be no real suspicion until your…*our* ship takes off."

After he had made love to Juba, she could see the sun was wheeling high, and in the temple they would begin to wonder a little. "We must hurry," she said, and she broke a budded branch off a laesa bush, so that later, when everything was strange, this bit of what she had been would be with her to surprise her. In strange places, but with this man.

She turned to smile at him, for her heart was full of love, and she felt that he was as much within her as he was within himself.

It was then that he grabbed her hands and tied them, and he tied her feet, and he lit a cigarette and stood for a moment, looking at her and laughing a little with his eyes.

Juba's mind was dark, very dark, as dimness after bright sunlight in the eyes. She spoke to him with her brows, afraid to ask out loud why he had done this, though there could be only one reason.

"Thanks," he said, "for all of it." Then, seeing her tears, he said, "Well, really, what did you expect?"

There was a sharp stone beneath her shoulder, and she moved against it, so that it would cut through her pain. And, feeling the blood warm on her skin her tears stopped, for it was the stone that had hurt her, and not the Man.

"You act," she said with a sneer, "as I would expect a man to act."

"And you," he said, walking off with his heavy steps, "have very kindly acted as I would expect a woman to act."

Thus it was that she opened her veins on the sharp rock. Not out of love. Not out of sorrow. Not even out of fear. Out of pride.

OF ALL POSSIBLE WORLDS
by Rosel George Brown

(Originally appeared in the February 1961 issue of *Fantasy & Science Fiction*)

I'm not sure what it was that first made me take note of Rosel George Brown. Maybe it was that the cover of her first novel, the 1966 science fiction mystery Sybil Sue Blue, reminded me of Picasso's portrait of Sylvette David, which I knew so well from the Bremen art museum. Learning that Brown had been a teacher like me and that she was from New Orleans, a city I love and where I spent some happy months as a young girl, made me even more interested in her fiction. Alas, I had never heard of Rosel George Brown before I stumbled across her work because she is not nearly as well-known as she should be.

In the late 1950s and early 1960s, Rosel George Brown was considered one of the most promising new voices in science fiction. She burst onto the science fiction scene in 1958 and was even nominated for the Hugo Award for the Best New Author in 1959. Sadly, she lost to "No Award," along with Brian W. Aldiss, Pauline Ashwell, Louis Charbonneau and Kit Reed, in what has to be one of the great oversights of Hugo history.

Two years later, "Of All Possible Worlds" appeared in the February 1961 issue of The Magazine of Fantasy & Science Fiction. *And even though Rosel George Brown had been publishing for not quite three years at this point, "Of All Possible Worlds" was already her fourteenth story.*

99

"Of All Possible Worlds," a philosophic tale of an explorer and the alien culture he encounters, is quite typical of Brown's work. Her protagonist is no ray gun wielding, gung-ho space hero, but a scholar who quotes Leibnitz and Bishop Berkeley. His mission is not to conquer, subjugate or trade—indeed, all of those things are made quite impossible by Brown's chosen method of space travel which does not allow for taking along anything but a single person – but to observe and learn. In fact, the quiet, intellectually curious protagonist, who is a far cry from the square-jawed space cowboys that are still all too common in science fiction, is a large part of what attracted me to this story.

The alien culture our protagonist encounters is not hostile and warlike either, but instead a gentle civilization whose people seem to live without conflict or possessions, perfectly at peace. Our explorer promptly goes native, only to learn that no matter how long or how closely he lives with them, he can never truly know the aliens.

Both the trip in a windowless one-person spaceship and the alien world itself are vividly described, making the reader feel as if they were there. The culture the protagonist encounters is both fully realized and truly alien, though both we and the protagonist do not realize how alien it truly is until the end (the title of Walter Ernsting's German translation spoils the ending; thankfully, this is not the case here!)

"Of All Possible Worlds" is a story that was ahead of its time, a story that is closer to the New Wave of the later sixties and the social science fiction of Ursula K. Le Guin than to the so-called Golden Age and the domestic stories Joanna Russ called "galactic suburbia" science fiction (though Brown certainly wrote domestic science fiction stories such as the 1959 story "Flower Arrangement"). In many ways, "Of All Possible Worlds" feels like a precursor to the sort of stories that Star Trek would dish up every week a couple of years later. Star Trek's "Prime Directive"

echoes the proscription against Brown's explorer inter-fering with the cultures he encounters.

In another universe, would Rosel George Brown have become as beloved and influential as her contemporaries Anne McCaffrey and Ursula K. Le Guin? It's certainly possible, considering how well regarded and how ahead of its time her fiction was. Alas, we will never know, because in our world, Rosel George Brown died of lymphoma in 1967 at the age of only 41. She left behind a small, but remarkable body of work: three novels, two of them starring the cool futuristic female cop and single mom Sybil Sue Blue, and twenty-one stories—two of which were included in this anthology so that you might rediscover and enjoy this unjustly forgotten writer.

—Cora Buhlert

I stirred in my colloidal suspension. I could feel the transverse waves I had created bound through my little universe and rebound against me again. I was waking up. I was nearing the planet, then. Algol II, was it? My thinking would be fuzzy for a while.

I began the exercises, slowly and carefully, uncoiling from the foetal position you assume naturally in suspension. I wondered if the child *in utero* had any such premonition of the bright, violent world to come.

First one leg. Then the other. Slowly, but still the colloid shook. I did not want to wake up too fast. It is easy to panic. To thrash about wildly and be buffeted by your own struggling waves. It is too much like a nightmare of suffocation. Or claustrophobia. And if you fight too hard, your metabolism rises to normal before it's time to get out and then you just die. Nobody wants to die.

I lay still again until I felt the waves subside and the slight nausea recede. I would be well within sight of Algol. It would be blazing along one hemisphere of my windowless monad.

At least, that's what I call it. Ever since I read Leibnitz the phrase has stuck in my mind like a label for which there was no carton. When I saw the one-man spacers, I pasted my label on them immediately.

What I should have done was read more Leibnitz. Or less. Or

refrained from mixing his ideas up with Bishop Berkeley's and my own.

Because when I saw the one-man spacers they were so perfect a symbol that I had an irresistible impulse to get in one. If anyone asks me why I travel about the galaxy, I say it is because I am an anthropologist and explorer. If anyone should say, No, *really* why do you do it? I would say, Because it is a quick way to be Somebody in the eyes of my fellow man and to make money. But if God should ask me, I would have to say, There was just something about those windowless monads that fascinated me.

I began to move my left now, slowly, slowly stretching it out from my shoulder, I imagined, damping the sense of excitement that wanted to boil within me, the green planet rushing out to meet me. Or my windowless monad falling down to meet the planet. It doesn't matter, of course, which way you look at it.

Because each of us, locked in the windowless monads of our senses, sees only what his brain chooses to record. And if we reach out, for reassurance, to touch the hand of a friend, there are only the empty spaces between the atoms that touch, and the little deceit our senses practice.

So used am I to the deceits of my senses, that I act as though I can communicate not only with my fellow man, but also with those other races of the galaxy whom we have not known well enough to call fellow man.

I did not know whether there would be intelligent life on Algol II or not. All I had was a chemical analysis of the atmosphere, the temperature and the gravity. But it was such a planet where, in blithe disregard of Lecomte du Noüy, life might very well evolve.

If there were nothing to eat on the planet, I would die. For my windowless monad was not a little cruiser I could navigate around space like a boat on a pond. That sort of thing was a government project all by itself. My monad would set me down, cough me up, let me back in after five years, Terran time, and take off again. With exactly and only enough energy for take off. Lots of them came back empty.

I faced it, in the dark dream where I floated to my sluggish exercises. Most of them came back empty.

After long, heavy hours that faded past uncounted, when I wondered if perhaps the mechanism had failed and I would hurtle through space forever, without warning I was ejected into a world of brilliant sunshine, green trees and moving figures.

My first reactions were instinctive. I rolled over on my stomach and coughed the fluid out of my throat, my eyes tightly closed against the unaccustomed light. The sun was hot, but I felt cold, dreadfully cold, and naked in the empty air, uncontrolled breezes blowing over my damp body, the long, wet strands of my hair hanging down my neck, for my hair had grown long, even at the slow rate of life in Suspension.

I lay there, in a state of partial shock, unable for a while to think of anything but my own acute discomfort. Then my body chemistry must have adjusted itself to the new environment, for I became aware of two sensations, as I lay with my head down in my hands, my eyes closed.

First and foremost, I was terribly hungry. Hunger was clawing at my innards and I felt that my very stomach was being ripped and torn. I was trembling with it.

The other thing I was aware of was a sound, a rushing sea sound, such as a sea shell makes in the ear.

I turned over weakly and looked at the moving figures. The sunlight flashed and danced crazily in my eyes, for they were still shocked by it. Through half-closed lids I saw figures that were unmistakably humanoid.

A grey, attenuated face came near mine. "Food!" I said, and pointed at my mouth.

A hand, too smooth and slightly scaled, helped me up. The hand wrapped twice around mine and I saw it was opposed thumb and tentacle. I believe that's all I noticed until something liquid was handed to me. I drank it and went to sleep with my head on a table.

I woke up on a couch, feeling a great deal stronger and with my eyes focusing properly.

There was a girl sitting beside me. I'm not sure how I knew it was a girl, for it was some time before I could tell one of these natives from another.

Up close she looked silvery and I saw the skin was not really scaled. It was composed of large, slightly thickened epithelial cells. She stared at me from cool, bluish eyes. This stare was one of the most difficult things I had to adjust to on Algol II. The natives stared openly and starkly, like a cat or a child. It was because they had no eyelids and in sleep the pupils contracted to shut out the light. The eyes were covered with a thick, translucent lens.

She spoke—a stream of glottal noises that sounded a little like German. Behind the noise of her speech was the muffled power of the sea sound.

I spoke, simply because it would seem ungracious not to, and she nodded her smooth, silver head, a gesture which I took to mean she did not understand me.

She handed me a white, stone bowl of liquid, which I drank. It was the same as I had had before. It tasted a little like barley. It was warm and good.

She pointed at some material hung over the back of my couch, rose and left the room. I noticed then that I had been covered with a sheet of soft fiber. I stood and put on what was obviously a garment. It was of a simple design of the sort found over and over in temperate climates. It was two pieces of material clasped at the shoulders and tied up at the waist with a sash. It was a little long, for these people were taller than I, but I pulled it over the sash at the waist and found it quite comfortable.

I wondered whether I should go out. It occurred to me that I was still barefooted and I looked about the couch and found a pair of sandals. They were large but the leather thongs held them on securely.

It would be better to stay where I was, I decided. Obviously the natives were friendly and solicitous of me, but I had no way of knowing what taboos I might break merely by the way I tied my sash or the position in which I held my arms.

I was, I noticed, not in a room but in a tent. The floor was sand. Green sand, rather coarse, and flashing like emerald where the sun caught it. For all I cared it *could* be emeralds. I could take nothing back with me in my windowless monad. Nothing but my knowledge, that is.

The tent was white leather, well made and carefully stitched. My first deduction was that I had found a desert nomad culture. There was the tent and the sand. But I had a vague memory of trees, where I had landed. And when I looked closely at the furniture I saw it was such as no pack animal could carry. The table and couch were solid rock, though the couch was, of course, cushioned.

I tried to lift the table, for I was amazed at how heavy it looked. I could not budge it. I dug down in the sand to find that it was carved from the living stone. So was the couch.

This was no nomad culture. There was the soup, too. A nomad culture does not cultivate grain, though of course they could steal it from neighboring peoples.

Still, despite the embedded furniture, there was a feeling of transience about the room. Perhaps I had been put into a vacant tent. Perhaps that was why there was nothing personalized about it. No unguent jars, no stray clothing hung up, no pictures, no statuary, no weapons.

But there was something about the tent that kept recalling the girl. The odor. That was it. A light fragrance that had been strong when she was near and I had only now remembered it. An odor like the crushed leaves of some plant whose name I had forgotten. An odor, really, more like herbs than flowers.

I hoped she would come back. There had been a grace and gentleness about her I had liked. The way she had offered the soup. The casualness with which she had spoken—simply to give me the reassurance of speech. And the modesty she had displayed in leaving the room when I dressed. Even these little things had told me a lot about the culture in which I found myself.

I heard the deep, sighing sea sound again and three natives entered. Not the girl. I discovered then where the sound came from. It was the noise they made breathing.

Then began the long, slow process of learning the language. If only I could have brought a linguaphone with me, it would have been merely a matter of hours. But an explorer can take nothing but his body and mind in a windowless monad. That is the challenge of the job.

And, in a way, it makes things easier. You do not find yourself looking at a crystal picturama and longing for home, or strapping on a ray gun and feeling superior to the natives. It is not possible to play God. There is no temptation to offer colored beads. You have nothing to offer but yourself. So you try to make that good.

That night the tall, silver girl came back and motioned me to follow her. We stood in line and were given a bowl and food of a more solid sort than I had had before. I followed her back to the tent and we ate in silence except for the sea sound of her breathing.

This, I discovered, was the Way to dine. The bowl never varied. Nor did the food, with slight exceptions.

She took my hand and led me outside. She pointed upward and we watched a yellow moon chase a green one slowly across forty degrees of sky. Then we took our bowls and returned them to the washing place and kitchen—a spring within the stand of trees near where I had fallen. The water was brought down to a huge, white bowl carved into the bedrock that was close to the surface. There was no artificial light, but the light of the twin moons gave this whole world a muted glow. The water flashed with colored bubbles and hung like jewels off the washed bowls.

It seemed to me everyone we passed stared at me with violent curiosity. But I later discovered their sentiment was one of only mild interest. The rest was the effect of those lidless eyes.

By the time we returned to the tent again the moons were about to set. The girl stood for a moment in the moonlight, her face holding an expression, but whose meaning I could, of course, not fathom.

"Grecthchra," she said, pointing at herself. This was obviously her name.

"David," I said, in turn, pointing at myself. She shook her head, meaning, I understood by now, she already knew my name. She had for some reason refrained from using it. Perhaps out of delicacy, when she had not yet made herself known to me.

She followed me into the tent and I realized, with horror, that she had probably been assigned to me for a wife. Such a custom is not unusual.

It was unthinkable, of course. I stood there in the dark, knowing there was no way I could explain it to her, but not wanting to hurt her feelings.

She led me to the couch, removed the coverlet and laid it on the sand. She slept on the coverlet. I would rather she had slept on the couch, but I did not know how to indicate this without possible misunderstanding. So I slept all night on the pillowed couch and felt almost as if I were in a ship, with the soft sea sound of her breathing in my ears.

Most of my days thereafter were full of language lessons, and someone, I'm not sure it was always the same person, took me about the village. It was a simple society, but very highly organized. The red-tinted tents of the hunters, looking like a Christmas decoration in the emerald sand, stood all together, farthest from the spring, or oasis. Closer were the clustered tents of the weavers. The potters did not make bowls of clay. They carved them from the hard stone and it was obviously slow, weary work.

I never saw the least sign of violence in the community. Nor the least expression of discontent, though I was never able fully to fathom the expressions of these mammalian-reptile-humanoids.

Everyone seemed to be occupied, each in his cluster of tents. Male and female worked equally and I learned to distinguish slight female characteristics these creatures bore.

I found myself, even after weeks of living with these people, still thinking of them as animals. I took myself to task about it. Was it prejudice? I have lived with animals, as a matter of fact, and thought of them as people. Why was I doing less for these intelligent, friendly creatures?

It struck me, finally, that just as the structure of their eyes deceived me into thinking they were staring, so the customs of their society deceived me into thinking they were depersonalized to such an extent that they called to mind an ant hill. They all wore, for instance, exactly the same kind of garment. In the morning it was returned to the Washing Place and turned in for a fresh garment. No one wore jewelry or ornamentation of any kind. They did not paint their faces or their bodies. Nor did they carry things about with them, such as we Terrans always do. No book, no wallet, no keys.

It is an odd feeling to possess nothing, to have no pockets and carry no pouch or purse. I would reach about unconsciously, when I prepared to go for a walk, for the things a civilized man needs to go about with. Money, keys, tickets, those minimal things. I had constantly, on this planet, the irritating feeling that I had forgotten something.

There was something about these people that still, even after weeks of living with them and even when I knew the language, eluded me. It is the ignorance a child feels in a room full of adults. As though there is some common, tacit knowledge available to everyone but him. And he doesn't even know how to ask for this knowledge, for he doesn't know the nature of it.

When, therefore, Grecthchra asked if I would like to visit the Temple, I was delighted. I had noticed not the least sign of religion in the community. There was a great deal of formality, but I could see no sacred significance to it. The Temple would, perhaps, communicate to me some meaning about these people I had missed.

I tried to ask Grecthchra about it as we walked over the green sands toward a dull red hill in the distance.

"What is your *purpose* in life?"

She was silent, as is customary when a question is asked to which one does not know the answer.

"What do your people hope to achieve?"

Indeed, these were clumsy questions to ask. It occurred to me that I would not quite know what to say if someone asked *me* these kinds of questions.

We passed a band of hunters, going out on foot to spear the hard-shelled desert animals that went into our one dish.

"We want," Grecthchra finally said, "to eat each day and in the end to procreate. That is the Way."

But I knew still there was something I did not understand. And I felt like pounding on the invisible walls that separate one consciousness from another, and demanding knowledge.

The entrance to the temple, I saw as we drew near it, was a huge, square orifice, carved into the rock, and completely bare of ornament. The rock was, however, squared off to a perfect edge and beautifully polished. I became very curious as to what kind of a god would be imagined by these people whose art was restricted to the most fundamental simplicity. A monolith? Or perfectly life-like statues?

I was totally unprepared for what we saw within.

It was an empty room.

An enormous, square, red room, carved from the living rock, and empty as the craters on Luna.

"Where," I asked, "is the thing for which your Temple was created?"

She led me to one huge wall and ran a tentacle over it. I saw there were carvings in the wall. Writing, obviously. No pictures at all. The writing surprised me, for I had seen no sign of books or inscriptions and I had assumed the culture was not literate.

"What does it say?"

"The things that the children need to know. How to make the tents. How to cook the meals. How to hunt. The times for silence. Many things."

The children! Why had I not noticed? Perhaps because I have none myself and have no awareness of them. "I have seen no children," I said.

"They are not yet conceived," Grecthchra answered.

"There are *no* children?"

"How could there be?" This was, really, a statement.

Grecthchra did not dislike my questioning. If she had answers she gave them to me. But most of my questions were meaningless to her.

"Are there no old people?" I asked her one day, for it had struck me that they all seemed to be the same age. It could be, of course, that there were signs of age I could not recognize. Still, there had been no funerals. The only death had been that of a hunter, who died of what appeared to me to be blood poisoning. He was buried with no ceremony.

My question was greeted with silence. Again I had asked a question with no meaning.

"Where is your mother?" I asked. "The woman who gave you birth?"

"I do not know."

We were occupied with the Morning Inspection. We stood watching a potter. He had polished the sides of his stone bowl. This must have taken years. He was now grinding out the inside with a stone. Every day the hollow was a fraction of an inch deeper. Every day he held it out for our inspection.

"It is well," Grecthchra said, as she did every day.

We were, I had gathered, part of the Ruling Class, though this tribe seemed to have no need of a ruling class. There was never a thing of which Grecthchra did not say, "It is well."

The function of the ruling class was mostly, as far as I could see, to express appreciation of what the others did. Whether the potter was pleased to be told, It is well, I do not know. I assume that he was.

Two things happened to me on this planet that can never be understood by those who have led only one life. Remember that I was newborn in nakedness and loneliness on this planet, and that all I had of my own world was a memory that, after a year or two (as I approximate the time), became almost unreal. Remember that I had not even a mirror to remind me that I was a Terarn.

The first thing that happened was that I became as static and formalized as the natives with whom I lived. I was not merely acting like them so as to study their culture. I all but forgot to study them. I was engrossed in the Morning Food Motions, the Morning Walk, the Watching of the Double Moons, and the rest of it.

The second thing that happened was that of course I fell in love with Grecthchra.

These things did not happen all at once but I became aware of them all at once, on separate occasions.

One night I had a vivid dream, a strong, real dream of home. I was in my apartment having a drink with Jack and Vivian Stall, my cocker spaniel nuzzled against my knee, the air tanged with the familiar smells of dog, tobacco and alcohol. Jack was asking, "How long will you be gone?" and suddenly a wild alarm spread through my body. I sat up with a thudding heart. In heavy blackness of the night, after the moons have set and the tent shuts out the stars, I had the illusion that I was struggling to open nerveless eyelids, or that I had gone blind.

The only reality was the slow, measured sea-keening of Grecthchra's breathing on the floor beside me.

HALFWAY MARK. The words spread across my mind.

It was, of course, the warning signal. I had no way of measuring time by Earth standards. But like anyone who has lived his life with clocks, I had a very good time sense buried too deep for me to consult consciously. The alarm had been planted by post-hypnotic suggestion.

110

There would be another when the five years were up. I would have a day to get to the monad.

But it was this alarm, and the dream that preceded it, that made me conscious of how completely I had given myself over to the culture of Algol II.

It had, as a matter of fact, become a habit.

There is nothing more dangerous than a habit.

It had been necessary for me to discard most of my Terran habits, from smoking to brushing my teeth. I was not aware, until the moment of the alarm, that I had replaced them with the cultural habits of Algol II.

And I had seen, on all Algol II, an area of about two miles in diameter. Only the hunters went further than this, and I was not a hunter.

I had made no systematic study of the culture. Because there were those questions I did not know how to ask and those questions I soon realized it was not proper to ask.

More, I had lost the spirit of curiosity and adventure that I had suddenly remembered possessing that night back in my old apartment back on Terra, discussing my coming trip with Jack and Vivian.

What, then, had I been doing for two and a half years? In the morning I rose, at the proper time, when the sun flashed off the emerald sand at the edges of my tent and made shadows like the sea on the roof Grecthchra and I folded our cushions and coverlets neatly, walked out and observed the sky from all directions. We observed, inevitably, that it would be a day without rain. After observing the sky, we observed the earth, always the same, glittering, green sand. Occasionally the light would be particularly interesting on a large piece of sand, perhaps the size of a marble. Then we observed, without criticism, the tents of our neighbors. One, perhaps, might be sagging slightly and need a pole shifted.

Then, in a leisurely fashion, we strolled over to the Washing Place, perhaps half a mile away. Here we handed our bedclothes to the Washer and went to separate tents where there were bowls of water for washing and fresh garments, all exactly the same.

We then lined up at the Cooking Place, received our food and

111

carried the heavy bowls back to our tent to eat with the single spoon that came with it. We ate slowly and in silence. After breakfast, we returned our bowls and spent the morning Inspecting.

Lunch was the same as breakfast. After lunch we walked each day to one of the red hills in the distance, all the hill into which the Temple was carved. Though they appeared red from a distance, there was a white rock folded in with the red.

We sat on a red or white boulder, rested, and looked about to the far horizon. Green sand, red hills and small outcroppings of trees were all that were to be seen. Occasionally one of the small, plated desert animals darted out of its burrow in the sand and across the desert. A few small birds wheeled in the sky, apparently reptilian in character, though I never saw one close enough to be sure.

Then came the walk back to the village and the social gathering. This was not formalized. All the tents were open, and the custom was to look in at random and if anyone were home, to visit. Socializing involved small talk. Very small talk. Remark upon the weather, which was always the same. Discussion of the progress of the weavers on a certain garment. The growth of the grain, which was artificially irrigated by the spring. The most interesting conversation was that of the hunters. How an animal was pursued. How caught. When one hunter died, as I have mentioned, that, too was small talk. Casually mentioned.

After Socializing came dinner, the same as breakfast and lunch. And every night, when I had brought my bowl to the Washing Place and returned to my tent, I was tired enough to sleep without thinking. I had, after all, spent most of the day walking in the open air.

And so I spent two and a half years doing exactly nothing, vaguely happy to drift from day to day in the inertial force of habit.

When the alarm came and reminded me of who and what I was, and a sense of time possessed me again, I was amazed at what I had done. One week of such purposeless activity on Terra would have driven me mad. And yet on Algol II I had so taken it for granted that I never for a moment felt time wasted.

Now, of course, I resolved to set out the next day to explore the planet further. Since I had two and a half years left, I could go a long way and still get back in time.

But the next morning something highly unusual happened. I awoke to a noise like Grecthchra's breathing magnified a thousand times, like an angry sea upon us. I sat up in the grey light and Grecthchra looked at me, nodding her head pleasantly.

"It is raining," she said.

We walked out for our breakfast as usual. The rain was warm. The whole world was gray, now, instead of green, and Grecthchra laughed when little rivulets dripped over her lidless eyes.

"The world," she said, "looks strange through drops of water."

The day's activities went on as usual and the rain stopped in the middle of the morning. The raindrops flashed so on the tents and the sand, when the sun came out, I could hardly bear to look at it.

It was during the afternoon walk that I abandoned all thoughts of leaving the village for an expedition further into the planet.

The desert had covered its face completely. As far as the eye could see, a heavy, bluish-green foliage had sprung up, and tiny red, yellow and white flowers opened their eyes to the sun.

Only the hills rose red and bare.

I could hardly bring myself to walk on the foliage. It seemed an almost sacred eruption of life after all the barren years.

But Grecthchra expressed no surprise. She did, however, have a spring in her step which I took to denote pleasure.

We set out for the hill. Grecthchra always chose which we would climb, and I always followed her. We clambered up the red rocks, noting little pockets of flowers where the sand had collected here and there. There was a tremendous burgeoning joy in the world, a color and promise such as had never been before.

A clear wind blew, and I looked around to see a little wave run through the sea of flowers. I felt as though the sunshine itself were running through my veins.

"Look!" Grecthchra cried from the top of the hill. Her voice was like a bell and I climbed to it.

I found her bent over a flower. It was a deep, gentian blue, tinged with black. It was the only blue one we had seen and it trembled a little under our breath as we watched it.

113

"It is blue," Grecthchra said, with wonder in her voice. Her face was full on mine. "Like your eyes."

Grecthchra held the soft blue flower in her strange, silver hand. The sunshine glittered on her silver skin. I knew that I had never seen anything so beautiful.

After that, my days and nights ran together in a silver stream. I did not know whether Grecthchra was more beautiful when she was like amber under the green and yellow moons, or when, lying on the emerald sand in the day, she was like a silver fish coming up from the sea.

A sense of time, oddly enough, returned to me. I felt as though we were running with a mighty wave, as though we must some day be flung up from the enchanted sea.

I could not get my meaning across to Grecthchra.

"A day and a night," she told me, "are like the day and night before and the day and night to come. Why would anyone count the number of them?"

"But Grecthchra, are you not to grow old? And die? Am I to grow old all by myself?"

"We do not grow old," she said, "like vegetation and animals. How could we?"

"There is something here," I said, "that I do not understand." Could they be immortal?

"Why should you understand?" She swapped her bowl for mine, a gesture of love. Indeed, when I looked at her I could care for nothing else. Not even understanding.

But the days and nights, as it turned out, were not all the same. Grecthchra, I think, could not have told me what was going to happen. But when things did happen, suddenly it was as though she knew it all along. Like the post-hypnotic suggestion which had waked me up in the middle of the night. It had been there and I was not aware of it. And by now I had forgotten it, for I was determined to live out my life with Grecthchra.

One night I woke to hear Grecthchra sobbing. I thought she was strangling, and it was like the sound of the sea struggling against the rocks.

"Grecthchra!" I reached out for her in the blind darkness but she was not there. I started to get up and feel for her, for I could see no faintest light.

"Stay there!" she cried. "It is the pain. It is not proper for you to be by me."

And so I lay there though the night, and late, late she crept into my arms, and slept.

In the morning I saw what it had been. There lay on the green sands a large, silvery egg, veined with blue.

Grecthchra seemed, somehow, proud, and so, though there was something a little ludicrous about it, I said, "It is well." I wondered if she realized that such was the difference in our races that this egg would never hatch.

We spent the days as we had been spending them, the egg remaining always in the corner of the tent.

In other tents, I noticed when we socialized, there were other eggs.

One morning we wakened suddenly before dawn. There was a wild, cold wind that blew through the flaps of the tent and spattered the sand against the sides.

It was gone in a moment, but it left a chill upon me and I held Grecthchra to me. Somewhere in the eternal summer, ice was forming.

That day was not as other days. The tents were empty. The weavers did not weave and the pots of the potters were stacked up neatly before their tents.

"Where are they?" I asked.

"They are preparing for the children," she said, as though she had known all along, though I am sure that when we went out she expected the potters to be in their usual places.

We walked to the Temple. Most of the village seemed to be there, working. They were bringing the green sand in from the desert and piling it in the rear of the Temple.

"Why are they doing that?" I asked.

"It is for the children," Grecthchra said.

Each day we went to watch them bringing in the sand. Each day the cold winds became more frequent.

In the mornings, now, we stayed in our tent after breakfast, and I clung to Grecthchra as though the end of the world waited outside the little summer of our tent.

By afternoon the sun reflected hot off the sands and we watched the workmen bringing the green sand into the Temple.

One morning Grecthchra said, "It is time." She picked up the silver egg and held it carefully in the folds of her garment.

I followed her to the Temple. The wind blew up a green dust and rattled the tents on their poles. It blew through the pores of my skin and made my bones feel brittle.

There was no joy in the world.

Grecthchra went into the Temple and I watched her bury the silver egg deep in the green sand.

Then we watched others do the same thing.

"It is well," Grecthchra said.

But I did not think so.

When all were finished and we stood outside the Temple, several of the men grasped one smooth panel of the entrance and began to tug on it. A wall of rock slid out—it must have been exquisitely balanced. They closed the entrance.

The sun, I saw, was now high in the sky. It must be long past the time for the second meal.

But it was cold even now, even with the sun hot on the sands. The wind was like currents of ice water.

"What does it say?" I asked, for there was writing on the door. Grecthchra looked at me. She drew me up to the door and the others drew back politely to let us through. They were reading disinterestedly, as though it were something they knew by heart.

Grecthchra took my hand. "It says, 'We have known a great science, we have changed the face of our planet many times. And yet, our own nature does not change. In the end, what is life? To be content, to live, to procreate, to die before life becomes a burden. Ours, then, is the best of all possible worlds. Go in contentment. It is well.'"

But the others were already starting.

"Where are they going?" I asked.

"To the sea," Grecthchra answered. "Do you not hear the waves?"

I had heard them since I came. But I did not know what it meant.

I followed after her. My breath trailed behind me in frosty plumes. When I breathed, the cold air came into my whole body.

Evening came early. The sky disappeared in a grey, looming mist. Grecthchra no longer glittered silver.

The grey evening congealed into a darkness so heavy I could almost feel it. There was no moonlight through the clouds.

I took Grecthchra's hand, for everyone walked on through the night. I do not know how they knew the way, but none faltered.

Grecthchra's hand was cold and without recognition. "The sea does not call to you," she said. "Go back."

But I could not leave her, though I could tell she had already left me. I clung to her hand and followed her on through the cold washes of the night.

Finally, I heard the waves. They became louder and more violent, and drowned out the sea sound of the breathing around me.

A white, bright dawn came up and I could see, far out, the dancing sea beyond a cliff. It was green, as the sands had been, and seethed under the yellow sun.

We drew closer, and there was no sound but the crashing sea as one by one the people of Algol II stepped over the cliff.

I tried to tug Grecthchra away.

"Don't!" I cried. "There is a whole life before us, Grecthchra."

"There is a whole life behind us," she replied, as though the matter had no interest for her.

I clung to her smooth hand until it slipped away from me and she fell into the sea. I stood there watching the bodies fade into black specks and finally fall into the heaving sea below.

I could not believe it. I sat hunched over, watching the blown foam for hours, not believing it.

I even tried to throw myself over the cliff. But I found I could not. I wished there were someone to push me. But there was no one.

I was alone in the world.

I do not know how I lived through the night.

I found my way, the next day, back to the village. I was so frozen I felt I must be dead and dreaming a nightmare of life.

All the way back there was the sea sound in my ears. So that for me the air was full of ghosts. And even after I returned to the village I still imagined I could hear it.

I looked through all the tents, running and shouting.

In our tent I looked for something of Grecthchra I could hold and remember. But there was nothing. She had had no possessions.

My windowless monad was still there—round, silent and closed in on itself. How long? Days? Weeks? Maybe a year or more? I had taken no account of time.

Time was now a gross, ponderous, living thing for me. I hated it. The days and the nights.

I tore up a tent to make clothes and still I was cold. I harvested the last shreds of grain in the dying field. I sought out the desert animals and found them hibernating in the sand. I pulled them out and killed them in their sleep.

I do not know whether it was days or weeks or months before the alarm brought me to my space ship.

I still wake at night with the sea sound in my ears. I think, now, that the sea was calling to me, too.

SATISFACTION GUARANTEED
by Joy Leache

(Originally appeared in the December 1961 issue of *Galaxy Magazine*)

You are about to read a full third of Joy Leache's bibliography. While she could have also written under a pseudonym, no evidence suggests this. You'll find no pictures, no birth certificate, no obituary—nothing to indicate she existed, let alone published, before 1959 when Future Science Fiction *published her first story, or after 1961 when* Galaxy Magazine *published her third and final story, "Satisfaction Guaranteed."*

By 1961, Galaxy's *flagship editor H. L. Gold had long-since shaped the magazine into a reputable publisher of science fiction, one which stood shoulder-to-shoulder with* Analog *and* Fantasy & Science Fiction. *He set some of the highest standards on the market, and his interest in socially-conscious works helped the genre evolve beyond John W. Campbell's scientific hero stories.*

Because of these factors, the publication of "Satisfaction Guaranteed" might not come as a surprise, and its plot does contain all the ingredients of a top-notch Galaxy *story. Yet female-written stories accounted for only 9% of* Galaxy's *1961 literary output, a proportion that wasn't unusual for the time. It leaves the conscientious reader wondering: where did Joy Leache come from, and, more importantly, where did she go?*

Perhaps the uphill battle of being a female writer in a

119

male-dominated industry became too much to bear. "Satis-faction Guaranteed" reveals that this was more-than-likely at the forefront of Leache's mind. Ms. Featherpenny, steno-grapher and de facto assistant to the incompetent marketer Andy, is introduced in an objectified state as "a passable figure [with] nice legs." While she is dismissed and demeaned on every page, the humor and fantastical nature of the story lure the reader away from just how grounded it is in the reality of the time: Andy is a bumbling Don Draper figure, and Featherpenny is there is there to look pretty.

Andy is tasked to devise a viable export for the planet Felix II, but he immediately becomes frustrated at the Fel-icians' refusal to enter into the tourist industry, something which would come easily to them considering their uncanny resemblance to leprechauns. Instead of solving the issue, Andy drinks himself into depression, dismissing Feather-penny's trenchant suggestions as those of a "stupid steno." At the end of the story, he notices he "can't seem to think unless [she's] around," yet she doesn't bother pointing out why this might be. Would it really have made a difference?

Female writers descend from a lineage that masked their ideas with masculinity. Mary Ann Evans wrote as George Eliot, Louisa May Alcott penned her favorite fiction as A. M. Barnard, and a slew of science fiction writers chose male pseudonyms. But while many female writers are in-delible members of the literary canon, their works are rarely taught to high school students. In the early 2000s, the only female writer my high school required me to read was Harper Lee, and while the female Scout narrates To Kill a Mockingbird, *her white savior father is the clear hero—and worst trope—of the story. I wouldn't discover the first two writers to positively influence my writing life until college. Both were exceptions to the ruling class of novelist: Zora Neale Hurston (who died penniless, buried in an unmarked grave) and E. M. Forster (who, unable to bear continuing to write about heterosexual relations, gave up writing fiction after penning* A Passage to India, *his most renowned novel).*

Perhaps with the cards stacked against her, Leache simply threw in the writing towel. We'll never know, but one of the Felicians in her final story provides heartbreaking insight when explaining why his people can no longer cater to tourists: "We weren't real to them. It became difficult for us to seem real to ourselves."

—A.J. Howells

Andrew Stephens was trying to think of two things at once, and it wasn't working out. An inspirational message (delivered by Crumbly, president of Planetary Promotions, Inc.) was mixing itself up in his mind with the probable difficulties of his first company assignment.

He hoped he was thinking, and not worrying. Crumbly said worry was fatal in the promotion business. It was fervor, not fret, Crumbly said, that had made Planetary Promotions, Inc. what it was today. And it was work, not worry, that would make it what it was destined to be tomorrow.

Andy Stephens stared at the farthest corner of his office (about four feet from his nose) and sighed. He didn't have a slogan in his body, let alone on (or off) the top of his head.

His assignment was an easy one, Crumbly had assured him. Planetary Promotions always started new men off with easy ones. Only fair.

Andy squared his narrowish shoulders in as close an imitation of Crumbly's desk-side manner as he could, and picked up the dope sheet.

It seemed there was a planet, Felix II, somewhere near the edge of nowhere. It wanted to join the Galactic Federation.

A laudable desire, Andy thought, but strictly a political matter, having nothing to do with Planetary Promotions, or Andrew Stephens.

However, it also seemed that a planet had to demonstrate that it would be contributing something to the Federation before it was allowed to join. In other words, Andy thought, you have to have something they want, or they won't let you in.

A buzzer squawked out of the dun-colored box on his desk. Andy jumped, and flipped the lever.

"The bus to the port will be at the door in seven minutes," the grim voice of the Lower Office Coordinator told him. "A stenographer will meet you on the ship."

"Thank you, Miss Ellis," Andy said meekly. He stuffed the dope sheet into his jacket and left the Main Office for Felix II.

"Excuse me," said a feminine voice. "Are you with Planetary Promotions?"

Andy looked up. A sandy-haired girl with a passable figure and nice legs was looking down at him. "Yes," he said. "I'm Andy Stephens."

The girl looked relieved. "I'm Edith Featherpenny from the steno pool," she said. "I was afraid I wouldn't be able to find you."

"Sit down," Andy invited.

He moved, and Miss Featherpenny moved. Between them, they unsettled a large woman eating an orange. When the juice had been mopped up and the woman apologized to, Miss Featherpenny squeezed in beside Andy.

"Is that the information on the case?" She indicated the dope sheet crumpled under Andy's arm.

"Yes." Andy tried to pull it out. "Were you issued one?" He moved his elbow and tried again.

The orange woman glared at him.

Miss Featherpenny shook her head. "Miss Ellis told me you'd tell me everything I needed to know."

Andy felt obscurely flattered. "It doesn't look too promising," he admitted.

Miss Featherpenny glanced at the dope sheet and found a ray of hope. "The Federation only requires that the Felician exports are nearly as valuable as their imports," she pointed out. "'Nearly' is a nice vague, maneuverable word."

"But," said Andy, "if the Felicians can't think of anything to sell, how do they expect me to?"

"Maybe they're too isolated to know what's in demand," Miss Featherpenny comforted him. "It says they won't authorize ships to land on the planet except by invitation."

"It might be isolation, I suppose," Andy doubted. He felt an urge to confide in Miss Featherpenny. She did, after all, look as if there might

122

be something besides fluff in her head.

"Look," he said. "This is my first assignment, on my fourth job, on my second career. I've got to make good. My father is beginning to get impatient."

Miss Featherpenny's eyes grew softer. "Fathers are usually more patient than their children think," she encouraged.

"But," Andy added morosely, "I have a brother, a salesman with Universal Products. He keeps getting promoted, and I keep getting fired. Dad must be conscious of the contrast."

"Maybe," Miss Featherpenny suggested, "your brother's been lucky. You know, being assigned jobs that were easier than they sound."

Andy glanced at her to see if he was being humored. He decided he was not, or not much. "I've tried to believe that," he admitted. "Unfortunately, Lloyd keeps proving me wrong. He got his last promotion for selling fancy food products to the Mahridgians."

Miss Featherpenny had obviously never even heard of Mahridge.

"They have a strong taboo against eating," Andy explained. "They swallow concentrates to keep alive, but it's still not quite decent. On Mahridge, it's the dining room, not the bathroom, that has a door with a lock on it for privacy.

"Is he married?" asked Miss Featherpenny, who didn't intend to be a steno all her life. "I mean," she added quickly, "his wife would get anxious about his selling something like that, that could get him put in prison, or killed. How did he do it?"

There was a certain coolness in Andy's voice. "He took a lead from the dope peddlers. He converted the adolescent Mahridgians first. It's all right to eat on Mahridge now."

Miss Featherpenny diplomatized. "I don't think that's ethical. Convincing people to do what they think is wrong."

Andy was still suspicious. He said, "Ethical or not, he got the promotion."

They stood at the edge of the only launching pad on Felix II, and surveyed the landscape. Thirty feet away, there was a barnsized stone building with a weedy roof. Aside from some rounded blue hills in the distance, and a Felician leaning against the building, there was not much to detain the eye.

Miss Featherpenny giggled softly in surprise. "He looks like a leprechaun," she said. "The sheet didn't say that."

"Tourist trade," Andy breathed, his eyes gleaming with the solution of his problem.

Since the two-foot-tall welcoming committee showed no signs of moving, they started toward him.

"My name," Andy said in Galactic, "is Andrew Stephens. I'm here from Planetary Promotions."

"I know," the Felician muttered ungraciously. "I came out from town to meet you. My name is Blahrog. Who's this?"

"My steno, Miss Featherpenny."

"Urk." Obviously Blahrog had never heard the term "steno" and was interpreting it freely. "I'm in charge of our admission to the Federation. That means I'm in charge of you." He eyed Andy unenthusiastically. "You haven't had much experience with this kind of thing, have you?"

Andy had a wild rush of hope. If the Felician government rejected him as a representative, he could go home without a failure on his record, and pray for a simpler assignment. Even P. P. didn't consider an agent responsible for the unpredictable whims of aliens.

"No, I haven't," he replied cheerfully. "I was hoping maybe you had."

Miss Featherpenny, who hadn't read the contract, gasped.

Blahrog, who had read the contract, replied, "I haven't. Let's get on into town where we can discuss the possibilities in comfort."

They set out, walking unequally through the thick white dust that passed for paving on Felix II.

"Don't you use ground cars?" Miss Featherpenny choked at the end of the first half-mile.

"Don't have technology," Blahrog growled, stumping grimly along. "The Everking has a car, but he doesn't use it much. No fuel."

As he walked, Andy composed a speech on the merits of the tourist business, to be delivered to the Everking.

Miss Featherpenny grew visibly more depressed with each mile. She uttered an involuntary cry when the guard of the city gate appeared with a slender mug in each hand.

"Felician ladies don't drink," Blahrog said gruffly.

"I can fetch you a glass of water," the guard offered, without enthusiasm.

"Thank you," said Miss Featherpenny, with an attempt at sincerity.

The contents of his mug made Andy choke. "Tastes something like cider," he gasped.

Blahrog downed his without a wink. "It's customary to give a guest a mug of Throatduster as a sign of gratitude because he walked so far in the dust."

"In this dust," Miss Featherpenny murmured to her second glass of water, "any distance is far."

"Thoughtful custom," Andy said quickly. "Could you export the beverage?"

"Sell Throatduster?" Blahrog was indignant. "It would be a breach of hospitality. Besides, Felix II can't produce enough second-rate stuff, let alone first-rate. Sometimes, in a bad year, we have to greet guests with water."

"What a pity," said Miss Featherpenny.

She became increasingly unsympathetic as Andy swallowed another Throatduster at the door of the Palace (a one-story building similar to a small barn), and yet another in the presence of the Everking (an eighteen-inch Felician with a beard-warmed paunch).

Andy watched the Everking dim and blur on his wooden throne. Swaying slightly, he muttered, "I wonder what proof this stuff is?"

"In short, Mr. Stephens," Blahrog was translating, "we cannot think of a single product which we could sell. Have you any immediate suggestions?"

Blahrog's expression indicated that he ought to say something, but Andy couldn't think of a thing, except that he didn't need any more Throatduster. "No," he said firmly, if faintly. "Thank you very much, but no." He passed out cold.

"I'm afraid the journey was too much for him," Miss Featherpenny put in.

"Ah, yes," Blahrog translated for the Everking. "Throatduster has that effect on some life forms. Perhaps he had better retire, and discuss the situation more fully tomorrow."

The Everking motioned to a pair of stout-looking guards (thirty inches tall, at least). They towed Miss Featherpenny's immediate superior out of the royal presence.

"They will show him to his room," Blahrog explained.

The Everking let loose a quick stream of Felician.

"Would you," Blahrog addressed Miss Featherpenny, "enjoy meeting my daughter? The Everking suggests it, since our affairs could hardly be of interest to you."

"I'd be very pleased." The words were not empty ones. Edith Featherpenny's education in coping with men had not extended to Felician males. Blahrog frightened her with a feeling of superior and incomprehensible intelligence.

Hrom, although seventeen inches tall and weighing perhaps eleven pounds, was definitely feminine and comprehensible.

"Why don't women drink Throatduster?" Miss Featherpenny asked, on the strength of a two-hour acquaintance.

"The men grow the grain here," Hrom explained, "and it's theirs as long as it's in the fields. However, we consider harvesting women's work. We also make the Throatduster. Then we sell it to the men. We don't drink because it is uneconomical."

"Does everyone grow his own grain?"

"Not any more. Town women have other sources of dress money. The custom started that way, that's all."

"If you'll forgive my saying so," Miss Featherpenny remarked, "that dress you are wearing must have taken a big chunk out of your pocket."

Hrom sighed. "In my mother's time, I would have thought nothing of it. Now, one such gown is all I can afford."

"I would have thought your father was one of the wealthier men on Felix II," Miss Featherpenny remarked.

"He is *the* wealthiest," Hrom said. "The richest man is always Minister of Finance. It's only reasonable." Her tone changed. "We're all poor now, since the tourist industry failed. It took every dnot we had to pay for the contract."

Invisible antennae shot from Miss Featherpenny's forehead. "You must be quite sure that Planetary Promotions won't fail you." She tried her best to sound casual.

Hrom smiled faintly. "Have another of these seed cakes," she said.

"Thank you. They are delicious." Miss Featherpenny took one, regardless of calories. "Of course, there is the guarantee clause: 'Double your money back.'"

Hrom busily fluffed a cushion. "One must have some insurance," she said, having her turn at sounding casual. "Tell me, are they wearing large or small hats on Earth this season?"

Miss Featherpenny conceded defeat. "It's all bonnets for summer," she said.

Her first impulse was to tell Andy that she thought the Felicians had bought the guarantee clause, not the contract. It died at her first sight of the morning-after Andy. The situation must be pretty desperate, she rationalized, when the wealthiest girl on the planet has only one dress. This is probably their last chance.

Andy tried to conceal his headache by being brisk and efficient. "Have you considered your natural resources?"

Blahrog, slow and shrewdly inefficient, said, "We mine soft coal. Enough for our own fires and to spare."

"No one within a hundred light-years of Felix II uses coal for fuel anymore," Andy said gently. "Do you have enough for the plastic industries?"

"We have four freighters surplus every season." Blahrog was evidently banking heavily on the coal.

Andy wondered if coal were the only surplus on Felix II. "What are you doing with your surplus at present?" he inquired tactfully, hoping that Blahrog would realize, without being told, the impossibility of supporting the population of Felix II on four freighters of soft coal.

"We store it up," was the crafty answer, "and sell it to the synthetics plants on Darius IV when the Ionian miners go on strike."

"How long since the Ionians struck?" If this economic event occurred regularly, the coal surplus could assist in meeting the Federation's requirements.

"Twenty seasons or so." Blahrog's tone was off-handed, but his eyes slid guiltily toward Andy and away again.

Andy sighed. "Any other resources?"

They went quickly through minerals, agricultural products and animal skins; established that Felicians could not teleport, levitate or read minds. They were technologically uneducated, and had no industry on the factory-system level.

"It is coal or nothing, Mr. Stephens," Blahrog said with finality. "Isn't there some way to make the Federation believe that our coal is superior to other coal, and worth more?"

"Do you, perchance, own a sizable proportion of Felician coal reserves?"

Blahrog nodded, guilty looking again.

"Well, forget it. There isn't enough."

The Everking, who had been holding Andy's translator to his ear in silence, burst into speech.

"His Foreverness says," Blahrog remarked cannily, "that it appears impossible for Felix II to join the Federation."

"We aren't through yet," Andy said quickly. "What about the tourist industry? If you'd allow visitors and advertise a little..."

"No," the Everking shouted, in Galactic.

"We tried that during the last reign," Blahrog said. "It didn't work."

"You're pretty far off the shipping lanes, I'll admit," Andy said, "but surely you could attract enough tourists from somewhere to show a profit."

"We showed a profit," Blahrog said morosely.

He translated a remark of the Everking's. "We made money hand over fist."

"Then why did you quit?" Andy was baffled. "Why did you restrict the planet?"

"Because of the way we happen to look."

"Like leprechauns," Miss Featherpenny explained. "And Hrom looks exactly like a little Christmas fairy."

Blahrog winced. "The tourists found us amusing. We weren't real to them. It became difficult for us to seem real to ourselves. Most of my generation couldn't grow up. The birth rate dropped. We closed the planet to keep the race alive. That's all there is to it."

"Surely," Andy protested, "if you handled it differently..."

"Tourists," Blahrog translated for the Everking, "are out of the question."

"I remember hearing about an intelligent life form that resembled teddy bears," Miss Featherpenny said thoughtfully. "Everybody loved them on sight."

"What happened to them?" Blahrog asked with interest.

"They became extinct."

Andy glared at her. How could he accomplish anything with a stupid steno butting in? She looked away, guilty.

"It's such a simple solution," he said. "It fits your situation perfectly."

"That's what we thought, until we tried it," Blahrog said, grinning sidelong at Miss Featherpenny.

"If you won't try tourists," Andy snapped at both of them, "I don't see exactly what you can do."

"Maybe you didn't cover everything in the special abilities list," Miss Featherpenny suggested softly.

Andy glared at her again. "All right, Blahrog. Can you think of anything you can do that most other species can't?"

Blahrog looked at the floor and considered. "We can walk a long way without getting tired," he offered.

Andy sighed, and wrote "Endurance?" on his scratch pad. It was scarcely saleable. "Is there anything else? Anything you know how to make? Besides Throatduster."

"We make good shoes," Blahrog said hopefully. "The tourists used to buy lots of them."

"Hum," Andy cogitated. "Here we have something for which a market already exists. If we can expand the market and the production facilities..." He nailed Blahrog with a finger, in conscious imitation of Crumbly. "How many pairs of shoes can Felix II produce in a single season?"

"If the reserves were called in to the Cobbler's Guild, it would be almost half the manpower of the planet..." Blahrog paused, doing mental arithmetic. "Four and a half million pairs, more or less." He sounded as though he were surprised.

129

"That ought to do it," Andy said gleefully.

"But where will we find that many pairs of feet?" Blahrog asked.

"There are eight million times that many pairs of feet in the Federation," Andy said. "Leave the advertising to Planetary Promotions."

"It seems sort of poetic," Miss Featherpenny romanced. "Leprechauns are supposed to be cobblers."

Blahrog snorted.

Andy turned and addressed her from the full distance between a promoter third class and a girl from the steno pool. "Miss Featherpenny, I will ask for your opinion when I want it."

Miss Featherpenny answered from her side of the gulf. "Yes, sir."

Andy had always despised rank-pullers. He turned to Blahrog "I'll have to send the dope back to the Home Office so they can put it through the computer and send me the ad-intensity index."

Blahrog looked a polite enquiry.

"That will tell us how effective the ad campaign will have to be to make a go of this. What's the fastest way to send a message to Earth?"

"Radiogram the satellite station," Blahrog answered. "They'll relay it to the next ship within range, and the ship will relay it to the next planet it nears with the radiogram facilities to send it to Earth."

"How long will it take to get an answer?" Andy asked.

"About twelve days."

They didn't stare at the sky while they waited for the answer.

Blahrog called the members of the Cobbler's Guild together, and delivered a series of lectures on their importance to the future of Felix II.

Foreseeing a return to political and economic power, the reserve members dusted off their lasts and aprons and got back into practice. For the first time in nearly thirty seasons, the applications for apprenticeship were too numerous to handle. New life showed on their faces.

The Master Cobblers (including the Everking and Blahrog) worked around the clock, fabricating plastic lasts. Miss Featherpenny and Hrom dug pictures and descriptions of the various types of Galactic feet that habitually or occasionally wore shoes out of old periodicals, located by members of the newly-organized ladies' auxiliary.

130

Felix II was humming, if not absolutely singing, with industry and good humor. Some of it rubbed off on Andy. He relented toward Miss Featherpenny to the extent of presenting her with a pair of Felician shoes, fabricated by the Everking. They were of the sensible walking variety, and not Miss Featherpenny's style. Nevertheless, she was extremely pleased with the gift. Like all Felician shoes, they fit her perfectly.

The Everking, backed by his Debators and ministers, issued public thanks to one Andrew Stephens, restorer of hope, and propagator of economic equality. The ladies' auxiliary gave a tea in Miss Featherpenny's honor. They were both showered with gifts from a grateful and admiring populace.

The reply to the message was signed by Crumbly himself. "Forlorn hope," it said unsympathetically. "Try something else. Computer indicates ad intensity of 0.94."

An ad intensity of 0.0001 means you sell someone something he wants anyway. An intensity of 1.0 means you have to make the consumer love something he thinks he hates.

Andy sent a young Felician on the run for Blahrog, and retired to the storeroom of Blahrog's dwelling, which housed two fair-sized plastic barrels of Throatduster.

"But you have to try," Blahrog insisted, finishing his second mug of hospitality.

"Snow good," Andy said, deep into his fifth. "Even Gray Flannel, ad man in legend, only got to 0.87. Simpossible."

Blahrog, who knew little about advertising or computers, repeated, "You must try. No member of the Cobbler's Guild has ever quit without trying."

Andy had been accepted as an apprentice of the Guild the night before.

"Dunno," he said. "Tell you simpossible."

Blahrog climbed off the barrel of Throatduster. "I'll go get Miss Featherpenny," he said. "Perhaps she can help you."

"Miss Featherpenny. Bah," Andy snorted. "What good would she be? Dumb steno." He tried to be fair. "Nice legs, I admit. But no brains."

"I'll go get Miss Featherpenny," Blahrog repeated firmly, closing the door behind him…

"What frame of mind is he in?" Miss Featherpenny looked uncertainly at the heavy door to Andy's store room.

"Drunk," Blahrog informed her coldly.

It takes an enormous quantity of Throatduster to intoxicate a Felician. Intoxication is therefore considered bad form.

"And belligerent," the Minister of Finance added.

"Oh, dear." Miss Featherpenny looked at the door again. "But what can I do?" she asked in a helpless voice. "I'm not a promoter."

"He said," Blahrog indicated the door, "that you were a dumb steno."

"Well!" Hrom exclaimed.

Miss Featherpenny's hackles invisibly rose. Her mouth visibly tightened. She turned away from the door.

Hrom said, "You ought to try to show him."

Miss Featherpenny looked at them, and at the surrounding examples of Felician landscape and architecture.

"Mr. Blahrog," she said suddenly, "you don't mind looking like a leprechaun, do you? As long as you don't have to meet people?"

Blahrog's silence was more than dignified.

"What do you mean?" Hrom asked.

"You wouldn't mind if we used a picture of a Master Cobbler in the ad, would you?"

Blahrog thawed abruptly. "You have an idea?"

"If you don't mind the picture."

"He doesn't mind," Hrom said, adding in Felician, "After all, Papa, we don't have to let any ships but the freighters land."

"Go ahead, then," Blahrog consented.

"Good luck," Hrom added.

"You," Andy welcomed her. "Bah." He shut his eyes. Most of him was sprawled out on the floor.

"Yes, me," Miss Featherpenny agreed, repressing an inclination to kick him. She sat down on one of the kegs, and opened her stenographer's book. "I came to take down the ad for the shoes," she announced.

"What ad?" Andy moaned. "The newest, biggest, brightest ads can't get over an 0.62. How can I manage an 0.94? You're crazy." He opened his eyes. "But you do have nice legs."

"Felix II is sort of quaint," Miss Featherpenny suggested. "Why not use an old ad?"

"An idea," Andy enunciated, without hope.

"It's sort of pretty too," Miss Featherpenny nudged.

"We could use a color picture of it," Andy said, kicking thoughtfully at an overturned stool.

"The Felicians are quaint looking, too."

"Sure," Andy said. "Put a Felician in the foreground, cobbling." He tried to sit up.

"I've seen ads like that in history books," Miss Featherpenny said, exuding admiration.

"It's so old it's new," Andy said, lying down again. "Old English lettering over the top. A real cliché." He considered Miss Featherpenny's ankle. "Peaceful scenery, Felician shoes?"

"Not quite," said Miss Featherpenny.

"Quiet field, Felician shoes?"

"Nope," said Miss Featherpenny.

"You're an aggravating woman," Andy said sweetly, "but you do have nice legs."

"What about Elysian fields?" Miss Featherpenny suggested.

Andy tasted it. "Elysian fields, Felician shoes." He tried to sit up again. "You got all that down?" he demanded.

"Yes," Miss Featherpenny lied. She had it in her head, but not on the steno pad.

"Then get somebody to send it off so we can find out if it's good enough. And come back soon." He wobbled on his elbow. "You do have…"

"I think I'd better attend to sending it personally." Miss Featherpenny opened the door. "You rest until you feel better."

Blahrog had gone, but Hrom was waiting for her. She looked more like a Christmas fairy than usual. A mischievous one.

"Did you manage?" she whispered.

"Barely." Miss Featherpenny looked grim.

"Drink this," Hrom ordered, holding out a mug of Throatduster.

Miss Featherpenny was surprised. "I thought ladies didn't drink on Felix II."

"There are," Hrom said, "exceptions."

The next twelve days of waiting for computer results were not as hopefully active as the first twelve. The Felicians finished setting up their manufacturing and storing systems, but they didn't start making shoes. The cattle drovers forbore to slaughter the beasts who provided the leather.

The Everking and his Debators all developed severe cases of beard-itch, a Felician nervous disorder. Since it is even more unseemly to scratch on Felix II than it is on Earth, they retired temporarily from public life.

Andy also retired from public life, biting his fingernails, an Earther nervous disorder. Blahrog joined him in the illness, which was new to Felicians. By the time the answer from Planetary Promotions came it was the most fashionable habit on the planet, in spite of the fact that Felicians have extremely tough nails, and a pair of bony ridges rather than true teeth.

The second message was also direct from Crumbly. It read: "Computer rates ad campaign at intensity 0.942. P. P. in action by the time you receive this. Stephens ordered back to Home Office; promoted to first class."

Four Earth months later, Miss Featherpenny entered Andy's ten by twelve office, her high heels clicking on the plastic tiles, and laid a memorandum on the new steel desk.

"They've been admitted," she announced.

"What? Who?" Andy said irritably. There were times when he thought her position as his private secretary had gone to her head.

"Felix II has been admitted to the Federation. The contract has been fulfilled." She smiled brightly. "Shall I mark the file closed?"

"Can't yet," Andy said. "Felix II won't be a permanent member of the Federation until they've been self-supporting for ten years."

"Why?" asked Miss Featherpenny.

"It's a precautionary measure," Andy began to explain. "Oh, let's go get some lunch and forget Felix II."

"Yes, Mr. Stephens," Miss Featherpenny said meekly.

He followed her out the door, admiring the effect of her glastic skirt. She did have nice legs...

Three years later, Edith Featherpenny was forced to remember Felix II. There was a communication on her mock-baroque desk. Felician shoes weren't selling. Felix II wasn't making enough money. The Galactic Federation was threatening to take steps.

She glanced at the impressive door to the inner office. Andy, she knew, was engaged in reading a letter from his brother Lloyd, who had just been promoted to vice-president of Universal Products.

She judiciously forged his initials on an order to put data on the Felix II failure through the computer.

In an hour and a half she had the answer. The Felicians hadn't changed the styles, and their shoes didn't wear out. Everybody had a pair.

She considered the door again. There was really little sense in disturbing Andy over such a simple matter. She forged his name on a message to Blahrog. "Change the styles of your shoes."

She then picked up some carefully selected problem sheets from the top of the filing cabinet, and went through the impressive door.

The next morning, Blahrog's answer was on her desk.

"Felician shoes are of the cut most suited to the feet that wear them. To change them would be both foolish and unethical."

It was a good thing, Miss Featherpenny thought, that Andy was feeling better today. She went into his office, padding softly over the carpet to his contemporary prestwood desk.

"Good morning, Edie," Andy said cheerfully. "What happened? Lightning strike you?"

"Practically," Miss Featherpenny said. "It's Felix II again." She handed over the sheaf of papers.

"Why didn't you tell me about this yesterday?" Andy muttered, reading them.

"I thought I could handle it." Miss Featherpenny made a face. "Until

135

I got that answer this morning."

"It sounds like typical Felician thinking," Andy said. "There's no sense trying to argue by mail." He sighed. "You'd better reserve a first-class passage for me on the first ship out."

"Can't I go?" Miss Featherpenny asked.

"Who'd run the office?"

"The stenos can stack stuff until we get back." Miss Featherpenny looked wistful. "I was in on the beginning of it. I want to see it through. Besides, I'd like to see Hrom again."

"Oh, all right," Andy agreed. "Make it two first class."

Blahrog was waiting on the long porch of the space port dining room.

"Have a nice trip?" he asked.

"What's all this about not changing the shoe styles?" Andy countered.

"As I told you in the message," Blahrog said impatiently, "We make our shoes in the best possible shapes for the feet that will wear them. There isn't any good reason to change them."

"You can't sell people two pairs of identical shoes," Andy insisted.

"You might be able to sell them if you changed them," Miss Featherpenny added, sounding reasonable.

"Save your arguments for the Everking," Blahrog said. "Come on to the car."

"Car?" Miss Featherpenny exclaimed. "The Everking's?"

"No, mine." Blahrog couldn't keep the pride out of his voice. "There are nearly two hundred cars on Felix II."

Andy went over the same ground in the presence of the Everking. It didn't help. The Everking, his minister and his Debators were solidly against changing the shoes. The ethics of the Cobblers' Guild were involved.

"If you won't follow Planetary Promotions' advice," he said at last, "the company can't be responsible for the outcome." He glared at the assembly. "In other words, the guarantee clause is cancelled."

There was an indignant and concerned buzz from the audience. Blahrog got up.

"Your Foreverness," he said, "honorable members of the government, Mr. Stephens. Three Earth years ago, Felix II gathered together all the money the government could find, and bought a contract with Planetary Promotions." He paused and shuffled his feet. "We did not expect the contract to be fulfilled. We needed money, and two for one would keep us going while we attempted to educate the young to be immune to the tourists. Of course, if Planetary Promotions found a way for us to be self-supporting without tourists, we would be equally pleased."

"I thought so," Miss Featherpenny murmured.

"Really," Andy said. "Why didn't you let me in on it?"

Blahrog cleared his throat to indicate that he wasn't through. "Since a way was found," he continued, "Felician self respect and content has increased along with Felician prosperity." He glanced uneasily at Andy. "We would like to continue as we are going."

"Unless you change the styles," Andy said flatly, "that is impossible."

Miss Featherpenny, realizing that they were starting over the same ground, slipped out the door and walked over to visit Hrom.

"So Papa admitted it," Hrom said, after Miss Featherpenny had admired the baby, and been shown over the house. "I almost told you myself, when I first met you."

"You told me enough to let me guess the rest," Miss Featherpenny said.

"Have some olgan seed cakes," Hrom offered. "Why didn't you tell Mr. Stephens?"

Miss Featherpenny took a cake. "Partly because of his almighty attitude, and partly because I was on your... Ow!" She clapped a hand hastily to her jaw.

"What's wrong?" Hrom asked, alarmed.

"Broke a tooth," Miss Featherpenny muttered, her face contorted.

"Does it hurt much?" Hrom's question was part sympathy and part curiosity.

Miss Featherpenny nodded. "I'll have to find a dentist right away."

"What's a dentist?"

"Man who fixes your teeth."

"But we don't have teeth," Hrom said.

"I forgot," Miss Featherpenny moaned. "Oh, Lord, I guess I'll have to go all the way back to Earth."

Hrom shook her head. "There are a lot of Earthers living on Darius IV. They must have a dentist. There's a ship every morning."

"Fine," Miss Featherpenny gasped.

"Can I get you something for the pain? Would an aspirtran help?"

"I'd better have two. Thanks."

"Here. Take the bottle with you." Hrom was frowning worriedly. "My, I'm glad we don't have teeth."

"I'll have to tell Andy—Mr. Stephens—that I'm leaving."

Inspiration dawned on Hrom's face. "I've hardly been out of the house since the baby was born. I'll leave him with my husband's mother and go with you."

"I'd be glad of the company," Miss Featherpenny admitted.

"Good. I'll find out what time the ship leaves, and tell Mother Klagom about the treat she's got coming. You go tell Mr. Stephens and then come back here for the night."

Miss Featherpenny heard them shouting before she opened the council chamber door.

"I suggest," Andy was saying, "that you either change the styles or go back to the tourist business."

She pushed the door open.

"Mr. Stephens," Blahrog said mildly, "the last time calamity was upon us, you solved the problem by drinking Throatduster until you got an idea. May I suggest that you try again?"

"Andy," Miss Featherpenny whispered.

"Well?" he snapped.

"I broke a tooth. I'm going over to Darius IV tomorrow, with Hrom, to have it fixed."

"Why Darius IV?" Andy demanded. "What's the matter with Felician dentists?"

"What's Hrom going to do with the boy?" Blahrog demanded.

"Hrom's leaving the baby with Mrs. Klagom," Miss Featherpenny answered, "and there aren't any Felician dentists."

"Mrs. Klagom is a silly woman," Blahrog disapproved. "She would do better to leave him with me."

"If you must, I suppose you must," Andy admitted grudgingly. "Where are you going now?"

"Back to Hrom's house to lie down."

"Tell her I'll mind the baby," Blahrog called after her.

As she closed the door, she heard Andy say, "Gentlemen, if you'll supply the Throatduster, I'll give it a try."

"It's awfully quiet," Hrom said doubtfully, looking around at the Felician spaceport. "Look at the tannery chimneys. No smoke."

Miss Featherpenny, her mouth in good repair, glanced into the bar as they passed it. "Only two shippers," she said. "There are usually dozens."

"They must have stopped production entirely," Hrom said.

"Maybe Andy thought of something."

"I wonder if Papa brought the car down for us."

He hadn't. They walked into town.

Blahrog was in conference with the Everking.

"I'd better wait for him," Miss Featherpenny said. "I want to find out what's going on before I talk to Andy."

"I'd better rescue Mother Klagom from the baby."

Blahrog was as long-winded as usual.

"Where is Mr. Stephens?" Miss Featherpenny demanded, as soon as she saw him coming down the hall.

"In his old storeroom," Blahrog said moodily. "He's quite drunk, I believe, but he doesn't seem to be getting any ideas."

"Then why did you stop cobbling?"

Blahrog did a Felician shrug. "We're waiting to see what happens. There's no sense making shoes any more if they aren't wanted."

"I have to talk to him," Miss Featherpenny said.

"Do you have an idea?"

"No," Miss Featherpenny lied. "But you'd let him drink himself to death, if he didn't think of anything."

"You want a lift in the car?" Blahrog asked, uninsulted.

"I'd be pleased, if you don't mind. I just walked in from the port."

Andy was not, as Blahrog had suggested, very drunk. He was only hung over. "Get your tooth fixed?" he asked cheerlessly.

"Yes."

"Good dentist?"

Miss Featherpenny nodded. "He had some entirely new equipment. Extremely powerful, and quite precise."

"Oh?" Andy straightened in the old arm chair. "I've been trying to think. And drinking. Throatduster isn't working this time." He paused to reconsider. "Except that it makes me drunk. Everything keeps getting fuzzy, and my head is wider than my shoulders."

"The dentist said," Miss Featherpenny persisted, "that he could pull a whale's tooth as easily and smoothly as he pulled mine."

"You had to have it pulled? Too bad." Andy made a face at the full mug of Throatduster on the barrel beside him. "The Felicians won't change their minds about the shoes, and they won't try tourists again. I can't think of anything else. And they can claim the guarantee. I was bluffing."

"I know," Miss Featherpenny said. She tried again. "The dentist claims even the tiniest species could do dental work on the biggest species." She paused, hoping it would sink in. "Providing the tiny species had sufficient dexterity."

"Blasted Felicians," Andy muttered. "Stubborn little pigs."

"That's part of their trouble, I think," Miss Featherpenny said. "Being little, I mean. But it doesn't always work against them. When they're doing delicate work..."

"Like those shoes," Andy agreed. "'Best possible shapes already,'" he imitated Blahrog.

"They're one of the smallest intelligent species," Miss Featherpenny said in desperation. "And their manual dexterity rating is one of the highest. Why, a Felician could get both hands inside an Earther's mouth."

"And steal his fillings..." Andy started. "Wait a minute. You've given me an idea."

Miss Featherpenny breathed relief. "I have? What is it?"

"Dentists! They can all be dentists."

"All?"

"Well, enough of them to provide for the planet's income."

"Why, that's marvelous," Miss Featherpenny said. "It won't matter that other species think they're cute. Everybody takes dentists seriously."

"Their appearance will work for them," Andy said. "Think of children's dentistry."

"Let's go tell them right away," Miss Featherpenny said, feeling like a Bobbsey twin.

Andy swayed upward.

"Sit still," Miss Featherpenny commanded. "I'll bring you some coffee."

Blahrog accepted the suggestion with Felician phlegm and ministerial greed. "We'll have to change the tax system, since most of our working population will be living off-planet."

"Maybe you could work out a rotation system, Papa." Hrom had sneaked into the council chamber.

"Wait a minute," Andy said uneasily. "How are you going to educate these dentists?"

Blahrog stopped and thought. "We'll use the hotels for schools," he said slowly. His face wrinkled with sly pleasure. "And we can sell the coal surplus to pay teachers and buy equipment."

The Everking made a wicked-sounding comment in Felician.

The entire assembly burst into loud, beard-wagging laughter. It had a nasty ring to it.

"What did he say?" Andy demanded.

"He said," Hrom giggled, "'Let them try to treat us like stuffed toys now.'"

"Disgusting," said Miss Featherpenny.

"Indecent, Edie," Andy agreed. "But never mind. Let's go home and get married."

"You're a little sudden."

Andy grinned. "I'll have a raise coming for this, and I'd like to keep you in the family. I can't seem to think unless you're around."

"Took you long enough to notice," said Miss Featherpenny. But she didn't say it out loud.

THE DEER PARK
by Maria Russell

(Originally appeared in the January 1962 issue of *Fantasy & Science Fiction*)

"The Deer Park" is Maria Russell's only published short story, appearing in the January 1962 edition of The Magazine of Fantasy & Science Fiction. *Unfortunately, the editor's intro makes no mention of her background, nor does it provide any commentary of her beautifully-written tale. I am grateful for the opportunity to finally rectify that oversight.*

Maria Russell's real name was Mary Russell Standard. Born in 1926 in Orange, Texas, she worked as a senior computer systems analyst in Connecticut for several decades, eventually being promoted to Vice President of Software Engineering. Clearly, she was a smart, steadfast and determined woman.

I can only speculate what inspired her to write this tale, but it seems likely that "The Deer Park" was influenced by her experiences as an intelligent woman working in a male-dominated environment. Through her skillfully-woven tale, Russell establishes a futuristic world in which a network of planets is protected by a highly advanced technological system—protected from what, exactly, is left ambiguous.

Our protagonist, a Minister of one of these planets, is adamant that the overly-protective systems are a wondrous marvel, even if means his world is insufferably predictable and sedate. The Minister's senses have become so dulled by the safety of his world that he doesn't even realize it, until an Envoy from a distant planet (one that does not rely on the same protections as his) arrives and challenges his point of view. The Envoy, a quietly powerful woman completely unlike anyone the Minister has ever met, questions his sense of safety when she posits, "Security is not a joy. Security is a disease."

Through the tale, Russell's astute perception of the human psyche shines. The more insecure we are, the more we try to control; the tighter our control, the more insecure we are that our grip will fail. She suggests that insecurity and self-doubt will forever endure despite the scientific advancements of humanity—and, in fact, our scientific advancements will end up enhancing our insecurities. In today's world, where self-worth can be rated by how many likes one's social media post achieves, it seems that Russell's theory has been proven correct.

The Envoy in the story makes a compelling argument that ultimate and absolute control over one's environment, one's companions and oneself is self-limiting. Freedom lies in the possibility of the unknown, even if it might lead to a disastrous outcome; unhindered liberty, she asserts, is always preferable over the uninspiring staleness of a predictably controlled environment.

"The Deer Park" is a beautifully haunting feminist tale of a self-assured woman cleverly needling at a man's insecurities to achieve her goals, pacing out for the reader an astute insight into the human mind and a prescient point of view. Russell demonstrates a mastery of prose that belies her short tenure as an author and leaves us yearning to read more from her.

—Claire Weaver

The day was a tender joy of green and gold, shot with flecks of blue that twinkled among the leaves of the tall old trees. The grass was long and soft (weaving itself into a carpet as proper grass should do) and the deer were warm shadows graciously drinking at the serene pool that lay in the end of the oaken tunnel. The Minister was very happy.

"It is," he said to his lovely companion, Ronde, "a great blessing to be the Minister of Defense for the Terrana Hegemony—for who else has as much time as I for such pleasant pursuits as these?"

Ronde agreeably dipped her flame-graced head, and squeezed the arm she held, just ever so little—just as she always did—to show that she was perfectly atune.

"It is," continued the Minister, "a grand and glorious blessing that the systems are so well protected, so well covered and concealed from whatever evil intelligences exist in the universe..."

"So well concealed from Nature," interposed Ronde. "How I hate the Old Ones! What nasty creatures!"

"And from the Old Ones," agreed the Minister, for, of course, Ronde had merely echoed his thoughts—thoughts which he had not yet had time nor inclination to express—echoed them just as she always did.

"And from Nature—that concatenation of the elder antagonists of man," he continued, "for, if such concealment were not the case, I should never have the opportunity to create or enjoy the dearest ideals of my heart." He was actually thinking of the deer park, but he pinched Ronde ever so slightly and gently, so that she could assume he was thinking of her. She squeezed his arm again. They were *perfectly* atune. But, after all, had he not created her?

They walked on, bending their steps into the winding footpaths, and stopping to fall upon a green and leafy bed beneath one of the giant trees and indulge themselves for a moment, or for many minutes. Then they would rise, and continue their strolling, pausing here to stroke the antlers of a royal buck, or there to tickle the ears of a wistful doe and coo and chuckle over the reedy helplessness of a tiny fawn. The scene was altogether pastoral, altogether pleasant, altogether picturesque.

When they had encountered their third couch of leaves—or was it boughs, perhaps?—the Minister found himself slightly bored with so much indulgence, and Ronde, atune as always, rejected him with a slight push from her white hand and sat up, brushing her exquisitely milky brow with the same white hand, and petulantly waving the other.

"I think, Vwal," she breathed, "I would rather not—at the moment. I think, instead, I would prefer to see a she-lion, or some such grisly animal, attack one of the deer—a buck, of course, for the battle would not be excitingly equal if it were a doe. Do find a lioness for me, Vwal! Oh, do!"

She rose, searching among the far trees for the sight of the beast, for, of course, she knew that he could, would do that very thing.

The Minister felt a delicious pain slide through him like a razored knife. A struggle! How marvelous...he should have known that this most precious puppet of his imagination would quite naturally discern the peak and crisis of satiation.

"No!" he cried, all outer sternness, all inner delight. "No, Ronde! how very immoral, how unethical of you! I will do no such thing!"

"Ah, please, dear, beautiful, most good Vwal!" Tears lept into her green eyes, and she clasped her little hands in a consummate attitude of supplication.

"Certainly not!" he said, calmer now, for he knew that he would consent, he knew the exact and fatal length to his endurance of this chasm in his being. It was an excellent and fantastic pleasure.

"Ah, Vwal," she murmured, sinking to her knees and clasping his, all in one graceful and generous movement, "I have never seen the frightful battle of these creatures, the torn flesh and the blood running, dripping on the greensward. I have never heard the cries of lust and terror, the piteous wailing of the wounded, felt the panic of the near-defeated. Let me know it. Vwal! Let me see, hear and feel!"

She pressed her supple body against his legs, and he was conscious of her breasts pleading with his tendons, her hands pleading with his thighs, her being—which was, of course, his own—pleading also. The pleasure boiled and bubbled, the pressure mounted, reaching the point of furtherest containment, and, with a gasp of relief, he flashed the image in his mind into the qopot; the she-lion roared down on the buck. The battle was a classic specimen, and, in the end—as he had willed it—the buck victorious. The Minister was satisfied. He disliked cats of any description.

When quiet had at last settled down like a contented hen, the Minister looked around him, sensations of distaste tickling his brain. What is duller than a climax past and half-remembered?

"I believe," he said, "that I shall go to sleep." And he lay down on the last-encountered couch, and Ronde curled herself beside him, in the crook of his arm.

The Minister awoke some ten minutes later, his arm numbed from the weight of Ronde. He raised his head, and looked at her with an expression compounded of the previous sensations.

"Oh...disappear," he muttered, a little sulkily. She vanished as dew from the grass, but more swiftly. The Minister sighed, rolled over, and went back to sleep.

He was awakened again, this time in half an hour.

"Sire," burbled the little pink flame of his fama, "there's a committee of persons to see you."

Who on earth would want to see me? thought the Minister, though he was as yet half asleep and really supposed that he must be dreaming still.

"Oh, no one on Earth, Sire," responded the fama with excruciating veracity. "These are very minor persons," it went on, answering with its usual alacrity the unformed queries in his mind, "from a very minor planet, from a very minor system—a one-time colony of Terra's. One has no idea what they want," it concluded with an apologetic flicker.

"Oh, dear," mumbled the Minister, "I suppose I should tidy up."

He directed another image to the qopot, and, as the cloth on his body smoothed itself free of dirt and wrinkles, so did the shreds and gobbets of the big cat carcass disappear and the grass fade from rusty crimson to its usual green. As an afterthought, the Minister reduced its hue to more nearly a springtime chartreuse.

"Show them in," he said, feeling the need for a spoken command. He tried to move his arm in an appropriately languid fashion toward what he thought was the entrance to the park.

But the roseal extension of his senses had already fluttered away in the opposite direction, and the Minister was left alone to attempt an attitude of comfort on the familiar boughs. He nervously summoned Ronde. She appeared a trifle tentatively, a trifle timidly, as if not certain that she was wanted. The Minister wasn't certain, either. His fingers were still numb, and, besides, he almost wished for a mind other than

146

his own to tender the support and courage necessary to cope with the bizarre situation. But Ronde was better than nothing.

The visitors intensified the wish by entering behind him. The Minister cursed his bad memory: he had forgotten that only the week before he had removed the gates of the deer park to the eastern wall, where they would open to the morning sun. Not that it mattered where he placed his sun, for doubtless a quadrillion fireballs spun beneath the mamiraj, but an innate sense of fitness caused him to create his private dawn always to the east. Unfortunately, now, he was facing west, and Ronde was the one to notice the appearance of the strangers.

"There they come, Vwal," she stated, and he followed the pointing of the slender limb, hand and outstretched finger. He was annoyed that she had seen them first, and he created a large strawberry mark on her wrist.

There were only five of them—four men, and their leader. A female. The Minister noted in distaste her pale hair, her lean and vital body, her confident stride. He decided that he disliked blondes.

The girl came straight towards him—tall as himself and nearly half as powerful. The Minister felt threatened, abused. He watched her swing her shoulders—gracefully, he had to admit on second thought, though, of course, he much preferred the slink and sloven walk of Ronde.

And worse still, the girl had an insolent nose, and brilliantly blue eyes...eyes blue as the—yes, it *was* sky! For he'd always made his own canopy that lovely, frightening color. He drew his glance away from the girl in confusion.

"Sire," announced the fama, "these are the persons from the planet Zzzt, which circles the star Osborne 542—a star, one understands, of eighteenth magnitude or perhaps nineteenth."

"Eighteenth," said the pale-haired girl, "and the true name of our sun is 'Sol,' after our parent." She smiled at the Minister with friendly abandon. The Minister stared back with shaky enmity.

"It is a *very* minor planet," soothed the fama, with a placating flicker, "and the only child of the star Osborne 542. A very insignificant piece of cosmic dust. Even today, their world is not within the mamiraj."

"You're not sealed?" cried the Minister. "How terrible!"

The girl smiled again, raw energy flooding from those disturbing eyes beneath that sun-frothed hair.

"We don't find it terrible at all."

"But...you live in the open," whispered the Minister, "under the... sky..."

"Yes," answered the girl, with simple truthfulness.

"It *is* blue, isn't it?" asked the Minister, suddenly confronted with the possibility that his sense of fitness had not functioned with perfection during the thousand-odd years of his life. "It is...blue?"

"Yes," answered the girl, again. "As blue as the skies of Earth. Though, of course," she added, quickly, "none of us have ever seen the skies of Earth."

"Nor have I," said the Minister, stiffly, "but I understand they're blue."

"Sire," murmured the fama, "these persons have come to implore your aid."

"Oh?" queried the Minister, uncertainly. "Well...perhaps you'd better sit down."

The four men gratefully arranged themselves on stump and log and fountain-lip. The girl tailor-crossed herself on the ground before the Minister.

"Sire," she began, without more ado, "for aeons we have lived, a peaceful people, tilling the soil, tending the herds, rearing our children and dying in our turn. The ways of space and the universe have been forgotten, much to our sorrow. The ships that brought us to Zzzt have been allowed to rust, until all we had left was an old creaking can of a vessel. It managed to return us to the worlds of Terrana before it fell to pieces at one tiny blast from the invader."

"Invader!" cried the Minister, shuddering at the thought of alien presence—which alien presence he could not have said— "well! such incidents are behind us, for we lie safe behind the mamiraj...as can the planet Zzzt."

"Sire," responded the girl, "Zzzt thanks you. But we require another type of assistance."

There was a pause—expectancy counterpoint to a basso of faint

148

terror.

"What type?" mumbled the Minister, but before he got his answer, Ronde was on her feet, her eyes blazing with emerald fire, her hair a contrasting aurora around her white, drawn face.

"Whelps of death!" she cried. "They wish to live in the ancient way, to be suckled and spat upon by the Old Ones!"

The girl seemed unperturbed.

"How else to see the stars?" she asked.

"We see them," snarled Ronde, "any day or night we please, and if, at any given moment, we don't care for them, we snuff them out."

"What joy in that," asked the girl, "to look at stars that may be dismissed like a candle flame caught between thumb and forefinger?"

"The joy of art, creation, power...security..." answered Ronde, calmly, framing her words in a triumphant smile.

"Security is not a joy," said the girl. "Security is a disease." She spoke very quietly, in the manner of one who is forced to utter a sad truth, which for the sake of politeness and pity were better left unsaid. She held her sight upward for a moment, staring at Ronde; then she looked at the Minister and smiled gently, once, and let her gaze drift downwards, across the pool and the lawn, until it rested on the ground in front of the Minister's feet. Ronde followed the sweep of vision to the end; then she turned her eyes to the Minister; they were the puzzled eyes of an antique child.

"You answer her, then," she said, pouting a little. "Well? Aren't you going to answer her?"

The Minister looked from one to the other for a long moment, listening painfully for the notes of the old harmony—his harmony, with its agreeably futile accidentals—and hearing only fantastic modulations far too potent for his comfort: strange sounds from a stranger's world. Suddenly, he put his hands over his ears; then he got down on his knees, and, with first his back and last his neck crooked at the necessary angle, he looked up at the girl.

"What type?" he repeated, and his voice rang cold and hollow—so hollow that it frightened him until he remembered that the palms of his hands were pressing a myriad molecules of air against his ear drums; he removed his hands at once. "What type," he said again, and was relieved to note that his words sang in the air—this time thinly, and with but a slight tremble.

"Ships!" The girl spoke eagerly. "Ships of space, new and bright and ready for battle."

"We...we have no such antiques." The singing voice became dry and whispery, and he could not have said whether it was from relief or sorrow.

But she pursued—over the inch of distance between them.

"You built them once!" she cried. "You must retain the skill!"

He retreated three inches—desperately.

"We...we do not need it. The qopot will create whatever we hold in our minds." And his throat choked—too late—as his brain grasped the implication of his words and the sense of that daring that had lain so deep within him that he had never recognized it before.

But the girl seemed to discover not victory, but defeat. Sadly she shook her head.

"Who can hold such a thing as a ship in his mind?"

Unsought release from unwanted duality flooded the Minister like the white rain of hope. He stood up on his feet once more, and stared down at the top of the girl's bent head.

"Exactly!" he crowed "You must have a toria, my dear child, a toria! and I've got none—none at all. I mislaid my entire collection at least six hundred years ago. Or was it five?" he mused. "No difference, I've not got any, so I'm really quite afraid we can't help you."

"Goodbye," said Ronde, haughtily waving her hand. At the sound of her voice, the strange notes clanged again, and the Minister wished to call out, "Wait!" but he said nothing, though the girl was now gazing up at him, sadness dampening her eyes.

"Sire," said the fama, "here is the toria you desire."

"*I* desire?" cried the Minister, falling back a pace, and it was with shock he noted, in truth, a queer little thought at the edge of his mind— so queer, indeed, that he did not even think to question the fama as to the whereabouts of that adolescent mislaying.

"No!" shrieked Ronde, and the strangers got to their feet.

For a thin little firey line was already uncurling from the center of the hovering flame. It wound itself into the qopot and nestled, layer on layer, around a whiling spoke. The Minister went closer and watched in horrified fascination, and he was the last to notice the look of shining wonder that appeared on the face of the girl as she looked down the great tunnel of trees to the end of the park.

There, there at the very end of the lane, by the little pool, was a pure loveliness, poised like a great silver butterfly or gleaming bird—a ghost of old, beckoning once again to the man that lived in the Minister. He took a step forward, and was surprised to find that the others did likewise, for they had all moved as one creature, drawn by the shimmering vision that seemed to dance in ecstasy at the water's edge.

Ronde whimpered once, and flung herself on the ground at the Minister's feet. He hardly glanced at her.

"Sire!" cried the girl, excitedly, "You've given us back our home!"

"I?" exclaimed the Minister, again. He was bewildered. What had he to do with that foreign thing caught from the little spinning reel in the qopot? Yet that tiny, odd thought was bobbing and bobbing around in his mind. He looked at the fama, almost as if for guidance.

"Their fleet awaits them," said the fama, "on the far planets, just as Your Honor wished."

The Minister did not protest this time, but only stared for a minute; then he turned on his heel, without another word, and left them.

"Thank you," whispered the girl, to no one in particular.

The Minister stood behind the bole of one of the larger oaks and watched their departure. He was not really looking at the girl, but at the sheen of her hair glittering through the shadows of the trees.

"Gold as the...sun," he whispered, and he followed the shining strands until they disappeared behind the moonsilver of the little ship.

And he continued to stare at the ship, for now, he thought, it lay like a poor, captured thing in the deathly beautiful embrace of the pool and gardens—eager for flight, but frozen to stillness.

A sense of sorrow overwhelmed him, and he watched, while the deer came, and nuzzled and grazed and cropped, unafraid and careless, so sure were they of the stranger's tameness and timidity.

Many minutes passed, and finally the Minister walked over to Ronde where she lay on the ground. He looked down at her, contemplation patterning his face. Experimentally, he changed one curl of her head to a more golden hue. Then a quiver of disgust crossed his heart, and he changed it back. She opened one eye, then the other, and gazed up at him.

"Have they gone, Vwal?" she asked.

"Yes," he answered, dully, "they've gone."

"Good!" she cried, and leaped to her feet, as if from a make-believe sleep. "Dear Vwal," she murmured, as she fastened herself to his arm, "what terrible people those people were."

"Yes," agreed the Minister, still dully. He was looking at the ship.

"Vwal!" she cried. "Destroy it, quickly!"

"Why...I don't know if I can," he answered in a mild, deceptive voice.

"Try, try!" she urged, but he shook off her grasp and started for the ship as steel starts for a magnet—slowly at first, then more and more swiftly. Ronde stood for a moment still as eternity. Then she ran after him.

The Minister ran faster than she, and Ronde caught up with him only when he reached the ship.

"Vwal!"

He turned.

"I only want to look," he said.

"No!" Her hands were clawing at him, her body seeking to pull him away from the enemy. "You must not!"

He looked at her, his eyes gone wild and glad.

"Why must I not?" he cried, even as his hands found the secret of the entrance and the little ship opened itself to his longing.

She answered nothing, but only stared at him with the green eyes of his coward soul. With a great cry, he leaped for her throat and tore the slender cylinder of snowy flesh to bits and pieces. She did not call out—not once—and he was amazed when once more she lay in the grass at his feet to find that his hands were not stained with blood. Somehow he had expected her to be complete.

"The battle was excitingly equal," he muttered to himself. It was an epitaph.

He pivoted, to enter the ship, but the flickering light of the fama caught his eyes. It was glowing with a harsher color, and seemed to be expanding before his very gaze.

And, as he stared at the fama, the queer little thought, dipping and rolling around in his mind, reached out, convulsively, for the knowledge of the fama—and the pink flame disappeared, sucked into the whirlpool that was the Minister.

Suddenly he was aware of a vision both within and without his skull, a vision of gigantic galaxies and entire universes—wonder on wonder, starry cloud on cloud, infinite on infinite. He found himself the focus of a tremendous pinwheel of sensation, of desire for the sweet vastnesses of space.

The wheel spun faster and faster, and curiously appeared to condense toward a point before his mind, and the energy of his emotion directed itself straight through that point to the qopot. Swifter and swifter grew the impetus which was himself, forcing the qopot to destroy the mamiraj, to burst those bubbles which confined the worlds of the Hegemony. It seemed to the Minister that there should have been a noise of sorts, but there was no sound at all. Not even a gentle sigh, or breath of expiration.

He looked around him. The park was as it should be, a little dimmer, perhaps, for the sunlight seemed to be fading. The deer still grazed at the side of the ship, chocolate against green and silver.

"A dream," he whispered, "it was all a dream."

And then he saw the star, twinkling at the edge of a cloud. He did not know that the star was Venus, and the cloud frightened him, for he had never seen such a thing before.

But his brief fright deepened to a chill foreboding of still greater happenings. For the star, too, was fading, and not through any will of his own. And the deer park itself had a peculiar look. It seemed to grow transparent, and, through the incipient diaphaneity he could see the outlines of mountains, and these mountains seemed also pellucid, and beyond them were forests and mountains of that same strange clarity—glass rock on tree on rock, wavering and receding into the distance.

With a sudden burst of awful knowledge he looked down at his feet—and through them, through his pseudo-earth to its inspiration, and through them all into the stars and distances that should, by all rights, grace only the skies of the antipodes. He looked at his hands, his arms, his torso, and the veins and arteries and skeleton itself seemed faintly discernable through the cloth and flesh.

"What's happening?" he cried. "Ronde, Ronde!" She did not answer, but his own mind did. And he wondered how the Old Ones—the very life and rhythm of the cosmos—had tolerated these worlds of dream and shadow for so very long.

He sighed and sat down by Ronde, for there was really nothing else to do. He took up a lock of the rusty hair, and stroked it gently, and the brown deer came and snuffled at his hands, and he reached in his clothing for the bit of food which the deer were expecting. It was, he thought calmly, as solid as ever.

While the deer licked at his fingers, his eyes travelled the circuit of the dimming horizon, swept the sky in pursuit of the fading suns and their satellites, and his mind observed, still calmly, that it had never known the boundaries of the Hegemony until this moment when they were only apparent by their swift disappearance.

The farthest reaches of the system seemed very faint now, but the deer park, strangely enough, remained clear in his vision. He watched in growing fascination as non-existence crept upon the mountains and the forest, crept closer and closer to the deer park, until at last there were only the oaks and the lawn and the gentle boughs and the little pool and benches, all glowing with a gay translucency, the whole wheeling and turning like a great room in empty space. He bent and kissed the strands of hair that lay across his palm, and waited for the darkness.

TO LIFT A SHIP
by Kit Reed

(Originally appeared in the April 1962 issue of *Fantasy & Science Fiction*)

When Kit Reed made her first sale of "The Wait" to The Magazine of Fantasy & Science Fiction *in 1958, she was 25 years old and a journalist writing for the* New Haven Register *and* Newsweek. *By the time she passed away in 2017, she had published 28 novels and dozens of short stories.*

Writing had always been Reed's life's ambition: She dictated a novel to her mother at the tender age of four-and-a-half, and she stated emphatically in a 2013 interview that she'd rather die than pursue another vocation.

Luckily, Reed had a charmed start to her career. Her first story was published right off the "slush pile" and she became a staple of F&SF *from then on. According to Reed, she never faced discrimination on the basis of her gender: "I never wanted to write like a woman. I wanted to write like a witch." Certainly,* F&SF *was not shy in announcing Reed's "Mrs." status in the same breath that they crowed about her "notability" and "authority." Nor were the fans put off: Reed was recognized as one of science fiction's best new authors in 1959 with a Hugo nomination, and by the end of her career, she was one of the genre's biggest names.*

As an SF luminary, it is appropriate that Reed had no trouble embracing the modern era, blogging frequently and maintaining an active presence on several social media platforms. I was lucky enough to have the opportunity to correspond with her regarding her early works, including the one you're about to read. "To Lift a Ship" is the story of Ike and Mary Lee, a pair of psychically adept but otherwise inconsequential people tapped to be psionic test-pilots.

Though there are no nuts, bolts, or any scientific under-pinning to the story, Reed described the piece to me as "hard science fiction," which I suppose it is when compared to the more literary, philosophical pieces that defined her later work. Her early work for F&SF *thus marks an interesting first stage of her career, when she was still writing science fiction that fit firmly within the mainstream, albeit unique in presentation and style.*

"To Lift a Ship" is my favorite story from this era of her work, and I think you'll like it, too.

—Gideon Marcus

It was a small, grey, drab, relatively unimpressive hemisphere. Later it would be fitted for cargo, passengers. It would be enlarged and fountains would flow in mirrored lounges and cabins would nestle where the dome met the flooring, open and ready for intrigue. But it was all but empty now, and the lines of the dome rose above them, pure, unadorned.

The man and the woman sat on metal stools at the center, knees touching, hands resting lightly on a metal bar. There was no other machinery in the ship.

Better turn back now. He canted one hand.

They turned the hemisphere together, minds meshing, and Mary Lee's delight pushed the ship into an extra little skip.

Skimming soundlessly, avoiding highways and buildings, they went on into the cloudy morning.

They circled over the field where Zorn waited, loath to set down. Troubled by something in the air of the ship, Mary Lee let herself look up, into Ike's face, sensing some deep restlessness that intruded at the back of his mind. Shaking her head, she touched his thoughts and the two of them pulled the ship into a rising, swooping turn and circled the field once more, lost in flight.

It was not as joyful as their first flight. When they first lifted the ship together Mary Lee had faltered, at the brink of all joy, all understanding, afraid if she looked too closely at what was happening it would dissolve and she would lose everything. Then Ike's thoughts had swelled and surged past her in the sheer exuberance of flight. The hemisphere had leaped forward, and laughing, she had given herself to the rush of the ship. Now, even as her happiness in what they were doing grew, Ike pushed the ship farther, faster, and she found herself frightened, sure that his growing impatience threatened their control of the ship.

What's the matter? He lifted his eyes from the bar between them, annoyed.

Nothing.

Shrugging, he inclined his hand.

They set the ship down with a bump.

Zorn was clattering out of the transmitter shack as they landed. He bounded across the field to meet them, small and rugged in a hairy tweed coat.

"You went like a dream," he said. "Not a bobble. And I was sending out a helluva strong signal." He gestured at the tower that rose at the far side of the field. "You didn't hear me at all?"

Mary Lee shook her head, wondering why he thought anything could distract them.

"Hum?" Ike had thrust his hands in his pockets, preoccupied.

Zorn pressed him. "My transmission. I thought it might jam you."

"Oh, that." Ike waved his hand negligently. "Didn't hear a thing. I told you nothing bothers us."

At his shoulder, Mary Lee drew herself up proudly, acutely conscious of the way they looked, standing together in the grey morning.

"I've hired a commercial pilot who can keep his mouth shut," Zorn went on, making notes. "Tomorrow he'll circle you and we'll see if *that* slows you down."

"I told you," Ike said with a flash of irritation. "Nothing bothers us." He lifted his dark face. "We can fly anywhere."

"We have to know just what you can do," Zorn said patiently. "And we have to know a little of the *why*."

"Testing. Talking." Ike's face was clouded. "We've been coming out here for three months."

Zorn's voice was quiet. "And you've only been flying for one. Do you think I can show this ship to anybody until we have some idea what makes it work? Why it works for you and Mary Lee?"

"It works for us." Ike leaned forward a little.

"Now. But for how long?"

Mary Lee fell back, oppressed by the idea that they might not always be able to fly, that the flights might stop.

"It works for us," Ike said determinedly. "That's enough."

Zorn put a hand on his arm. "Then flying should be enough for you, for now."

"When nobody sees us?" Ike shook free, jaw thrust forward. "We can fly anywhere. Why in hell don't you let us?"

"We have to take our time." Zorn said. "We have to test."

"Test..." Ike growled.

Mary Lee put up one gentle hand to stop him, but he was gone.

Zorn turned to her, eyes pleading. "Do you feel the same way?"

She shook her head, almost blinded by the memories of flight. "Flying's enough, Mr. Zorn. It's..." She lifted her hands expressively. Then, running them over her pale hair, she talked in a spurt, trying to explain. "He wants somebody to *see* us. He wants to make money. Mr. Zorn, I don't think he can *afford*... "

"Afford!" Zorn snorted. "My laboratory's pouring thousands into this project. Do you have enough money to live comfortably, Mary Lee?"

"Yessir. More than I ever made at the flower shop..."

"Well Ike is getting twice as much. He made next to nothing at that gas station. He can afford to come here every day. He can afford to take orders, too." He headed toward the shack where his equipment was stored. "Call him to come back here and help you put the ship away."

She sent out the call. Then she looked anxiously from Zorn to the edge of the field, wondering if there would be more hard words when Ike came.

Seeing her distress, Zorn spoke more gently. "We have to do things in their own time, Mary Lee. Every pirate in the world would be after you and that ship if we turned you loose now, and the people who weren't trying to buy or steal you would be trying to discredit you. We have to take our time." He touched her hand. "I'll get out of the way now, before Ike comes back. Try to calm him down, will you? Oh—and tomorrow—don't try to outrace that pilot I hired. There are some things I'll need to know."

By the time Ike came across the field to help her with the ship, Zorn was gone.

For a wild moment, when they touched the bar together, she thought they were going to take the ship and run with it, fly until there were just the two of them, the ship and the sky, but then Ike cleared his throat, jaw set in remembered rage, and they eased the little hemisphere into the low shed hidden at the edge of the field. After the ship came to rest Mary Lee sat for a few minutes, still touching the bar. When she shook herself to attention and left the ship, Ike was gone.

She killed the rest of that day in the park, in shops, in the movies, and the world outside seemed no more real than the black-and-white shadows that moved on the screen. She slipped through the streets like a ghost, marking time until the next morning, when she would be in the ship with Ike, and everything would seem real again.

Her landlady nodded as she went by, ticking off one more boarder home from work. "Nice day, Miss Addison?" The voice ordered her to stop.

"Yes'm," Mary Lee said reluctantly, wishing she could escape the old woman and go inside.

"Come." The old woman was imperious. "Come sit down." She fixed her eyes on Mary Lee until the girl took a chair beside her on the creaking porch. She talked on and on about goings on in the neighborhood and Mary Lee tried to give the appearance of listening, but the yammering woman was no more than a shadow to her, moving shadowy lips. "...and he hasn't seen you in the flower shop for weeks."

"Um?" Mary Lee shifted uncomfortably.

"He likes you, you know. You two should—get together." The old woman shaped her hand suggestively. "By the way..." Her eyes

159

narrowed, almost disappearing in greasy, wrinkled folds. "...If you haven't been at the shop, where *have* you been?"

Mary Lee gnawed at the inside of her mouth.

"I mean, a girl who isn't working regular..."

"Oh." May Lee got to her feet. "If that's what you're worried about." Zorn had paid her that morning. She fished in her pocket. "Here. Here's the rent."

She thrust the money at the old woman and fled into the house. A couple passed her on the stairs, quarreling, no more than a pair of chattering wraiths.

In her room things seemed even less substantial. Curtains flopped at the window, a grey film, and the sounds of the street flowed in and about her, never touching her. She moved from chair to table with no apparent plan, fluttering her hands over their surfaces, and even the furniture seemed indifferent to her. She moved on and on, trying to find something in the room that mattered, almost overcome by her isolation, sure for the moment that she herself was no more than a shadow, until finally, if only to prove her reality, she sent out the call. *Ike? You anywhere around?*

Zat you, baby? She could tell he was surprised.

Hi. Oh, Ike, hi. I just had to...

He cut her off. *Can't talk now. Got a date.* As if to soften it, *We'll really show them in the morning, won't we, baby?*

Her pride sang in the air. *We sure will.*

And she forgot his abruptness, and clung to that. She knew she gave his thoughts more meaning than she should, but she couldn't stop herself. And she felt somehow that their flights together underscored the meaning, that what they were doing pointed toward a future that, for her, couldn't help but be better.

She stayed at the window for a long time, thinking about Ike. She remembered the first hostility, the suspicion. Ike, with arms crossed in a black tee shirt, black hair swept back, menacing. The look in his eyes that told her he had already dismissed her as a drab little girl, a nothing. And the sharp surprise when she found herself fully aware of his scorn. She had looked up, biting her knuckles, to see the glint break in his eyes as he realized that he was not alone with his thoughts. Bristling, they had faced each other.

Who are you? The question had no words.

And Zorn, still not sure they were different from the hundreds of others he had tried, had introduced the unlikely team—a cocky, swaggering boy who seemed little better than a thug and a plain, frightened girl, wondering why his processing staff had ever selected them.

By the time the weeks of testing were over they had reached some sort of brusque, businesslike truce, barely tolerating each other, each rigid for fear the other would slip past all barriers, into the unguarded mind.

Then there had been weeks in the field, trying to lift the ship.

Then there had been the first flight.

With it hostility became a memory. In the air they were a team, a man, quick and strong, with a profile like a blade, and a woman, sure and perceptive, now, unaccountably, almost beautiful. And for Mary Lee, at least, from that moment, there was nothing but Ike and the ship.

She left the window long after dark, not even hungry, and composed herself on the bed, clearing her mind, shutting out the room and street and the drab expanse of the shabby neighborhood, waiting for morning.

"Morning, baby." Ike sprang over the grass, hair tumbled in the sunlight.

"Ike. Hi, Ike." She went to meet him, half-skipping.

The sun struck lights from the ship.

Above, a biplane was circling. Zorn was stationed at the edge of the field, adjusting a pair of expensive binoculars. He was expansive this morning, anxious to see what they could do, grinning. He had an assistant with him, who drew a drafting pencil over a series of graphs. At a signal, Mary Lee and Ike were to go into the ship.

They flew like angels. They dipped and swooped around the small plane, confounding the pilot, oblivious of the electronic device Zorn had planted in their ship, not even aware that the tower was beaming the strong signal Zorn had designed because if anything could, it would curb their flight. Ike shouted for joy, and then, before Mary Lee was fully aware of what he intended, he had brought the ship down hard on the tail of the biplane. Laughing, they chased it home, circling twice high above the airstrip before they turned back to Zorn's field.

Zorn was on the ground to meet them, furious. He turned on Ike. "You acted like a fool."

"You wanted to see what that plane would do to us." Ike slouched, grinning. "I showed you what we could do to the plane. Any plane."

"You went too near that airfield." Zorn shook his binoculars. "What if you were seen?"

Ike drew himself up. "What if we were? It's time somebody saw us."

"You know you're not ready."

"Who the hell says we're not ready. You're keeping us hidden like a couple of..." the word eluded him. He shrugged. "It's time people saw this thing. People with money. I didn't come into this for peanuts, and I'm not going to settle for peanuts just because you're scared." He jammed his face into Zorn's. "Scared."

"If you bring this thing out in the open you'll blow it for all of us." Zorn's face was set in anger.

"I know why you're afraid," Ike said. "Your contract's no good. You're afraid somebody will cut you out. If you keep us hidden, nobody can get to us to tell us what suckers we are."

"Tomorrow some people from the plant will be out for observation," Zorn said, dangerously quiet. He was making notes.

"We're suckers!" Ike swelled with rage.

"You and Mary Lee will be on the field at eight," Zorn said in level tones. He turned on his heel.

"You're afraid, Zorn, afraid," Ike roared.

Mary Lee shrank from his thoughts.

"Without us you're nothing, Zorn." Ike's voice seemed to fill the field. "That's why you're afraid."

May Lee stood at the edge of the field after Ike and Zorn had gone, too weak to move, awash in the waves of their anger.

Her landlady was lying in wait for her, like a fat spider.

"Man was here for you," the old lady said, licking her lips, "Sweetheart?"

"What..." Mary Lee forced the words. "What did he look like?"

"Like trouble, that's what he looked like. Dark hair, black shirt..."

The old woman ran her thick tongue back and forth.

"Oh." Mary Lee could feel the blood leave her face. "I…"

"If that's the kind you're hanging around with… If that's the reason you're not working…" The old woman made an obscene gesture. Her face seemed filmed over with grease.

"Stop!" Strangled, Mary Lee ran to her room.

She tried to shut out the woman, the house, in memories of the flight, but try as she could, she couldn't call them up. There was a sound on the stairs. Step, snuffle. Step, snuffle. The old woman was coming up, heading toward her room. She heard fingers fumbling at the door, heard her landlady's sharp, ugly bark. Just then Ike's call came into her mind, and she ran out the door, past the sweating old woman, and went without question into the streets. She didn't even hear the woman shouting after her.

He was at a small park, one of the last pretty places in the neighborhood, trembling with urgency.

Come on, baby, come on.

Where, Ike? Even before he touched her hand she knew she didn't care.

Hands still touching, moving in silence, they boarded a bus and rode to the field and the ship. Dazed, Mary Lee stood by while Ike did something to the guard and they were in the shed, at the door of the hemisphere, in the ship.

It lifted like black lightning, hurtling into the night, and they flew on without direction, faster than they had ever gone, eyes turned inward, on their own preoccupations, hearing dulled by the rush of wind against the hemisphere. Mary Lee lost herself in the plunge forward, the feeling of oneness with Ike, knowing that she had found in flight with him something she would never find at any other time, in any other place, in any other human being. She didn't care how far or fast they went, and she didn't care (for she had read it in his mind) that the ship was theirs now, not Zorn's, and they would never go back.

She was ready to fly on forever, until the ship disintegrated and the wind took them, until their power failed and they plummeted into the sea, because as long as they flew she was with Ike and he was with her, and she knew now that she was in love with him, and there was nothing outside herself but Ike, and the ship. She threw back her head as the ship went on and on, forgetting everything now but the immediacy of the flight, dreaming, until suddenly, in the half-light of the ship Ike lifted his eyes from the bar and looked at his watch, and she realized he had some plan.

It's time. And he put a direction into her head.

They turned the ship together and Mary Lee could make out in his mind the picture of a vast field, a geometric array of building, elaborate wires and towers and a knot of expensively dressed people on the ground, waiting for Ike. Soon she could sense the excitement of the watchers, and when she glanced at the viewport, she saw the field below them, and the knot of people. As they swooped low, one of the watchers waved a flag.

Let's show them.

Ike lifted one hand from the bar to touch her face, and then unfurled an intricate pattern of dips and turns, of rises and falls, and bending their minds together, they moved the ship into a parabola. She was uneasy now, because what they did seemed important to Ike only because there were powerful men watching from below. But in the next second she saw that his plan for the ship's motion was beautiful, and because she loved him she threw her heart into it.

Mary Lee could sense the excitement of the watchers, and Ike swelled with pride. Expanding in his strength and happiness, she helped him pull the ship into a wild dash for the ground, to hover, two feet above the field, to pull up suddenly in a free, headlong rush for the heavens.

Ike. Oh. Ike.

Pretty good, baby, pretty good. But the swoop and the dive seemed to mean little to him. He was intent on the men below.

Who are they, Ike? She was uneasy.

Never mind, baby. It's not important.

But it was, she could tell, and she fought back the feeling that there were other things for Ike, things more important than her and the ship.

Hey... His delight at their power rang in her head like a bell. *Let's show 'em what we can do.*

And they dipped and turned in a dizzying pattern and then slowed, to hover above the field.

The thoughts of the watchers crowded into the ship and Mary Lee shrank from them. The expensively dressed men couldn't believe what they had seen, couldn't wait to run their hands over the ship, to touch the fliers, to own both. Their minds were mirrors of greed.

Ike. She called him, with a sense of foreboding. *Let's go...*

He was distracted by the thoughts from below, and she couldn't reach him. There was the fragment of an answer. *After I fixed this up?*

A short command came from the signal tower. *Come down.*

No. Mary Lee clung to flight. *Ike, let's get out of here.*

Another fragment... *ready to go into production.*

Come down. The signal intruded. *Come down.*

Ike, it's no good. She pushed a picture of endless skies into his mind.

We'll show 'em how it works, train new pilots... he was slipping away from her.

We don't need all that, Ike. The ship's all we need. She pleaded, eyes burning fiercely. *Ike?*

Come down. The signal was imperious.

She tried to touch his mind but it was driving ahead now, closed to her. *Ike.* Nothing. *Ike, look.* And she laid her mind open, showing him everything—the love, the drive, the most secret things—and begged him to look into it, helpless, vulnerable in her appeal.

And in that second he swept the control away from her, nosed the ship down with such power and drive that she knew she and the ship had never been enough for Ike, and their time for flying together was ended.

She sat numbly in the ship while Ike, swaggering a little, went across the field to talk to the chairman of the board. He brought the man, encased in tweed, redolent of tobacco, into the hemisphere. He stood by politely as the industrialist sniffed at the unimpressive metal, the simple controls, Mary Lee.

Ike looked at her indifferently. "We could jazz up the inside a little bit," he said bluffly, waiting for the offer.

Finally, when the man touched the end of his cigar to the bar, knocking a thick ash on the floor, Ike grew tired of waiting, and spoke again.

"Well?"

"It looked pretty good up there." The man stepped on the soft ash. "But this…" He waved a hand around the control room. "Let me go along this time. Before I make an offer I want to be sure what you can do." One of his lackeys brought a camp stool and set it up at one edge of the hemisphere.

Without looking at Mary Lee, Ike settled himself at the bar.

Numbly, still blinded by love, Mary Lee bent her will to his. She put leaden fingers on the bar. She could still sense his tension as they strained together, trying to lift the ship. There was no sound but the throb of their bodies, the breath of the man on the camp stool. Both willing the ship to lift, they pushed again.

They worked together for several minutes, straining, trying, until finally, without looking at Ike, Mary Lee put her head down on the bar and wept.

The industrialist left the ship.

Maybe now. Ike was desperate, unbelieving.

And they tried once more.

Then, black with rage, he turned without another word for her and stamped outside, already framing the explanations he would make. Broken, still sobbing, not even aware of what she was doing, Mary Lee lifted the ship blindly and started back to Zorn's field.

THE PUTNAM TRADITION

by Sonya Hess Dorman

(Originally appeared in the January 1963 issue of *Amazing Stories*)

"The Putnam Tradition," published in Amazing *magazine in 1963, was Sonya Hess Dorman's first published work, the predecessor of a line of metaphorical stories and poetry. Born in New York City on April 6, 1924, Dorman lived a fulfilling life as a writer and was recognized with many awards for her talents, including the Rhysling Award and a nomination for the James Tiptree Jr. Retrospective Award. Though her name ultimately became well-known and acknowledged, Dorman initially wrote under her initials, perhaps to avoid discrimination from publishers for being a woman.*

Putnam touches on themes of sexism, but in ways that may surprise you. The story follows the hardened grandmother Cecily Putnam and her extreme distaste for where her world is going. She dislikes her granddaughter's husband and the progress he brings. Her biggest worry is for her great-granddaughter, who may not carry the family tradition that has been passed through generations of Putnam women. A story of trials overcome by the strength and love of a family, it is heartwarming to say the least.

It isn't often a story can be read many times over and still bring new meaning each time, but that is the case with Sonya Dorman's "The Putnam Tradition." Every sentence leads you around another corner and keeps you hooked. Its themes on the intimidation and fear that comes with change are timeless, and along with its eloquent writing, this is a story that will make a deep impression. It is an expert, twistily crafted piece that will leave you with questions, and also answers you didn't know you needed.

—Lorelei Marcus

It was an old house not far from the coast, and had descended generation by generation to the women of the Putnam family. Progress literally went by it: a new four-lane highway had been built two hundred yards from the ancient lilacs at the doorstep. Long before that, in the time of Cecily Putnam's husband, power lines had been run in, and now on cold nights the telephone wires sounded like a concert of cellos, while inside with a sound like the breaking of beetles, the grandmother Cecily moved through the walls in the grooves of tradition.

Simone Putnam, her granddaughter; Nina Putnam, her great-grand-daughter; the unbroken succession of matriarchs continued, but times the old woman thought that in Simone it was weakened, and she looked at the four-year-old Nina askance, waiting, waiting, for some good sign.

Sometimes one of the Putnam women had given birth to a son, who grew sickly and died, or less often, grew healthy and fled. The husbands were usually strangers to the land, the house, and the women, and spent a lifetime with the long-lived Putnam wives, and died, leaving their strange signs: telephone wires, electric lights, water pumps, brass plumbing.

Sam Harris came and married Simone, bringing with him an invasion of washer, dryer, toaster, mixer, coffeemaster, until the current poured through the walls of the house with more vigor than the blood in the old woman's veins.

"You don't approve of him," Simone said to her grandmother.

"It's his trade," Cecily Putnam answered. "Our men have been carpenters, or farmers, or even schoolmasters. But an engineer. Phui!"

Simone was washing the dishes, gazing out across the windowsill where two pink and white Murex shells stood, to the tidy garden beyond where Nina was engaged in her private games.

168

She dried the dishes by passing her hand once above each plate or glass, bringing it to a dry sparkle. It saved wear on the dishtowels, and it amused her.

"Sam's not home very much," she said in a placating voice. She herself had grown terrified, since her marriage, that she wouldn't be able to bear the weight of her past. She felt its power on her and couldn't carry it. Cecily had brought her up, after her father had disappeared and her mother had died in an unexplained accident. Daily she saw the reflection of her failure in the face of her grandmother, who seemed built of the same seasoned and secure wood as the old Putnam house. Simone looked at her grandmother, whom she loved, and became a mere vapor.

"He's not home so much," Simone said.

Her face was small, with a pointed chin, and she had golden-red hair which she wore loose on her shoulders. Nina, too, had a small face, but it was neither so pale nor so delicate as her mother's, as if Sam's tougher substance had filled her out and strengthened her bone structure. If it was true that she, Simone, was a weak link, then Sam's strength might have poured into the child, and there would be no more Putnam family and tradition.

"People don't change that easily," the old woman said.

"But things—" Simone began. The china which had a history of five generations slipped out of her hands and smashed; Sam's toaster wouldn't toast or pop up; Simone couldn't even use the telephone for fear of getting a wrong number, or no number at all.

"Things, things!" her grandmother cried. "It's blood that counts. If the blood is strong enough, things dissolve. They're just garbage, all those things, floating on the surface of our history. It's our history that's deep. That's what counts."

"You're afraid of Sam," the young woman accused.

"Not afraid of any man!" Cecily said, straightening her back. "But I'm afraid for the child. Sam has no family tradition, no depth, no talent handed down and perfected. A man with his head full of wheels and wires."

Simone loved him. She leaned on him and grew about him, and he supported her tenderly. She wasn't going to give him up for the sake of some abstract tradition—

"—it's not abstract," her grandmother said with spirit. "It's in your blood. Or why don't you sweep the floors the way other women do? The way Sam's mother must?"

Simone had begun to clean the house while she was thinking, moving her hand horizontally across the floor, at the height of her hip, and the dust was following the motion of her hand and moving in a small, sun-brightened river toward the trash basket in the kitchen corner. Now Simone raised her hand to her face to look at it, and the river of dust rose like a serpent and hung a foot below her hand.

"Yes," she agreed, "at least I can clean the house. If I don't touch the good china, and look where I'm going."

"Phui," the old woman said again, angrily. "Don't feel so sorry for yourself."

"Not for myself," Simone mumbled, and looked again toward the garden where her daughter was doing something with three stones and a pie plate full of spring water.

"I do despair of Nina," Cecily said, as she had said before. "She's four, and has no appearance. Not even balance. She fell out of the applerose tree, and couldn't even help herself." Suddenly the old woman thrust her face close to her granddaughter. It was smooth, round, and sweet as a young kernel of corn. The eyes, sunk down under the bushy grey brows, were cold and clear grey.

"Simone," the old woman said. "You didn't lie to me? You did know she was falling, and couldn't get back in time to catch her?"

A shudder passed through Simone's body. There was no blood in her veins, only water; no marrow in her bones, they were empty, and porous as a bird's. Even the roots of her hair were weak, and now the sweat was starting out on her scalp as she faced her grandmother and saw the bristling shapes of seven generations of Putnam women behind her.

"You lied," the old woman said. "You didn't know she was falling."

Simone was a vapor, a mere froth blowing away on the first breeze.

"My poor dear," the old woman said in a gentle voice. "But how could you marry someone like Sam? Don't you know what will

170

happen? He'll dissolve us, our history, our talents, our pride. Nina is nothing but an ordinary little child."

"She's a good child," Simone said, trying not to be angry. She wanted her child to be loved, to be strong. "Nina isn't a common child," she said, with her head bent. "She's very bright."

"A man with his head full of wheels, who's at home with electricity and wires," the old woman went on. "We've had them before, but never allowed them to dominate us. My own husband was such a man, but he was only allowed to make token gestures, such as having the power lines put in. He never understood how they worked." She lowered her voice to a whisper, "Your Sam understands. I've heard him talk to the water pump."

"That's why you're afraid of him," Simone said. "Not because I'm weak, and he might take something away from me, but because he's strong, and he might give us something. Then everything would change, and you're afraid of that. Nina might be our change." She pointed toward the garden.

Following the white line of her granddaughter's finger, Cecily looked out into the garden and saw Nina turn toward them as though she knew they were angry. The child pointed with one finger directly at them in the house. There was a sharp crackle, and something of a brilliant and vibrating blue leaped between the out-stretched fingers of mother and daughter, and flew up like a bird to the power lines above.

"Mommy," Nina called.

Simone's heart nearly broke with wonder and fright. Her grandmother contemptuously passed through the kitchen door and emerged on the step outside, but Simone opened the door and left it open behind her. "What was that?" she asked Nina. "Was it a bluebird?"

"Don't be silly," Nina said. She picked up the pie plate and brought it toward them. Cecily's face was white and translucent, one hand went to her throat as the child approached.

Brimful of crackling blue fire with a fluctuating heart of yellow, the pie plate came toward them, held between Nina's small, dusty hands. Nina grinned at them. "I stole it out of the wires," she said.

Simone thought she would faint with a mixture of joy and fear. "Put it back," she whispered. "Please put it back."

"Oh Mommy," Nina said, beginning to whine. "Not now. Not right away. I just got it. I've done it lots of times." The pie plate crackled and hissed in the steady, small hands.

Simone could feel the old woman's shocked silence behind her. "You mustn't carry it in a pie plate, it's dangerous," Simone said to her child, but she could see Nina was in no danger. "How often have you done this?" She could feel her skirt and her hair billow with electricity.

"Lots of times. You don't like it, do you?" She became teasing and roguish, when she looked most like Sam. Suddenly she threw back her head and opened her mouth, and tilting up the pie plate she drank it empty. Her reddish gold hair sprang out in crackling rays around her face, her eyes flashed and sparks flew out between her teeth before she closed her mouth.

"Nina!" the old woman cried, and began to crumple, falling slowly against Simone in a complete faint. Simone caught her in trembling hands and lowered her gently. She said to her daughter, "You mustn't do that in front of Grandy. You're a bad girl, you knew it would scare her," and to herself she said: I must stop babbling, the child knows I'm being silly. Oh isn't it wonderful, isn't it awful, O Sam, how I love you.

"Daddy said it would scare you," Nina admitted. "That's why I never showed you before." Her hair was softly falling into place again, and she was gazing curiously at her great-grandmother lying on the doorstep.

"It did scare me," Simone said. "I'm not used to it, darling. But don't keep it secret anymore."

"Is Grandy asleep?"

Simone said hastily, "Oh yes, she's taking a nap. She is old, you know, and likes to take naps."

"That's not a nap," Nina said, leaning over and patting the old woman's cheek, "I think she's having a bad dream."

Simone carried her grandmother into the house. If that old, tired heart had jumped and floundered like her own, there must be some damage done to it. If anything happened to her grandmother, the world would end, Simone thought, and was furious with Nina, and at the same time, full of joy for her.

Cecily Putnam opened her eyes widely, and Simone said, "It does change, you see. But it's in the family, after all."

The old woman sat upright quickly. "That wicked child!" she exclaimed. "To come and frighten us like that. She ought to be spanked." She got up with great strength and rushed out to the garden.

"Nina!" she called imperiously. The child picked up one of the small stones from the pie plate now full of spring water, and came to her great-grandmother.

"I'll make something for you, Grandy," she said seriously. She put the stone in the palm of her hand, and breathed on it, and then held out her hand and offered the diamond.

"It's lovely. Thank you," the old woman said with dignity, and put her hand on the child's head. "Let's go for a walk and I'll show you how to grow rose-apples. That's more becoming to a young lady."

"You slept on the step."

"Ah! I'm old and I like to take little naps," Cecily answered.

Simone saw them disappear among the applerose trees side by side. She was still trembling, but gradually, as she passed her hand back and forth, and the dust followed, moving in a sparkling river toward the trash basket, Simone stopped trembling and began to smile with the natural pride of a Putnam woman.

THE PLEIADES

by Otis Kidwell Burger

(Originally appeared in the February 1963 issue of *Fantasy & Science Fiction*)

As a writer for the Galactic Journey, I have a complex relationship with Time, living as I do in two eras. Perhaps no other author is more suited to examination in this dual context than Otis Kidwell Burger. Born in 1923, and very much still active, Ms. Burger has been a bastion of twentieth century women's literature in New York for over fifty years, rubbing elbows with the likes of Kurt Vonnegut and Norman Mailer, hosting literary parties and poetry circles, advocating for the female perspective in American intellectualism.

Burger's foray into science fiction was actually quite brief, with the tales "The Pleiades" (1961), "Love Child" (1962), and "The Zookeeper" (1963) appearing in The Magazine of Fantasy & Science Fiction *and "Servant Problem" (1965) published in* Galaxy. *The author is perhaps better known as an acclaimed poet.* Love is a Season, *a sonnet cycle she wrote in 1957, rediscovered and published only recently, is hailed as some of the most moving poetry in Shakespearean meter since the bard himself, weaving an emotional relationship to nature and love. It's no wonder that her tale "The Pleiades" delves deep into the meaning of being human.*

This story calls to the reader with all the brazen confidence of a carnival barker: Come one, come all, to the

Greatest Show in the Universe! The Seven Sisters, daughters of Atlas, will beguile you with their timeless dance in the stars as Ms. Burger weaves a tale with veiled machinations. Let the "Eh, Eh" of the Beasts lull you into the monotonous perfection that has become Man in this distant future.

Ms. Burger will take you on a journey where your desires are flipped upside down, and the crowds clamor for a taste of death. Thrill on a world starved for the march of Time, and ask yourself: what happens to humankind if we are all as agelessly beautiful as we dream?

—Gwyn Conaway

"Hurry, hurry, hurry, the Greatest Show in the Universe…" Junior's voice echoing outside; the sussurru of the crowd passing.

"Where'd you put that lipstick?"

"Aniides! my shawl…slippers, make up, hot pack, g-string."

Under the sagging contours of the hot little tent, the Pleiades, literally and figuratively the hottest show in the universe, struggled to put itself together. Seven sisters. Only six of them there now, again, for the ten millionth time, maybe; aided by the bustling figure of the dresser, Aniides (eight-armed, and of course chosen for so being) who pushed among them bearing necessary articles, a strange tree-full of gauzy, gaudy feminine garments. But they had had stranger figures in that dressing room that had, for who counted how many years now, been set up on so many strange planets.

The lurid carnival lights painted hectic colors across the battered tent; thrust scarlet searchlights into its rents; and, brushing across the rim of jungle, turned across the youthful faces of the crowd, and met in huge kaleidoscopic arcs of color in the night sky above the sprawling fairgrounds.

Before the next tent, the Taanist fire-swaller glowed eerily; born on a near-dark planet, and; like many dark-living creatures, translucent, he thrust his many-colored fires down his throat; all his internal workings, like a glass man's, outlined in cerise, umber, gold. Close by, the old lion roared, and was answered by the Eh, Eh, of two toad-like furry beasts in the next cage. Actually, derision; they were on the payroll, and

175

after the show, played cards with the roustabouts and the other freaks: voluntary freaks, with all human privileges, including the Pill. Only the lion, involuntary beast at every circus since time began, roared out his weariness and anger all alone.

Having finished his preliminary spiel, Junior came rushing in among the frantically dressing Sisters. "Girls, girls. C'mon now, Time. We gotta crowd, and where are you dames as usual, fussin' over your looks." His gloved clown's hands clapped, softened, impatient. Handsome, like all the people those days, but a little short (perhaps why he had aligned himself with the Sisters?), he had exaggerated his defect with immense padding under a shocking-pink-and-green checked suit; a too-small straw boater perched on his head; a huge putty nose. Con man and clown, with sweat and greasepaint like dissolving flesh running down his cheeks, toad-squat in his monstrous costume, he waddled among them, summoning. "Girls, girls..."

"Eh, eh," derisively, the beasts outside.

I would have spat on him once, Maia thought. She took her black wig from one of Annides' appendages, and settled it, trembling, over her head and shoulders. I would have spat on a Junior then; a freak. We had all the men in the universe at our feet.

Over and around her mirror, lapping and overlapping like scales of some strange, tired beast, the curling photographs, mementoes of one night stands on how many forgotten bars in almost nameless planets. Frontier bars, pasted together out of odd materials-at-hand, dug out of jungles, deserts, snows; hermetically sealed against alien atmospheres and lifeforms; but always nostalgically, improbably, recreating from unlikely materials the half-remembered décor of the habitat most familiar to the rough crews of early space ships. Rows of bottles, with gut-searing contents fermented, after patient experiment, from local flora; heads of strange beasts over improvised mirrors of polished metal; the bars themselves made of packed muds, packing cases, trees, and, in one picture, of bone. Here and there, tacked boldly over this littered pictorial tribute to Man's ingenuity, were more presentable photos of longer engagements, in settled towns whose bars boasted genuine wood, and mirrors flown from Home (over what incredible dazzling blackness of space); in these the Pleiades showed themselves quite clearly.

The Pleiades Stars of a universe, lovely even among a beautiful People, long of hair and leg, their long bodies so breathtaking that they had never needed to bother much with costumes, or talent; it was enough, in those early Frontier towns, for them merely to prance across the stage. For the men, starved by long years, nights, eons alone on strange planets, to stare at them. Jam-packed audiences, night after night; and the silence of the audiences like that of space itself.

The Seven Sisters! (Not, of course, sisters) black haired, long-limbed, dressed in little but sequins and top hats; prancing like a matched team of trotters, pulling the dubious vanguard of civilization. Descending, as luminous and unlikely and mythical as their starry namesakes, from the empty skies (sky still so new each man re-membered it as visceral as hollow hunger, a nameless fear, under his ribs), to dance and show the reality of their flesh to men in make-shift bars across the universe. Life. So strange a habit at best; so unfamiliar here, in alien worlds. To be seen, craved, touched, in that long line of trotting girls.

"Never enough men," Maia articulated, half aloud, through the weight of grease paint. Enough anything, then. She put out her hand, but Aniides had already passed on. Slut. Both Taygete and Electra were screaming for Aniides, the blare of a loudspeaker called the crowd's attention to the beast charmer; now the long wavering wailing of his instrument, and the derisive "Eh, eh" of the beast as they rose to dance.

"You ready?" Junior cried, anxious. "You're fine, great, kids. C'mon. Whatta dames always hang around so long for?... we gotta show to do..."

Outside the flimsy canvas door, the night roared. Criss-crossing lights competing with three silent moons, blare of canned music against the humming edge of jungle, counterpointed by the solitary radio of a clown who'd already finished his act, in the next tent. The too-sweet voiced babble of the crowd. A moan from the old lion.

Alycyone, Maia, Electra, Taygete, Sterope, Celaneo. How many million times thus, in lockstep, brazen under the spotlights, their black

177

sequined cloaks concealing pyraminds below painted faces... they had pranced out, glittering shadow-selves under Junior's baton. Dazzling grimace-smile across each face. Black top hat. Tantalizing fragment of black-stockinged leg.

A small, disinterested buzz of applause rose from the audience.

"Laydeez and gentlemen." Junior, on his rostrum. "I am here to show you, tonight, the most, the absolutely most amazing and compelling show left in this weary universe. You have all, I am sure, seen girly acts before. (Pause for titter.) They are part of every circus since time began, bless 'em. And these girls, like all of you out there tonight, have been around nearly that long. Well, can they show you anything new? Who can? (Pause for a lower buzz.) Laydeez and gentlemen, I would like to tell you a story. (Slight shifting in audience.) Once, many many years ago, before things were organized as they are now, we all had to take pills... I wonder how many of you remember? (five or six hands). Or else. Well, one day these seven lovely sisters here..."

Alycyone began to dance, solo. The black cloak whirled up about her legs.

... "the toast of a universe, the beautiful, talented Seven Sisters..."

One by one, the other Pleiades whirled slowly after her.

... "who spent their lives entertaining our poor boys over in space (and how many of you have ever spent time in a real space station? You'll know what a generous action it was, for these kids)... Well, for those of you who don't remember, suppose we stop just a moment, while I show you how it was."

He waved the girls into a cluster at one side.

On the screen outside the tent, the huge 3D picture flashed into sputtering, glowing color; the old picture of Earth, accompanied by Junior's rasping spiel; the "educational" build up to the act. "Laydeez and gentlemen, you see here a picture of old Mother Earth, in the days when..."

The cities, sprawling miles deep over Earth and oceans; a monstrous steel-chrome-glass growth of thrusting spicules and steel spines, like the skeletons of extinct microscopic diatoms, ever farther and farther out, into the air, into the rock below. Growing. Like something alive, only there was nothing else alive then, except people, and a few house-pet plants and animals.

I was poor, Maia thought. Raised mostly in a nursery in the Lower East 2nd level at the city's bottom depth; 15 years before I grew up, won a talent show, and was taken up to the 50th level with some other kids to give a show for a producer...and saw the sun, the real sun, for the first time. And the stars."

...And can you folks imagine what that first look at the stars, the stars from which they took their names, finally, meant to these poor kids?

"What did it do to me? What it did to millions of others. I dreamed of them, as everyone else did, then. They were our only hope. We had the Invention, but not the technical means of spaceflight; and Earth was on the verge of Revolution. The Earth so full already; suicides, hysteria, starvation, everything, but still short of the War we could not afford, for we were then as all-entwined as some monstrous green-growth plant. So that at first, the Invention became almost a religious ceremony, its possibilities being too terrifying to contemplate otherwise... When you became 21, there was a special ceremony; a priest, relatives, cakes, flowers and you were given the Pill, your first full-strength Pill in a sort of casket with velvet lining. Very fancy. Everyone wept. It was a Coming of Age for all time. And after that, you took the Pill every day, and you were immortal. Unless you forgot. And some did. (How many, Unwilling to see older friends, like my sister, born too soon to take the full course of Pills, die...or unwilling merely to suddenly take on the full burden of life forever, because when a race has planned as if life has an end, and suddenly, it hadn't...)

"Now all of you out there," Junior rasped on, "can't imagine that time, of course. You're all just given an injection at birth; no one need worry about forgetting. It's as sure as birth itself, part of your heritage."

...And then, Maia's thought furring out faintly, picking up the voices, the books, of long ago men; then the real Revolution; the discoveries that open the universe to men. With space ships, the Long Sleep, and Life eternal finally all discovered, Life's new lease came up at how long long last. And the pent up rush began; out, away! The black miles opened; new worlds opened; light years and other planets to colonize. And how many died like lemmings, lost, drowned in the dark oceans of no-air; dead asteroids orbiting forever in foam-rubber-plastic-food pill tombs around unknown worlds, or forever wandering. But some came home. To other atmospheres, worlds, enough alike to sustain the uneasy habit we call life. And so the frontier towns came into being. Lusty, ravenous for what the men had never thought to see again; life, in its rawest forms; drink, and violence, and girls.

And so the Seven Sisters came into being...

The screen sputtered into darkness. The crowd drifted, aimless, before the platform. All arrested at 21, all beautiful from long breeding, they wore not only similar garments (a Greek chlamys, variously fastened, and the same family lineaments) but the same air. Poised, yet settled. Half bored. They had already said to each other whatever individual things they had to say. Childhood's solitudes had long since been annealed in the group. So had the love affairs, rivalries, and intellectual and spiritual adventures. They lived together in perpetual maturity, knowing all secrets about each other (except the minute grass-root changes of temper and mind, except their ultimate destinies), conscious as any communal animal is conscious, of the beings des-ignated to be its mouth, mind, reproductive powers, or outer tendrils.

Drifting and gazing, they rarely touched. Flesh is no different, exciting, or more taboo than mind, to beings of an indefinite lifespan. Philosophers of the past talked of universal mind, transcending earthly, perishable mind; did any speak of universal, eternal flesh? Men clutch what goes quickest; but now flesh and mind, for eternity, were one. There was no longer a need to gratify flesh while it lasted, or seek immortality for less perishable mind by forging it into books, buildings, ideas. In reaching for eternal life, Man had finally reached only stasis, emptiness, a common shared loneliness.

Yet even ultimate safety breeds its nettles; the liers on beds of physical and spriritual nails, the joiners of the circus, or dangerous expeditions. And, the commentators, the poets. Though most real poets had been reduced (by lack of poetry's necessities; the sense of that brief friction between the individual and time) to pretty, flaccid, involved verses, some still lurked among all the other non-poet revolutionaries...life's eternal counter swell; the restless, the questioners, the merely crazy. The now nearly-mute voices of protest and revelation; voices dammed in darkness, in eternal day, and ever ready to break loose.

While the People, cool and silent, merely waited, to be entertained.

"...And so one day these kids, who had spent their lives entertaining a universe..." Junior adjusted the spotlight, sweating, "Well, one day the space ship on which they were traveling was forced down. Crashed and burned. But by a miracle, all escaped unhurt. Well, almost all. On a green planet, where they could eat and breathe; but it was off the main route. And of course, their pills... Ran out. Laydeez and Gentlemen..."

Now Alycyone began to whirl again across the small stage, a shrouded pyramid in her black cloak, under the flickering light; the others followed.

A gasp, a ripple spread across the audience. All the beautiful young faces turned, frozen; the shapely bodies in their simple tunics like marble. Greek statues in man's image of the Gods, the immortals watched now from the chorus, as on stage, the Thing, the dread no-more existent prime Taboo, began to unveil itself.

Old Maia began to strip.

The line of prancing girls, following her under the dull light, in their slow wheeling parody of dance, began to strip, too. First the cloaks, then the hats, sailing out over the audience. Now at a slow drum-beat roll, in unison, almost jauntily, off came the wigs. Bruised light glittered on their bald wrinkled skulls; they tapped and turned again; and now with quickened fingers as the music mounted, tugged at bras and g-strings and straps until layer by layer their naked bodies appeared. Sagging, dug-fallen, pot-bellied, veined and scarred, a monstrosity of flesh, so withered and mauled that it was as though time had striped and beaten them with some incredibly fine whip, leaving its imprint in a maze of wrinkles extending from crown to toe down the gross acreage of time-punished and falling flesh. Six crones, six old cronies of Chronos, pinched and bedeviled by their old bedfellow Time, till their carcasses showed the weight of his caresses, their bodies falling grotesquely down around their bones like carelessly anchored stockings; halfway arrested on gravity's inexorable downward way to the grave. And now, off with the face paint and cheek-straps (chapfallen; now their false teeth out; the whole structure of face sagging into lappets and jowls, the fantastic rumpling of some 700 years of life); denuding themselves finally of the last scrap of false eyelashes and eyebrows. Out of hollow eye-sockets, their Death's eyes stared sadly, grimly, over the stilled carnival.

Somewhere in the audience a baby; there weren't many, reproduction was limited; began to cry: and in the otherwise now total hush the sighing sound of the audience's breath rasped in and out, like the air from one pair of lungs, like the wind off a meadow, after a hot day. A loudspeaker nearby crackled suddenly, splitting the hush like the first distant rumble of thunder. Time, held up, suspended forever in grey barren eternity, now crackled for an instant across the frozen mob; sparked between two opposite poles.

... "And carking," the loudspeaker said... "And carking Death
will find you out
And nibble life up, doubt by doubt..."
"And that," Junior began hastily, trying to drown the sound, "is what your new life has saved you from, Laydeez and Gentlemen; the skeleton in the closet, so to speak, that mankind..."
"...And strip the senses, one by one (the loudspeaker went on, ignoring him)
Till sense itself is left undone..."
"Shut him up," Junior said.
From the audience, a bearded face rose, detaching itself suddenly; a voice gleefully, powerfully, roared back at the PA,
"And freakish age
Will pull our teeth
And bare the withered
Bone beneath..."
"And bed us down..." the loudspeaker cackled back.
"...Safe from stars and skies at last,
To rest
In other springs, on Earth's
Warm breast..."
Pandemonium. Shouts and jeers. The bearded man went down under a mob, was raised by an opposing mob and brandished like a flag.

Someone stifled the loudspeaker in a final squawk; after a brief sound of scuffling, bland carnival music blared forth again.

"Laydeez and gentlemen!"

"Hurrah for death!"

"Laydeez and..." Junior sweating, flung cloaks over the girls, harangued the audience. "Please! Puleez! The show is not over. For those of you who have enjoyed our show, who have found that it has brought new meaning into their lives, there is still..."

"Death and liberty for all!"

"...another part of the show, if you will kindly step this way, for just ten spantans more, the tenth part of a..." Sweating, he trundled the box containing the seventh sister into its niche on the side of the tent. "In this box, the sister that unfortunately..."

"The people's right! No freedom without death!"

"...did not survive the crash of the rocket ship. A fascinating and unique specimen, Ladeez and Gentlemen, and the only one of its kind in the universe (will someone shut up the joker out there?), where Death and old age no longer exist, and where everyone has an equal right to *Life*, ladeez and gentlemen, and there is no need for such suffering, as you see here, only to remind you, in this educational spectacle, of what mankind had to endure in his Dark Ages."

More than two thirds of the audience came up to file past the narrow coffin, padded in faded stage velvet, where Merope's mummied body lay in state, grinning at the stars; and stood for awhile to shift, perhaps, the weight of eternity from their feet. In another's misfortune, one's own often looks brighter.

The six surviving old women sat back in their tent again, huddled in their cloaks, sipping tea. Life's conscience; spooks, antiques, ghosts, from the world of death and time, they were pensioned by the government. Because of them, the dissenters and poets had been discovered and dispersed.

"Great show tonight, kids," Junior called, trotting past. Merope's coffin had been wheeled into the tent; as he passed, he was now stripping off his putty nose. The crowds had gone home. "Always like to give folks something to make them Think."

The old women did not look up from their tea. Outside, the hard brilliant starlight loomed over the littered darkness of the fairgrounds. Most of the other freaks had gone to bed. But from the poker game two tents down came the faint, derisive eh, eh, echo, of the Eh beasts; and from a nearby cage, the mournful, solitary roar of the old lion.

NO TRADING VOYAGE
by Doris Pitkin Buck

(Originally appeared in the May 1963 issue of *Fantasy & Science Fiction*)

*Doris Pitkin Buck, born in 1898, was one of the new women of the twentieth century. She graduated from Bryn Mawr in 1920 and embarked on a career as an actress on stage and screen before her marriage. In an age when women were expected to quit the world of work after marrying, she defied custom. She was always seeking new opportunities, from being a museum publicist, "paintings on the way to work—books and objects all old and rare" to working for the Department of the Interior "getting all dolled up and eating shrimp in front of a camera." (*The Magazine of Fantasy & Science Fiction, Feb. 1964) When not otherwise employed, she wrote freelance, her husband occasionally illustrating her articles. One imagines her floating through the public sphere, impeccably dressed and carrying the conversation.*

Somehow amidst all that, she was a founding member of the Science Fiction Writers of America. Her story "The Little Blue Weeds of Spring" was on the ballot for the first annual Nebula awards. Her dozens of stories have been translated into German, French and Croatian.

Her first short story, "Aunt Agatha" appeared in F&SF *in 1952, to some acclaim, yet the introduction to her story "Come Where my Love Lies Dreaming" in 1964, her eighth short story published in that magazine, mentions her as a*

185

poet first, a member of the rare group of authors published both in prose and poetry in that magazine.

It's not surprising. She wrote nearly as many poems as stories. Her last publication was a poem. "Travel Tip" was published in 1981, the year after her death, in the self-same F&SF magazine that had printed her so many times. At the age of 82, she was still contributing to the genre.

Her work deals often with women's emotional lives, and with the role of mother or lover over time and in extra-ordinary situations. She was unafraid to leave room for the reader to interpret incomplete information, which lends her writing a touch of the postmodern before its time. Ironically, the woman who never gave up her public life wrote time and again about women forced to choose between their families and caregiving and a more wild life. Be a grandmother or an immortal winged alien? Take a pill to become a mental dinosaur or take her son to the beach? These heroines don't always choose the kids, but I suspect her editors preferred when they did.

"No Trading Voyage" feels prose-like to a modern poetry reader, but it uses its skeletal narrative form to effectively tell a tale that might have been weighed down in story form. The very sparseness forces the reader to confront each unvarnished detail. We are left with the bare facts of an extraordinary journey, leaving our hands forever empty, grasping for the tragedy between details.

—Marie Vibbert

There being little
or perhaps nothing now,
no tithe no tittle to sell or barter,
I cannot make the usual report
on outgo or on intake
but what I say may be
not less important:

On the fourth globe that circles great Pleione
the inhabitants are grey, with cobalt eyes.
They see
all streams or waves sent out from any sun;
so to them space is never night,
not dun but dimly gleaming dawn,
save where among charted immensities
it dazzles with full daylight in a star.
These beings live their lives
in contemplation. That is their sole art.

We passed Albireo and met the pirates
haunting the nearby dust clouds.
They loosed trained *virlacs*, taught to capture
what can be held for slaves.
They never maim.
They bound us and then sold us in the markets
of what is our Pole Star.
Our tongues learned tunes of language
from lipless mouths.
We have been fed
on flakes of scentless *leel*, have gnawed
small *raphor* bones and watched Aldebaran,
cursing us as we watched.
We also quarried
the *arluk* mines of Mira.
They sold us once again.
I do not know what sun we headed for,
what comet glow.
We mutinied—then freed,
headed the ship upon a half-guessed course
to reach unknown Antares.

Upon our way, we found one nameless world,
a continented place of plants and insects
where flowers outglory even Earth's.

Through its black caves
our band was led by vines—
tender as women, wise as Solomon.
With their ringed tendrils
they clasped our human hands
and now in all worlds
this hand of mine feels empty.
We went on.

About Antares there are many planets
which to their cores are ocean.
They have never heard
even of islands. In bubbles
sucked by vast *nerhth* beds from the upper air
creatures like birds have being
and live their span on never-tiring wings.
The depths of green
press each imprisoned word
into a sphere.
Such calm and mindless beauty
was like a net to snare us—

yet we came through, whole and refreshed and young,
to sing with mirth,
a crew made ready for any voyaging
even return
to the doomed cradle that its ghosts call Earth.

CORNIE ON THE WALLS

by Sidney van Scyoc

(Originally appeared in the August 1963 issue of *Fantastic Stories of Imagination*)

Bookstores in the United States during the late 1950s and early 60s were as much accessible to women as they were to men. Their plethora of weird fiction, horror, fantasy and science fiction were marketed to anyone with the money to pay a meager sum of one to two dollars for the latest gothic reprint or the first edition of a 20th century counterpart. It's ridiculous to even argue that only men took a serious interest in any of these genres given that mail order subscriptions to anthology magazines like Galaxy *and* Imagination *were commonplace during this period. And yet, why do many of the names in this book sound unfamiliar to you, the casual reader?*

Even if the recognition for their works comes fifty (or more) years after their premier publication, I hope that Rediscovery *will bring to light the numerous works of female contributors to the malleable genre of science fiction. In particular, I hope that this anthology will revive interest in one particular author whom I have come to greatly admire—Sydney Van Scyoc.*

Like many women then and now, this powerhouse of talent, known by her middle name, Joyce, to her friends and family, wrote (and writes!) under the neutral name Sydney

189

Van Scyoc to side step the damage her career could take if her gender were transparent. She launched her writing career in fantasy and science fiction with the bitter and nihilistic tale "Shatter the Wall" in the February 1962 issue of Galaxy. *To date she stands as the creator of 11 novels and 31 short stories published between 1962 and 2005. Her works have been distributed globally in English, Croatian, Dutch, French, German, and Italian. A dynamic lady, she even took time in the 1990s and early 2000s to undertake a venture into the jewelry making business, selling her handmade earrings and bracelets at fairs and conventions.*

As an author Sydney J. Van Scyoc has an intensity in her stories that is hard to match. In an almost stream of consciousness style her characters' emotions and thoughts spill onto the page with sadness, love, need, and ambition. Of particular note are her early short stories, populated with women who are unfulfilled and angry, despite (and in part because of) the comfortable trappings that surround them. They are hungry, but they don't necessarily understand what is gnawing at them. They are haunted and haunting, both ungraspable and impossible to forget. The following story is one such work of Scyoc's that showcases her unique style, as well as her penchant for memorable female characters who say much through their individuality.

"Cornie on the Walls" was originally published in the August 1963 issue of Fantastic Stories of the Imagination. *Bluntly, it is a trial by fire initiation into Scyoc's writing style. Not content to speculate solely upon future culture and society, Scyoc takes into consideration the changes that could occur in our inner dialogue as language evolves. As a result, reading her stories is not unlike a Middle English speaker trying to understand contemporary English. Her sentence structures and words are sometimes difficult to parse, but in writing this way Scyoc is getting at a poignant aspect of science fiction literature—exploring conceivable changes in human jargon and slang.*

Despite her volumes of works and the experimental quality of her writing, Sydney J. Van Scyoc was plagued by harsh to mediocre reviews. At a time when New Wave science fiction was gaining momentum in the early 1960s, it is frustrating to think that such a talent (and that of her peers) was not more readily lauded. However, thanks to her inclusion in Rediscovery *it is my hope that this will soon be remedied.*

—Rosemary Benton

Sometimes she looked at him from his own walls, with monkey bright eyes and pensive face. He knew she couldn't be there, but she was, fleetingly.

Sometimes he saw a glow, a passing of light, on a far wall. When he focused on it, it was gone, but he knew it had been Cornie, watching.

Sometimes she came to his chamber floor. She came thin, a stick drawing of herself, then grew and flowed until she was a monstrous Cornie drawn over the entire chamber floor. All he could do when that happened was close his viewports, because wherever he looked, in the kitchen, in the service halls, in her quarters, there she spread, her hair, her foot, something of her.

Sometimes he heard her footsteps coming down the service hall, approaching Central Control where he lay paralyzed, desensitized, and wired into Central Control Panel. Once when he looked he saw only a shadow on the wall, fading.

But now the bell was ringing, singing through his halls as Cornie had sung. He made the thought necessary to view the singer. She had a bull's massive high shoulders, hair of rusted fine wire, and someone had thumbed her nose down. She glared into his viewport as if he had been that someone.

He slid the door anyway and murmured her in. She stalked his hall, glowering at the good pictures he thought on the walls.

Reaching the main chamber, she dropped heavy and uncompromising to the settee, which sat in the center of the otherwise bare room. Her voice was a fingernail drawn across rusting screenwire. "You the one wants a housekeeper?"

His speakers murmured, "I am." Unhappy violin talked around his words, because his reasons for wanting a housekeeper were sad ones. "Unfortunately my wife—"

"Here I come clean across town and against my better judgement," she said, "and you play music."

The violin died. So did his voice.

"Well, you want to see my papers?" She thrust them at the nearest viewport.

Sighing, he examined them. She was qualified and highly recommended, and he was weary of interviews. But he did not want her.

"Well?" she said.

He sighed again. He would compromise. He would take her, if she would satisfy the one condition which could make her presence tolerable.

He stated his condition, as nicely as he knew how.

Alas, his voice hung lame.

"Not for any job," she hissed when she could purple and swell no more.

She was so angry she would not look at the good pictures he thought for her, pictures of her rewiring Central Control with smooth plastic hands, smiling for the tourists with a smooth plastic face, polishing his floors in a lithe plastic body.

"You want a good dependable housekeeper, okay," she said. "You want a female to show off, get one's already fit for it. You listen. You let them freeze up your God-given body and program you into one made by the sinful hand of man, you condemn your everlasting soul."

"You must consider—"

"There's some consider this you're doing sinful too," she said darkly. "I figure as long as you stay in your own body, it's your business whether you got wires running out your head and tubes going in your stummik."

"Surely—"

"I got the papers," she did. "Do I get the job?"

He hesitated. "I'm sorry," he said. "In your present condition—"

She was up and stalking. He was relieved to slide the door after her. "You decide you want a good, dependable housekeeper, you know

192

where to call," she cried back.

He was alone.

He shuddered and was still, listening. Hearing nothing, he turned to practice, thinking upon his sensitive electronic walls and floors the intricate and shimmering scenes his mind gave him, viewing them critically, making small corrections to bring them to perfection.

Someone was watching.

Cornie.

He was working on the north wall, viewing from the south viewports. He switched, stealthily, to north viewports.

She wasn't there.

She was somewhere. He knew. He felt it.

Rapidly he thought through all his viewports, click, click, click; secondary gallery, kitchen, Cornie's quarters, service halls. She was nowhere.

The bell rang. He hesitated, then thought the thought necessary to view the singer.

Cornie's friend Nora stood on his step, tight-lipped, contained too tightly by black.

It was only courteous to admit her. He slid the door, murmuring.

She acknowledged neither his greeting nor his presence, until she reached the main chamber. There she stopped, gasped, raised a face darkening with anger.

Cornie was everywhere, on the walls, on the ceiling, on the floor. There were dozens of her young and bony with fine, straight black hair. But there was no monkey's gleam in her eyes, no hesitant smile at her lips. She was Cornie stylized, unliving.

"How could you?" Nora cried. "You've destroyed everything that was Cornie. You've left nothing but arms and legs and nobody's face. You've killed her again."

Abruptly she collapsed to the settee, sobbing into her handkerchief. "I told her you cared for nothing but your own walls and floors," she sobbed. "I told her, and now you've taken everything she was and used her to decorate yourself."

Suddenly she was up, running down the service hall to pull the handled door and glare into the bladed metal interior of the Central Power Unit. She jumped back, gnawing her handkerchief. "I don't believe it," she said faintly.

So he made pictures for her on the wall beside the Unit, pictures of awkward Cornie probing into the Unit with tools she insisted she knew how to use, pictures of her dress catching on a fan blade, of her foot, as she moved to free her dress, reactivating the main switch, which she had deactivated before beginning work, pictures of her dumb and whitened face, pictures of blood and fingernails and pieces of fine, straight black hair.

Nora had the decency to run outside to be sick.

Then she couldn't come in again. She gnawed her handkerchief and tried to put her foot over the threshold, but it would not go. Finally she left.

The dead Cornies faded. But she was still there, somewhere.

He would purge himself of her.

He gathered himself, gathered all his power of mind. And he released himself in black pictures of torture and death. He covered his walls with death, felt certain that even his body quivered in its chamber, his body that had been surgically paralyzed the day they had wired him into Central Control.

When he was certain she was purged, he let blood and death wash down his walls into puddles which faded from his floors, leaving him clean, white and alone.

But he was not alone.

Blood dripped still from the northwest corner of the chamber, dripped and ran down the wall in a pattern which was Cornie.

He couldn't cry. His body lay paralyzed, and tears thought on sensitive walls were but a formalized expression of sorrow. Cornie, he demanded, what could I do but what I did?

The blood began to fade.

Tourists were coming.

They were three, a man, a woman, an impertinent small boy. He slid the door before they could ring. His murmuring was urgent; his hallway burst into a frenzy of color and motion. Forms grew, merged, faded, pulsed, in every color he could think. Forms shimmered, glowed. Forms became people, people forms.

Never had a house thought such forms for tourists. For critics, perhaps, for connoisseurs, but never for tourists. They were stunned and slow in his hall. So he thought a jungle and a jungle village in his main chamber, and he let it leak into the hall, now a native's cry, now an abstraction of zebra, running. That drew them from the hall into the scene he had created.

Ah, such a scene it was.

He viewed it with understandable pride.

Then he saw her, dripping from the same corner, dripping through the good green foliage he had made there.

The tourists hadn't seen. They were dazed by his extravagance, by life that crept through underbrush, by hunters who returned chanting with game, by kettled village fires, by women at crude looms, by the naked brown child who played at jungle's edge.

He had to hide the dripping Cornie.

A lion crept through the brush, silent and listening. The child looked up, saw the animal's approach, puckered, began to wail. The tourists turned at the sound, turned to see the lion crouch and spring, to see the gush of baby's blood, to see the lion lope through dense vegetation, to see him run up the trunk of a leaning tree, to see the child's blood, as his body was torn, drip through the foliage to cover the Cornie dripping there.

The mother seized her child and hurried him out the door. The father stared, then backed after them.

Through the closed door he could hear the mother's scolding. He could hear the child's shrill protest, "But I wanta see the lion eat the baby!" He could hear the father plead, "Honey, they've always been okay before."

He had no time for their squabbling. He knew how to be rid of the Cornies. Hadn't it been her fondest desire, always, to see him happy?

He thought the jungle away.

He thought upon his walls the housekeeper he wanted. She was young, fit, sure, with level eyes and crisp neat brown hair. He thought her and let her guide tourists efficiently through his rooms, let her polish in his kitchen with strong, sure hands, let her rewire the Central Control with deft fingers. He let his yearning violin say, This is what I want, now that Cornie is gone.

When he looked again, Cornie was fading. A moment, and she was gone.

He had done it. The girl on his walls began to caper, to jig. His violin fiddled, and he made copies of his own thin body to dance with her.

Then, into the eye of one dancing girl came a gleam he knew. Over the lips of another settled a sad, quivering smile. The crisp brown hair of another became fine and black.

How could she, when she knew he wanted this neat, efficient brown-haired girl instead?

She danced nevertheless on his walls, smiled her bright, tentative smile, and the other girl's body became hers, long, bony and awkward.

There was a pounding, a ringing. He channeled his thoughts to the door.

Nora flounced his hall. Inspector Woodrow of Living Houses Bureau, balding and weary, trailed behind. "Look, they told you at the office," he said. "The police investigate every case of accidental death. Thoroughly. What do you expect me to find after they've been over the place?"

"And I tell you he did it intentionally," she said. "He cares for nothing but his walls and floors. Before he was wired he tolerated her because she did not interfere with his painting. Then he was selected, and it was different. She was his hostess. But she had no style. She had only to step into a room and everything went awry. And when she guided tourists, she didn't treat them as worms or slugs. She took them even into the service areas, which hurt his pride, to have tourists examining his units. She explained to them everything she knew, how he was wired directly into Central Control, how he could think scenes and sounds, how he could hear and see, how the machines cared for his body. They listened more to her than they looked at him, so he killed her."

Woodrow glared at the fading Cornies. "You have no new evidence then?" he said. "You dragged me here for words only?"

"Haven't I given you a motive?" she demanded.

He sighed heavily. "You have not. A motive is love, money—"

"He cares nothing for money!" she cried. "Don't you see? He lives for his walls and his floors. Money is nothing!"

"You take a unique view of the human situation," he said. "You must tell me more, when I have no houses to inspect." He turned to go.

She caught his sleeve. "He could have short circuited," she said. "He could have shut himself down and saved her."

He removed her hand. "Short circuiting, since you seem to have skipped your homework, is roughly comparable to self-induced convulsions followed by complete unconsciousness. Not an easy state to achieve voluntarily." He stalked out the door.

"But he's shorted before. She used to tell me."

He didn't turn.

"No one cares," she cried after him. "He murders in cold blood, and no one cares."

Then they were gone.

So was Cornie.

She was nowhere. He switched from viewport to viewport, click, click, click.

It was no use beginning anything. She would come to interrupt.

She did not come.

But every time he decided, Now I can make scenes, now I can speak with my violin, he thought he felt her beginning to come.

Then, as if the sun had penetrated a dark corner of his mind, he remembered what he had known all along. She *couldn't* come, not of her own volition. Only he could draw her from his walls and floors, because only he could draw anything from his walls and floors.

He had been bringing her himself. Not consciously, but she had come from his own mind.

It was with difficulty that he refrained from making celebration on his walls. For to be rid of her he had only to vow, solemnly; From this moment I will never again remember—

197

He was careful not to remember who it was he would not remember.

Having vowed, he sat quietly and walled her, a faceless someone, into a single, closed chamber of his mind.

But he had made a mistake. He had not decided what to remember in her place. If he wiped away her very existence, did he not wipe away a considerable portion of his own existence too? Couldn't he safely remember that she had existed, that she was now gone, without going on to remember the details—her face, her body.

He made black pictures on a secret wall, trying to decide. He pretended she had never existed. Painstakingly he remembered all the details of the bachelor life he had lived. But it was futile. She *had* existed.

He tried to remember instead the life he had lived with someone who had not been Cornie. That too was futile. He too carefully endowed the other woman with all the traits Cornie had not possessed. Everything she was reminded him of what Cornie had not been.

He was still deciding when the students came. They were a dozen, with notebooks and their own folding chairs. They clattered into his chamber and their zealot instructor darted among them arranging their chairs in a semi-circle facing the south wall.

But when he made his designs they sat sullen because each was convinced that he could do as well, given the opportunity, and each resented not being given the opportunity. Their wooden faces irritated him. Their presumption in coming to sit sullen infuriated him. He couldn't restrain himself. His speakers growled. His walls burst into flame. The chamber grew hot and crackling with anger.

The flames purified him, burned away anger and inhibiting anxiety, left him leaden with unexpressed urgency. He thought advanced designs, feverishly. He covered himself, from service halls to front door, with intricate, difficult designs, worked them into complex scenes which grew, faded, glowed, until he dissolved them back into designs and from those designs brought new scenes. Color and action tumbled from his mind, crowded against themselves and each other on his walls.

He covered himself with scenes that told of everything he knew. He brought scenes that told all of life and death. He brought scenes of love, fury, pain and death.

Never had a house made such scenes for students, never for such a small and undistinguished group, never with such lack of restraint.

At last he was spent. He let his walls blank. He sank into a dumb, half-conscious state.

The instructor's face twitched. "Questions?" he snapped.

The students blinked stupidly. Then a knobby, tall boy cleared his throat and stood. "Sir, perhaps I'm speaking out of turn, but what if he should work himself into a breakdown?" he said.

The instructor scowled. "Perkins," he said coldly, "this man is linked directly into a care system devised to control and eliminate any physical condition not requiring drastic surgery. He enjoys better health than anyone in this room. If you have no intelligent question, be seated."

Perkins lowered his knobby head. "I meant a mental breakdown, sir."

The instructor stared, unbelieving.

"Insanity, sir," Perkins muttered.

That was when he saw her. She was staring into his viewport, a tall, bony girl with a frightened small smile beginning to quiver at her lips.

"We will forget you said that, Perkins."

"But sir, I noted a definite preoccupation with blood, death and the end of all things. Perhaps I misinterpreted but—"

"There is no question of insanity!"

Perkins lowered his head. "Sir, you always tell us not to close our minds."

She was staring directly at him. Her eyes were the wise, bright eyes of a monkey.

She knew.

She knew he could have shorted, as he had shorted every other time her inaptitude had placed her in serious danger. She knew he had restrained himself when every instinct had cried for him to short. She knew he had deliberately let her die.

"There is no question," the instructor said emphatically.

"But sir, don't you feel that an individual isolated from normal

199

human contacts, wired into a setup like this and all his senses cut off, getting everything secondhand through viewports and mikes, might become more susceptible to mental illness than—"

"Perkins, I shall forget everything."

Her blood had begun to drip down his walls. Wherever it dripped it became a small Cornie. Each small Cornie screamed in a small voice and bled, and where she bled there was another Cornie. His walls covered themselves. His rooms filled her screams.

"Sir!" Perkins exclaimed in horror.

The instructor gulped. "Class dismissed!" Cornie drowned his words. Gesturing wildly he herded his open-mouthed students to the door.

The girl and Perkins remained. The girl smiled Cornie's pleading bright smile, and her eyes were swimming. Every Cornie on his wall smiled back at her. Every Cornie laughed softly, mockingly, though Cornie had never mocked. The girl choked, gasped, and she too began to laugh, a shrill, hurting laugh. Perkins seized their chairs and pulled her to the door.

Outside her laughter died. She choked and gasped again. She threw her head back. She screamed and screamed. Perkins dropped the chairs, slapped her twice, hard. When she collapsed to his shoulder he hurried to the bus, leaving the chairs behind.

What could I do? he wanted to cry after her. You were awkward and bony. You wore squaw dresses with silver rickrack, and your hair was cut ragged. You were a monkey in my halls. You couldn't make my kitchen shine or my floors glow. You couldn't repair or rewire without disaster. You dripped solder, dropped tools, made connections that never held. Yet when I wanted to hire a professional housekeeper, you cried. You insisted you could do it yourself. But you banged my walls with cleaning equipment, seared my countertops with hot pans, let tourists smoke in my room.

What could I do? You smiled at each man wistfully, as if you were his small child whom he had not loved enough, at each woman the same, and everyone let you have his heart. They listened to you with indulgent smiles and gentle faces. They lingered at the door with questions, just to hear your voice.

They never saw me for you.

What could I do? he wanted to cry. I loved you. Yet you asked every tourist, every critic, every student to love you too, asked with your smile, your eyes, your shy, whispering voice.

I knew you really asked their love for me. I knew you asked them to enjoy and remember and appreciate me.

But when you were here, they never saw me.

Now you know. I let you die.

Come back.

But the bus left, and she didn't glance back as it went.

Had she understood? Had she heard?

The other Cornies faded. He was alone.

Then she was coming up the walk. She didn't look at all like herself. She was blonde and dumpy with pale eyes, but he knew it was her.

He slid the door joyously. "You understood! You came." His violin frolicked around his words.

She frowned into his viewport. "I heard you needed a housekeeper," she said warily.

"But I'll need no one, now that you've come. Drip solder, drop tools, set hot pans on my counters. I don't care."

"I've got all my licenses and very good recommendations," she said, still more warily. "I'm a graduate of Granly-Hopkins School of Living-House Care."

"I know. I remember. You brought your slides and tapes from school each evening. We watched and listened, you on the settee and I from Central Control. I explained to you the care and construction of a living house. You rumpled your ragged hair and could understand nothing. But I don't care."

He told her other things too. But she backed away, turned and ran down the walk. He cried after her. She ran anyway.

She would come again. He knew she would.

A busload of tourists came. She wasn't with them, and he wouldn't slide his door. "No," he said. He knew she would be back.

She was, often. Sometimes she came alone, sometimes several of her came together. Sometimes she came with a man or men or with children. But she wouldn't come through his door. He welcomed her.

He told her all the things he remembered. He pleaded, "Don't you remember too?" But she wouldn't come.

After a few days more and more of her came. She stood in groups, with men, with children, with women who weren't her. Sometimes the others whispered or laughed, but she didn't. Sometimes the others said, "Mad house" and tittered. But she didn't.

Once the instructor returned with Perkins. Their faces were grave. The instructor pressed the bell.

She wasn't with them. "No," he said.

"Sir—" Perkins ventured.

"He is tired. He has exhausted himself. There is no question of insanity," the instructor said.

She wasn't with them. "No," he said.

UNWILLINGLY TO SCHOOL
by Pauline Ashwell

(Originally appeared in the January 1958 issue of *Astounding Science Fiction*)

Unwillingly to School *is so unusual as to be unique.*

To begin with, it's a science fiction story penned by a woman. That's not as uncommon these days, but in 1958, only a tiny fraction of the stories coming out in the likes of Fantasy & Science Fiction, Astounding, Galaxy, *et al were penned by female authors. Though forty stories might be released across multiple digests in a given month, perhaps one or two were by women.*

Secondly, Unwillingly to School *is not only written by a woman, it stars one—a rare science fiction story, indeed.*

Thirdly, the lead is a woman with a disability. Disabled characters are hardly seen in fiction of any kind, and when they are, the disability is usually the point of the story. In this ingenious tale, however, the main character's disability doesn't even show up until about halfway through. It affects the story, but it is not the point of the story.

Given all this, it may sound unbelievable, but there is one other story I can think of that was penned by a woman in that era and starred a woman with a disability: Anne McCaffrey's The Ship Who Sang. *However,* Unwillingly *has one more quality that sets it apart and makes it truly stand alone: humor. It is laugh-out-loud funny. There are plenty of science fiction stories that intend to be funny, but not many that actually succeed. Even fewer of them contain* humor that stands the test of time. The protagonist's wry observations peppered throughout the piece are positively delightful, leaving the reader chuckling helplessly despite themselves.

You may be turned off at first, as I was, by the writing style. I implore you to give it a chance! It's clearly a deliberate choice on the author's part, and it rings oddly to those that are used to more formal wording even in their fiction. As the protagonist herself notes, "Man to man with my tutor at least I can make him laugh, he says The rugged unpunctuated simplicity of my style of writing is not suited to academic topics even when leavened with polysyllables end of quote," but while the rugged unpunctuated simplicity of her style may not be suited to academic topics, it's perfectly suited to this clever, lighthearted story.

The attendees of the World Science Fiction Convention in 1959 apparently agreed. They nominated Unwillingly for a Hugo award that year in the category of Best Novelette, and Ashwell herself in the category of Best New Author. She was one of the first women to be nominated for a Hugo, along with two others in the Novelette category (Zenna Henderson's Captivity and Katherine MacLean's Second Game, which was co-written with Charles V. DeVet), and with Rosel George Brown and Kit Reed for the Best New Author of 1958. In the end, Clifford D. Simak's The Big Front Yard took home the Novelette rocketship, and no one ended up with the Best New Author award—the voters chose "No Award" that year.

The nominees in the "Best New Author of 1958" category are particularly interesting, as Pauline Ashwell is listed twice: once as Pauline Ashwell, and once as another pseudonym she wrote under: "Paul Ash" (Ashwell was discovered by John Campbell and wrote for Astounding/ Analog under both "Paul Ash" and "Pauline Ashwell" throughout the late 50s and 60s.) One hopes that those who tabulated the totals were sensible enough to add together *the votes for Paul and Pauline (and indeed, the Hugo website lists only one entry, "Paul Ash (aka: Pauline Ashwell)," in its list of nominees that year, suggesting that they were). Also of note is the fact that the nominee list had more women than men, with Ashwell, Brown and Reed being joined by Brian Aldiss and Louis Charbonneau. Though the readers chose "No Award," Brian W. Aldiss received a plaque as the official runner up.*

If you end up falling in love with the indomitable protagonist of Unwillingly to School, *you can read more of her adventures in a fix-up Ashwell put together in 1993 titled* Unwillingly to Earth. *Though it's out of print, copies thankfully aren't hard to find.*

—Janice Marcus

This may look like a moviegram of Brownian Movement but no such luck; it is Russett Interplanetary College of Humanities Opening Day, four thousand three hundred twenty-seven other freshers milling around and me in the middle with a little ticket on my chest says Lee, L. because my given name is something not to mention; they say these kids came from one hundred twenty-four planets just to study at Russett but personally of all points in the known continuum this is the one I would rather be any place But.

Freshers come all sizes, all colors but a fair number are girls so there is one thing we will be finding in common anyway.

This may come as a surprise, that I am a girl, I mean. My tutor at Prelim School says my speech is feminine as spoken but written down looks like the kind of male character who spits sideways.

I reply that I talk like my Dad he is a character all right, male too but does not spit, if you spent your formative years with a filter in your kisser neither would you.

He says my flair for seeing the functional significance of the minutiae of behavior is obviously what got me chosen for the Cultural Engineering course.

Huh.

I know what got me into that all right I am not so dumb as I look.

You think I flatter myself? Brother, by what goes on I look dumb indeed. Maybe this is because of my hair, curly and pale colored—all right, blond. My eyes are blue as they come which is by no means sky color whatever books say, my skin is pink some places white others when washed and a visitor we had once said I had a rosebud mouth.

I am seven then, I do not hold it against her right away there are no roses where I grew up; when I landed here on Earth I hunt one up to see was it a compliment.

Brother.

I find later they come other colors but this one is frostbite mauve, and the shape!

I wish to state here my mouth has two lips like anyone else.

Where I grew up is Excenus 23, how I got hauled off it is due to a string of catastrophes but the name of the biggest is D. J. M'Clare.

Excenus sun is what they call a swarmer, ninety-seven small planets in close orbits plus odd chunks too many to count, Twenty-three is the biggest, gravitation one point oh seven Earth diameter a fraction less, if you ever heard of the place it was because they mine areopagite there. Ninety-four percent production for sale in the known volume of space comes from mines on Twenty-three; but for that, no reason to live there at all.

My Dad started as a miner and made his pile, then he took up farming and spent the lot, he has it all back again now.

Areopagite forms only in drydust conditions meaning humidity at ground level never above two and one half percent rainfall. None, hence from this farming on Excenus is something special, but miners are like other people they have to eat too.

When Dad started there was him and Uncle Charlie and their first year they fed two thousand men, nowadays the planetary population is eleven thousand three hundred twenty and there are seven other farmers, most of them started working for Dad and graduated to farms of their own. Nobody on Excenus eats trucked concentrates now.

Uncle Charlie is Hon as in secretary meaning no real relation. He is an engineer, when Dad met him down on his luck but able and willing to build diggers, harvesters, weathermaker for ten thousand acres out of any junk to hand. Had to be done like that because Excenus Haulage

Company, the big company did all the shipping in and out of the planet, sold food concentrates. No competition welcome therefore no shipments seeds, agricultural, machinery, all that, would have been allowed through.

It takes Charlie two years to do his job, meanwhile Dad bones up the agricultural side. Nowadays there are a lot of books on drydust farming, they cover soilmaking, microbiology, economical use of weather, seed selection, plenty more; at that time then: were fewer and Dad read them all.

If he had sent for the usual texts E. H. C. might have caught on and had a little accident in transit, so Dad gets them in as *books*, I mean antique style, chopped in pieces and hinged together down the side. They are labeled Curio Facsimiles and disguised with antique picture covers mostly show the damnedest females you ever saw, dressed in bits and pieces mostly crooked; some of them dead. People collect these things for some reason. Dad has one or two put on top with texts to match the outside, rest are textbooks on agriculture like I said.

Charlie offers to make reader-reels from them but Dad turns it down. He still has all those books packed in a row, when l was little he used to tell me how he learned all his farming studying that way, without using machines, it just showed you could still do it if you had to. Dad never had any education and it bothers him; l used to think that was why he kept on telling me this.

Well there are plenty of troubles not least with E. H. C. but Dad is not the type to give up; reason he started farming in the first place was he caught on E. H. C. were making it impossible for anyone to do just that; Dad does not like people who try and stop him even if it was not what he wanted in the first place.

I am born soon after the farm is really set, my mother walked out when I was three. She was fresh out of college with an agricultural degree when he met her, maybe the trouble was Dad caught on she knew less about drydust farming than he did, maybe other things. Excenus 23 is no place for a woman they say.

It is O.K. by me but I was born in the place.

Dad and Charlie raised me between them like the crops, this is to say carefully.

There are plenty more people now in Green Valley where the farms are, thirty or so and they change all the time. People who come out farm for a bit make their pile then go. We even get women some times. Peoples' wives from Town come out to board sometimes, Dad lets them because he thinks they will Mother me.

Well mostly I manage to steer them off and no hard feelings, it is my home after all they got to be reasonable about it if they want to stay. Seems they do as a rule, Town is kind of tough to live in. Several stayed a year or more. So it is not true to say I grew up in a wholly masculine environment, I knew up to seven women for quite a while.

Green Valley is outside the mining area and about six hundred miles from Town. This has to be, Town gets most of its water combing the air and so do the weathermakers for the farms; anyway mining and farming do not mix so good. The Valley is twenty miles each way hedged by hill ridges up to seventy feet high. Outside is stone flats, dust bowl and tangle-mats of *Gordianus* scrub. Forty miles round about I know it pretty well but the rest of the planet is about the same, except for Town.

This is where I was born, I was all set to stay there till Dad had his accident, first catastrophe on the way to this place.

I am up one day in a helivan watching the harvest on a thousand—acre strip at the edge of the farm, there is a moderate wind blowing from over the hill, so we are keeping the weather-lid over each row until just before the harvester gets there so as to keep the dust out of the grain. I am directing this.

Here at the edge the weather-lid is just above the com, it runs from the weather-maker in the middle of the farm in a big cone like a very flat tent, fifty feet high in the middle and four miles across. You cannot see it of course unless the wind blows dust across, or there is rain inside; the lid is just a layer of air polarized to keep dust one side, water vapor the other; just now you can see plainly where puffs of dust go skittering across.

The harvester gets to the end of a row on the far side from the road. I signal Biff Plater at Control and he draws the weather-lid in twenty yards. The harvester lifts its scanner at the end of the strip, wheels, and comes through the next swathe, with the big cutter pushing six inches above ground, stalks sliding back into the thrasher bagged corn following on the trailer behind.

Then I see Dad come along the road riding the biggest kor on the farm. Kors are *Pseudocamelopus hirsutinaris* part of the indigenous fauna we started taming to ride on about a year ago. Dad does not really enjoy it, he cannot get used to having no brakes but he will not give up. I see right away he is having trouble, the kor slipped its bridle and navigating on its own, long neck straight out and Dad slipping to and fro in the saddle; his mouth filter is bumped out and waving behind.

The harvester is half up the field. I do not want the kor to be scared I yell to Biff, Turn it off quick! but the controls are on the other side of the shack from the weather ones.

Then the kor sees the scanner rearing on its stalk, it is not frightened at all thinks this is the great great grandfather of the species and charges straight across to say hello.

I am yelling to Biff and got my eyes shut, then he is yelling right back, I have to open them and look down.

The kor has gone straight into the cutter the second before it stopped. Dad has been thrown and the harvester stopped with one tread a foot from his head and a corner gone over his arm.

I bring the heli down yelling for help on all frequencies.

Dad is breathing but flat out; fractured skull, ulna and radius like a jigsaw puzzle, multiple injuries to the chest; the kor is in three pieces mixed up with the machine.

We call the hospital in Town and they direct first aid over two way visiphone while the ambulance comes. It takes seventy minutes and I am swearing to myself we will hire a permanent doctor if we have to shanghai him, after this.

The ambulance arrives and the doctor says we have done as well as can be expected, fortunately Dad is tough but it will be a two-month hospital job at the least.

They crate him up in splint plastic and load him into the ambulance. Buffalo Cole has packed me a bag, I get in too.

I am out again first thing, passengers not allowed.

I get out the long-distance heli and go straight to Town, I am waiting

209

in the hospital when they arrive. I wait till they have Dad unpacked before I start to inquire.

These hospitals! It is all they will do to let me look at him, when I do he is lying in a kind of tank; his chest is the wrong shape, there is a mass of tubes round his head running to a pump, this is for resorption of blood clots in the brain; more too the other end for external aeration of the blood, he is not going to use his lungs for a bit.

I think this does not look real, Dad in all this plumbing; then I hear my breathing goes odd, next thing you know the doctors steer me outside.

They say it will be a week before the blood clots go and Dad wakes up but they will report by visiphone every day.

I say No need they can tell me when I visit each day.

They are deaf or something, they repeat they will call Green Valley each morning at thirteen o'clock.

I say Is that when they would prefer me to call in?

At last they have got it, they say Surely I will not fly six hundred miles every day?

I say No I shall be stopping right here in Town.

Then they want to know what friends I am stopping with, I say at a hotel of course.

Consternation all round No place for young girls to stop in this town, they make it out the toughest hellhole in the known volume.

I say Nuts there are hotels for transients and their wives too.

They flap wildly in all directions and offer me a bed in the nurses' hostel which is men only ordinarily but they will make an exception.

I say thanks very much, No.

In the end they tell me to go to the Royal Hotel it is the most respectable of the local dumps, do not on any account make a mistake and go to the Royal Arms which is a pub in the toughest quarter of the town; they tell me how to go.

I put my luggage bag in my pocket, for some reason I have clutched it throughout; and I go. Way I feel I do not go to the hotel straight off, I walk around a bit. I have been into Town of course shopping with Dad, maybe twice a year, but I do not seem to know it so well as I thought.

Then I find I have got to the Royal Arms or just near it anyway.

It is now late evening the sky is black except for stars, planets, and meteors crashing through every minute or two. The town is lit up but there are few in the streets, quiet folk are home in another quarter the rest still fueling up indoors. Way I feel is some toughery would suit me fine to take my mind off, because taming kors was my idea in the first place. Maybe I will get a chance to try out that judo trick I learned from Buffalo Cole.

So I slip through the noise-valve doors one after another and go into the pub.

Brother.

The noise trap is efficient all right, outdoors no more than a mutter so there is a real wallop inside. Every idea in my head is knocked clean out of it, even the thought I might go away. Among other things are three juke boxes in three corners going full blast and I cannot hear them at all.

Part of the decibels come from just conversation, part is encouragement to a three-way fight in the middle of the floor. I am still gaping when two of the parties gang up on the third and toss him all the way to the door. I dodge just in time, he rebounds off the inner valve and falls right at my feet.

Everyone turns and sees me, and the juke boxes all become audible at once.

I go down on my knees to see if the character I have just missed meeting is still breathing or not. His pulse is going all right but his face is a poor color wherever blood lets me see, I yell for water but competing with the juke boxes get nowhere. I am taking breath to try again when someone turns them off at the main, silence comes down like cotton-wool.

I ask for water in a whisper, someone brings it and tries to take me away.

I find I am clinging to the guy yelling He is hurt he is hurt! There is blood balling in little drops on my evercleans and smeared over my hands, I am trying to wipe it off with a disposable; not suited to this of course it crushes and goes away to dust and then the cotton-wool feeling in my ears spreads elsewhere.

Then I am lying on my back with water running down my chin and a

211

sensation of hush all round.

I try to sit up and something stops me. Someone murmurs soft nothings that fail to make sense.

I keep quiet till I have it sorted and then I figure I have fainted clean away.

Me, Lizzie Lee.

I sit up and find I am on a couch in a sort of backroom and there are faces all round. Half of them seem knocked out of shape or with knobs on, bashed recently or previous.

The faces all jostle and I hear they are telling those behind She is sitting up! and the glad news getting passed along.

Someone pushes through the faces carrying a tray with food for six, I deduce they think I fainted from hunger or something.

I would put them right on this when I realize the feeling in my middle is because I last ate ten hours ago.

I weigh in and they appear pleased by this.

So I feel an explanation is owed and I tell them my Dad is in hospital with an accident, you would not think they could get so upset about a perfect stranger, sure this will not last but it is genuine feeling just now for all that.

There is more buzzing and a kind of rustle and I find they are taking up a collection.

I am horrified, I cry No, no, they are very kind but I truly cannot accept.

And they think this is proper pride or something, they start to mutter again and someone says Well then no need to worry, Knotty will give me a job as long as I need it, won't he? Knotty is in the crowd somewhere, seems he is keeper of this pub. His seems to agree and I figure out he'd better.

I do not see why they are so sure I am indigent until I happen to glance down. I am still in my work evercleans I was wearing when Dad got hurt; also it breaks on me suddenly this is the worst quarter of the town no girl would come here if she could afford to be elsewhere, even then not into the Royal Arms unless full of sweet innocence or something.

And I cannot speak.

When a bunch of strangers are mooning over your problems because you are a poor young thing you cannot tell them you walked in to look for a fight.

Truly, I could swear out loud.

In two shakes of a vibrator they have it fixed, Knotty will give me a job as long as I need one and I can have a room above the pub and at least fifty husky miners have sworn a personal guarantee no one within miles will lift a finger in any way I could not wish.

So what can I do?

I thank them and I walk out into the bar and when I get there I find the laws of human nature are not wholly suspended, there is a fight going on.

My bodyguard behind me gives a concerted roar and the fight stops and they look sheepish at me.

It is so clear they expect me to look shocked and sorrowful that I cannot help it, this is just what I do.

I ask the cause of the fight and they shuffle and the bigger one says he is very sorry and would like to apologize Miss.

It turns out he has come in since I arrived and wishes to get drunk with the minimum delay, the assembled party tell him Damsel in distress back of the bar and he says to hell with that, she is probably faking it anyway; he sees this was error and regrets it very much.

And I have to make a production over forgiveness, he will never believe me unless I do.

So I am stuck.

You think all this will wear off in a day or two? Brother, so do I. At first, that is. But it does not. I have reformed the place overnight.

I begin to think getting drunk each night and working it off by fighting are not really their personal choice, all they need is a little stimulus to snap them out of it; such as the influence of a good woman maybe and looks like I am elected.

I get so busy listening to assorted troubles and soothing fights before they come to the boil, apart from any job Knotty can give me such as putting glasses in the washer and dishing the drinks, I hardly have time to think about Dad except at the hospital each day.

He is dead out for seven days just like they said, while the blood clots get loose from his brain; also they set his ribs and arm and tack up things inside. My miner friends all cheer me up they say This is a good hospital and tell me all the times they have been put together again themselves, I say Oh and Ah so often I am quite tired it seems to please them anyway.

Then Dad comes awake.

He does not do it while I am there of course, but I am allowed to sit with him two hours the day after, they have shifted him out of the tank into a proper bed, and taken the plumbing away. Towards the end while I am there he comes round and says Hello Liz how have you been?

And I want to cry but I am damned if I will, I say I am fine. And he is already asleep again.

I ring home like I do every day. Charlie is out so I leave a message, then I go back to the pub. I feel truly I could sing all the way, I do not notice until Knotty says so that I am singing anyway. Knotty is in a sour mood but when I tell him about Dad he fetches out half a smile and says will I be leaving then?

I say No Dad has another one month and twenty-one days in hospital to go.

At this his face falls under three gravities and he says All very well for me. I say why? can he not afford to pay me?

He says what troubles him is the pub. Since I came liquor drinking is down two-fifths, if anybody starts to get drunk the rest stop him in case something occurs to sully my pure girlish mind, it becomes clear that to Knotty this sobriety is not pleasing at all.

Well it is far from being my wish either, at least I think that at first then I think again Do I really want my pals back to the old routine drunk every night dead drunk Friday to Monday? This do-gooding is insidious stuff.

I go on thinking about it when I have time, this is not often because the boys are so pleased to hear Dad is better they allow each other to get quite lit, I have to head off one row after another.

I begin to think anyway this situation cannot last long, the pressure is building up visibly something is going to blow they need outlets for aggression and getting none just now. Also I must do something for

Knotty. I could tell him Dad will pay back his losses but Knotty's head is solid bone; if I once got into it I am not a dear little down-and-out, he would let it out again at the diagrammatic wrong time.

Things have got to end but they have got to end tidy with no hard feelings, I shall need help for this.

I got out that night as soon as Knotty is in bed and get to a public visiphone. I dial home, never mind it is one in the morning I want Uncle Charlie.

What I get is Buffalo Cole looking sleepy, he lets out the yip he learned from an old stereo and asks where I am and where I have been so long and so loud I cannot tell him for quite a while.

Then he tells me Charlie is here in Town.

He has assumed I am staying at the Hospital. They phoned today as usual, he asked for me and found I was somewhere on my own; he busted into Town straight off like a kor calf into a cornfield and been hunting for me all over tearing out hair in bunches.

He is staying with a friend the far side of Town, I ring.

Brother.

Now he has found me he has no wish to talk to me I am to stay in the visiphone booth and not move till called for well I suppose can wiggle my ears if I like.

Charlie arrives in a heli four minutes later and mad enough to burn helium, he gives me the kind of character my pals sketch for each other when I am not supposed to be by.

He is not interested in excuses, he will get me out of whatever mess I am in for my father's sake; I will come to a bad end someday but I can have the grace to keep it till the old man is on his feet again. I have learned something these last few days, I do not yell back. I say I have been very foolish and I need advice.

Do not think this fools him but he is taken aback slightly. I get something said before he recovers and in the end I tell the whole thing hardly interrupted at all.

At the end he gives me a peculiar look like when one of his hatcharia gave birth to a parrot and says nothing at all.

I say Look Charlie my idea is this; he says Liz your ideas are the start of this trouble in the first place, you have been getting ideas ever since I knew them and every one worse than the one before, just let me think about this.

Then he says Well if you leave without explanations I suppose we will have these desperate characters hunting for you all over Town and if the truth gets out there will be a rumpus because of that, I guess you better go back there for tonight anyway, how are you going to get back in?

I say I have a key, does he think I crawled out of the window? From his look I rather gather he does. Men are children at heart.

All the same I go back quietly and sleep like a tombstone.

In the morning I see Charlie at the hospital and he says he has an idea but seems he prefers to sit on it and see how will it hatch, I do not tell him what I think of this.

Then Dad wakes and says a few words and things look brighter and afterwards Charlie swears he has a real idea how I can get out of this without any hurt feelings, it just needs a bit more work on it.

I go back to the Arms thinking my troubles are half over, Brother what error, this is where they begin.

That evening I am chinning to some types who cut up yesterday, I tell them how shocked I am how surprised how sad because they have backslid, they are always sure I feel like this. If I do not say it they get upset because they suppose my feelings too deep for words; I can do this sort of thing no hands now.

Just the same it takes some concentration, when the stranger comes in I hardly notice him at all.

He is a tall chap in the usual evercleans with filter mask over his shoulder, all that is strange is I have not seen him before, men stick to their own pubs as a rule.

He slides into a corner and swaps words with the regulars and I forget him altogether

The clock strikes twelve, two hours to midnight closing, enter a tall dark stranger.

Short hair and big shoulders and the face that launched the campaign for Great Outdoors Shampoo, maybe twenty-two years old, he takes a

216

quick look round and I guess he does not think much of the place.

Well he should have seen it a week ago, now there is only one single juke box going and people are just chatting over drinks, not a fight in the place.

He comes up to the bar and taps someone on the shoulder to make way; try touching anyone a fortnight back and stand well clear! This time the fellow stops his fist before it goes six inches and then moves over an inch or two and I am face to face with the stranger over the gap.

He looks at me and registers more surprise than I thought his face could hold, I say What are you drinking sir?

He swallows hard and says Beer please; something is displeasing him like mad but I cannot see how it is me.

I give him his beer and he gives me an unloving look and moves away, he horns in on one of the gatherings and starts to chat.

I am busy but I keep an eye on him and it seems to me the chat is getting too emphatic for health, I beckon over a miner called Dogface and ask what goes on.

He says That character been annoying you Liz? I say No is he annoying anyone else? Dogface says he asks too damn many questions someone will paste him any minute now.

I sign for another miner called Swede, these two are the steadiest around; I say Ride herd on this character and keep him out of trouble.

They say How? I say get into conversation and stop him talking to anyone who is prone to get mad.

They look doubtful so I tell them to talk to him, he is asking questions well tell him answers, tell him about life on Excenus you can see he is a fresh-out Terrie, tell him about mining; that will be instructive for him.

Next time I look Dogface and Swede are one on each side of him talking away, the other types have all drifted off.

The stranger stays for an hour and they stick by him all the while, when he leaves no one has laid a finger on him, I have done a good deed this day. Dogface and Swede say they never knew they had so much to talk about, just the same the stranger did not look grateful to me.

217

Next day I go to the hospital as usual wondering if Charlie has hatched his idea.

Halfway there I feel eyes on the back of my neck. I look round and there he is again, the tall dark stranger I mean.

He strides up and says he wants to speak to me.

His tone is such that I think of Buffalo's judo trick but he looks the type to brush it off with a careless reflex, I could wish there were more people around.

I say What about?

He says I know damned well what about, this is poaching and he will not stand for it, he will complain to something I do not catch.

I say he must be thinking of somebody else.

He sizzles behind his teeth and says I need not think I can get out of it by playing innocent because he will be able to trace me perfectly well. I obviously come from that establishment for muddy minded morons Pananthropic Institute of Social Research; everybody knows Excenus is Russett's fieldwork place and no other school would crash it, let alone homing in on a practical that way.

Furthermore the dodge I am using was corny in the Ark of earlier.

I am much perplexed but more angry and ask what he is proposing to do.

He says Don't worry I will find out later, I guess he does not know either; but before I can say so he goes striding away.

I walk on getting madder as I go, this mystery on top of everything else is enough to drive me round the fourth dimension, and he will catch on to his mistake and I shall never hear it explained; however when I arrive I forget him because Dad is awake and fit for talking to.

Several times I wonder Shall I tell him the whole thing? but he is still sick, this is no time to tell him I am serving in a bar in the toughest part of the town.

We talk quietly about the farm and plans for next year and things we did when I was little, all of a sudden I want to cry.

Then Charlie comes. One visitor at a time I have to go, Charlie needs some instructions about the farm.

I think I will go out and walk around, I do not like waiting in the hospital they think women belong some other place. I am halfway down

218

the outside steps when there is a shadow over me and a voice says Excuse me, Miss Lee?

I turn and stare.

Brother what is this, are they making a stereo on Excenus; this is the handsomest man I ever came across. He makes the one this morning look like a credit for twenty all from one mold, I am certain I never saw him before.

He says We met last night though that was hardly an introduction, he is glad of an excuse to make my acquaintance now.

I think No this cannot be, yes it is, this is the gink I hardly noticed last night; same face same voice same hands and I never looked at him twice, how in Space is it done?

Brother, he called me Miss Lee!

I say there must be some mistake and turn towards the hospital again.

He says the hospital clerk told him my name and he saw me come out of the Royal Arms this morning.

Sing Hey for the life of a hunted fawn, now I am good and mad, just crazy. He says he thinks a talk would be mutually profitable, what I think is something quite different and I say it out loud. He has a way of doing things with his eyebrows to look amused, men have been killed for less.

He says What would the clientele of the Royal Arms think of that?

I say what the hell is that to him?

He says he will be delighted to explain if I will give him the opportunity but this is hardly a suitable place to talk.

There are no places suitable and I tell him so.

He says he has a helicar there, if I would care to drive it anywhere I like he will give me the key.

I begin to see what will happen if this specimen opens his face to Knotty and Co; I must know what his game is; I say O.K.

We are just getting into the heli when the air is sundered, Liz! here is Uncle Charlie and my reputation in pieces again.

He charges across and my companion says Mr. Blair? which is Charlie's name though I hardly remember, and he hands over a card with a name and some words on it.

Charlie reads it and looks baffled but not mad any longer.

I sneak a look at it, it says D. J. M'Clare and a string of initials, Russett Interplanetary College of Humanities, Earth, it has Department of Cultural Engineering in little letters lower down.

Charlie says Liz what in Space are you doing now?

M'Clare says he has to make Miss Lee a rather complicated apology, this being no place to do which he has suggested a ride, it will be much better if Mr. Blair will come along too.

I do not know how it is done but ten seconds later Charlie is inviting him for a drink to the house where he is staying and I am tagging along behind.

The house is close to the hospital and well to do all right the air is humidified right through. I choose lemonade to drink, I never cared for alcohol much and I am more tired of the smell; when Charlie has done bustling with drinks M'Clare begins.

He says he understands Miss Lee had an encounter this morning with his pupil Douglas Laydon.

I say Great whirling nebulae not the lunatic who called me a poacher? He says Very likely, Laydon came here to do a practical test and finding I had anticipated him was somewhat upset.

He explains that students in Cultural Engineering have a fieldwork test after two years, this one had to make a survey of the principal factors leading to violence and try out short-term methods for abating same in a selected portion of the community on Excenus 23 namely the Royal Arms pub.

M'Clare says Excenus 23 is a very suitable spot for this kind of fieldwork, the social problems stay constant but the population turns over so fast they are not likely to catch on.

Charlie nods to show he gets this, I get it too and start to be angry; not just mad but real angry inside, I say You mean that dumbbell came out here to push people around just for the exercise?

He says fieldwork is an essential part of the course for a Cultural Engineering degree, I say Hell and hokum nobody has any right to interfere with people just for practice, he says Not everybody possesses your natural technique Miss Lee.

I say Look that is different, I was not trying to find out what makes people tick then fiddle with the springs and think I done something clever.

Charlie says Shut up Liz.

This man does not believe me, well I did not start this on purpose but now I remember all the times I listened to someone tell me his troubles and thought What a good girl am I to listen to this poor sucker, how wise how clever how well I understand; I do not like thinking of this.

Then I find Charlie has started to tell M'Clare the whole thing.

I will say for Charlie he tells it pretty fair, he does understand why I cannot just let my pals find out I have fooled them, whatever he may have said; but why does he want to tell it to this character, who will not see it at all?

Then he says Well, Professor, if I understand what Cultural Engineering stands for this is a problem right in your line, I would very much welcome advice.

M'Clare says nothing and Charlie says it is a very minor matter of course, M'Clare says There he does not agree.

He says if these tough types caught on that their dear little down-and-out was really rich it would not stop at personal unpleasantness, the whole relation between the mining and farming communities might well be upset.

I would like to sneer but cannot because it is perfectly true, Dad is pretty rich and has a big effect on local affairs; if the miners think his daughter been slumming around making fools of them no knowing what comes after.

M'Clare says However it should be easy enough to fix things so no one can catch on.

Charlie says it is not so simple, Liz has to be got away where no one will chase after her; fortunately very few people in Town are in a position to recognize her, but where can she go now.

I say Look that is easy give me a job on the farm.

Charlie says Suppose they take a fancy to visit you, you think Buffalo Cole is going to remember you are the hired help came there last Tuesday? That is the one place you can be certain sure someone will give you away.

Besides just at present they know your name but have not connected it with Farmer Lee. No, Liz we have to get you a job as companion or something to someone here in Town, a respectable woman the miners will keep right away from.

I say Charlie there are maybe three respectable women in Town; if you park me on one all my pals will come round to make sure I have not hired into a brothel by mistake. How will your lady friend care for that? Charlie says What worries him is where to find a woman anyone could believe had voluntarily saddled herself with a hellcat like me.

M'Clare makes a little cough and Charlie says What does he think?

M'Clare says our solutions are too prosaic and too partial, this is a classic example of the fauntleroy situation and should be worked out as such.

I say What the hell is a fauntleroy?

He says this means a situation in which one younger and apparently weaker person exerts influence over a group of adults by appealing to their protective instincts.

Appeal hell! he says. Unintentionally, no doubt. He says the situation can only be properly resolved if the subject appears to be in no further need of protection against the trouble, whatever it may be; in this case financial.

Charlie says You mean we should tell them Liz has come into money and moved to a hotel?

M'Clare says that again would be only a partial solution, he thinks it would be better if Little Orphan Liz and her sick father were rescued by a Rich Uncle arriving next Wednesday from Earth.

Charlie says Why is Liz short of money if she has a rich uncle ready to assist? M'Clare says he is also a long-lost uncle only recently made his pile and just managed to trace the one remaining relative he has looked for ever since.

I say Why is this better than he died and left me the cash? He says Money for nothing morally unsatisfactory and a bad ending, this way you give something in return; also your lonely uncle can take you and your father straight off to Earth and leave nothing for anyone to ask questions about.

I do not believe anyone will swallow this hunk of cereal, too convenient all round.

According to M'Clare that does not matter, it is the right kind of improbable event for this situation. My pals will think it quite right and proper for their little ray of sunshine to be snatched up into unearned affluence and cheer the declining years of her rich relative and bring him together with his estranged brother-in-law; right ending to the situation. Statistical probability irrelevant to the workings of Destiny.

Charlie says Where will we find an uncle? He himself is too well known, to hire an actor means going off the planet. M'Clare says as it happens he has to leave the planet this afternoon and will be returning next Wednesday himself.

Charlie says You mean you'd do it? That's really wonderful what do you say Liz? What I want to say is, I will not have this cultural cork-screw add himself to my family, but the lemonade tangles in my epiglottis; people have died that way but Do they care?

M'Clare says of course he must get Mr. Lee's permission for this masquerade; I just thought of that one now I am left with nothing to say except Hellanhokum I ought to be back at the bar.

I do not trust M'Clare one Angstrom I could see he was thinking of something else the whole time, probably What interesting opportunities for fieldwork if the whole thing got given away; if Dad is really over his concussion he will put a stopper on the whole thing.

Does he hell!

Charlie takes M'Clare along, never mind visiting hours are over, they spill the whole thing to Dad before the professor catches his ship.

Well I will say they made a job of it. When I go along in the morning absolutely no bites in the furniture, Dad is still weakened of course.

He says Liz, girl, you are as crazy as a kor-calf, you got as much sense as a shorted servo, the moment I take my eye off you you stir up more trouble than a barrel of hooch on a dry planet. It is a long time since I was surprised at anything you do; here he goes off into ancient history not relevant to this affair.

This business, he says, has put the triple tungsten-plated tin top on it, even you must know what could have happened to you going into a place like that, Liz girl how could you do such a thing?

I say Dad I know it was crazy but you have it all wrong, miners may be tough but those types were real good to me.

He says Liz your capacity to fall on your feet is what scares me the worst of all, one of these days the probabilities will catch up with you all in one go. Look at this Professor M'Clare probably the one man in the Universe would know how to get you out of this with no one catching on, and he turns up here and now.

Well I was all set to get out myself with Charlie helping, but it seems to soothe Dad to think about M'Clare so I let him. That smoothy put himself over all right.

It develops where he has gone is Magnus 9 in the next system to let an examinee loose on some suckers there; he has left a list of instructions with Charlie, and Dad says I am to order myself according to these and not dare to breathe unless so directed.

They are all about what I am to do and say, Charlie stands over me while I learn them by heart, he does not seem to trust me but Hellanall does he think I want to fluff in the middle of a script like this?

Tuesday evening is when the scene starts, my pals ask What is on my mind they hope my old man is not worse is he?

I say I have had a message from a ship just coming within communicator distance and is landing tomorrow. I am to meet someone, whose name got scrambled, at the Space Gate at five-thirty A.M.; I cannot think who this can be it worries me a little Dad has so many troubles already.

At this my pals look grim and say If it is debts I can count on them and if it is anything else I can still count on them, I feel ashamed again.

Five-thirty is a horrible time to start. I am yawning and chilled through, the night breeze is still up and dust creeping in among the long pylon shadows in little puffed whirlwinds; the three ships on the field got their hatches down and goods stacked round and look broken and untidy.

First a little black dot in the sky then bigger and bigger covering more and more stars, it does not seem to come nearer but only to

224

spread, then suddenly a great bulging thing with light modeling its under side and right over head, I want to duck.

It swings across a little to the nearest pylons. They jerk and the arms come up with a clang, reaching after the ship. There is a flash and bang as they make contact just under the gallery where it bulges, then a long slow glide as they fold and she comes down into place like a grasshopper folding its legs.

I find my breathing hitched up, I take a deep lungful of cold morning dust and start coughing.

My pals rally round and pat me on the back.

I thought there were only three present but there seem to be more, I cannot see the passengers get off until half are into the Gate, M'Clare is not in sight hell he did not see me perhaps he has ditched me.

The speaker system makes with a crack like splitting rocks and says Will Miss Lee believed to be somewhere around the Gate come to the manager's office at once please?

I take another deep breath more carefully.

My pals seem to think it is sinister, I now have seven on the premises and they wish to come too. In the end they elect Swede and Dogface bodyguards and the rest wait outside.

I cannot remember one single word I ought to say.

In the office is a man in uniform and another one not, I guess I look blank but not as blank as I feel the human face could hardly, how has he done it this time?

It was several seconds before I recognized him at all. He looks older and kind of worn you would guess he had a hardish life and certainly not cultured at all.

I say I was called for, my name is Lee.

He says slowly, Yes, he thinks he would have known me,

I am very like my mother, and he calls me Elizabeth.

Every word is clean out of my head, fortunately my pals take over and wish to know how come?

M'Clare looks at them with a frown and says neither of them is James Lee, surely?

I say No they are friends of mine, does he mean he is my mother's brother because I thought he was dead?

225

This is not the right place for that the script is gone to the Coalsack already.

M'Clare says Yes he really is John M'Clare, he brings out papers to prove it. My friends give them the once over several times and seem to be satisfied, then they want to know sternly Why had he not helped us before?

M'Clare brings out letters from a tracing firm that cover two years and a bit, I will say he is a worker he has vamped all this stuff in three days with other things to do, I suppose Cultural Engineering calls for forgery once in a while.

My pals seem satisfied.

I say Why was he looking for us seeing he and Dad never got along? This is the script as originally laid down.

M'Clare alters the next bit ad lib and I don't take it in but it goes over with my pals all right, they tell him all about Dad's accident which they think happened prospecting, and about me and the bar; just then in comes M'Clare's acquaintance well to do in business locally meaning Uncle Charlie, apologizing for being late though M'Clare told him how late to be.

My pals shuffle and say Well Miss Lee you will not want us now.

I say What is this Miss Lee stuff you have been calling me Lizzie for weeks. I had to tell them my name or they will call me Bubbles or something.

M'Clare says he has a great deal to discuss with his niece and Dad, not to mention Charlie, but he wants to hear all about my doings and I will want to tell all my friends; maybe if he calls round to the Royal Arms in the evening they will be there?

They shuffle but seem gratified, they go.

Charlie sits down and the manager goes and Charlie says *Whew!* I sit down and do not say anything at all.

Well Knotty will be pleased to get rid of me that is one life brightened anyway.

I do not want another day like that one, six hours doing nothing in a hotel. I see Dad about five minutes, he uses up the rest of visitor's time with M'Clare or Charlie in and me out, then Charlie flies back home to get something or other and I want to go too, I want to go home! I will never come to this town again, I can't anyway until my pals have all left the planet. I wish all this lying were over.

Evening M'Clare and I go out to the bar.

Knotty has had a letter from me all about it and of course everyone knows, minute we get inside the door I see everybody is worked up and ready to fight at the drop of a hint, fauntleroy situation or not if they think my rich uncle is trying to snoot them all the trouble missed during the last fortnight will occur at one go.

Then M'Clare spots Dogface and Swede at the back of the crowd and says Hello, five minutes later it is drinks all round and everything Jo-block smooth, I could not have done it better myself.

Then he is making a speech.

It is all about Kindness to dumb creatures meaning me, I do not listen but watch the faces, judging by them he is going good. I hear the last words, something about Now he has found his niece and her father he does not want to lose sight of them and his brother-in-law has consented the whole family goes back to Earth in two days' time.

It occurs to me suddenly How am I going to get off the ship? They have found some sick cuss wants to get to Earth and will play my Dad ten minutes to get a free passage, but my pals are bound to turn up to see me off how am I to slip away?

Then I stop thinking because Dogface says slowly So this is the end, hey Liz?

And someone else says Well it was good while it lasted.

And I cry, I put my head down on the table among the drinks and cry like hell, because I am deceitful and they are kind to me and I wish I could tell the truth for a change.

Someone pats me on the back and shoves a disposable into my hand, I think it is one of my pals till I smell it, nobody bought this on Excenus! I am so surprised I wad it up and it goes to dust so I have to stop crying right away.

I even manage to say Good-by and I will never forget them. They say they will never forget me.

We say about ten thousand good-byes and go.

Next day the hospital says Dad overtired, they have sedated him, seems he was half the night talking to M'Clare and Charlie what the hell were they thinking of to let him? My uncle will call for me. I expect Charlie what I get is M'Clare.

We are to go shopping buying some clothes for me to wear on Earth, it seems to me this is carrying realism too far but I do not want any more time in the hotel with nothing to do.

Fortunately the tailoring clerk does not know me, we have a machine out at the farm; he takes a matrix and slaps up about ten suits and dresses; they will be no use here at all, no place for condensers or canteen I cannot even give them away.

However I am not bothered so much about that, M'Clare is all the time trying to get me to talk, he says for instance Have I ever thought about going to College? I say Sure, I count my blessings now and then.

We are somehow on the subject of education and what teaching have I had so far? I say Usual machines and reels, I want to get off this so I start to talk about Excenus he cannot compete there. I tell him about our manners, customs, morals, finance, farming, geography, geology, mining of areopagite, I am instructive right back to the hotel I hope now he has had enough of it.

In the evening they let me see Dad.

They say You really ought not to be allowed in he has had his quota of visitors today already, I say Who? but need I ask, it was Mr. M'Clare.

The nurse says I am allowed to see Dad because he refuses to go to sleep until he has told me something, but I must be careful not to argue it will retard his recovery if he gets excited again.

Dad is dead white and breathing noisy but full of spirit, the nurse says You may have five minutes and Dad says No-one is rationing his time for him when he is ready he will ring. The nurse is a sturdy six footer and Dad is five foot four, they glare it out. Dad wins in the end.

Well I intend to keep it down to five minutes myself, I say Hello Dad what cooks?

He says Lizzie girl what do you think of this M'Clare?

I think quite a number of things but I say He is very clever I think.

Dad says Sure he is clever, Professor at a big college on Earth gets students from all the planets in the known volume, I been talking to him

228

and he says you have a flair.

I say Huh?

Dad says I have a flair for this cultural engineering business, Professor M'Clare told him so.

I say Well I promised you already I will keep it under control in future.

Dad starts to go red and I say Look two minutes gone already, what did you want to tell me? say it straight, and he says Going to send you to College, girl.

I say What!

Dad says Liz, Excenus is no place for a young girl all her life. Time you seen some other worlds and I cannot leave the farm and got no one have an eye to you, now M'Clare says he will get you into this College and that is just what I need.

I say But—!

Dad says They got schools on Earth for kids like you, been on an outback planet or education restricted other ways, they are called Prelim Schools; well you got the Rudiments already; M'Clare says after three months Prelim you should be fit to get into Russett College of Humanities, he will act as your official guardian while on Earth. Do not argue with me Liz!

The nurse comes back and says I must go in thirty seconds not more, Dad is gray in the face and looks fit to come to pieces, I say All right Dad of course you know best.

He says Kiss me Lizzie, and good-by.

Then the nurse chases me Out.

This is M'Clare's doing playing on Dad when he is mixed in the head, he knows damned well this thing is impossible if he were only in his right mind. I go tearing back to the hotel to look for M'Clare.

I find he is out.

I sit there seething one hour twenty-seven minutes until he comes in. I say I have to speak to him right now.

I do not know if he is looking bored or amused but it is an expression should be wiped off with rag, he says Certainly, can it wait till we reach his room?

229

We get there and I say Look what is this nonsense you have talked Dad into about taking me to some College on Earth or something? Because it is straight out crazy and if Dad were right in the head he would know.

M'Clare sits down and says, "Really, Lysistrata, what a spoiled young woman you are."

Who the hell told him, that name is the one thing I really do hold against Dad.

M'Clare goes on that he did not understand at first why my father refused to have me told about the scheme until it was all fixed, but he evidently knew the best way to avoid a lot of fuss.

I say I am not going to leave Excenus.

M'Clare says I cannot possibly avoid leaving Excenus I have got to go on the ship tomorrow haven't I?

I say they can send me back by lifeship, he says it is far too late to arrange that now.

I say then I will come back from the first stop on the way.

He says he is officially my guardian from the moment we leave the planet and he cannot allow me to travel alone, reason for all this rush is so he can see me to College himself, What is the matter with me don't I want to see the World anyway?

Sure, some time, but I don't have to go to College for that.

M'Clare says that is my mistake, Earth had such a rush of sightseers from the Out Planets entrance not permitted anymore except on business, only way I can get there is as a student except I might marry an Earthman some day, I say Hell I would rather go to College than that.

Just the same when I have had enough of it I am coming straight back home.

M'Clare says I will do no such thing.

Great whirling nebulae he cannot keep me on Earth if I want to go! he says On the contrary he has no power to do anything else, my father appointed him my guardian on condition I was to do a four-year course at Russett. Of course if I am determined to return to Excenus home and Dad rather than make the effort to adjust myself to an environment where I have not got everyone securely under my thumb there is an easy way out, I have to take a Prelim test in three months and if I fail to make it no power on Earth could get me into Russett, and he would have to send me back home.

We have to start early in the morning so Good night.

I go to my room, if there was anything I could bite holes in that is what I would do.

I will pass that exam if it takes twenty-eight hours a day, no this is to be on Earth well all the time that they have; I will get into M'Clare's class and make him Sorry he interfered with me.

What does he think I am? Dad too, he would have sent me to school long ago except we both knew I would never make the grade.

I am next thing to illiterate, that's why.

Oh, I can read in a way, I can pick up one word after another as they come up in the machine, but I cannot use it right; Dad is the same.

Dad used to think it was because he learned to use it too late, then when I was old enough to learn he found I was the same, some kink in the genes I suppose. Both of us, we cannot read with the machine any faster than an old-style book.

I did not know this was wrong until I was eleven. Dad hid the booklet came with the machine then one day I found it, part of it says like this:

"It has sometimes been suggested that the reading rate should be used as a measure of general intelligence. This is fallacious. The rate at which information can be absorbed, and therefore the rate at which words move across the viewer, is broadly correlated with some aspects of intelligence, but not with all. Mathematicians of genius tend to read slower than the average, and so do some creative artists. All that can safely be said is that people of normal intelligence have reading rates somewhere above five thousand and that it is exceptional for anyone to pass the ten thousand mark: the few who do so are usually people of genius in a narrowly specialized field."

My reading rate is so low the dial does not show, I work out with a stop watch it is eight hundred or thereabouts.

I go and ask Dad; it is the first time he let me see him feeling bad, it is all he can do to talk about it at all, he keeps telling me it is not so bad really he got on all right and he cannot read properly any more than me; he shows me those old books of his all over again.

After this we do not talk about it and I do not want to talk about it

231

now. Not to anyone at all.

That is the longest night I remember in my life, nineteen years of it.

In the morning we got to the Gate. My pals are there seeing me off, I do not cry because I have just found something makes me so mad I am just waiting to get in the ship and say what I think to M'Clare.

Then we go into the ship.

I cannot say anything now we have to strap in for takeoff. The feeling is like being in a swing stopped at the top of its beat. I cannot help waiting for it to come down, but after a bit I grasp we are up to stay and get unhitched.

In the corridor is a crewman, he says Hello miss not sick? I say Ought I to be?

He asks am I an old traveler? when I say First time up he makes clicking noises to say I am clever or lucky or both.

We are getting acquainted when I feel eyes on my backbone and there is M'Clare.

M'Clare says Hello, Lizzie not sick?

I say I do not have to pretend he is my uncle anymore and I prefer to be called Miss Lee. I will not have a person like him calling me Lizzie or in fact anything else, as of now we are not speaking anymore.

He raises an eyebrow and says Dear him. I start to go but he hooks a hand round my arm and says What is all this about?

I say I have been talking to that poor sucker come out of hospital and pretending to be my Dad. He is a heart case thinks he will be cured when he gets to Earth able to get around like anyone else, I know if he could be cured on Earth he could be cured on Excenus just as well, he will simply have to go on lying in bed and not even anyone he knows around, it is the dirtiest trick I ever knew.

Well he is not smiling now anyway.

He asks have I told the man he will not be cured, I say What does he take me for?

He says, I could answer that but I won't. You are quite right in thinking that it would do very little good to take a man with a diseased heart to Earth, but as it happens he will not be going there at all.

Close to Earth, M'Clare goes on, there is a body called the Moon

232

with approximately one-eighth the gravitational pull, there is a big sanatorium on it for men like this one, the rare case not curable by operation or drugs: and if he cannot live a quiet normal life he will at least be able to get out of bed and probably do some sort of job, this has been explained to him and he seems to think it good enough.

Sweet spirits of sawdust I have heard of that sanatorium before, why does the deck not open and swallow me up.

I say I am sorry, M'Clare says Why?

I say I am sorry I spoke without making sure of the facts.

I do not beg his pardon because I would not have it on a plate.

M'Clare says my uncle gave him a letter to deliver to me when the ship was under way, he shoves it in my hand and goes away.

It is written with Dad's styler, he fell on it during the accident and the L went wobbly, what it says is this.

Dear Liz,

About this College, I know you said I know best but did not mean it at all, just the same I reckon I do. You got to look at it another way. When they got the readers out at my old school and found I could not use them they reckoned I was no good for learning, but they were wrong. There is more to being educated than just books or you could sit and read them at home.

You and I are handicapped same way so we have to use our heads to get over it. All that is in books came out of somebody's head, well you and I just got to use our own instead of other people's. Of course there is facts but a lot of books use the same facts over and over, I found that when I started to study.

There is another thing for you, they told me at school I would never be any good for studying but I reckon I did all right.

It is high time you saw some other worlds than this one but I would not send you to College if I did not think you could get through. M'Clare says you have this Flair. We will look forward to seeing you four years from now, don't forget to write. Your loving father, J. X. Lee. P.S. I got a list of books you will want for Prelim School and Charlie had Information

Store copy them, they are in your cabin. J. X. Lee.

Poor old Dad.

Well I suppose I better give it a try, and what's more I better get on with it.

The reels are in my cabin, a whole box of them it will take me a year to get through, the sooner the quicker I suppose.

I jam one in sit down in the machine put on the blinkers and turn the switch.

There is the usual warmup, the words slide on slow at first then quicker then the thing goes click and settles down, the lines glide across just fast enough to keep pace with my eyes. I have picked myself something on Terrestrial Biology and Evolution, I realize suddenly I will be among it in a couple of weeks, lions and elephants and kangaroos; well I cannot stop to think now I have to beat that exam.

Most of those weeks I study like a drain.

They have cut day-length in the ship to twenty-four hours already. I have difficulty sleeping at first but I adjust in the end. Between readings I mooch round and talk to the crew, I am careful not to be the little ray of sunshine but we get on all right. I go and see the man with the sick heart a few times, he wants to know all about the Moon so I read up and relay as well as I can.

It sounds dull to me but compared to lying in bed I can see it is high-voltage thrill.

He thanks me every day for the whole voyage, I keep saying we only did it because we wanted someone to impersonate Dad. I think there ought to be ways for people like him to get enough money to go to the Moon how can you earn it lying in bed? he agrees with this but does not get ideas very much, I think I will write about it to Dad.

We stop at the Moon to put him down but no time to look round, M'Clare had to be back at Russett day before yesterday, I suppose he lost time picking me up; well I did not ask him to.

Dropping to Earth I am allowed maybe half a second in the control room to look at the screen, I say What is all that white stuff? they say It is raining down there.

More than half of what I see is water and more coming down!

When the Earthbound ask what interests me most on Earth I say All that water and nothing to pay; they do not know what it means getting water out of near-dry air, condensing breath out of doors, humidity suit to save sweat on a long haul: first time on Earth I go for a walk I get thirsty and nearly panic, on Excenus that would mean canteen given out rush fast for the nearest house.

They told me it was raining; all the same when we walk out of the ship I think at first they are washing the field from up above, I stand there with my mouth open to see; fortunately M'Clare is not looking and I come to quite soon.

Seems all this water has drawbacks too, round here they have to carry rainproofing instead of canteens.

I spend three days seeing sights and never turn on a book.

Prelim School.

Worst is, I do not have a reader of my own now, only reading rooms and I have to keep it private that I read more than two hours a day or someone will catch on and I will be Out before I have a chance to try if what Dad says will work out.

There is more to teaching than books for one thing Class Debates, these are new to me of course but so they are to the others and these I can take. Man to man with my tutor at least I can make him laugh, he says The rugged unpunctuated simplicity of my style of writing is not suited to academic topics even when leavened with polysyllables end of quote, but it is all these books are getting me down.

In the end I get a system, I read the longest reel on each topic and then the other one the author doesn't like, that way I get both sides to the question.

Three months and the exam; afterwards I keep remembering all the things I should have said till I take a twenty-four-hour pill and go to bed till the marking is over.

I wake up and comes a little blue ticket to say I am Through, please report to Russett College in three days for term to begin.

Well, what am I grinning about?

All this means is four years more of the same and M'Clare too added on.

I go for a walk in the rain to cool off but I keep on grinning just the same.

It comes to me as a notion I may not get through Russett term without telling M'Clare all about himself, so I get round and see as much of Earth as I can; more variety than at home.

So then three days are up and here I am in Russett entrance hall with more people than I ever saw in my life at one time.

There are these speaker mechs which are such a feature of Terrestrial life all round the room. One starts up in the usual muted roar like a spacer at a funeral, it says All students for Cultural Engineering Year One gather round please.

This means me.

Cultural Engineering is not a big department, only fifty of us coagulated round this mech but like I said they come all kinds, there is one I see projecting above the throng so brunet he is nearly purple, not just the hair but all over. What is the matter with him he looks like the longest streak of sorrow I ever did see.

Well there are other ways to get pushed into this place than through basic urges thalamic or otherwise, just look at me.

The mech starts again and we are all hanging on what drops from its diaphragm, it says we are to File along corridor G to Room 31 alpha and there take the desk allotted by the monitor and no other.

This we do; even by Terrie standards it is a long hike for indoors.

I wonder what is a monitor, one of these mechs without which the Earthbound cannot tell which way is tomorrow? Then we are stopped and sounds of argument float back from ahead.

That settles it, Terries do not argue with mechs and I am conditioned already, it is a way to get no place at all: there is someone human dealing with the line.

We go forward in little jerks till I can hear, it is one of those Terrie voices always sound like they are done on purpose to me.

We come round the comer to a door and I can see, this Monitor is indeed human or at least so classified.

Here we go, it is only me this could happen to.

Each person says a name and the monitor repeats it to the kind of

236

box he carries and this lights up with figures on it. I wonder why the box needs a human along and then I remember, one hundred twenty-four different planets and accents to match. I guess this is one point where Man can be a real help to Machine.

I am glad I saw him before he saw me: I tell him Lee, L. and he looks at me in a bored way and then does a double take and drops the thing.

I pick it up and say Lee, L. in cultivated tones, it lights up just the same, Q8 which means the desk where I have to sit.

The desks are in pairs. When I track Q8 to its lair Q7 is empty, I sit and wonder what the gremlins will send me by way of a partner.

I do not wait long. Here she comes, tall and dark and looks like she had brains right down her spinal column, she will have one of those done-on-purpose voices in which I will hear much good advice when the ice breaks in a month or so. Brother this is no place for me.

She looks straight past my shoulder and does not utter while she is sitting down.

I cannot see her badge which is on the other side. She has what looks to me like a genuine imitation korhide pouch and is taking styler and block out of it, then she looks at me sideways and suddenly lights up all over with a grin like Uncle Charlie's, saying as follows, "Why, are you Lizzie Lee?"

I do not switch reactions fast enough, I hear my voice say coldly that my name is Lee, certainly.

She looks like she stubbed her toe. I realize suddenly she is just a kid, maybe a year younger than I am, and feeling shy. I say quick that I make people call me Lizzie because my real name is too awful to mention.

She lights up again and says So is hers, let us found a Society for the Prevention of Parents or something.

Her brooch says B Laydon, she says her first name will not even abbreviate so people here got to call her just B.

I am just round to wondering where she heard my name when she says That stuffed singlet in the doorway is of course her big brother Douglas and she has been wanting to meet me ever since.

Here Big Brother Douglas puts the box under his arm and fades gently away, the big doors behind the rostrum slide open as the clock turns to fourteen hours and Drums and Trumpets here comes Mr. M'Clare.

B Laydon whispers I think Professor M'Clare is wonderful do not you?

Brother.

I know M'Clare is going to deliver the Opening Address of the Year to Cultural Engineering students, it is my guess all such come out of the same can so I take time off for some thought.

Mostly I am trying to decide what to do. Prelim School was tough enough, so this will be tough[2], is it worth going through just to show M'Clare I can do it?

Sure it is but can I?

I go on thinking on these lines, such as what Dad will say if I want to give it up; I just about decided all I can do is wait and see when suddenly it is Time up, clock shows 1500 hours exactly just as the last word is spoken and Exit M'Clare.

Some thing I will say.

I look round and all the faces suggest I should maybe have listened after all.

B Laydon is wrapt like a parcel or something, then she catches me looking at her and wriggles slightly.

She says We have been allotted rooms together, sharing a study, do I mind it?

I assume this is because we come together in the alphabet and say Why should I?

She says Well. On the form it said Put down anyone you would like to room with and she wrote Miss Lee.

I ask did she do this because mine was the only name she knew or does she always do the opposite of what Big Brother Douglas tells her, she answers Both.

O.K. by me anyway.

Our rooms are halfway up the center tower, when we find them first thing I see is a little ticket in the delivery slot says Miss Lee call on Professor M'Clare at fifteen thirty please.

Guardian or no I have seen him not more than twice since landing which means not more than twice too often; still I go along ready to be polite.

He lets me sit opposite and looks thoughtful in a way I do not care for.

He says "Well, Miss Lee, you passed your qualifying exam."

I say Yes because this is true.

He says, it was a very economical performance exceeding the minimum level by two marks exactly.

Hells bells I did not know that, marks are not published, but I swallow hard and try to look as though I meant it that way.

M'Clare says the Admission Board are reluctant to take students who come so close to the borderline but they decided after some hesitation to accept me, as my Prelim Tutor considered that once I settled down as a student and made up my mind to do a little work I should get up to standard easily enough.

He says However from now on it is up to me, I will be examined on this term's work in twelve weeks' time and am expected to get at least ten percent above pass level which cannot be done by neglecting most of the work set, from now on there are no textbooks to rely on.

He presents these facts for my consideration, Good afternoon.

I swagger out feeling lower than sea level.

It is no use feeling sore, I took a lot of trouble to hide the fact that I did a lot of work for that exam, but I feel sore just the same.

The thing I want to do most is get one hundred percent marks in everything just to show him, I got a feeling this is just exactly how he meant me to react, because the more I think about it the more sure I am very few things happen by accident around M'Clare.

Take rooming, for instance.

I find very quickly that most people taking Cultural Engineering have not got the partners they put in for, this makes me wonder why B got what she wanted, meaning me.

Naturally the first thing I think of is she has been elected Good Influence, this makes me pretty cagey of course but after a day or two I see I must think again.

B always says she does not *look* for trouble. This may be true, she is very absentminded and at first I get the idea she just gets into a scrape through having her mind on something else at the time, but later I find she has Principles and these are at the back of it.

First time I hear about these is three nights after Opening, there is a knock at my bedroom window at maybe three hours. I am not properly awake and do not think to question how somebody can be there, seeing it is five hundred feet up the tower; I open the window and B falls inside.

I am just about ready to conclude I must be dreaming when B unstraps a small antigrav pack, mountaineering type, and says Somebody offered her the beastly thing as a secondhand bargain, she has been trying it out and it doesn't work.

Of course an antigrav cannot fail altogether. If the space-warp section could break down they would not be used for building the way they are. What has gone wrong is the phase-tuning arrangement and the thing can be either right on or right off but nothing in between.

B says she stepped off the top of the tower maybe an hour ago and got stuck straight away. She stepped a little too hard and got out of reach of the tower parapet. She only picked that night for it because there was no wind, so she had no chance of being blown back again. She just had to turn the antigrav off, a snatch at a time, and drop little by little until the slope of the tower caught up with her. Then she went on turning it snap on and snap off and kind of slithering down the stonework until she got to about the right floor, and then she had to claw halfway round the building.

B says she was just going to tap at the window above mine and then she saw that frightful Neo Pueblo statue Old Groucho is so proud of, then she came one farther down and found me but I certainly take plenty of waking.

Well I am wide awake now and I speak to her severely.

I say it is her career, her neck, neither of them mine, but she knows as well as I do jumping off the tower is the one thing in this University is utterly forbidden and no Ifs.

B says That's just because some idiots tried to jump in a high wind and got blown into the stonework.

I say Be that as it may if she had waked up Old Groucho—Professor of Interpenetration Mechanics ninety last week—she would have been expelled straight away, I add further she knows best if it would be worth it.

B says she is a practicing Pragmatist.

This turns out to mean she belongs to a bunch who say Rules are made mostly for conditions that exist only a little bit of the time, e.g. this one about the tower, B is quite right that is not dangerous except in a high wind—not if you have an antigrav I mean.

B says Pragmatists lead a Full Life because they have to make up their own minds when rules really apply and act accordingly, she says you do not lead a Full Life if you obey a lot of regulations when they are not necessary and it is a Principle of Pragmatism not to do this.

B says further it is because Terries go on and on obeying regulations unnecessarily that Outsiders think they are Sissy.

I say Huh?

B says it is not her fault she never had any proper adventures.

I remark If her idea of an adventure is to get hauled in front of the Dean why did she not go ahead and wake up Old Groucho instead of me?

B says the adventure part is just taking the risk, everybody ought to take some risks now and then and breaking rules is the only one available just now.

This causes me to gawp quite a bit, because Earth seems to me maybe fifteen times as dangerous as any planet I heard of so far.

There are risks on all planets, but mostly life is organized to avoid them. Like back home, the big risk is to get caught without water; there is only about one chance in one thousand for that to happen, but everybody wears humidity suits just the same.

On Earth you got a sample of about all the risks there are, mountains and deserts and floods and the sea and wild animals and poisons, now it occurs to me Terries could get rid of most of them if they really cared to try, but their idea of a nice vacation is to take as many as possible just for fun.

Well later on it occurs to me I should never have understood this about Terries but for talking to B, and I look round and find a lot of the

241

Terries got paired up with Outsiders for roommates and maybe this is why.

I say to B some of what I think about risks and it cheers her up for a moment, but she goes on getting into trouble on Pragmatic Principles just the same.

Me, I am in trouble too but not on principle.

The work at first turned out not so bad as I expected, which is not to say it was good.

Each week we have a different Director of Studies and we study a different Topic, with lectures and stereos and visits to museums and of course we read Books.

Further we have what are called Class Debates, kind of an argument with only one person speaking at a time and the Director to referee.

Terries say this last is kid stuff, the Outsiders met it mostly in Prelim School if then so they really study hard so as to do it good. Next thing you know the Terries are outclassed and trying hard to catch up, so a strenuous time is had by all, I begin to see there is a real thing between the two groups though no one likes to mention it out loud.

Class Debates I do not mind, I been used to arguing with Dad all my life, what gets me is Essays. We do one each week to sum up, and all my sums come wrong.

Reason for this is we get about fifteen books to read every week and are not allowed more than three hours a day with a reading machine, this is plenty for most people but I only get through a quarter of the stuff.

If you only know a quarter of the relevant facts you get things cockeyed and I can find no way round this.

My first essay comes back marked Some original ideas but more reference to actual examples needed, style wants polishing up.

The second has Original!! but what about the FACTS, style needs toning down.

More of the same.

After three weeks I am about ready to declare; then I find B gets assorted beefs written on her essays too and takes it for granted everybody does, she says Teachers always tell you what you do wrong not what you do right, this is Education.

I stick it some more.

I will say it is interesting all right. We are studying Influences on Cultural Trends, of which there are plenty some obvious some not.

Most of the class are looking forward to becoming Influences themselves, we have not been taught how to do this yet but everyone figures that comes next. It seems to me though that whatever you call it it comes down to pushing people around when they are not looking, and this is something I do not approve of more than halfway.

There is just one person in the class besides me does not seem to feel certain all is for the best. This is the dark fellow I noticed on Opening day, six foot six and built like a pencil. His name is Likofo Komom'baraze and he is a genuine African; they are rare at Russett because Africans look down on Applied studies, preferring everything Pure. Most of them study Mathematics and Literature and so on at their own universities or the Sorbonne or somewhere, seems he is the first ever to take Cultural Engineering and not so sure he likes it.

This is a bond between us and we become friendly in a kind of way, I find he is not so unhappy as he looks but Africans are proverbially melancholy according to B.

I say to Komo one time that I am worried about the exams, he looks astonished and says, But, Lizzie, you are so clever! turns out he thinks this because the things I say in class debates do not come out of any book he knows of, but it is encouraging just the same.

I need encouragement.

Seventh week of term the Director of Studies is M'Clare.

Maybe it makes not so much difference, but that week I do everything wrong. To start with I manage to put in twice the legitimate time reading for several days, I get through seven books and addle myself thoroughly. In Debates I cannot so much as open my mouth, I am thinking about that Essay all the time, I sit up nights writing it and then tear the stuff up. In the end I guess I just join up bits that I remember out of books and pass that in.

B thinks my behavior odd, but she has caught on now I do not regard M'Clare as the most wonderful thing that ever happened.

The last debate of the week comes after essays have been handed in, I try to pay attention but I am too tired. I notice Komo is trying to say something and stuttering quite a bit, but I do not take in what it is about.

Next day I run into Komo after breakfast and he says Lizzie why were you so silent all the week?

What we studied this time was various pieces of Terrie history where someone deliberately set out to shape things according to his own ideas, I begin to see why Komo is somewhat peeved with me.

Komo says, "Everybody concentrated on the practicability of the *modus operandi* employed, without considering the ethical aspects of the matter. I think it is at least debatable whether any individual has the right to try and determine the course of evolution of a society, most of the members of which are ignorant of his intentions. I hoped that the discussion would clear my mind, but nobody mentioned this side of it except me."

I know why Komo is worried about this, his old man who is a Tartar by all accounts has the idea he wants to re-establish a tribal society in Africa like they had five hundred years ago; this is why he sent Komo to study at Russett and Komo is only half sold on the idea.

I say "Listen, Komo, this is only the first term and as far as I can see M'Clare is only warming up, we have not got to the real stuff at all yet. I think we shall be able to judge it better when we know more about it, also maybe some of the stuff later in the course might be real helpful if you have to argue with your Dad."

Komo slowly brightens and says "Yes, you are a wise girl, Lizzie Lee."

Here we meet B and some others and conversation broadens, a minute later someone comes along with a little ticket saying Miss Lee see Professor M'Clane at 11.30 hours please.

Wise girl, huh?

Komo is still brooding on Ethics and the conversation has got on to Free Will, I listen a bit and then say, "Listen, folks, where did you hatch? you do what you can and what you can't you don't, what is not set by your genes is limited by your environment let alone we were not the first to think of pushing people around, where does the freedom come in?"

244

They gape and B says Oh but Lizzie, don't you remember what M'Clare said on Opening Day?

This remark I am tired of, it seems M'Clare put the whole course into that one hour so Why we go on studying I do not know.

I say No I did not listen and I am tired of hearing that sentence, did nobody write the lecture down?

B gasps and says there is a recording in the library.

It was quite a speech, I will say.

There is quite a bit about free will. M'Clare says Anyone who feels they have a right to fiddle with other people's lives has no business at Russett. But there is no such thing as absolute freedom, it is a contradiction in terms. Even when you do what you want, your wants are determined by your mental makeup and previous experience. If you do nothing and want nothing, that is not freedom of will but freedom from will, no will at all.

But, he says, all the time we are making choices, some known and some not: the more you look the more you see this. Quote, "It has probably not occurred to you that there is an alternative to sitting here until the hour strikes, and yet the forces that prevent you from walking out are probably not insurmountable. I say 'Probably' because a cultural inhibition can be as absolute as a physical impossibility. Whatever we do means submitting to one set of forces and resisting others. Those of you who are listening are obeying the forces of courtesy, interest or the hope that I may say something useful in examinations, and resisting the forces that tend to draw your minds on other things. Some of you may have made the opposite choice. The more we consider our doings the more choices we see, and the more we see the better hope we have of understanding human affairs."

Here are examples how people often do not make the choice they would really prefer, they are got at for being sissy or something. Or social institutions get in the way even when everyone knows what should be done, Hard cases make law and Bad law makes hard cases too. M'Clare says also You are always free to resist your environment, but to do so limits all your choices afterwards, this comes to Make environments so they do not have to be resisted

There is lots more but this bit has something to do with me, though you may not think so yet.

If I have any choices now, well I can throw my hand in or try to work something out; all I can think of is telling M'Clare how I cannot use a reading machine.

I am not so sure that is a choice, when he said Inhibitions can be absolute, Brother no fooling that is perfectly true.

Right now I can choose to sit here and do nothing or go and get some work done, there is a Balance of forces over that but then I go along to a Reading Room.

I have a long list of books I ought to have read, I just take the first, dial for it and fit it in the machine.

I think, Now I can choose to concentrate or I can let my mind go off on this mess I got into it and What Dad is going to say, no one in their senses would choose that last one. I set my chronoscope for twenty past eleven and put the blinkers on.

I switch the machine on, it lights and starts to go.

Then it goes crazy.

What should have warned me, there is no click. There is the usual warmup, slow then faster, but instead of a little jump and then ordinary speed it gets faster and faster and before I realize it I am caught.

It is like being stuck in concrete except this is inside me, in my head, and growing, it spreads and pushes, it is too big for my skull it is going to *burst*

and then I have let out a most almighty yell and torn out of the thing, I find later I left a bit of hair in the blinkers but I am out of it.

There is no one around, I run as though that machine had legs to come after me, I run right out in the campus and nearly crash with a tree, then I put my back to it and start breathing again.

Whatever I have done until now, judging by the feel of my ribs breathing was no part of it.

After a bit I sit down, I still have my back to the tree, I leave thinking till later and just sit.

Then I jump up and yell again.

I have left that crazy machine to itself, someone may sit in it this minute and get driven clean out of their head.

I run back not quite so fast as I came and burst in, someone just sitting down I yell out loud and yank him out of it.

It is a Third Year I do not know, from another class, he is much astonished by me.

I explain.

I guess I make it dramatic, he looks quite scared, meanwhile a small crowd has gathered around the door.

Along comes Doc Beschrievene expert at this kind of machine to see Why breach of the rule of silence in this block.

He trots straight in and starts inspecting the chair, then he says Exactly what happened, Miss Lee?

I say My God I have to see Mr. M'Clare!

I have been scratching my wrist for minutes, I now find the alarm of my chronoscope is trying to make itself felt, once again I am breaking records away from there.

I arrive one minute late but M'Clare has a visitor already so I can even get my breath, I also catch up on my apprehensions about this interview; seems to me the choice is get slung out as a slacker or get slung out as moron and I truly do not know which one I care for less.

Then the visitor goes and I stumble in.

M'Clare has a kind of unusual look, his eyes have gone flat and a little way back behind the lids, I do not get it at first then I suddenly see he is very tired.

However his voice is just as usual, not angry but maybe a little tired too, he says "Well, Miss Lee, they say actions speak louder than words and you certainly have given us a demonstration; you've made it quite clear that you could do the work but you aren't going to, and while it would be interesting to see if you could gauge the requirements of the examiners so exactly this time I don't think it would justify the time taken to mark your papers. What do you want to do? Go back to Excenus straight away or take a vacation first?"

I simply do not have anything to say, I feel I have been wrapped and sealed and stuck in the delivery hatch, he goes on, "It's a pity, I think. I thought when I first saw you there was a brain under that golden mop and it was a pity to let it go to waste. If only there were something that

247

mattered more to you than the idea of being made to do what you don't want to—"

It is queer to watch someone get a call on a built-in phone, some do a sort of twitch some shut their eyes, M'Clare just lets the focus of his slide out through the wall and I might not be there anymore, I wish I was not but I have to say something before I go away.

M'Clare has been using a throat mike but now he says out loud, "Yes, come over right away."

Now he is not tired anymore.

He says "What happened to the reading machine, Miss Lee?

I say "It went crazy." Then I see this is kid's talk, but I have no time to put learned words to it, I say "Look. You know how it starts? There is a sort of warmup and then a little click and it settles down to the right speed? Well it did not happen. What I think, the governor must have been off or something, but that is not all—it got quicker and quicker but it did something else—look I have not the right expression for it, but it felt like something opened my skull and was pasting things on the convolutions inside."

He has a look of wild something, maybe surmise maybe just exasperation, then Doc Beschrievene comes in. He says "Miss Lee, if it was a joke, may we call it off? Readers are in short supply."

I say if I wanted to make a joke I would make it a funny one.

M'Clare says "Ask Miss Lee to tell you what happens when you start the reader."

Beschrievene says "I have started it! I connected it up and it worked quite normally."

Now the thing has gone into hiding, it will jump out on someone else like it did on me, I have no time to say this; M'Clare says "Tell Dr. Beschrievene about the reader."

I say "It started to go too fast and then—"

He says Start at the beginning and tell what I told before.

I say "When you sit in a reader there is normally an initial period during which the movement of the words becomes more rapid, then there is a short transitional period of confusion and then the thing clicks audibly and the movement of the words proceeds at a set rate, this time—"

Here Doc gives a yell just like me and jumps to his feet.

M'Clare says What was I reading in the machine?

I do not see what that has to do with it but I tell him, then he wants to know what I remember of it and where it stopped.

I would not have thought I remembered but I do, I know just where it had got to, he takes me backwards bit by bit—

Then I begin to catch on.

M'Clare says "What is your usual reading rate, Liz?"

I swallow hard, I say "Too low to show on the dial, I don't know."

He says "Is your father handicapped too?"

I lift my head again, I am going to say that is not his business, then I say Yes instead.

He says "And he feels badly about it? Yes, he would. And you never told anybody. Of course not!" I do not know if it is scorn or anger or what. Beschrievene is talking to himself in a language I do not know, M'Clare says Come along to the reading room.

The chair has its back off, M'Clare plugs in a little meter lying on the floor and says "Sit down, Liz."

There is nothing I want less than to sit in that chair, but I do.

M'Clare says "Whether or not you have a repetition of your previous experience is entirely up to you. Switch on."

I am annoyed at his tone, I think I will give that switch a good bang, I feel I have done it too.

But the light does not go on.

M'Clare says patiently "Turn on, please, Miss Lee."

I say "You do it."

Beschrievene says "Wait! There is no need to demonstrate, after all. We know what happened."

Then M'Clare's fingers brush over mine and turn the switch.

I jump all over, the thing warms up and then click! there is the little jump and the words moving steadily through.

And you know, I am disappointed.

Beschrievene says He will be the son of a bigamist, I jump out of the chair and demand to know what goes?

M'Clare is looking at a dial in the meter, he turns and looks at me with exactly the same expression and says, "Would you like to repeat your previous experience?"

Beschrievene says "No!"

I say "Yes. I would."

M'Clare bends and does something inside the machine, then he says again "Sit down, Lizzie Lee."

I do, I hit the switch myself too.

There it is again, words slide across slow and then quicker and quicker and there is something pressing on my brain, then there is a bang and it all goes off and Beschrievene is talking angry and foreign to M'Clare.

I climb out and say Will they kindly explain.

M'Clare tells me to come and look, it is the reading-rate dial of the machine it now says Seven thousand five hundred and three.

Beschrievene says How much do I know about the machine? seems to me the safest answer is Nothing at all.

He says "There is an attachment which regulates the speed of movement of the words according to the reaction of the user. It sets itself automatically and registers on this dial here. But there is also another part of the machine far more important although there is no dial for it, unless you fit a test-meter as we have done: this is called the concentration unit or Crammer."

I did know that, it is what makes people able to read faster than with an old-style book.

He says, "This unit is compulsive. When the machines were first made it was thought that they might be misused to insert hypnotic commands into the minds of readers. It would be very difficult, but perhaps possible. Therefore in the design was incorporated a safety device." He pats one individual piece of spaghetti for me to admire.

He says, "This device automatically shuts off the machine when it encounters certain conical wave-patterns which correspond to strong resistance, such as is called forth by hypnotically imposed orders; not merely the resistance of a wandering mind."

I say But—

He looks as though I suddenly started sprouting and says "M'Clare this is most strange, this very young girl to be so strong, and from childhood too! Looks are nothing, of course—"

M'Clare says "Exactly so. Do you understand, Miss Lee? One of your outstanding characteristics is a dislike of being what you call pushed around, in fact I believe if somebody tried to force you to carry out your dearest wish you would resist with all your might, you are not so set on free will as you are on free won't. The Crammer appeared to your subconscious as something that interfered with your personal freedom, so you resisted it. That isn't uncommon, at first, but not many people resist hard enough to turn the thing off.'

I say "But it worked!"

Beschrievene says that the safety device only turns off the Crammer, the rest of the machine goes on working but only at the rate for unassisted reading about one-tenth normal rate.

M'Clare says "You, my girl, have been trying to keep up with a course designed for people who could absorb information seven or eight times as fast. No wonder your knowledge seemed a bit sketchy."

He sounds angry.

Well hells bells I am angry myself, if only I had told somebody it could all have been put right at the start, or if only the man who first tried to teach Dad the reader had known what was wrong with the way he used it, Dad would have had ordinary schooling and maybe not gone into prospecting but something else, and—

Then whoever got born it would not have been me, so where does that get you?

Beschrievene is saying "What I do not understand, why did she suddenly stop resisting the machine?"

M'Clare says Well Liz?

It is a little time before I see the answer to that, then I say "We cannot resist everything we can only choose the forces to which we will submit."

They look blank, M'Clare says Is it a quotation?

I say "Your speech on Opening Day, I did not listen. I heard it just now."

This I never thought to see, his classical puss goes red all over and

251

he does not know what to say.

Beschrievene wants to know more of what was said so I recite, at the end he says "Words! Your students frighten me, M'Clare. So much power in words, at the right time, and you are training them to use such tools so young! To use them perhaps on a whole planet!"

M'Clare says "Would you rather leave it to chance? Or to people with good intentions and no training at all? Or to professional ax-grinders and amateurs on the make?"

I say How do I stop doing it?

Beschrievene rubs his chin and says I will have to start slowly, the machine produced so much effect because it was going fast, normally children learn to read at five when their reading rate is low even with the Crammer. He says he will take out the safety but put in something to limit speed and I can have a short session tomorrow.

I say Exams in four weeks three days why not today?

He laughs and says Of course I will be excused the exam—

M'Clare says Certainly I will take the exam, there is no reason why I should not pull up to pass standard; work is not heavy this term.

Beschrievene looks under his eyebrows but says Very well.

After lunch I sit down in the doctored machine.

Five minutes later I am sick.

Beschrievene fusses and gives me antinauseant and makes me lie down one half hour then I start again.

I last twenty minutes and come out head aching fit to grind a hole, I say For all sakes run it full speed it is this push and drag together turns me up, this morning it only scared me.

He does not want to do this, I try all out to persuade him, I am getting set to weep tears when he says Very well, he is no longer surprised my will was strong enough to turn off the machine.

This time it comes full on.

The words slide across my eyes slow, then quicker, then suddenly they are running like water pouring through my eyes to my brain, something has hold of me keeping my mind open so that they can get in, if I struggle if I stop one micro-second from absolute concentration they will jam and something will *break*.

I could not pull any of my mind away to think with but there is a

252

little corner of it free, watching my body, it makes my breath go on, digs my nails in my hand, stops the muscles of my legs when they try to jerk me out of the chair, sets others to push me back again.

I can hear my breath panting and the bang of my heart, then I do not hear it any longer, I am not separate any longer from the knowledge coming into me from the machine.

and then it stops.

It is like waking with a light on the face, I gasp and leap in the seat and the blinkers pull my hair, I yell What did you do that for?

M'Clare is standing in front of me, he says Eighty-seven minutes is quite sufficient come out of that at once.

I try to stand and my knees won't unhinge, to hear M'Clare you would think it was his legs I got cramp in, I suppose I went to sleep in the middle of his remarks anyway I wake tomorrow in bed.

In the morning I tell it all to B because she is a friend of mine and it is instructive anyway.

B says Lizzie it must have been awful but it is rather wonderful too; I do not see this I say Well it is nice it is over.

Which it is not.

Four weeks look like a long time from the front end but not when it is over and I have to take the exam.

I have made up my mind on one thing, if I do not pass I am not asking anyone to make allowances I am just straight off going home, I am too tired to think much about it but that is what I will do.

Exam, I look at all the busy interested faces and the stylers clicking along and at the end I am certain for sure I failed it by quite a way.

I do not join any postmortem groups I get to my room and lock the door and think for a bit.

I think That finishes it, no more strain and grind and Terrie voices and Please Tune in Daily For Routine Announcements and smells you get in some of this air, no more high-minded kids who don't know dead sure from however, no more essays and No More M'Clare, I wish they would hurry up and get the marks over so I can get organized to count my blessings properly.

However sixty four-hour papers take time to read even with a

Crammer and M'Clare does them all himself, we shall get the marks day after tomorrow if then.

There is a buzz from the speaker in the study and B is not there, I have to go.

Of all people who should be too busy to call me just now it is Mr. M'Clare.

He says I have not notified him of my vacation plans yet.

I say Huh?

He says as my guardian he ought to know where I am to be found and he wants to be sure I have got return schedules fixed from wherever I am going to so as to make certain I get back in time for next term.

I say Hell what makes you think I am coming back next term anyway.

He says Certainly I am coming back next term, if I am referring to the exam he has just had a look at my paper it is adequate though not outstanding no doubt I will do better with time. Will I let his secretary have details of my plans, and he turns it off on me.

I sit down on the floor, no chair to hand.

Well for one thing the bit about the vacations was not even meant to deceive, he did it just to let me know I was Through.

So I have not finished here after all.

The more I think about studying Cultural Engineering the more doubtful I get, it is pushing people around however you like to put it more fancy than that.

The more I think about Terries the more I wonder they survive so long, some are all right such as B but even she would not be so safe in most places I know.

The more I think—

Well who am I fooling after all?

The plain fact is I am not leaving Russett and all the rest of it and I am so pleased with this, just now I do not care if the whole College calls me Lysistrata.

1958 HUGO AWARDS BALLOT

HUGO AWARDS ——————

This is your 'Hugo' awards ballot. Each year at the World Science Fiction Convention an award called the 'HUGO' is given for outstanding acheivement in each of the following fields. The selections listed here have been chosen for nomination to this years awatds list by fandom at large. This is your chance to vote for the final award.

RULES

1. You can vote for only one selection in each category.
2. No write in votes will be counted.
3. It was very apparent from the nominations ballots that in some categories there was no particularly outstanding selection. Because of this we have included a choice called, "No award in this category".
4. The ballot must be signed to be considered as a vote.

Mail your ballot to: DETENTION, James Broderick, 12011 Kilbourne St, Detroit 13, Michigan.

BEST NOVEL OF 1958 – Vote for one – Five nominations:

A Case of Conscience	James Blish	Ballantine Books
Have Spacesuit, Will Travel	Robert Heinlein	F. & S. F.
Time Killer	Robert Sheckley	Galaxy Magazine
We have Fed Our Seas	Poul Anderson	Astounding S.F.
Who	Algis Budrys	Avon Books

BEST NOVELETTE OF 1958 – Vote For One – Eight nominations:

Big Front Yard	Clifford Simak	Astounding S.F.
Captivity	Zenna Henderson	F. & S.F.
Deskful of Girls	Fritz Leiber	F. & S.F.
Rat In The Skull	Rog Phillips	If Magazine
Reap The Dark Tide	Cyril Kornbluth	Vanguard
Second Game	Katherine MacLean & Charles De Vet	Astounding S.F.
The Miracle Workers	Jack Vance	Astounding S.F.
Unwillingly To School	Pauline Ashwell	Astounding S.F.

BEST SHORT STORY OF 1958 – Vote for one – Ten Nominations

Edge Of The Sea	Algis Budrys	Venture
Nine Yards of Other Cloth	Manly Wade Wellman	F. & S.F.
Rump-Titty-Titty-Tum-TAH-Tee	Fritz Leiber	F. & S.F.
Space To Swing A Cat	Stanley Mullen	Astounding S.F.
The Advent on Channel Twelve	Cyril Kornbluth	Venture
The Hellbound Train	Bob Bloch	F. & S.F.
The Men Who Murdered Mohammed	Alfred Bester	F. & S.F.
Theory of Rocketery	Cycril Kornbluth	F. & S.F.
They're Been Working On...	Anton Lee Baker	Astounding S.F.
Triggerman	J. F. Bone	Astounding S.F.
No Award In This Category.		

PRO-MAG OF 1958
- Astounding S.F.
- Mag of F.& S.F.
- Galaxy Magazine
- Infinity
- New Worlds

BEST PRO-ARTIST
- Ed Emshwiller
- Virgil Finlay
- Frank Kelly Freas
- Van Dongen
- Wally Wood

BEST HOLLYWOOD MOVIE OF 1958
- The Fly
- The Horror of Dracula
- The 7th Voyage of Sinbad
- No Award this year

BEST AMATEUR MAGAZINE
- Cry of The Nameless
- Fanac
- Hyphen
- Science-Fiction Times

- JD Argassy
- Yandro

BEST NEW AUTHOR OF 1958
- Brian W. Aldiss
- Paul Ash
- Pauline Ashwell
- Rosel George Brown

- Charbonneau
- Kit Reed
- No Award in this Category

sign here _____

CONTRIBUTOR BIOGRAPHIES

Doctor Laura Brodian Freas Beraha

Doctor Laura Brodian Freas Beraha was a voiceover artist and classical music personality on radio stations in San Francisco and Los Angeles, and was also the voice of Delta Symphony and Delta Jazz for Delta Airlines. A past President of the Southern California Early Music Society, she is degreed in Music, but also attended art classes at Indiana University's School of Fine Arts and at the California Art Institute. Her cover and interior artwork has been published by, among others, *TSR, The Easton Press, Analog Magazine of Science Fiction/Fact, Weird Tales*, and *Marion Zimmer Bradley's Fantasy Magazine.* Laura was a co-recipient (with Frank Kelly Freas) of The Association of Science Fiction and Fantasy Artists (ASFA)'s Chesley Award for Best Cover of the Year. Laura has also served as ASFA's Western Regional Director. She is a judge in the L. Ron Hubbard "Illustrators of the Future" contest.

One of her passions is costuming. She is a former Director-at-Large of Costumer's Guild West, a WesterCon Masquerade Winner, and a WorldCon Masquerade Judge. She also founded the Collinsport Players performing troupe when she was the MC at the first annual Dark Shadows Festival.

Another of her passions is English Regency Dancing, which she also teaches in Pasadena, California. Laura founded the (San Francisco) Bay Area English Regency Society and the (San Fernando) Valley Area English Regency Society. A member of the International Association of Astronomical Artists, Laura is the widow of famed science fiction illustrator, Frank Kelly Freas, with whom she co-edited the fourth volume of his collected works, *Frank Kelly Freas: As He Sees It* in

2000. She and artist Bob Eggleton are producing a new Kelly Freas art book, *The Complete Frank Kelly Freas*, to be released in 2019. In 2012 Laura Freas married school teacher Steven Beraha in Los Angeles.

Gideon Marcus: Founder of the Serling Award-winning and twice Hugo-nominated historical web project, Galactic Journey, Gideon Marcus is a science fiction writer and space historian. His alternate history story, "Andy and Tina," is the lead tale in the Sidewise-nominated anthology, *Tales from Alternate Earths 2*. He lives in the San Diego area with his wife and their prodigy daughter as well as a matched pair of cats.

The easiest places to find him are at the galacticjourney.org website, @journeygalactic on Twitter, and, of course, galacticjourney.press.

Natalie Devitt: Natalie Devitt works in education. Having graduated from film school, she writes for the Hugo-nominated fanzine Galactic Journey, where she covers The Twilight Zone and The Outer Limits. Her interests outside of television and film include reading, hunting for new record shops, playing guitar, blowing all of her money on concerts and fan conventions, and visiting her local antique shops. She lives in California with family and her crazy tuxedo cat named Ziggy.

Erica Frank: Erica Frank is a gamer (tabletop RPGs and point-and-click adventures, mostly), filker, blogger, slashfic reader and occasional writer, occultist of various interests, and 8–5 office worker. She lives in the SF Bay Area, with many of the clichés that implies. She's been an avid science fiction reader for more than 40 years, growing up with Heinlein, Asimov, Niven, and Herbert. Her preferences gradually shifted from space adventure to the evolution of society as she discovered authors like Le Guin, Tiptree, McCaffrey, and Butler. She is the archivist at Galactic Journey, where she occasionally writes articles.

Erica Friedman: Erica Friedman is the Founder of Yuricon, former manga (Japanese comics) publisher at ALC Publishing. She has written and spoken about lesbian-themed Japanese comics and animation for Japanese literary journal *Eureka*, *Animerica* magazine, the Comic Book

Legal Defense Fund, Dark Horse, and contributed to *Forbes*, *Slate*, *Huffington Post*, and *The Mary Sue*. She has edited "Dangerous Women," an anthology of lesbian super-villians for Northwest Press.

She writes about lesbian-themed Japanese animation and comics on her blog, Okazu.

T.D. Cloud: Cloud began her professional writing career in 2016 with *Brontide*, an LGBTQA+ fae romance novel set in a world of politics, betrayal, and folklore. From fae to Drow to vampires to witches, all of her works include diverse gender identities, sexualities, and immersive world building to satisfy those in need of a break from reality for a few hundred pages. She currently has seven novels out with many more in the works including an eight-book vampire series, a dark romance between a familiar-less witch and a chaos god, and a dhampir story set to the tune of a melancholic mystery.

Check out her work at tdcloudofficial.com.

Andi Dukleth: Andi Dukleth is a San Diego indie comic book creator and video journalist at the local NPR affiliate, KPBS. Born and raised in Oceanside, CA, she attended California State University San Marcos where she majored in Art and Technology. From there, she initially got a job as a video editor and news photographer for KUSI News, transitioning to greater responsibilities at ABC 10 News, and now KPBS. Ever passionate about storytelling, she has also worked in collaboration with the Accidental Aliens Comic Studio to produce and publish three anthology books.

She credits Hayao Miyazaki, Joe Hill, and CLAMP as her biggest influences.

Cora Buhlert: Cora Buhlert was born and bred in Bremen, North Germany, where she still lives today—after time spent in London, Singapore, Rotterdam and Mississippi. Cora has been a science fiction fan for as long as she can remember and blogs about SFF both at her own site and Galactic Journey. Though she writes in various genres, science fiction and fantasy will always be her first love.

Cora is the author of the "In Love and War" space opera series, the

"Shattered Empire" space opera series, the "Silencer" series of pulp style thrillers, the "Thurvok" sword and sorcery series, the "Helen Shepherd Mysteries" and plenty of standalone stories in multiple genres. When Cora is not writing, she works as a translator and teacher. Visit her on the web at http://www.corabuhlert.com or follow her on Twitter @CoraBuhlert.

A. J. Howells: A. J. Howells is the publisher and general editor of Makeshift Press (MakeshiftPress.org), publisher of Fredric Brown's *The Office*. A.J.'s prose has appeared in *The First Line*, *South 85 Journal*, *Rhetoric Askew*, and two volumes of *Workers Write*. RhetAskew Publishing will soon release his horror-comedy novella *Alley Bats*, and his poetry has been featured in *Eunoia Review* and *The Offbeat*. He lives with his wife, two children, and two cats, in the woods of northern Virginia where he spends far too much time reading comic books and listening to Sun Ra. In his spare time, he teaches full time.

Claire Weaver: Claire Weaver is a British-American screenwriter, journalist and author. She has written for sci-fi media magazines *SciFiNow* and *Death Ray*, as well as a host of websites including Nerd Like You, Infinity Plus and Broad Universe. She was the Features & Production Editor for the British Science Fiction Association's *Matrix Magazine*, and was a member of the judging panel for the Arthur C. Clarke Award in 2007 and 2008. Her short story, "The Tollhouse," was published in the communication-themed anthology *Myth Understandings*. She recently co-wrote a virtual reality sci-fi/horror miniseries, Into The Blind; penned several episodes of the animated children's series Eddie Is A Yeti; and was a contributing writer for *Celebrity Ghosts & Notorious Hauntings*, a non-fiction book about the paranormal.

Lorelei Marcus: Lorelei Marcus is a fifteen-year-old young woman taking on the world. A veteran artist, she started her comic career at nine years old with the famous *Blue Bird* (the inspiration for the current DC Comics character of the same name). Studying and proficient in both traditional and digital art, she likes visual media best, but music is a close second. She has written two songs with a third on the way, and she regularly performs live.

A frequent writer for the Hugo-nominated fanzine, Galactic Journey, she is an activist at heart, and she hopes to leave an impression on the world by educating, inspiring, and providing for the community.

Gwyn Conaway: Gwyn Conaway is a costume designer in Los Angeles, California, specializing in fashion history and entertainment design. A member of the Costume Designers Guild, her work primarily consists of period and genre film design and 3D costume simulation consultation. She is a cultural guide for the National Partners of American Theatre, curating a national award for design excellence that takes students at the top of their craft to Seoul, South Korea every year. Conaway is also a professor at Art Center College of Design, where she teaches history of fashion for entertainment designers. Her publications focus mainly on the psychology of fashion expression throughout Western history, and the process of culture-building for entertainment.

Marie Vibbert: Marie Vibbert's fiction has appeared multiple times in Analog, F&SF, and other markets. She's a computer programmer who played for the Cleveland Fusion women's tackle football team. The Oxford Culture Review called her work "Everything Science Fiction should be." Currently she's working on a statistical analysis of women writing as women in speculative fiction magazines over time, shopping around three novels, serializing a fourth on Curious Fictions, and working feverishly with her husband Brian on Tinselfly, a MYST-like game that should be available for PC and Mac next year, through Whitethorn Games.

She lives with her husband Brian Crick, his brother John, her sister Terrisa, and niece Jennifer in a house that's nearly 100 years old and doesn't have enough cats.

You can learn more at marievibbert.com or follow her on Twitter @mareasie.

Rosemary Benton: Rosemary Benton is an oncology clinical research assistant and freelance writer harboring ambitions of one day having her own science fiction and horror stories published. She is an associate writer for the science fact and fiction blog Galactic Journey where she reviews Silver Age novels and films. Prior to that Rosemary was a monthly contributor to Comics Bulletin where she wrote a column on horror manga and a column on imported comics featuring female protagonists. She is a graduate of Mount Holyoke College, and in 2012, graduated from Simmons College with master's degrees in both history and library and information science.

Janice Marcus: By day Janice is a mild-mannered writer of romance, mystery and science fiction. She's also the editorial backbone of the Serling-Award winning and twice Hugo-nominated web project, galacticjourney.org. At conventions you may find her cosplaying, moderating Galactic Journey's presentations, or participating on panels with topics ranging from fanfiction to copyright to queer themes in pop culture. In her spare time she loves to sing karaoke and practice pole dancing.

Janice has a degree in Japanese Studies and an ongoing interest in Japanese pop culture. When she's not writing, editing, singing, or dancing, she's usually out enjoying the sun in San Diego county or helping support her daughter's dreams of becoming a musician, a comic artist, and taking over the world.

ABOUT JOURNEY PRESS

Ten years ago, I started the project of getting through the huge trove of science fiction magazines that my father left me. I wanted to make sure I read them all, so I held myself to one simple rule: I'd read every magazine for the current month exactly 55 years prior, allowing for the fact that the publication date was usually a month or two ahead of when a magazine was printed.

Thus, in February 2009, I started with the March 1954 *Imagination*, and I've been keeping up ever since. *Astounding, Fantasy & Science Fiction, Galaxy*…you name it, I've read it.

In 2013 (1958), I decided to start the blog, Galactic Journey. It was just a convenient repository for my thoughts, a way of fixing in print what I thought of the stories I was reading. I figured that, at best, I'd have a few readers.

Six years later, the Journey has won the Serling Award and been nominated for the Hugo twice. From its humble beginnings as a place for magazine reviews and space news from 55 years ago, the blog has become a bonafide phenomenon, with some twenty writers, global coverage, even a fashion column.

Over the course of Galactic Journey's production, I read a number of great stories that are still considered classics today. But I also encountered dozens of authors, and countless excellent pieces, that I'd never heard of. In particular, the several dozen women who were writing SFF; I'd never heard of Sydney van Scyoc, Sondra Dorman, Kit Reed. I'd never seen the stories that put Rosel George Brown on the map.

While Galactic Journey has spotlighted these works in its articles, that still didn't do much to bring the stories back to life. I wanted them to be living things again, printed and widely available. And that's why *Rediscovery* exists.

Now that I've started, though, I've realized I don't want to stop. I have so many great stories I want to share with you, both stories from the past and stories yet to be written. More anthologies in the *Rediscovery* series. Modern themed anthologies and SFF novels with creative spins on classic ideas. Short stories and novellas—the kind with awkward lengths most outlets don't like to publish, but which used to be common (just the right length for a short plane flight or a long wait in a doctor's office.)

And above all, good stuff. Work that stands toe to toe quality-wise with the classics we are reprinting.

It's a new Journey, but one we're excited to be starting. We're so glad you decided to join us at the beginning, and we hope you'll stay with us for the rest!

—Gideon Marcus

CPSIA information can be obtained
at www.ICGtesting.com
Printed in the USA
LVHW030415020421
683199LV00003B/21